A VILLAGE SECRET

Julie Houston

HEAD
of ZEUS

An Aria Book

This edition first published in the UK in 2022 by Head of Zeus Ltd,
part of Bloomsbury Publishing Plc

Copyright © Julie Houston, 2022

The moral right of Julie Houston to be identified as the author
of this work has been asserted in accordance with the Copyright, Designs
and Patents Act of 1988.

9 7 5 3 1 2 4 6 8

A catalogue record for this book is available from the British Library.

ISBN (PB): 9781801101905
ISBN (E): 9781788549820

Cover design © Jessie Price
Illustration © Robyn Neild

Typeset by Siliconchips Services Ltd UK

Printed and bound in Great Britain by
CPI Group (UK) Ltd, Croydon CR0 4YY

Head of Zeus Ltd
First Floor East
5–8 Hardwick Street
London EC1R 4RG

www.headofzeus.com

For Ben and Georgia

PROLOGUE

November 2020

'*Jen? I'm so desperately sorry you've had to sit through all this. All this utter rubbish that's come out, in there, this afternoon.' Laurie Lewis, my husband of sixteen years, ran down the steps and through the milling crowd towards me, pulling me towards him, desperate to protect me from the melee that was insistent on reaching out greedy, intrusive arms and hands in my direction.*

'You know, don't you Jen?' Laurie was vehement, pulling my face up towards his own, those incredible navy eyes of his blazing into mine, despite the crowd moving in on us. 'I love you? Will always love you? That all this…' he gestured an arm to the seething throng determined to reach its goal, '…means nothing. It's you and me that mean everything…' He broke off, arms still around me as the media reached us.

'What do you think of the verdict, Jennifer?'

'Did you know about all of this, Jen? What do you think about it all…?'

I batted away the intruding mikes and cameras,

blindly pushing my way through the crowd, while Neville Sanderson, Laurie's advocate, urged me none too gently towards the waiting car.

Neville stopped briefly, almost toppling from the wet and slippery leaf-strewn pavement into the road as the media surged forwards, on and around him like a baying pack of wolves. He was about to address the reporters, when Laurie himself pushed forwards and, arm wrapped protectively around me once more, began to speak. 'This whole trial has caused enormous damage to myself and my family. My whole reputation has been besmirched, but we're not leaving it there. This decision will be appealed...' Laurie paused... 'and we will fight on to show that I am, in fact, innocent of all I've been accused of here in court today...'

ACT 1

I

September 1999

'I'm up here, Dad: East Range, staircase I up on Angel Court.' I actually laughed at the expression on my dad's face at the thought of his having to carry all my suitcases, bin liners, bags and other paraphernalia needed for my final year studying English Literature at Trinity College, Cambridge.

'Aren't you glad to be back in college rooms again instead of that awful house you were renting last year?' Dad hauled in as much as he could in one go while my mum brought up the rear with a couple of black bin bags, one already split and in danger of spilling its contents of bras and knickers onto the floor of the double-set room I'd been allocated through the main ballot the previous term. Jeremy, my only brother, and roped in to help when he just wanted to be at home with his mates playing football, was plugged into his Sony Walkman and being absolutely no help with the bags. Or anything else.

'Totally glad.' Struggling with a mountain of duvet,

3

pillows and bed linen, I dropped the stuff onto the floor before bouncing on the bed in order to ascertain its springs. 'God, I reckon there's been a whole load of others before me on this bed. Mind you, a veritable oasis of comfort compared to that dreadful bed I endured on Roxburgh Road last year.'

'I'm glad you're out of that place, Jenny.' Dad frowned. 'I worried about you all the time while you were living there. It was such an awfully dark and dismal road with those back entrances where anyone could have been waiting to jump out at you.'

'Dad, stop treating me like a little girl.' I tried again to find some bounce in the bed but without much success.

'I'm not, darling. I just think, if you're at Cambridge, you should be taking full advantage of living in these fabulously historic buildings, instead of some dingy backstreet terrace. Making the most of being right here, in the midst of it all.'

'You know your father never got over ending up at a Midlands poly rather than a university.' Mum laughed. 'Just indulge him a bit, Jen. Let him live the dream with you a while longer.'

'I think he's done alright for himself despite that, don't you? *And* he's got three years of Jeremy being somewhere to indulge himself from next year.' The three of us glanced at my seventeen-year-old brother who was now slumped, eyes closed, in the one somewhat tired looking armchair, and laughed.

'I've bought you one of these new mattress toppers,' Mum said, rummaging around in a bin liner as I jumped off the bed and wandered over to look at the view from my window, hoping to get a glimpse of the Trinity College clock, Chapel Fountain or the statue of Henry VIII.

I was over the moon I'd been allocated Great Court for my final year at Cambridge. I loved the feeling of actually living within the history of the place, to be a part of what was reputed to be the largest enclosed courtyard in Europe, completed in the early seventeenth century.

Disappointed that I couldn't see the actual Chapel Fountain itself, I was about to turn back to the room and suggest Jeremy might like to get the hell off my bed – where he'd now moved himself to – and make himself useful, when I both heard and saw a crowd of students gathered in the court below. I was immediately drawn to the dark head of the taller of the two men whose arm was thrown nonchalantly round the shoulders of a tiny brunette. 'Lucky girl,' I thought wistfully as the dark-haired man, obviously sensing he was under scrutiny, looked directly up at my window. He apparently didn't see anything of interest and immediately gave all his attention back to the girl at his side, turning her towards himself and kissing her so thoroughly I felt myself grow quite hot with lust.

Had I finally found Byron?

Two years previously, after A-Levels and wildly excited about leaving home and taking up the offer of three years at Cambridge to study English Literature, I'd taken the usual flight with my parents and Jeremy in order to spend the summer at our house in Kefalonia. Three weeks in, and bored with the premise of yet another day sitting under the relentless, seemingly inexhaustible heat of the Greek August sun, I'd decided I needed some time to myself and had taken the early morning three-hour ferry and bus ride from the island across the water to Missolonghi. I'd crossed to the mainland lots of times before of course, but always accompanied by my parents and Jeremy, who they'd inevitably had to entice with promises of ice cream or coke in order to get him to visit the historical sites for which Missolonghi was famous. Now, with a new sense of freedom and independence, I looked across at the breath-taking natural landscape of the mainland, feeling the hot late-morning breeze in my hair as the ferry creaked its way slowly into port.

English Literature had always been my main love, but History came a close second and that morning, suffused with the hot Greek sun and the heady tang of lemon balm, fresh bread and coffee fighting for precedence, I fell in love.

With a two-hundred-year-old man.

Well, to be accurate, a man who had been *dead* almost two hundred years. After a strong Greek coffee which set my pulse racing, I crossed over to the square of *Markos Botsaris*, stepping out of the heat and into the cool interior of the city's Museum of History and Art. Vryzakis' interpretation of the welcome of Lord Byron to Missolonghi stopped me dead in my tracks. Here, then, was the man: the embodiment of all the erotic dreams that had taken me by surprise (as well as taking the place of the reams of history facts and literature quotes) once the A-Level exams were over. I felt quite overwhelmed with the feeling and moved around the museum, hunting for, and taking in, everything I could find about George, Lord Byron. The more I gazed at his broodingly devastating good looks, the curl of his upper lip, the scowl on his brow, the dark hair and the piercing blue eyes, the more I knew I was spoilt forever for the acne-faced, cheese-and-onion-breath boys – boys not men – I'd snogged, and one I'd eventually lost my virginity to, one cold damp evening in the back of a car after too much Bulmers (sweet) cider.

I made the return ferry journey back to Kefalonia a different girl – no, I told myself, a sensually aroused woman – determined, once I got to Cambridge in the following weeks, to find a Byron of my own. And how fortuitous, I sighed deliciously to myself, that Byron had actually himself been at Cambridge. And at Trinity too. It was an omen, I knew.

Despite constantly searching for my own living manifestation of Byron, I was, it seemed, set to be disappointed on that score. My first two years at Trinity College passed like any other student's there. I made new friends, had several affairs, broke a couple of hearts – including that of the mainstay of the Cambridge Blues, Beau O'Farrell from Texas. Bloody daft name, I'd thought, as I finished the relationship after six months, much to my parents' chagrin – they'd adored him more than I ever had. At the end of each term, I took back to Berkshire not only the mandatory piles of dirty washing, but also a disappointment that my heart had yet to be captured by a living embodiment of the Byron oil paintings that had so entranced me in the museum in Missolonghi: the *mad, bad and dangerous to know* lover I so longed for remained, two years on, simply a figment of my over-romanticised imagination.

I glanced across this new room of mine where my parents,

totally unaware of this iconic moment in their daughter's life, were bouncing a truculent – and unfortunately flatulent – Jeremy from the rigid single bed in order that Mum could try out the new mattress topper which she'd bought for a fortune in John Lewis the previous week. Mattress topper? I closed my eyes briefly, despairing at the very notion of such banal, everyday goings on when George, Lord Byron's double, had just passed by outside my window.

'Right, darling? Usual place for lunch is it, before we set off back down the M11?' Dad picked up his car keys and wallet and smiled in my direction.

'Fine, yes, lovely.' I could feel myself almost at fever pitch to get lunch over with, say final farewells to my parents – who were always reluctant to let me go again after four months back in their company – and then sort myself out in my new room before setting out to find friends in adjacent courts. 'Let's go.' I gave Jeremy, who was now slightly more animated at the mention of food, a sisterly punch on the arm to make sure he really was alive and, taking one final glance out of the window in the hope that Byron might still be under it, followed my parents and brother back down the stairs and into the early autumn sunshine.

Working in the City of London, my dad was often given recommendations for the best places to eat both in and outside of the capital and once I started at Trinity, and being a bit of a foodie himself, he had been more than willing to take up the recommendation suggested by one of his company's accountants that they give Midsummer House, a newish restaurant on Midsummer Common right on the banks of the River Cam itself, a visit. With its elegant and spacious, light-drenched conservatory dining room, the

Victorian villa had immediately become a firm favourite and was traditionally booked at the start of each new term that I was taken back to university.

Both Dad and Jeremy would have preferred to drive the distance to the restaurant but Mum, wanting to stretch her legs before the two-hour drive back to Berkshire, and I, desperate to bump into Byron, as I'd now dubbed the beautiful dark-haired man, both insisted we walk the three-quarter of a mile route via St John's Street.

'Are you looking for someone?' Mum asked as she and I walked behind the other two. 'Your head's going left and right like a dyslexic nodding dog.'

'I was hoping I might see Gudrun or Annabelle,' I lied, forcing myself to look ahead and stop this daft searching for someone who probably, when it came down to it, looked nothing like Byron at all. I'd only seen the top of his head and, briefly, his face, but the way he'd been kissing that girl had sent shivers right the way down to my toes and back up to where it really mattered.

The maître d' greeted Mum and Dad like long lost family, ushering us to our reserved table in the choicest part in the restaurant, flapping starched white napkins like starter flags and generally making us feel like we were the only people that mattered. Even Jeremy deigned to unplug himself from his music, his seventeen-year-old boy's appetite trumping his desire to appear cool and laidback.

'I love this place,' Dad beamed, as he always did. 'You'll have to make sure you get that place at Cambridge, next year, Jeremy. I want at least another three years of all this once your sister leaves...' He broke off from perusing the menu as the restaurant door opened and six people walked in to accompanying laughter and banter, rendering Jeremy's – not overly polite – retort to Dad inaudible. The four of us looked up, as did everyone else in the restaurant, and my heart started hammering. He was here. Byron was actually *here* and every bit as gorgeous as I'd thought from that very first glance up at me from below my college room window. He still had his arm around the incredibly tiny girl who was apparently confident enough in her own – beautifully tanned – body to wrap it in tight satsuma-orange pedal pushers topped with a white corset-type bustier. Only someone as slim and self-assured as this dark-haired beauty could get away with an outfit like that. The pair were very obviously the main act while the other four – three men and one other girl – were merely walk-on attendants. As my heart continued to hammer, I found I was unable to take anything more than shallow breaths and, for a moment, actually wondered if I could possibly be having a heart attack. I buried my crimson face in my glass of water while attempting to breathe normally once more.

'What's up with you?' Jeremy was staring as only a post-adolescent can stare. 'Seen someone you know? Someone you fancy?' He lowered his voice, 'Someone you've *shagged*?'

'For heaven's sake, Jeremy, behave yourself.' Mum, catching this last retort, slapped my brother round the head with the heavy menu.

I peered over my own menu at the laughing, chattering party of six opposite, willing Byron to turn so I could examine his features more clearly. When he did, stroking the brunette's face sensually with a lightly tanned hand, I found I couldn't look away and when, sensing again he was under strict scrutiny, he turned slightly in my own direction,

I blushed scarlet once more, diving behind the maroon leather-bound menu, the words swimming before my eyes in a maelstrom of confusion.

On my third attempt at saving all his features for future reference – the sharply chiselled cheekbones, the longish, black curling hair, the startlingly navy eyes – Mum glanced from me and then back to the object of my scrutiny.

'Your Byron at last, darling?' she whispered, taking in the beautiful dark-haired man as well as the obvious effect he was having on me. While Mum had been fully aware of my long-running passion for George, Lord Byron, she'd always been mightily relieved, she said, the man was a fantasy from the realms of history and actually *dead*, unable to wreak havoc on her innocent daughter. This new Byron, she eventually admitted, this imposter, this flesh and blood young stud stroking the arm of the girl on the opposite table, had appeared a very different matter: very much alive and, from the quivering mass that I had become, quite possibly nothing but trouble ahead.

'He can't be that gorgeous, Jen.' Gudrun frowned, upending the bottle of cheap white wine into three glasses, before placing it empty on the floor and looking round for the second. She shifted her long legs, raked bitten nails through her short-cropped hair and settled herself back on the heaped floral cushions on the floor of my room.

'Oh, he is, he definitely is. I know exactly who she means and she's absolutely right.' Annabelle sighed. 'Long dark, curling hair, crinkling blue eyes...'

'Oh, for God's sake,' Gudrun tutted almost crossly.

'Listen to the pair of you: crinkling blue eyes. Eyes can't *crinkle*. The purple cellophane wrapper on the chocolate Brazil nut in a tin of Quality Street *crinkles*...'

'He's a sort of Michael Hutchence...' Annabelle went on.

'I hope not,' Gudrun smirked. 'He's been dead two years.'

'Byron's been dead two hundred,' Annabelle sniffed, 'but that doesn't stop Jen fancying him.'

'So, Jen,' Gudrun pointed out, 'if he's so gorgeous, how come we're into our third year and he's only just come to your attention? I don't think *I've* ever seen this demi-god you can't stop going on about.'

'There are well over twenty thousand students in Cambridge,' I said patiently. 'And, you must admit, we've tended to socialise mainly with people from Trinity.'

'Which college does this Byron bloke light up then?'

'Fitzwilliam. I've been doing my research. He's big into *Footlights* apparently.'

'Oh, an actoooor, is he?' Gudrun raised an eyebrow dismissively, lengthening the vowels on the word to show her cynicism. 'No wonder we've not seen him around; he'll spend all his time down on Park Street at the ADC club.'

'So, that's why we're going to enrol down there.' I laughed nervously, taking a big gulp of wine so as not to meet the others' eyes.

'You are joking!'

'No way!' Annabelle and Gudrun spoke as one.

'The last time I was on stage was when I was an angel in the Reception Nativity,' Gudrun said gloomily. 'I was already so pissed off at not being Mary, I broke my cardboard halo, took a swing at Joseph and got really told off by the old boot in charge. If you look at photos of me on stage, I'm scowling throughout and giving everyone black looks while I refuse to sing.'

'Not much changed there then,' Annabelle said dryly.

'You've never heard me sing.' Gudrun was put out.

'Exactly,' Annabelle said.

'Listen, Jen,' Gudrun paused only to finish her glass of wine, 'there's absolutely no way I'm setting foot in that place. I don't have the time, the energy or the inclination. I've got piles of work outstanding and then I've got months on hospital wards. I honestly don't know how these people spend so much time down there, letting it take over their lives, and still manage to come out with a degree.'

'But they *do*,' I said enthusiastically. 'Look at Tim Brooke-Taylor, David Frost, Eric Idle and John Cleese. All started their acting careers in Footlights.'

'But I don't want a career in acting,' Gudrun said in some exasperation. 'I'm going to be a doctor if you remember.'

'Alright then,' I racked my brains for others who'd gone on to fame and fortune. 'Norman Hartnell.'

'Who?' Annabelle and Gudrun again spoke as one but then Annabelle said, 'Oh wasn't he the first Dr Who?'

'No, that was *William* Hartnell. Norman Hartnell was the Queen's dress designer. Made her wedding dress.'

'Well, there you go then,' Gudrun said comfortably. 'The last thing I want to end up doing is designing bloody wedding dresses for royalty. I am, if you remember, against any elitist monarchical society. *Vive la republique!*'

'OK, OK, well at least come with me to watch what they're up to. There's the "*Fortnightly Smokers*" sessions – the next one is on Thursday – for freshers who want to show what they can do.'

'Well, if it's for freshers, your Byron's not going to be there then, is he? Do you actually have any idea what he's called?'

'Laurie Lewis.' I almost purred his name. 'What a beautiful name, don't you think? And, no, of course he's not a fresher. He's in his final year and from somewhere in the Yorkshire Dales. Katy Foster says he's got the most wonderful Sean Bean accent. She's told me all about him.'

'Yorkshire? Hell, that's a long way away. Isn't it near Scotland?'

I tutted. 'You obviously didn't do Geography A-Level, Gudrun.'

'Too busy trying to get the sciences and maths I needed for medicine.' Gudrun said tartly.

'So,' I pleaded, 'will you both come with me?'

'What's it worth?'

'Half a pint of Guinness in The Eagle?'

'What do you reckon?' Gudrun turned to Annabelle.

'Make it a pint, Jen, and we'll take you down there and hold you up if this demi-god of acting stoops to looking your way.'

I beamed. 'Brilliant. You might even enjoy it.'

'Right, is this it then?' Gudrun asked as we made our way to our seats. 'It's a bit small, isn't it?'

'It *is* small,' Annabelle agreed. 'You can't believe Norman Hartnell was designing the Queen's clobber in here, can you?'

Gudrun laughed out loud at that. 'Either of you two got any chocolate while we're sat here waiting?'

'Eighty seats apparently,' I said, not daring to look round to see if Byron was sat on one of them.

'And is he here?' Annabelle asked, having no similar compunction not to.

'I don't know.'

'Well, there's some bloke who looks a bit like Michael Hutchence by the stage…'

'Michael Hutchence? As if…' Gudrun snorted derisively. 'Michael Foot, more like. Look at that hair and those glasses. Oh, hang on, hang on, bloody hell, yep…' For once Gudrun appeared lost for words as a dark-haired man appeared at the first man's side 'You win, Jen. Byron and Michael Hutchence rolled into one.'

I took a surreptitious look towards the edge of the stage indicated by Gudrun and there he was, apparently helping organise this first freshers' stand-up comedy evening of the new Michaelmas term. My pulse raced and my heart hammered.

'He's coming over, Jen.' Annabelle almost spluttered the words.

Laurie Lewis, dark hair curling onto the collar of his leather jacket, was certainly heading our way. Oh, dear God, I thought, nervously biting my bottom lip and throwing back my hair in panic, please don't let Katy Foster have said something to him. I briefly closed my eyes while Gudrun and Annabelle on either side of me both surreptitiously reached for a hand each.

He walked right up to us… and then carried on walking. Walking all the way past, before gathering up and kissing the same girl he'd been with in Midsummer House on my first day back in Cambridge. It was a perfectly executed gathering up and kissing, centre stage almost, and sure to attract as much attention possible from the now full auditorium.

'Blimey, I bet he's rehearsed that move,' Gudrun whispered. 'See how he made sure he was in the best position to be seen before he kissed that girl?'

'He's an actor.' Annabelle was quick to defend my love object. 'It must just come naturally to him to be so overtly affectionate in public.'

'Make your mind up,' Gudrun hissed. 'He can't be both acting natural *and* being an actor at the same time.'

'Can't he?' Annabelle looked puzzled.

'Right, when do the laughs start?' Gudrun was becoming impatient. 'We've seen Byron, sussed out the opposition – sorry Jen, not convinced you're in the winning lane there – and now can we watch some comedy?' She looked at her wrist watch. 'I've an essay on rectal carcinoma to tart up before hopefully *not* seeing it in the actual flesh on the ward tomorrow.'

I wanted to cry: Laurie Lewis was obviously deeply entrenched with the sultry dark beauty. At five-foot-eight and a good size 10, I felt myself a sturdy roan carthorse compared to the little glossy show pony now possessively linking arms with Laurie Lewis and disappearing backstage with him.

'She's a midget.' Annabelle patted my left arm sympathetically.

'She'll have a terrible time in labour,' Gudrun added knowledgeably, patting my right. 'Come on, cheer up; curtain's going up.'

'Apparently it's a good idea for your opening joke to

have a broad appeal,' Annabelle whispered after the first three acts had been and gone, the first two accompanied by forced, highly inflated laughter from their mates in the audience.

'I don't think the last one had any friends to support him,' Gudrun concluded 'and, to be honest, Annabelle, I don't find jokes about flatulence *broadly appealing*. All three have hit the Holy Trinity Jackpot of being left, feminist, anti-monarchy and finding breaking wind funny.'

'That's a Holy Quadrant,' Annabelle pointed out.

'Why don't we have just *one* who admits to being Tory and racist?'

'They wouldn't dare. Shh, shh,' Annabelle hissed. 'Don't be so harsh. It's their first time on stage.'

'And hopefully their last,' Gudrun sniffed. 'What do you reckon, Jen?'

'It's good. It's fine. It's very funny.'

'But you're not laughing one bit, are you? Had enough? I think there'll be a break soon. We can slide out and give our seats to that lot standing over there. Do you want to go?'

I nodded, making to stand at the same time as there was movement around the stage and Laurie Lewis jumped up on to it. Mesmerised, I sat down once more, the other two glancing in my direction and then at each other, before taking their seats again themselves.

Oh, but he was beautiful. He spoke easily, his flattened northern vowels almost purring as he read out the agenda for both this, as well as the ADC Theatre's for the coming term. I couldn't take my eyes from him as he joked of the most important production coming up just before Christmas, that of *Gawain and The Green Knight*, 'the part of Gawain himself – that pinnacle of humility, piety, integrity, loyalty and yes, honesty – being played, somewhat superbly, by yours truly…'

'Eh, lad, ah dint realise yon King Arthur's pal were from oop north,' a wag at the back yelled out to much laughter and applause, Gudrun joining in with delight.

'OK, OK, I get it,' Gudrun eventually conceded through her laughter. 'Even I can see he's pretty gorgeous. But come on, let's get out of here while we can. I'm sorry, Jen, but I think he's well and truly spoken for.'

Being, on the whole, a level-headed sort of girl, and knowing that my dream job in publishing would only come about if I stopped thinking about Laurie Lewis and instead buckled down to hours of intense study, I forced myself to concentrate on the vastly increased workload that invariably comes with being a final year undergraduate at Cambridge, determined to get the First I'd promised myself – and my dad – I was in line for.

A damp, foggy November morphed into an even gloomier December, an irrepressible icy east wind blasting its way across the flatlands of East Anglia for what had seemed days on end. Instead of chasing ridiculous dreams of my Yorkshire Byron, I concentrated on the one from the nineteenth century – together with my ten-thousand-word dissertation: '*Byron and the women who loved him*', spending ludicrous amounts of time in the library, accessing research and the precise referencing of sources, bibliographies and possible footnotes in order to provide accurate description and explanation of the phenomenon that was the nineteenth-century poet, politician and freedom fighter.

And then it was suddenly the end of term and Dad was on his way to pick me up. I'd bumped into my Texan, Beau, earlier that week and had agreed to meet him for a quick Christmas drink in *The Eagle* before being picked up by Dad there.

'I thought you were trying to discourage the Texan chap,' Gudrun said, her voice slightly accusatory. 'You're dolled up to the nines for a date with someone you've professed no interest in.'

'It's not a date and I'm certainly not trying to *encourage* him,' I countered tartly. 'I need to be ready to go straight on to some drinks do Dad's been invited to up in London. He has contacts with Wesley and Brown Publishing in Westminster and thought, as I'm desperate to get into publishing once I graduate, I might like to join him.'

'Nothing like a bit of the old nepotism to get you where you want to be, is there?'

'Bit bitchy that, isn't it?'

'I'm sorry, Jen, ignore me. I'm just shattered and premenstrual.' Gudrun gave me an apologetic hug. 'I want to go home too, but I've another week on the wards before I can head back to Sussex. You look absolutely gorgeous. I love that brown leather skirt. Goes so well with your auburn hair and brown eyes.'

'Mum bought it for me last birthday. Not convinced it's really me.'

'Oh, go knock 'em dead.' Gudrun smiled, obviously

slightly embarrassed at the unusual handing out of such praise. 'I'd employ you to publish any book of mine the minute I set eyes on you...'

'Right, I'm off.' I hugged Gudrun back and looked at my watch before shrugging myself into my jacket. 'Have a good Christmas. Don't work too hard...'

I ran down the stone stairs, gave a cheery wave to the porter reading *The Daily Mirror* in his lodge before dashing down the Christmas-decorated streets, turning onto King's Parade and then Bene't Street before going into *The Eagle* and bounding up the stairs to the function room at the top, where I'd arranged to meet Beau.

He was already there, his face suffused with smiles the minute he spotted me. I moved to kiss him chastely on the cheek and, as I turned slightly to ask for a glass of white wine, stood stock-still, the blood pounding in my ears as my eyes met another pair.

Laurie Lewis was standing, alone, just a few feet away, his blue eyes staring at me with such intensity I couldn't do anything but stare, totally transfixed, right back.

2

'Hey, Jenny, you alright there?' Beau touched my arm solicitously, turning me back towards him as he handed over a glass of white wine. 'You look as though you've seen a ghost.'

'Sorry?' For a second, I couldn't quite work out where I was, how this huge bear of a man smiling down at me with such affection, was anything to do with me.

'You're actually shaking.' Beau was now concerned. 'Are you ill? You've gone quite white.'

'I'm fine. Really. Slight headache, that's all,' I lied. I didn't dare turn back to where Laurie Lewis had been standing, staring at me: he'd probably gone, melting into the heaving crowd of students determined to have one final meet-up before heading for home and Christmas or, worse, he'd been joined by his exotically dark girlfriend, the pair wrapped around each other, oblivious to anyone else but themselves, or even worse still, he'd never been there at all.

I'd made him up, for heaven's sake; a total figment of my imagination.

'Excuse me, could I get past you to the bar?' My heart raced once more as Laurie Lewis's hand rested briefly on my arm before he attempted to make his way through the throng standing two deep waiting to be served. Having moved past me, he turned, his eyes searching out my own before raking my face with such intensity I thought I might just fall in an embarrassing heap onto the wooden floor amongst the fag ends, spilled beer and abandoned crisp packets. Laurie smiled across at me (and no, Gudrun, the purple Quality Street wrapper *does not* have a monopoly on crinkling), his navy eyes still fixed on my own.

'Sure.' Polite as ever, Beau made way for Laurie, moving towards me and allowing the other man to walk past and, in doing so, blocking my view of Laurie with his huge height and expanse. 'Jenny?' Beau took my hand. 'Can I persuade you to fly out to meet my family after Christmas...?'

'Excuse me again,' Laurie's northern flattened vowels were a direct antithesis to Beau's extended deep southern drawl. He smiled directly at me, placing a lingering hand once more on my arm as he manoeuvred himself past to stand at a newly vacated space over by the window. I fancied I could still feel the heat of his touch on my jacket sleeve seconds after he'd moved away.

'Jenny? Jennifer?' Beau was looking concerned once more. 'What do you think?'

'What do I think?' I turned reluctant, dazed eyes away from Laurie Lewis's retreating form and tried to concentrate on what Beau was saying. 'About what?'

'New Year? Back home? Ma daddy would just love...' Beau broke off as a pair of arms went round me, one of them shooting out to shake his own.

'Beau. Good to see you again.' Dad hugged me once more. 'Are you ready, sweetheart?

We could do with heading straight back to London before we get stuck in traffic.'

'Good to see you too, sir.' Beau shook Dad's hand with such enthusiasm, Dad winced slightly before manging to withdraw it. 'Ah was just saying 'bout Jennifer – with your permission, sir – coming out to Wilbarger County for the New Year celebrations?'

'You don't need to ask my permission, Beau. Sounds a great offer. Jen?'

I glanced at my watch, reluctant to leave any room where Laurie Lewis was still in situ. 'You're very early, Dad. We've only just got our drinks.'

'Let me get *you* one, Mr Baylis.' Beau was already scanning the crowd at the bar for a way through. 'A coke, maybe?'

'It'll have to be a quick one.' Dad turned back to Beau but he was already on his way to the bar. 'Is it all back on, Jennifer?' Dad lowered his voice. 'You know, with the Texan? Your mother will be delighted.'

'No, it isn't,' I hissed. 'And don't you go encouraging him, Dad. Right, off to the loo…' I set off, pushing through the throng gathered around the session poet.

'You can't.' Laurie Lewis was stood in front of me, blocking my passage through.

'I can't what? Go to the loo?' Oh hell, bloody stupid thing to say.

'Go without telling me your name. Go without giving me your number.' Laurie reached out a slim hand, taking a stray lock of my long auburn hair in his hand before carefully placing it back behind my ear. 'You are the most beautiful girl I have ever seen.' He continued to gaze down at me, seemingly unable to tear his gaze away from my own.

'Oh, I bet you say that to all the girls.' Another bloody stupid banal thing to say. I mentally kicked myself.

'I most certainly do not.' Laurie grinned a lazy, lopsided smile and I felt my stomach slide away somewhere in the direction of my tan leather boots. 'Is that your dad? Has he arrived to whisk you away?'

'Yes, we have a drinks do to go to in London.'

'London?' Laurie grinned again. 'I'm on my way to King's Cross myself. I saw you come in here and just had to follow you in to see if you were as gorgeous as I saw at first glimpse. You've made me miss my train. But you're actually driving to London this minute…?'

'Oh.' I felt myself go pink. He wanted to drive to *London* with me? What was I supposed to reply? Giving a lift to Laurie Lewis would be like having a tiger on the back seat: what if he pounced? Wonderful but terrifying. Was he having me on? It was all a bit too much for me: the reality of actually standing next to Laurie Lewis after months of dreaming about him, after endless scenarios I'd acted out where he would set eyes on me and instantly fall in love with me, was actually a bit overwhelming. Especially as it seemed he was now suggesting he might join my dad and me on the journey home. As he shifted slightly, turning his head to lift his glass, I took a discreet glance up at his face. I wasn't disappointed: his mouth was full and sensuous, his olive skin unblemished, his eyes the blue of my favourite sweater. Laurie Lewis, remarkably, was every bit as gorgeous close up as from a distance.

'I have to go.' I saw Dad start to say his goodbyes to Beau and about to head in my direction.

'But I still don't know your name?'

'Jennifer.'

Laurie bent down and kissed my cheek, whispering in my ear: 'Jennifer, please may I have your number?' He smelt of wine and some unknown aftershave, of peppermint and French cigarettes.

'I don't have a pen on me.'

'I do.' Laurie took a Parker pen from the top pocket of the well-cut black jacket he was wearing over his white T-shirt. 'Fire away.'

'You've nothing to write on.'

'I want this number close to my heart.' Laurie grinned, turning the pen to the palm of his hand before writing down the number and, still holding my eyes, pressed his hand somewhere in the general direction of his chest, just as Dad and Beau appeared at my side.

Flushing with embarrassment that my father and, particularly, Beau, might have witnessed this little drama, I overcompensated, smiling inanely in welcome towards the pair of them.

'Jenny?' Beau turned a stricken face towards me. 'You've not said whether you'll come or not? To Wilbarger County…?'

Obviously sniffing a rival, Laurie Lewis thrust out a hand, first to Beau and then to Dad. 'Hi, friend of Jennifer's. Must go, I've got to get to King's Cross for the train home to Yorkshire and I've already *missed* one train.' He executed a winning smile in Dad's direction.

'Oh, shame I've got your mum's car, Jen. We could have given your friend a lift to London.' Dad turned to Laurie, taking in the other's incredibly good-looking face, the dark, almost gypsy-ish, hair and the apparent effect this boy was having upon his only daughter. 'Two-seater, I'm afraid.' He turned back to Beau who was hovering. 'Good to see you, Beau.' Dad patted my arm firmly. 'I'll be in the car, darling. We need to get off.'

'I really have to go,' I said. 'Beau, I'm so sorry, I have so much work to catch up on… and I'm nowhere near finishing. I must go,' I said again, reaching up on my tiptoes to give Beau's cheek a firm, and what I hoped was conclusive, kiss. I turned back to Laurie Lewis, unsure what to say or do next.

'See you, Jennifer,' Laurie smiled. He held up his right hand, my phone number marked in large digits on the palm. 'I'll ring you.' He bent down, replaced the lock of hair behind my ear once more and kissed the corner of my mouth. It was enough to have my heart racing and more than enough for Beau to get the intended message from this rival for my affections.

It was only when we'd picked up my luggage and were motoring down the A11 and just passing Saffron Waldon, that I realised Laurie Lewis had never introduced himself, never actually told me his name. He had, I further realised, assumed – rightly – I'd know exactly who he was.

I spent the days before Christmas in a state of feverish excitement and anticipation waiting for the phone to ring, swinging like a pendulum from the highs of the remembered subtle kiss, the writing of my number on his hand, his saying I was the most beautiful girl he'd ever met, but oscillating to the depths of despair when I remembered Laurie Lewis's sultry dark-haired girlfriend, before totally crashing when, by Christmas Eve, he still hadn't rung. Maybe he thought the phone number was for the halls of residence and what he'd *meant* was he'd ring me on my return to Cambridge? Or maybe, and far more likely, seeing I'd given a Sonning dialling code, he'd washed his hands both literally and metaphorically of me and was, even now, in the arms of the tiny sultry beauty somewhere, not giving me – Jennifer Baylis, five-foot-eight carthorse – another thought.

'Is this your Byron from the restaurant?' Mum finally asked when I had yet again raced down the stairs to the ringing phone only to end up in a seemingly interminable debate with Great Aunt Agnes re the merits of sage and onion stuffing versus chestnut and apricot for the turkey.

'Is *what* my Byron from the restaurant?' I snapped as I retraced my steps up to my room where I'd been trying, without much success, to make notes on the coming Lent term's module on post-colonial texts and theory.

'The reason why you're high as a kite one minute and about to slit your wrists the next?' Mum suddenly realised what she'd said and, staring at me, asked, 'You're not, are you?'

'Not what, Mum?'

'About to do anything silly.'

'Oh, for heaven's sake…'

'It's just that Dad said you were talking to an exceptionally attractive dark-haired man in The Eagle and poor old Beau didn't appear to be getting a look-in. Was this your Byron?'

I nodded miserably. 'I've finally met him, Mum. He said I was the most beautiful girl he'd ever met. He wrote my number on his hand…'

'On his hand?'

'...and now I'm worried he forgot and washed it off.'

Mum laughed at that. 'Well, progress indeed, darling. If he's that serious, if he wants your number, he'll find a way of getting it.'

'I'm off for a walk,' I said. 'I can't concentrate on any of this.'

'I could do with a hand with tomorrow's veg,' Mum said mildly. 'There are twenty of us tomorrow, you know.'

'I'll help when I get back. I just need to clear my head.' I headed back down the stairs and into the boot room where I pulled on my old pair of Hunters and Mum's Barbour, whistled for Paddy, our Golden Retriever, and set off.

I walked upstream from Sonning Bridge, where Dick Turpin was rumoured to have hung out at one point – not literally, I smiled to myself, recalling he'd actually been hanged at York. York, Yorkshire: home to the Vikings, the Romans, the Brontës, Sylvia Plath and Ted Hughes and now Laurie Lewis. God, I thought, as I passed St Andrew's church in its prime location on the Thames and where Jeremy had been christened, I wished I could stop thinking about him. I pulled Paddy from a particularly engrossing smell behind a wooden bench on the muddy footpath and, after giving me a mutinously hang-dog look, he allowed me to turn round and head back in the direction of home.

Dusk was setting in as I rinsed accumulated mud from the dog's legs and belly with the outdoor hose, before walking through the kitchen door. The house seemed unusually quiet, devoid of people, music or TV white noise. Jeremy appeared at the top of the stairs.

'Where are Mum and Dad?'

He shrugged. 'Gone out somewhere. For drinks with somebody.'

'That's helpful. *Not*.' I looked at him with some suspicion. 'What are you up to?'

'Nothing.' He appeared shifty and I sniffed the air suspiciously. He'd either been smoking, doing drugs or that other thing seventeen-year-old boys got up to when alone in their bedrooms.

'Anyone called?'

Jeremy shook his head. 'Oh, yes, someone from Neighbourhood Watch wanting Dad to join them for a Christmas sherry.'

'No one else?'

'Nope. Oh yes, hang on...St Andrew's saying Mum missed her turn to do the flowers.'

'That it?'

'Yep.'

'You sure?'

'I said. God, you could be a stand-in for Hanns-Joachim Gottlob Scharff...'

'Who?'

'Master interrogator for the Luftwaffe during the Second World War.' Jeremy was doing A-Level Modern History.

'Right.'

'Do you fancy pinching some of Great Granny Enid's advocaat? You know, get pissed?'

'On advocaat?'

'Granny Enid's not coming tomorrow; nobody else drinks it...'

'Well, no, obviously. Being dead these past six months does usually put a stop to any potential Christmas visiting.

Or drinking.' Mind you, it was tempting. I could drown my sorrows in eggnog rather than finishing making notes. Or attacking the two great bags of sprouts that were looking at me accusingly from where Mum had strategically left them, together with a sharp kitchen knife and a pan, on the kitchen worktop. 'Go on then. I'll get it.'

'Already got it,' Jeremy smirked, disappearing into his room. I climbed the stairs and followed him in, pulling a face as I met a fug of cigarette smoke, sweaty trainers and flatulence.

'For god's sake, open the window, Jez. Mum'll have a fit if she comes in.'

Jeremy poured two huge mugfuls, handing one to me and downing the other. Oh, what the hell. I raised the coffee-stained mug and went for it, enjoying the cloying but soothing taste of brandy and egg as it hit the back of my throat.

'Oh, somebody did ring for you.' Jeremy squinted through the professional-looking smoke ring he was intent on sending to the ceiling.

I felt my pulse race. 'Who? Who was it?'

'Erm, some woman? Some woman you met the other day at the publishing place up in London? Wants you to give her a ring after Christmas?'

Total disappointment that it wasn't Laurie was only slightly tempered by the fact that Tara Tremayne, from Wesley and Brown Publishing, had actually been in touch and appeared possibly interested in discussing an opening for me once I'd graduated in the summer.

'God, you're hopeless, Jeremy.' I made to rise from the depths of the armchair I was lying across, but the alcohol from the sickly advocaat appeared to have rushed straight to my legs and I settled back once again. 'Did she say anything else? Did she leave a number?'

'Yes, downstairs on the pad.' Jeremy stubbed out his cigarette and reached for a CD. 'Next to the number from some dude that rang for you.'

'Some dude?' I sat bolt upright. 'Some *dude*?'

'Didn't get his name… northern accent.' Jeremy lay back on the bed, banging his head rhythmically into his pillow as Def Leppard burst forth into the room. 'Not Scottish… Lancashire…? Yorkshire…?'

I jumped off the bed, raced down the stairs and into the hallway, scrabbling amongst the detritus on the table for the notepad that always sat by the side of the phone, scanning the page feverishly until I found what I was looking for. I took a deep breath, tearing off the bottom of the page with its very obvious area code and number and galloped back upstairs to my room where I ran a brush through my hair, applied lip gloss and liberally sprayed Dior's Dune. I looked at my reflection in the mirror, hastily added blusher to counteract the spots of red on my cheeks caused both by the advocaat and the shock of Laurie Lewis actually contacting me and went into my parents' bedroom where there was a second house phone.

I sat for a good minute on my mother's *Nina Campbell* counterpane, following the fabric's blue and yellow pattern with my finger while gathering the nerve to actually push the buttons on the phone.

'Daisy Royd Farm.' The man's voice was curt, northern.

'Oh, I'm so sorry,' I apologised. 'I must have got the wrong number.'

'Who you after, love?'

'Sorry,' I closed my eyes. Bloody stupid Jeremy had obviously written down the number incorrectly. Now Laurie would think I wasn't interested in getting back to him. There was always the *Yellow Pages*... But how many Lewises must there be in Yorkshire? Mind you, thank God he didn't live in Wales...

'Who you after?' the man repeated.

'Laurie Lewis?'

'Laurence,' the man shouted. 'Phone.'

Hope flared as I heard the man speak to someone. 'Keep it short, lad, would you? I need to get on to a couple of people who've not picked up their turkeys yet.'

'Hello?'

'Hello, it's Jennifer Baylis. You rang? You left your number with my brother?'

'Jen-ni-fer.' Laurie spoke my name, breaking it down into its three syllables, almost caressing each one with his lovely northern accent. 'I'm so glad you rang.'

'You live on a farm?' I asked, not quite sure what else to say.

'Yes. Sheep mainly, and cattle. My family has farmed here for centuries.'

'Oh, how *lovely*.' I had a sudden wonderful image of rolling Yorkshire dales, long-horned, rusty-brown cows chewing the sweet unpolluted northern grass, while hundreds of sheep were herded safely and lovingly down from the surrounding hills by a sharp-eyed, but caring, black and white farm dog. 'And turkeys?'

'Turkeys?' I could almost hear Laurie frown. 'Oh, my father rears a few around this time of year. Keeps the villagers happy at Christmas. Listen, Jennifer, I'm speaking to several people in the know up in London – TV companies and the like – between Christmas and New Year. I'd love to meet up with you.'

'Really?' I felt myself grin with happiness. The advocaat and adrenalin were doing their work. 'In London?'

'I could come over to you in Berkshire once I've had lunch with the producers in London.'

'Come to Berkshire?' I felt a slight wave of panic. 'To stay?'

'If that's alright with you? And your parents don't mind.' Laurie's voice adopted its silky persuasive tone once more. 'I've done nothing but think of you since seeing you in The Eagle last week, Jennifer. I'm not sure I can wait until we get back to Cambridge.'

'I could perhaps meet you up in London?' My mind was absolutely racing: I just couldn't imagine Laurie Lewis here with my parents. With *Jeremy*. While Mum and Dad had always encouraged my friends to stay, had always been more than welcoming to anyone I'd brought home (they'd adored having Beau to stay one long, tedious weekend when he'd followed me around the house like a love-sick puppy), let's face it, Laurie Lewis was a whole different ball game.

'I'm booked in for a chat with some guy at the BBC next Wednesday. Of course, acting is the only way forward for me and I'm looking at RADA after I graduate, but I'm investigating all possibilities, you know? Examining every way and means to get where I need to be. So, I've looked up train times from Paddington to Berkshire. Whereabouts are you?'

'Erm, I'm not sure my parents…'

'I totally understand. They don't know me from Adam. Look, just say if it's not convenient.' Laurie's tone was regretful. 'I've contacts in London; people who'd be happy to put me up for the night. I just thought it would be a great opportunity to spend some time with you? Get to know you?'

The thought that Laurie might lose interest in me, now that he'd found me, had me backtracking, assuring him that yes, of course, my parents would be more than happy to let him stay.

After another ten minutes on the phone, where Laurie flattered, teased and flirted with me, I ended the call fizzing with lust, happiness and anxiety as my parents walked in, slightly tipsy from their afternoon drinks do.

'Byron?' Mum asked, seeing my face.

'I thought Byron had been dead and buried these last two hundred years?' Dad frowned, as I floated back up the cream-carpeted stairs to my room.

'I think this one is very much alive and kicking,' Mum said, picking up the bag of unpeeled sprouts with a loud sigh.

3

When, four days after Christmas, it started snowing, I swung from despair that Laurie Lewis wouldn't actually be able to make it down from the Frozen North (where, from my southern-centric stance, Yorkshire had taken on the mantle of the Arctic Circle) to utter relief that he wouldn't actually now be coming to stay with my parents – and Jeremy – for the anticipated few days after his meetings in London.

'He's coming to stay?' Mum had asked through the growing mound of peeled sprouts once I'd advised her of the imminent guest. 'Here?'

I'd nodded, not quite able to meet Mum's eye.

'But is that wise, darling? What do you know about him? Have you spoken more than one sentence to him?'

'Of course I have,' I replied hotly, repeatedly denuding one sprout of its outer leaves until it resembled nothing more than a pale green nut. I could repeat, verbatim, the ten or so sentences that had actually passed between us.

'And where is he going to sleep?'

'We have *two* spare bedrooms for heaven's sake, Mum.'

'Yes, and Aunt Agnes will be in *one* of them.'

'You *are* joking?' My head flew up and the knife sliced through my finger rather than the vegetable. 'Bugger, now look what you've made me do. Please tell me she'll have gone by the time Laurie gets here?'

'No, Jennifer, she won't,' Mum said firmly. 'And you're bleeding all over those sprouts. She's decided she's staying here until the New Year before moving on to that friend of hers in High Wycombe.

I'd actually closed my eyes in despair at the very thought. How could I put Laurie in the tiny box room as well as subject him, as the whole family was annually subjected, to Great Aunt Agnes and the ancient stertorous-breathing pug that accompanied her wherever she went?

'Well, I suppose if you've invited this actor...'

I hadn't dared tell Mum he'd invited himself. In my mother's book, this was, I knew, the most heinous of crimes, the height of bad manners.

'... at least we should be able to have a decent game of Charades.'

After at least three changes of outfit, I finally settled on a pair of bottle-green cargo pants, my precious brown Doc Martens and a skimpy green vest that allowed free rein to my midriff. And then, terrified that Laurie might actually see it as an *open invitation* to my midriff, pulled on the oversized bottle-green sweater I'd bought Dad for Christmas.

'Doing a stint down on the docks, sweetheart?' Dad peered over *The Times* and drained his second cup of coffee. 'Wasn't that sweater a Christmas present for *me*?' he added, mildly.

'You need to wrap up, Jennifer.' Aunt Agnes broke off

another tiny piece of toast, buttering it lavishly and adding marmalade from the decanted mound on her plate before taking one bite and giving the rest to Winston, wheezing asthmatically at her feet. 'Young girls,' – she pronounced it *gels* – 'like you need to watch their kidneys, going out in the snow without a vest.'

A total blue-stocking, rumour had it, Agnes Fellowes – Mum's paternal aunt – had been recruited straight from Girton College, Cambridge, where she'd studied Maths, to join the growing band of codebreakers at Bletchley Park during the war. She'd never openly verified or denied this rumour, but enjoyed the notoriety that accompanied it, promising me, as a fellow Cambridge academic, she would reveal all when I was ready, in order that I could write up her exploits and, in Aunt Agnes's own words, *make a killing in the Sunday Times Best Sellers*.

'Do you want me to drive you to the station?' Dad now asked. 'The roads won't have been gritted.'

'Can I take the Defender?' Living where we did, down a Berkshire country lane that could be cut off for days when it snowed, Dad had bought an old 1970s army surplus Defender which had not only enabled him to thwart the snow and thus get through to Twyford station and up to London, but had been perfect for teaching me, and now Jeremy, to drive in the large paddock adjoining our garden.

'No, really, I'll be fine.' God, heaven forbid that I have my father in tow to pick up Byron, as was most often the case when a friend from school was coming for a sleepover. I glanced at the kitchen clock. I was ridiculously early, I knew, but nerves and Aunt Agnes were combining to send messages of escape to my booted feet. I dashed upstairs to the second spare bedroom to check all was in order – God, it appeared so provincial. *And* he'd have to share the bathroom with Jeremy. The bathroom! Hell, Jeremy was notorious for not flushing the lavatory.

I dashed in there, pulled a face of utter disgust at the contents of the toilet bowl, flushed, washed my hands and collected the wet towels the little sod had abandoned on the floor, depositing them in the laundry basket before fetching a matching clean pile from the airing cupboard. I got my revenge, using Jeremy's soggy flannel to wipe round the scum and bum-fluff debris left deposited round the basin before tossing it wetly by its corner to join its fellow towels in the basket.

'Mum, tell Jeremy to be *pleasant*.' I picked up the Defender keys from the hook by the back door. 'And if he can't be pleasant, tell him to... tell him to... oh I don't know, tell him to *shut it*. And to flush the bloody loo.'

'Darling, calm down.' Mum advised, taking a chocolate cake from the oven. 'You're making *me* nervous. His train doesn't get in for another hour.' She frowned. 'He can't have come down from Yorkshire just this morning?'

'No, he had various interviews yesterday with the BBC and... and... other people...' I couldn't imagine who these people were. 'RADA, I think.'

'RADA? Four days after Christmas? Surely not?'

'*I* don't know, Mum,' I said crossly. 'Whoever will take him on after he graduates.'

'Right.' Mum put up her hands in silent acquiescence. 'Whatever.'

'And he stayed with friends in London last night. In Chelsea, I believe. Actor friends.'

'Lovely. You get off and drive safely and I'll put sticking plaster over Jeremy and Aunt Agnes's mouths.'

The wheels of the Defender spun in protest once I managed to get the car into gear and actually moving. It was like manoeuvring a tank after driving Mum's little MX5 and I quailed somewhat as the lane ahead rose steeply, glinting frostily in the late morning sunshine. You can do this, I told myself and put the car into second gear, trundling slowly up the lane as I clutched at the rock-like steering wheel with my gloved hands. Once at the top of our lane, I was able to drive along country roads that appeared to have had at least a smattering of grit thrown at them, and then I was onto the main road and driving the two or so miles to Twyford Station where I'd arranged to pick Laurie up from the London train.

I parked the Defender in the Station Road car park as near to the main entrance as I could and, realising I had a good half-hour to wait before the train was due in, pulled on my pink bobble hat and gloves, cursed the car for its lack of heating and reached into my bag for the book of Byron's poetry I always kept in there, settling myself into the poet's words, rhythm and rhyme. I was soon totally immersed, the outside world fading into total insignificance. I'd just read and, with closed eyes, was repeating out loud the immortal words:

Love will find a way
through paths where wolves fear to prey

when there came a loud knocking on the passenger seat window and I jumped in panic.

'Thought it was you,' Laurie grinned as he opened the door and heaved himself and an overnight valise onto the seat. 'There was a train in when I got to Paddington so, rather than freeze my tush off on the platform, took a chance that you might be here early. Oh, my God, Jennifer, you're even more beautiful than I remembered.' He pulled off my pink woollen hat, throwing it into the back of the Defender and, wrapping my long auburn hair around his hands, bent to kiss my mouth. Caught off guard, I did the one thing I'd been dying to do ever since that morning I'd first seen him below the window of my room at Cambridge, and returned his kiss with an intensity that surprised us both. I'd kissed numerous boys and men in my almost-twenty-one years but never had a kiss left me reeling as this one was proving to do.

'Jen-ni-fer.' He smiled that wonderful lazy crooked smile and went in for a second kiss which, if a couple of giggling kids, peering in on tiptoe as they waited for their mother to open the boot of the adjacent car hadn't interrupted, might have led to a third initiated by myself.

I finally sat back in the driving seat, breathed out in order to bring back some semblance of normality to my wildly beating heart and adjusted my seatbelt before pulling a slightly trembling hand through my hair. I stole a quick glance across at Laurie as he fiddled with his own recalcitrant belt, and wasn't disappointed. He was everything – and more – I remembered and my heart continued to knock almost painfully as I took in the perfectly oval and symmetrical features, the longish black curls, the large navy blue eyes fringed with ridiculously long black lashes. He was buttoned into an expensive-looking navy overcoat and I wondered, not for the first time, how a student such as he could afford such classy clothes and meals out in Michelin-starred restaurants. I took in the yellow woollen scarf wrapped artistically around his neck, and came to the obvious conclusion that Laurie Lewis, like me, came from a family wealthy and generous enough to provide these little luxuries. I feasted my eyes on his profile as Laurie continued to struggle with the Defender's ancient seatbelt. A glimpse of black stubble graced his cheeks, chin and upper lip and I knew Aunt Agnes would more than likely raise an eyebrow at the lack of a morning shave. I didn't care; I loved everything about Laurie Lewis.

'Sorry about there being no heat in this thing,' I finally managed to say as I swung the Defender round a drift of exhaust-and-grit-encrusted snow and headed for the station exit. 'Mind you, I suppose you're used to tractors and farm vehicles living on a farm?'

Laurie nodded vaguely. 'I'm not sure how we managed to escape this snow in Yorkshire. We've had none so far this year.'

I felt vaguely disappointed. The images I'd romantically conjured up of Laurie driving the smart red tractor loaded with myriad bales of sweet-smelling hay up into the snow-ridden Yorkshire hills and dales on Christmas Day, faded to nothing.

'Great house,' Laurie said as I finished bumping along the frozen ruts of the lane and skidded through the huge wooden gates and onto the drive of *Mayfield Manor*. 'Have you lived here long?'

'We left Fulham when I was about four,' I said. 'I don't remember much about actually living in London itself. My brother, Jeremy, was only a baby when we moved here.'

'What does your father do?'

'Dad?'

Laurie nodded and I took in the stunningly-elegant grade-two listed manor house – seeing it, perhaps for the first time, through another's eyes – stretching itself like a particularly smug cream cat in the winter sunshine.

'He works in the city. Finance,' I said vaguely, never completely sure what Dad actually did. 'Come on, come and meet Mum. I'm afraid my Great Aunt Agnes is staying as well. She's a bit of a rum old bird; don't let her get you into any political discussion. Oh, and just ignore my brother, Jeremy.'

'Chocolates? For me? Really, you shouldn't have. I know how broke you students always are...' I heard Mum trail off as she took in Laurie's obviously expensive overcoat and silk scarf together with the gift-wrapped box of Harrods' dark chocolate truffles. She appeared unsure what to actually do with them, now they were in her hand. She glanced in my direction before placing them on the hall table, giving Laurie the opportunity to place a hand on her arm and move in for a well-orchestrated kiss on her cheek.

'So lovely of you to invite me.' Laurie offered up that winning smile of his. 'Especially after the day I had yesterday up in London with the BBC. Goodness me, what a day. All good stuff though, I'm sure. Promising, you know?'

I stared at Laurie as Mum politely tried to free herself

from his hand on her arm which appeared to have accrued a limpet-like quality. Was his voice different? There were still the obvious northern undertones, the flattened vowels, but a certain affectedness, as though he was acting out a part, was present. Perhaps he was.

'Ah, we meet again. How are you? Good Christmas?' Dad shook Laurie's hand firmly and Mum made her escape to the kitchen, raising another eyebrow in my direction until I actually felt the heat start to rise in my face. 'Jen tells us you've been up in town having interviews with the BBC? Been worthwhile?'

'I think so. Had lunch with the producer of a new drama that's being cast at the moment.'

'Really? Lunch? Good of them. Thought the Beeb had no money at the moment? They're always crying the poor tale when it comes to Radio 4.' Dad laughed. 'Where did they take you?'

Laurie appeared to hesitate. 'Oh, some little bistro place, can't quite recall the name.'

'Well,' Dad went on, 'I'm assuming you need to get with an agent? Get yourself an Equity card?'

'Oh, I already have one of those.' Laurie assumed an air of nonchalance.

'Really?' I was delighted. 'Gosh, I thought they were like gold dust?'

'Hen's teeth actually.' Laurie gave the two of us the benefit of his own, beautifully straight and white ones.

'So, er, how've you managed that?' I asked. 'I thought you had to be a professional actor?'

'You are going to finish your degree at Cambridge, aren't you?' Dad interrupted, looking worried. 'You can't give it up at this stage when you've only a couple of terms left to go.' It was a statement rather than a question. Narrowly missing out – according to his estimate at least, and we'd always teased him about this – on a place at Cambridge and spending three years, instead, at some former polytechnic university in the Midlands, had rendered my dad almost apoplectic at any wasting of opportunity on the part of those actually lucky enough to land a place at Oxbridge.

'Absolutely,' Laurie said smoothly. 'I have no intention of coming out without a First.'

'Right.' There was a protracted silence as Dad and I, as well as Mum, from the depths of the fridge where she was in the process of removing pâté and cheese for lunch, digested this self-proclaimed nugget of information, broken only by a latterly-risen Jeremy descending the stairs, simultaneously scratching at his groin and unwashed hair and proclaiming he was starving.

'So, how *have* you managed to get an Equity card?' I asked as I walked with Laurie along the same – now snow-covered – path I'd taken with the dog down by the church a week or so earlier. I glanced across at this beautiful man now several yards ahead of me, not able to quite believe he was here, with me. With *me*. With Jennifer Baylis. Jennifer Lewis. Jennifer Baylis-Lewis. I tried out the different combinations as Laurie walked ahead and I bent to scoop up the noxious dropping Paddy had deposited by his favourite bench.

'Do you really *have* to do that?' Laurie visibly shuddered as I deftly tied the black handles of the poo bag and swung it from my gloved hand in anticipation of the dog litter bin ahead of us on the icy path.

'And you a farmer's son?' I teased. 'I'd have thought you'd have been used to piles of the stuff around you?'

'Not *dog* crap. I've a bit of an aversion to this new mania for the constant clearing up after their pet pooches the middle classes appear to have taken on.' Laurie's Sean Bean vowels were back in place. 'What's wrong wi' just kicking it under the 'edge?'

'Is *that* what you do up in the Yorkshire Dales? Go round kicking cow shit under *the 'edges*.' I started to laugh at the thought of Laurie and his family following their cows around the fields, clearing up after them. When Laurie didn't seem to find either this, or my adopting what I thought was a pretty decent Yorkshire accent, remotely funny, I asked again about the Equity card.

'I model.' Laurie said with some pride.

'Model what?' I pulled the dog and caught up with Laurie. 'Aeroplanes? Railways? Villages?'

'I *am* a model.' When I still didn't quite understand what he was saying, Laurie went on, 'I've been a photographic model since I was a child.'

I stopped dead in my tracks, causing Paddy to look up at me in some surprise. '*That's* why I recognised you. *That's* why I knew your face.'

Laurie gave a slight smile. 'It comes to most people eventually. They know they've seen my face somewhere.'

'I thought I knew you from Greece.' I felt a tiny sliver of disappointment. 'From Missolonghi...'

'Greece? I've never been to Greece?' Laurie frowned.

'You've always reminded me of George, Lord Byron. We have a house on Kefalonia...'

'A house there as well? Your own? You own one?' Laurie

appeared much more interested in this fact than that he had a possible doppelganger in a museum on the mainland of Greece.

'Hmm, we've had it years. It belonged to my maternal grandparents originally. I suppose it'll pass down to Jeremy and me to share eventually.' I paused. 'Mind you, the little toe-rag's never shared *anything* with me. Apart from nits... Oh, and an out-of-date bottle of advocaat,' I amended, remembering. 'So, because you've been a model, you're allowed an Equity card? I never knew that.'

'The main reason I've kept the modelling work going all these years. It can be bloody tiresome and time consuming suddenly getting a phone call from my agent and then having to spend days freezing in some Scottish Highland dressed only in a pair of boxers.' (I gave a little involuntary shiver at the lust-making image of Laurie dressed in nothing but his pants.) 'But it does pay for life's little luxuries.'

'Ah, I see.' Things were beginning to fall into place. 'Well,' I said brightly, 'if you don't succeed in your acting career, at least you can always continue having your photo taken.'

Laurie's face darkened. 'There's no question I won't succeed,' he snapped. 'I just *have* to, Jennifer. That's why I'm putting all these feelers out now – writing letters, making phone calls, taking part in everything that's any good through Footlights. Look at Hugh Grant...'

'Wasn't he at Oxford, rather than Cambridge?' I frowned. 'But, absolutely. I could look at *him* for ever.'

'Exactly.' Laurie took my gloved hand. 'Mind you,' he bent to kiss my open mouth, 'I'd much rather you looked at *me*,' he added, grinning down at me. 'I don't know what you've done to me, Jennifer Baylis, but whatever it is, I want you to carry on doing it.' He kissed me hard, one warm and determined hand snaking stealthily up the back of my Barbour before finding its way beneath the hem of my shirt.

Loving the kiss, but hearing Paddy start a growling rumble in his throat (I reckon my dog thought Laurie was attempting to eat me) I pulled away first. I was also a bit embarrassed at the thought of being seen by friends from school or, even worse, friends of my parents or our neighbours who all walked dogs down this path. 'So,' I said, pulling down my shirt and adjusting my coat, 'I bet your mum and dad are very proud of you? You know, doing the photo shoots? Do you have brothers and sisters? Have they been to Cambridge as well?' I wanted to know everything about him. When Laurie didn't reply, didn't give any indication that he wanted to talk about his family back in Yorkshire, I suddenly stood stock-still, remembering. 'But you have a girlfriend, Laurie. I've seen you with her…'

'*Had* a girlfriend, Jennifer. It's been coming to an end for months.'

'And does she know? You know, that it's *coming to an end*?' I hated the idea I might be the cause of someone else's unhappiness.

'Don't worry, it really is over. Mind you, you've not said how *you* feel about me? I mean, I saw you outside The Eagle and ended up missing the train back to Yorkshire because I just couldn't *not* follow you inside.' He turned me towards him, gazing into my eyes with such intensity I eventually just had to – regardless of any randomly wandering neighbours – reach up and kiss him back.

Laurie eventually looked at his watch. 'I'm frozen. Should we be getting back? I don't want your dad to think I've run off with you. And I could murder a drink.'

4

'A new year. A new century. A new sodding millennium for Christ's sake.' Gudrun rolled over on my bed as though she meant to get up off it but then obviously thought better of it and, instead, reached for her bag, taking out a tin of tobacco and Rizla papers before rolling a few thin whisps of tobacco into an anorexic excuse for a cigarette.

'Well, *yes*, Gudrun,' Annabelle interrupted, 'if you hadn't noticed, we're actually three months into it. Mind you, nothing momentous seems to have happened to mark this fact. Well, for you and me, anyhow.' She looked meaningfully across at me.

'I thought you were giving up the fags, Gudrun?' I said, flapping my hands and going to open the window. A cold, miserably wet couple of months in the virgin millennium had morphed into a March which suddenly seemed to be bursting forth with new light and new life. And new hope for my future ahead. And even though, coming to the end of the Lent term, I was laden down with so much coursework and exam revision I sometimes felt I was drowning under the very weight of it all, I was also filled with a buoyant excitement for my life once I'd finished university. Three months on from him hunting me down in *The Eagle*,

Laurie Lewis and I were together, and what I suppose you would call a pair. We were together, he was my boyfriend, my partner, the man of my dreams. Give him any title you wanted, he was, he constantly assured me, his.

'You can't call these fags,' Gudrun said dismissively. 'They're just paper carriers of a little bit of light relief to get me through all of this. Jesus, if someone had only told me, when I was doing A-Levels and filled with a burning desire to save the nation's health, how bloody hard it all is...'

'Hate to tell you this, Gudrun, but you ain't seen nothing yet.' Annabelle pulled one of her faces. 'Just you wait until you're a registrar and constantly on call all night. You'll have helped whip out someone's appendix, had five minutes' sleep, no breakfast and then you'll be faced with a gall bladder *no one* should have to look at, let alone someone who's not yet had their Coco Pops.'

'Do you think I can change courses and do English Literature like you lot?' Gudrun glanced across at me from under almost closed eyes. 'How the hell does Byron get through all his work and pass exams when he's either fannying around, pretending he's an actor, or off posing for photos?'

'He doesn't *pretend* he's an actor,' I tutted. 'He *is* an actor.' I shrugged, not sure myself how Laurie managed to stay on top of everything. 'He appears to get by on not a huge amount of effort. And certainly not much sleep. One of those naturally clever people, I suppose. He'll suddenly panic, realise he's got a backlog of work and stay up all night on coffee and Red Bull. He seems to be able to pull it off.'

For a good fifteen seconds or so the only voice in the

room was that of Jennifer Lopez as the three of us digested Laurie's way of working through the final leg of three years at Cambridge. It had suddenly hit both Annabelle and me that we were on the last lap of our educational run and about to be thrown out of the cloistered womb-like world of Cambridge and into the real one – with all that went with it. I wasn't quite sure whether to be envious of or be commiserating with Gudrun who had another two years at university before her seemingly never-ending long haul to be a consultant ended.

'Well, it looks as though *you're* set up, Jen.' Annabelle was glum. 'And yes, I am bloody jealous: a job in publishing up in London and a gorgeous man in tow to boot. You couldn't make it up.'

'Still got finals to get through,' I said.

'Oh, come on, Jennifer, you know as well as I do, you're on for a First. Professor Dixon was singing your praises only yesterday.'

'Really?' The often sarcastic, and always taciturn, Professor John Dixon had never given any intimation he thought my thesis '*Byron and the women who loved him*' was up to much.

Annabelle nodded. 'I think he'd had a sneaky celebratory sherry with Professor Morgan –she's had some new work published, apparently – and it had loosened his tongue. He obviously shouldn't have been discussing another student's dissertation with me, so for heaven's sake don't let on I've told you, but yes, he said especially as you're going into the world of publishing, he wouldn't be surprised to see your Byron work morph into something much bigger in the years to come.' She laughed. 'Hey, you could end up doing a documentary for the BBC from your family's place in Greece.'

Although Annabelle was being totally over-the-top ridiculous – and I obviously didn't tell her this – the same thought had been buzzing round my head for weeks. How wonderful if I could actually eventually turn my dissertation into a published book, and then have it optioned for airing on TV. Maybe Andrew Davies, who'd done the fabulous job with *Pride and Prejudice* on the BBC, might be interested... And I knew exactly who'd be playing *my* Byron: Hugh Grant may have played Byron in the film *Rowing With the Wind*, but Laurie Lewis would be the perfect choice for my drama...

'Are we having that takeaway or what?' Gudrun finally rolled off my bed and brought me down to earth with a bump. 'KFC or a fart-worthy Vani's Vindaloo Special?'

'For Christ's sake...' Laurie stood at the bar in Trinity where I'd arranged to meet him. It was seven in the evening but incredibly quiet, everyone I knew in a total panic about the final exams we'd be sitting almost immediately after the Easter break, which commenced in a couple of days' time. Although Mum was wanting me home for the full five weeks' vacation, telling me she'd tiptoe round me while I revised, and bring me lovely things on a tray to keep me going, I'd applied for and been given permission to stay on in my room at Trinity for at least the first week of the vacation. Easter was the latest it could possibly be that year, being the very last weekend in April, I'd reminded Mum, and I reckoned I could cram in so much more work if I was left alone for the first week. I'd be home for the actual Easter weekend where, even though Jeremy and I were no longer children, Mum still insisted the Easter bunny would be a-visiting and there'd be an egg hunt around the garden and a huge Easter Sunday lunch to rival what we got through at Christmas.

'I suppose Byron is staying on as well for the vacation and not going back up to Yorkshire?' Mum knew me so well. 'Is that the real reason you're not coming home immediately?'

'I have no idea what Laurie has planned,' I'd lied. I knew perfectly well Laurie wasn't returning north at all and I was really looking forward to spending our nights together once we'd spent all day cramming. Laurie, who never worried about a thing, I'd come to realise, was suddenly in a panic about finals. Although he would never admit it to me, I knew he knew he hadn't got through the work he should have done. He'd returned, only the previous day, from a full week away on a photo shoot in Mallorca and I'd missed him terribly, counting the days until his return, immersing myself fully in the edits for Byron in order to feel Laurie that bit nearer to me, as well as going to bed with the navy cashmere sweater he'd left behind in my room.

Laurie stood impatiently at the bar, bad temper and tension emanating from every bit of his body while trying to get the attention of the barman who was intent only on his crossword. He was like a coiled spring. 'For heaven's sake…' he said out loud, raising his eyes to the ceiling as the barman disappeared through the open door behind the bar. Although he'd somehow managed to acquire a bit of a tan to complement those incredible blue eyes of his, Laurie was actually looking tired, puffy-eyed, seedy even. He was, I could see, about to erupt.

'You OK?'

'It's my dad.'

'Your dad?'

'Been taken into hospital, apparently.'

'Oh gosh, is he OK?'

'I would imagine so.' Laurie was dismissive. 'Oi, mate,' he shouted as the barman reappeared with a crate of mixers, 'who d'y'ave to sleep with round 'ere to get served?' His broad Yorkshire accent was out on full display. If ever Sean Bean needed a stand in, Laurie Lewis would surely be it.

'You offering?' the barman replied lasciviously and, if Laurie hadn't been in such a foul temper, I'd have laughed out loud.

'Certainly not,' Laurie snapped. 'This gorgeous girl here is more than enough for *anyone*.'

'What's wrong with your father?' I took his hand. 'Is it serious?'

Laurie downed the glass of red wine the barman finally put in front of him and he appeared to relax a little. He leaned towards me, taking my face in his hands, stroking my face in just the way he knew had me a quivering jelly. 'Jennifer,' he sighed into my hair. 'My mother obviously needs me back in Yorkshire; there's so much to do on the farm at this time of year.'

I'd hoped Laurie would be with me in Berkshire for the Easter weekend although, to be honest, when he'd accompanied me home for Dad's birthday the previous month, I'd found it a bit hard going. Laurie seemed to put on an act, determined to show my parents how wonderful he was. His Yorkshire accent became less pronounced with each hour that passed until, by the end of Sunday lunch, after several glasses of my dad's cherished Malbec, Laurie appeared more of a Home Counties resident than the rest of us. At which point Jeremy had snorted loudly over the cheese board, muttered something under his breath and left the table. Followed, minutes later, by Dad professing an urgent phone call to America that couldn't wait. Laurie had continued to advise both Mum and myself of his future plans for life and career in London once he'd graduated, and I'd just gazed at his beautiful face while he held my hand, praying these plans might involve me.

'Your father?' I repeated, bringing myself back to the present. 'Is it serious?'

'I need to go back up to Yorkshire to be with my family. They'll need me if something happens…' He dropped a kiss onto my head and sighed.

'Of course you do,' I said, stroking his face sympathetically. 'Gosh I know how awful I'd feel if it was *my* dad. You *must* go now.' I paused, an idea forming. 'Would you like me to come with you?' I asked. I was desperate to see the seductively charming farm in Yorkshire; to meet his parents and his three sisters. To see where Laurie had grown up. 'You know, I'm pretty much on top of my work now…'

'Hell, I wish *I* was,' Laurie scowled. And then smiled. 'No, no, I really don't want to take you from your studies. Your parents would never forgive me, and neither would you if you missed out on that First. I'll travel up in the morning and do a lot of work on the train.' He turned my face to his. 'You can't begin to imagine how much I've missed you, Jennifer. I should be going back up to Yorkshire this minute but I'm going to be really selfish – I need to be with you, if only for just one more night.'

I sometimes had to pinch myself that all this was real: that Laurie Lewis, beautiful man of my dreams, was actually with me, professing his love for me, putting off going back to see his sick father in the north in order to spend one more night with me.

We abandoned any further idea of spending the evening cramming in the library together and, instead, headed, arms round each other, back to my room with a bottle of wine picked up from the off licence on the corner. While Laurie helped himself to my one remaining clean towel – I had bags of laundry ready to take home to Mum – and disappeared along the corridor to the bathroom, I quickly brushed away the toast and peanut butter crumbs from the previous evening's late-night munchies, sprayed copious amounts of perfume both over myself and my sheets and smoothed down the pillows and coverlet.

Laurie was back in ten minutes, wearing just the navy towel wrapped around his hips, his black hair slicked back like an otter's, a dark mat of hair rising from the depths of his groin. That wasn't the only thing that was on the rise. I shivered slightly and Laurie smiled.

'Come here,' he said softly, 'we've got all night ahead of us before I leave for Yorkshire.'

I don't think I'd ever loved Laurie Lewis more.

'Jennifer, you're like a damned bear with a sore head. Go out for a walk. Take the dog with you and go out and get some fresh air, for heaven's sake.' Mum attempted to walk through the pile of screwed-up file paper, abandoned books, half-eaten sandwiches and empty cups before picking up several plates and a couple of mugs of untouched coffee, now cold and with a residual scummy rim. 'Surely you've done enough work today? You've been at it since five this morning.'

'I can never have done enough,' I said, almost in tears. 'If I don't get a First, I'll have let myself down…'

'Stop being so hard on yourself.' Mum paused, lifting and pushing back a lock of greasy hair from my forehead: I don't think I'd had a shower for a couple of days. I glanced out of the bedroom window, a slanting ray of light cheering up the garden and fields after several days of on-off April showers. The last of the daffodils were bobbing maniacally in the stiff breeze and the first tulips, still scarlet, yellow and mauve buds on slender milky-green stems, were manfully trying to compete. Everywhere I looked, new life was burgeoning forth and it was passing me by.

'OK, you're right,' I sighed, leaning back, stretching and catching hold of Mum's hand. I'd bitten her head off several times when she'd come in for a chat or just to tell me to go to bed when it was two in the morning. 'Sorry I've been such a cow.'

She laughed. 'I was just the same when I was doing my finals, sweetheart, but all *I* wanted was a good Two-One. A First from Cambridge, Jen, is pretty much pie in the sky… not that I don't think you're capable of it, darling,' she added hastily. 'And this job in London you've been promised isn't dependent on you getting a First, you know.'

'I know, I know.'

Mum hesitated. 'Why don't you have a break?'

'Yes, I'm going to,' I said. 'Going to have a shower, wash my hair, go for a walk with the dog and then do nothing but drink a whole bottle of Bulmers sweet cider and catch up with *Coronation Street*.'

Mum hesitated again. 'No, I mean a real break.'

'What? Like a mini break to Bournemouth?' I laughed at that.

'Dad's driving up to Leeds in the morning. Why don't you go with him?'

'Do they do mini breaks to Leeds?' I smiled as Mum tutted.

'I know you were hoping Laurie was going to turn up over the Easter weekend,' Mum went on, picking up a couple of books and straightening the folded dog-eared pages as she'd always done ever since I was a little girl and into *Hairy Maclary* and then *The BFG*.

I was desperate to see Laurie, and had spent the first couple of days back home expecting a phone call saying he was on his way down from Yorkshire for the Easter weekend but it – and he – never arrived. Eventually, once Easter Monday had been and gone, together with the surfeit of chocolate I'd anxiously nibbled at while debating whether I should ring him up in Yorkshire, I finally rang the number he'd left with Jeremy four months previously. And rang and rang, but to no avail. I looked up Daisy Royd Farm in Yellow Pages and it was the correct number but, despite that, it was either permanently engaged or ringing unrestrainedly into the ether.

Dad had bought me my very first mobile phone – a rather snazzy little Nokia – as an Easter present, tucked into a hollow chocolate egg which he'd then carefully rewrapped in its blue tinselly paper. I couldn't work out why he was encouraging me to break into the egg even before breakfast on Easter Sunday and why Mum wasn't standing over me telling me not to – we had a huge Easter leg of lamb to get through and I wasn't to spoil my appetite gorging on chocolate – as had been the case every other previous Easter morning.

A mobile phone, I soon worked out, wasn't much use when other people (Laurie) didn't also have one, but Dad assured me that by the time I was living and working in London the following autumn, to not have one could be compared to him not having a Filofax when he first started up his business in the city in the Eighties. According to Mum, Dad had been a true – if a little ageing – Yuppie, down to the blue striped shirts and red braces, a Perrier in one hand, his bulging leather-bound Filofax in the other.

'So, why don't you go up with Dad?' Mum finished rubbing at a coffee ring on my desk, leaned against the chair and folded her arms.

'To Leeds?'

'Yes.'

'For what reason?'

'You know why. It sounds to me as though Laurie is having some problems at home. With his father in hospital… he could have even died?'

'Mum!'

'Just saying, Jennifer. The last thing the poor boy needs when his finals are imminent.'

'Poor boy? I didn't think you were that keen, Mum.' Mum

had never actually told me what they thought about Laurie, but my parents' jointly raised eyebrows and exchange of glances whenever his name was mentioned told me enough.

'I've never said that, Jennifer,' Mum protested. 'I can totally understand what you see in him, darling; he's ridiculously attractive and quite the most charming...'

'But?'

'But *nothing*,' she said firmly. 'And, if knowing what's going on in his life is going to help you settle down to your work – and stop you biting my head off – then why not take the day off and go up with Dad?'

'I can't just do that, Mum.' I was horrified at the very thought. 'Just turn up, unannounced?'

'Well, go up to Leeds and have a day's shopping then. It's always good to see a new city. Or get Dad to drop you off in Haworth so you can see where the Brontës lived. Just have a day off from it all. Clear your head.'

'No way, Mum. I've far too much work to do, and as far as I know Laurie lives miles away from Leeds. Or Haworth. And, I wouldn't dare just turn up out of the blue. Sorry, Mum, daft idea...'

5

'This is a ridiculous idea of Mum's.' I glanced across at Dad. 'I should never have gone along with it.'

'Well,' Dad said cheerfully as he put his foot on the accelerator and moved the powerful BMW out into the overtaking lane on the M40, 'I'm not turning back now. Just go with the flow, Jen, and enjoy a day out with your old dad.'

'If you manage to get us there in one piece, I might. You don't half speed, Dad.' I looked out of the passenger window, at the streaks of red and yellow just beginning to appear in the sky to the east. The last two days had been particularly mild – warm even – for late April and it looked as though this one was heading that way too.

'Roads are pretty clear this time of the morning,' Dad argued.

'Morning? It's the middle of the night. It's still dark out there.'

'We should be in Leeds before nine. I'll buy you a nice breakfast and then you can decide what you want to do with the day. I've a meeting at nine-thirty in Leeds city centre but the next one isn't until the early afternoon, over near Midhope.' Dad glanced across at me. 'More than happy to drive you to Haworth so you can look round the Brontë parsonage before I set off for my meeting at one, if that's what you fancy?'

'It's a hell of a lot of driving for you, Dad.'

'Just what I need. I've been cooped up in the office in London for months and this car needs to have its head – show what it can do.' He put his foot down once more, giving the BMW free rein.

'You'll get done,' I said, closing my eyes and feeling the centrifugal force of the acceleration pin me back into my seat. Dad had always loved any form of speed, whether it be driving, skiing or when he took out his beloved speedboat moored down at the port in Kefalonia. Although he was a speed freak, he wasn't rash and every move was planned, measured.

'So,' Dad went on once he'd brought the car down to a slightly less law-breaking 8omph, 'You can do what I've suggested...'

'Or?'

'Or, once I'm out of the meeting in Leeds, I'll drive you over to Laurie's parents' place and then come back for you late afternoon when I'm done.'

I felt my pulse race at the very thought. 'I don't know, Dad. It's just not on, is it? I mean, what do I do? Knock on the farm door and say "Hi, I just happened to be in the area and is the kettle on?" Laurie would think I was mad. Think I was stalking him.'

'I'm sure I brought you up to be brave. Well, I hope I did.'

'Why are you and Mum encouraging me in this? I know for a fact you both don't like Laurie as much as you did Beau.'

'And your mum and I both know that you've fallen head over heels in love, Jennifer. And, while, yes, OK, Laurie might appear a bit flashy, a bit full of himself, we don't really know him. Quite possibly he's just been showing off to try to impress us. You know, as your parents, he wants to put himself in a good light with us. I can understand that. And, Laurie's only going to bother to do that if he feels the same way about you as you do about him.'

I'd always been able to talk to my dad about anything: school, boyfriends, drugs, and the rest. I was very lucky, I knew, especially when friends had commented there was no way they could confide in their fathers with anything like what Dad and I talked about.

'You seem to know a lot about this sort of thing.' I smiled, patting his arm.

'Well, I went through it all with your mum.'

'Did you?'

'Well, you know what your grandfather Fellowes was like.' Dad frowned as he remembered. 'Your grandma may have been a sweetie – and she *was*, but they'd had your mum, their only child, quite late on in life, and, especially when Aunt Agnes was thrown into the mix, I tell you, it was pretty hard going meeting up with that family. I came along, an Essex boy in red braces who'd been at a Midlands poly, and they weren't a bit impressed.'

'Really?' I suppose I knew all this, but not to the extent they hadn't wanted Mum to end up with Dad.

'Your grandpa was made lieutenant-colonel during the war as you know, and he expected his daughter to marry some Hooray Henry from the Home Counties, not a wide boy – spiv, even, as your grandfather liked to dub me – from Billericay.'

'And so this is why you're now driving me two hundred miles up the M1, to prove that you're not like Grandpa Fellowes?'

Dad laughed at that. 'Maybe. Who knows? Anyway, with Laurie at Cambridge – your grandfather would have been over the moon at that – and from farming stock into the bargain, he'd have been welcomed into the family fold in the way I never was.' Dad paused. 'Mind you, I'm not convinced Arthur Fellowes would have appreciated the northern accent or the long hair.'

'That's what I love about him, Dad.' I smiled, the thought of seeing Laurie again, surprising him on his home territory, sending shivers of delight and terror in equal measure down my spine.

'I know you do.' Dad patted my arm once again before fiddling with the car cassette player to find his favourite music. 'So, Westenbury village is it, then, rather than Haworth?'

'Do you think this is it, Jen?'

'No, it can't be.' I'd checked out Daisy Royd Farm in Yorkshire in the *Yellow Pages*, tallying it with the one precious phone number I had for Laurie and which I'd been constantly trying to get through to during the past week. 'I was under the impression Laurie's parents' farm was in the

Yorkshire Dales…' Not here, I didn't add, and what Dad was surely thinking, in a backwater of scrubby fields somewhere between Leeds and Manchester. It was now going on for early afternoon, the actual finding of Daisy Royd Farm, on the edge of the village of Westenbury, having taken us seemingly forever. We'd passed through several stunningly pretty villages once we'd left the M62, descending into a valley green with April rain, masses of daffodils and early blossom welcoming us into a part of the country I'd never before ventured. I hadn't, I thought somewhat guiltily, ever really been further north than Watford Gap, apart from flying up for a long weekend skiing break to Aviemore in Scotland when I was thirteen. Once off the main roads, we'd had to stop several times, asking for directions from helpful pedestrians who'd turned out, not so helpfully, to not know their left from their right or their T-junctions from their crossroads.

'Try the number again,' Dad advised, staring doubtfully at the mean-looking grey-stoned house standing somewhat balefully across from a windswept field filled with a few miserable looking sheep. It didn't help that the promise of another warm, sunny spring day down in Berkshire hadn't materialised up here in the countryside around West Yorkshire, where a lowering sky stretched overhead as far as the eye could see – an uninterrupted sheet of grey lead. 'You've got your new phone with you, haven't you?'

I pushed the digits on the Nokia which, after a week of constantly pressing, I now knew by heart. The same persistently engaged tone I'd been met with over the past few days rang out once more.

'What do you want to do, Jen? Turn round and head

down into Midhope town centre itself?' Dad looked at his watch. 'I'm already a bit late for my appointment, sweetheart...' He broke off as a figure, dressed from head to toe in rainwear, appeared at his side of the car, followed by a knocking on the driver's window.

'Can I help you?' The woman peered in as Dad opened the car window, dripping slightly from her raised wet arm and sending droplets onto Dad's black pinstriped suit trousers.

'We're looking for Daisy Royd Farm.' Dad turned to me. 'What's Laurie's last name, darling? I've forgotten.'

'Lewis,' I mumbled, totally embarrassed now and just wanting to turn round and get the hell out of there. It would have been enough, I now realised, just to see where Laurie lived. Just so I could picture where he was, until I saw him on his return to Cambridge. 'Come on Dad, let's go...'

'The Lewis place,' Dad said. 'We're looking for the Lewis place. Daisy Royd Farm?'

'You've found it then. You're here. Are you after some hens?'

'Hens?' Dad looked slightly startled. 'No, *Laurie*. My daughter here is a friend of Laurie Lewis...'

'Oh god, not pregnant, is she? You're not after Laurence with a shotgun, are you?' She started to laugh. 'Because, I have to warn you, my dad's pretty nifty with his own shooter. Can hit a rat in the hen house at fifty paces.' She chortled again. 'And that's when he's got a couple of pints inside him.'

'Right.' Dad and I exchanged glances.

'So, is the Boy Wonder expecting you?' The woman who, when I managed to get a good look at her beneath her rain hood, didn't appear much older than me, bent her head and looked across Dad towards me.

'Boy Wonder?'

'Laurence. Come on, I'll take you up to the house.' She addressed Dad once again. 'I wouldn't bring this shiny machine of yours through the gate. You might never see it again.' And when it was obvious Dad was beginning to think he'd brought me up to some northern den of car thieves, and was about to make his excuses and reverse us back down the lane we'd just come up, she went on, 'Mud. Acres of the stuff. Always is after a wet winter and spring. You'd get stuck, and we wouldn't be able to pull you out, as Dad appears to have knackered the bloody tractor once again.'

'I need to go, Jen.' Dad looked as he had on my very first day at Queen Alexandra's Girls' School when I was eleven, not wanting to catapult me out of the car and into a totally strange environment, but knowing he must. 'Decide what you're doing. You've got your phone.'

'Come on, love.' I didn't realise, until the woman took the hand of a somewhat vacuous-looking toddler, that she wasn't actually speaking to me. The child's face, as flat and pale as a saucer of skimmed milk, was almost hidden beneath the red hood of a quilted anorak. I hadn't realised the child – of indeterminate gender – was even there, so silent and still had it been throughout the whole conversation with its mother – well, I assumed she was its mother – and was further surprised when, taking a deep breath, grabbing my jacket and exiting the BMW, I saw the woman also had with her a baby in a pram.

'Ring me when you're done,' Dad said through his

still-open car window and, giving a forced cheery wave of encouragement just as he'd done when I was eleven, put the car into gear, executed a rather flashy three-point turn and roared off down the lane.

'Come on, let's see if we can find your Uncle Laurence,' the woman said to the toddler, who stared up at me with flat, expressionless eyes before dutifully trotting alongside his mother and her accompanying pram. I felt sick with nerves. What on earth was I going to say to Laurie: Surprise, surprise, it's me?

'Laurie doesn't actually know I'm coming,' I twittered, trying my best to avoid the muddiest parts of the path that led up to the house. My best tan leather boots were already splattered in oozing noxious mud and my leather skirt – the one I'd been wearing when I first met Laurie in The Eagle – was now sporting black dots. 'My father, somewhat fortuitously, had meetings in Yorkshire and I hitched a lift as it were... thought I'd surprise Laurie... have a break from all the studying I've been doing...'

The woman glanced my way. 'You don't have to explain: there's always been a stream of broken-hearted girls making their way to our door. My mum's used to it. And,' she paused, grinning, 'you lost me at *fortuitously*, love...'

Embarrassed, I followed her the rest of the way in silence as she led me round towards what I supposed to be the back of the house. A very large, untidy garden, full of row upon row of bedraggled-looking vegetables – potatoes, leeks and cabbages I guessed at a glance – stretched beneath a washing line of, presumably now very much wetter, sheets, men's socks and underpants. They stretched in a never-ending line (oh, God, no, that was Wordsworth's daffs, wasn't it?)

towards a broken-down wall separating the garden from the meadow beyond.

Our arrival signalled a cacophony of hysterical barking from two black and white farm dogs that, I was thankful to see, were actually tethered on chains. 'Shut it,' the woman shouted without much enthusiasm, and the dogs slunk back to their resting place at the entrance of two ramshackle kennels.

At the bottom of the three steps leading up to the back door, Laurie's sister – she still hadn't introduced herself, and showed little interest in knowing my name or how I knew Laurie himself – stopped, pulled a pink bundle from the pram and, with it tucked under one arm, took the toddler by the same hand, using her spare to open the back door with an accompanying kick to its base from her Wellington-shod foot. 'Always sticks,' she added cheerfully, pushing me, with the help of the pink bundle, into a warm but very untidy kitchen. She walked, I noticed now, with a very slight limp. 'Mum,' Janice – I was eventually appraised of her name – shouted up the stairs that led from the hallway next to the kitchen. 'Where's our Laurence? There's a friend of his arrived in a big posh car from London.'

'She's not here – she's just popped down to the Co-op for something – and neither's our Laurence.' A small, but fairly rotund man, red face clashing startlingly with a wisp of sparse ginger hair atop his otherwise quite bald head, appeared at the kitchen door, leaning heavily on the metal walking frame he'd used to propel himself forward from the room beyond. He turned to me. 'Hello, love, does our Laurence know you're coming?'

'No, no, not at all. I just, you know, happened to be in the area… thought I'd just call in…' I trailed off, wanting the ground to open up and swallow me as the two of them exchanged knowing looks.

'How's the leg, Dad?' Janice hoisted the pink bundle in front of her, peeling back several layers of fabric until a baby was finally released, its bald and wispy gingery head a mini replica of the man's who stood appraising me in the doorway.

'Bloody painful,' he sniffed. 'Could do with a cup of tea if you're putting the kettle on. Do you want one, love?'

'No, no, I'm fine thank you. Really.'

'I can see you're *fine*, love, but what I was asking was if you wanted a cuppa?'

'Thank you.' I felt myself redden. 'That would be very nice.'

'Milk? Sugar?' Janice sat the toddler down on the tiled kitchen floor, rummaged in one of those vast baby bags that all mothers seem to have with them, then whipped out a dummy and successfully stoppered the baby's mouth before it could actually protest. Then, expertly tucking the baby under her arm once more, she went to fill the kettle before placing it on the huge, curmudgeonly Aga to her left. I wouldn't, I decided, want to get into an argument with either Janice *or* the rusting, glowering Aga.

'Hello?' The kitchen door opened and a very tall, dark-haired woman with Laurie's unmistakable navy eyes smiled across at me as she proceeded to divest herself of her red coat and pick up the still – somewhat scarily – immobile toddler from the floor. Weren't kids this age normally into everything?

'Friend of our Laurence's,' Mr Lewis said, matter-of-factly. 'Come up from London.'

'Jennifer?' Mrs Lewis smiled. 'Laurie's told me all about you.'

'Oh. Has he? All good I hope.' Oh God, bloody banal thing to say.

'I didn't see any car, love? How've you got here? A taxi from the station?'

'No, my father drove me up. He had meetings in Leeds and Midhope. Once he's finished down there, he'll pick me up.'

'And does Laurie know you're here? Our phone's been down over a week – something else that's on its last legs.' She glanced across at Laurie's father and the look wasn't overly pleasant.

'That's why I came up. As far as I knew, Laurie was hoping to be with us for the Easter weekend...'

'I *bet* he was,' Janice interrupted. 'Anything to get out of giving a hand up here when it's needed. He'd much rather be fannying around thinking he's Brad Pitt, or pretty-boy posing for Armani in his undercrackers. Right, where are the tractor keys, Dad? I'll go and see if I can sort it.' She handed the pink baby to her mother. 'Oh, look, here's the man himself. Someone to see you, *Laurie*.' She threw a look at the kitchen door as Laurie, black hair plastered to his head, rain running in rivulets down his navy Barbour, shook himself like a wet dog.

My pulse raced. Every time I saw and reconnected with Laurie after time away from him, I wondered anew at the very beauty of him. He stood, startled, went very pale and then, very unusually for him, flushed pink. 'Oh, Jennifer? Where've *you* appeared from?'

'I've been trying to ring you all week...'

'Phone on the blink again, I'm afraid.' He still stood, as if rooted to the (badly balding) doormat.

'Unpaid phone bill more than likely,' Janice called over her shoulder as she passed him. 'Why not tell it as it is?'

Rita Lewis came to Laurie's aid. 'Jennifer's father has had a couple of meetings in the area, Laurie. She thought she'd take a break from all that studying and come and see you before he comes to pick her up.'

'Your dad's been here as well?' Laurie looked slightly sick.

'He just dropped me off, that's all.'

'Laurie, take Jennifer into the front room. I'll bring you both some coffee.' Rita Lewis frowned at the chipped mug of strong orange tea Janice had handed me and which, after one mouthful, had almost knocked my socks off.

Laurie led me through the kitchen and into a neat but very chilly room which, it was pretty obvious, was kept only for Sundays, Christmas and guests, expected or otherwise. A floral Sanderson-covered three-piece suite almost filled the room and, as we walked in, a huge ginger Tom (perfectly co-ordinated with the ginger heads prevalent in the kitchen) gazed up at us with insolent, hooded eyes, daring us to move him.

'Go on, get off,' Laurie said, bad-temperedly, clapping his hands before swiping at the mass of ginger and white hairs left on the sofa. He didn't meet my eye but said, 'Let me get out of these wet things, Jennifer. I've been working out in the fields.' For a second, I had a lovely romantic vision of Laurie out threshing and collecting the corn in the manner of Angel Clare in *Tess of the d'Urbervilles* and the words, "*He was surprised to find this young woman – who had just*

*that touch of rarity about her which might make her the
envy of her housemates ..."* sprang immediately to mind.
The illusion – and quote – lasted all of a second as Laurie
went on, 'Fucking cat' and, without another glance at me,
left the front parlour.

I sat there for seemingly ages, not daring to move but
getting colder by the minute. Eventually Mrs Lewis came
in with a tray of coffee in rose-decorated china cups and
with a plate of red- and silver-paper-wrapped biscuits. 'Oh,
it's freezing in here, love. Hang on, let's put the fire on.' She
bent down to the gas fire, turning a knob at the side and
waiting with a lighted match until there was a loud pop
and the fire sprang into life. She turned back to me. 'I bet
you've been studying like mad? Laurie tells me you finish
this time too and have a job in London? In publishing? I
envy you: I *love* reading.' She sounded wistful. 'I was so
sorry to have to drag Laurie back up here when he's got his
own finals in a few weeks but Terry – that's Laurie's dad
– fell again a couple of weeks ago. I thought we'd be able
to manage, but Janice – that's Laurie's sister who you've
just met – Janice's husband, Darren, who usually helps out
with the hens and the sheep, decided to leave...'

'To leave?'

'Hmm. Ran off with the travel agent who was planning
their summer holiday to Magaluf. Dreadful place by all
accounts, and even more dreadful customer relations as it's
turned out...'

'Goodness.' I couldn't quite work out if Laurie's mum
was being totally serious or recounting what had happened,
slightly tongue in cheek.

'... And then, with the phone off, and the tractor finally

giving up the ghost, I was at a bit of a loss. I hoped we'd be able to manage with Lorraine and Cheryl helping out but, in the end, I had to get Janice to ring Laurie at college.'

'Lorraine and Cheryl?'

'Laurie's other two sisters?'

'Oh yes, of course.' I knew Laurie had three sisters but he really hadn't spoken much about any of them.

'But Lorraine is pregnant and I really don't want her near the hens…'

Was this for Lorraine's benefit or the hens? I didn't like to ask.

'And Cheryl, who's a support assistant at school, has enough on her plate with a new husband and a new job.'

'Yes, I can see that.'

'So, I'm afraid it fell to Laurie to help. I'm sorry he wasn't able to come to your parents' for Easter.'

'Oh, don't worry about that.' I balanced my china cup and saucer in one hand while Mrs Lewis was insistent I take a chocolate biscuit with the other.

I glanced across at her as I bit into the cushiony biscuit, chocolate breaking off and falling onto my hand and plate, and I chewed nervously before swallowing a mouthful of sticky marshmallow and milk chocolate. Mrs Lewis's thick dark hair had faded and was shot with grey, but her cheekbones were high, her mouth still full and sensuous and those amazing blue eyes, which Laurie had obviously inherited, were clear and intelligent.

I decided, on first appraisal, I liked her very much.

6

Laurie finally reappeared, showered and dressed and looking more like the Laurie I knew and had fallen in love with. I'd rather liked seeing him as a farmer, although I knew he'd been deeply embarrassed at my turning up and seeing him at what he probably construed to be his most vulnerable. He was still on edge.

'It's stopped raining,' Rita Lewis said, smiling as Laurie came into the front room. He was ill at ease, not quite sure what to say or do with me. 'Why don't you take Jennifer out for a walk? She can borrow a pair of my wellies.'

'What time's your dad coming back for you?' Laurie asked, still seemingly unable to meet my eye.

I looked at my watch. 'Oh, a good couple of hours at least. He'll ring me when he's setting off.'

'Ring you?'

'New phone.' I took the Nokia from my coat pocket.

'Right. OK. Come on,' he said. 'We'll take Mum's car and go down to the village. Is that alright, Mum?'

'Yes, I don't need it. Are you coming back to eat with us, Jennifer? You're more than welcome.'

'That's really kind...' I started.

'We'll drive down to The Jolly Sailor in Westenbury,'

Laurie interrupted. 'Jennifer's dad can pick her up from there. Much easier for him than driving all the way out here again.'

'If you're sure.' Rita seemed disappointed.

Laurie disappeared for a few seconds and returned wearing my favourite leather jacket and dangling car keys. I stood up to make my exit.

'Really lovely to meet you, Jennifer,' Rita smiled. 'Do come again when Terry's back on his feet and we're not in such a mess with it all.'

Laurie bent to kiss his mother's cheek. 'See you later, Mum. If anything needs doing, Janice is here to help. I won't be too long.'

We walked back through the room off the kitchen where Laurie's father had returned to his original position on the sofa, leg up on a chair, pork pie moving methodically from its resting place on his large belly to his mouth, his eyes never once leaving the small black and white TV in the corner of the room where the racing from Kempton Park had him totally engrossed. The toddler had joined him on the sofa, eating his own – much smaller – pork pie, his eyes on the TV screen moving in perfect synchronisation with those of his grandfather as the horses jumped the nine obstacles and ran to the race's conclusion. Of the pink bundle baby, there appeared to be no sign.

'Nice to meet you, Mr Lewis,' I said as we walked past.

'And you, love.' He didn't look up but, instead, took a swig from his can of Tetley's before reaching for the pork pie once more.

The rain had moved away, washing the sky and leaving

patches of blue through which a weak sun was endeavouring to make an appearance, but it was still wet underfoot.

'Enough blue to make a sailor's trousers,' I smiled, running to catch up with Laurie who was striding ahead. He didn't reply. Across the yard, Janice appeared to have had some success with the ancient red tractor, which was now coughing asthmatically, noxious diesel fumes belching from its overhead chimney.

'You off?' she shouted down from the cab over the growl of the tractor as we headed for the small blue Fiat parked ahead.

'Nice to meet you, Janice,' I shouted back.

'Was it?' She frowned and then grinned. 'See you again, no doubt. You appear to have made progress with the Boy Wonder where others have tried and failed.'

'Fuck off, Janice.' Laurie swore at his sister and, grinning, she retaliated by revving the engine once more, sending further plumes of diesel in our direction.

Laurie still didn't say a word as I opened the Fiat's door and hunted for a seatbelt. The car smelt of oil and wet carpet with undertones of some chemical which I realised was coming from the green turtle car odouriser hanging by a suction pad on the windscreen in front of me. The combination of all three was almost overwhelming and I wound down my window before hunting for the seatbelt docket.

'Broken,' Laurie said tersely. 'Just pull it across your chest and hold it there so we won't be stopped for you not being strapped in.'

'Right, OK.' I turned to Laurie. 'I'm sorry, I shouldn't have come.'

'No.'

'I missed you. I was worried about you.'

'Well, I'm sure you can see there's nothing to worry about. I'm fit and well and living the good life.'

'Have you managed to do any revision?'

Laurie nodded as he put the Fiat into gear and drove across the muddy yard, through the farmgate and out onto the lane where Dad and I had sat deciding what to do an hour earlier. 'Once I've helped Mum and Janice with the hens and the sheep – there were a couple of troublesome late lambings this week and we had to get the vet out – then I've generally worked in my room until the early hours. I should have done more when I was in Cambridge,' he added, shaking his head almost in despair. There were dark smudges of fatigue underneath his eyes which, to be honest, as if it were kohl, only added to his beauty. I took a surreptitious look as Laurie commandeered the narrow country lanes and unexpected bends. Was it *actually* kohl?

'Your mum's lovely,' I said as Laurie continued a brooding silence.

'She is. She's put up with all this shit for years.'

'You mean your dad's leg?'

'I mean my dad generally. He's a drunken, lazy sod.'

'I don't suppose he can help breaking his leg.'

'Oh, I think he can,' Laurie almost growled. 'After a boozing session down at The Red Lion, one Sunday dinner, two years ago, he attempted to mend a gutter on the hen house. He fell off the ladder and broke his leg. Had a gammy leg and bad back ever since. Or so he says. He wouldn't have bothered going up the ladder to get to the gutter – would have much preferred sleeping off his skinful all afternoon, knowing him – but even Janice was on to him that water was pouring into the large battery hut.'

'Even Janice? What do you mean, *even* Janice?'

'Thick as thieves those two. Always have been. Eldest daughter and all that.' Laurie glanced in my direction. '*You* know what it's like being a daddy's girl...'

Is that how I came over? A bit of a daddy's girl? I suppose I was in a way. Did my brother Jeremy resent my relationship with Dad? Anyway, I couldn't imagine the formidable Janice being *anyone's* girl, but I could see Terry Lewis would jump – and ask how high – if she told him to.

'I *am* very lucky how I get on with my dad,' I said a little stiffly.

'You certainly are.' Laurie smiled for the first time that afternoon. 'Driving you all the way up here just so you can work out why I wasn't answering the phone?'

'I was worried about you. And I wanted to see you...' I trailed off. What if Laurie really wasn't bothered about seeing me? I looked out of the car window, at the plethora of acid green meadows, pink cherry blossom and miles of dry-stone walling sectioning off the landscape. Daffodils, their glory long over in the warmer south, were in their element up here, every lay-by and cottage garden ablaze with different shades of yellow.

'It's very Wordsworth round here,' I said, when Laurie didn't respond to my telling him how much I'd missed him.

'You're a hundred miles south of Wordsworth country, here,' Laurie said dryly. '*And* the wrong county.'

'Never was much good at Geography,' I said, slightly embarrassed at my apparent romanticising of the West Yorkshire countryside.

'Jennifer,' Laurie said, almost as if speaking to a child, 'There's *nothing* academically you're not very good at, so don't give me that.' He gave me one of his looks and then smiled, patting my arm. 'You can't imagine how much I wanted to see you too,' he said softly. 'I paid for the phone to be reconnected this morning – managed to fit in an unexpected but rather lucrative photo shoot in Manchester this week – and I was going to ring you...'

'Really?'

'Of course.'

Laurie didn't expound further as we appeared to have reached our destination. He pulled the Fiat into the car park of The Jolly Sailor which was, apparently, the village of Westenbury's only pub, nestled in between the village school and the very pretty church. Laurie glanced at his watch. 'It's only two-fifteen,' he said. 'We've almost an hour before closing time.' I let go of the seatbelt across my chest which, I realised, I'd been clutching onto for dear life, and followed Laurie across the tarmac, through a deserted beer garden – its wooden tables and chairs awash with puddles from the morning's rain – and into a low ceiling-ed, very traditional pub. The main bar area was almost deserted apart from two old codgers sitting silently over their half-pints of bitter and a dark-haired waitress carrying a couple of scampi-in-a-basket type meals on a tray. 'I'll be with you in a minute, Laurie.' She smiled winningly in his direction and then stared at me long and hard before carrying on into a back room – presumably where the bar meals were served and eaten.

We stood at the bar, which was gloomy and dusty, and I wished we'd been able to sit outside in the spring sunshine which was soaking up the remains of the morning's April showers. 'Right, what can I get you?' The waitress reappeared at the other side of the bar and, ignoring me, smiled again at Laurie. She was incredibly pretty, quite tiny and with a red ribbon tying up her abundant, very dark hair. I had the same feeling of being an overgrown carthorse next to Black Beauty as I had when I'd compared myself to Laurie's exotic former girlfriend in Cambridge.

I glanced across at Laurie who was now sharing some, obviously private, joke with the girl. Was he flirting with the barmaid?

'Jennifer, this is Jess, the landlord's daughter…'

Jess, the landlord's daughter, plaiting a dark red love knot, into her long black hair… I knew I was staring – as well as misquoting one of the most wonderful lines in English poetry – but she was so uncommonly striking, I couldn't help but drink her in.

'Jess and I were at school together,' Laurie said. 'Primary school, round the corner, as well as over at Westenbury Comp.'

'But whereas Laurence here was always top of the class in everything he did, and ended up at bloody Cambridge for heaven's sake, I left after GCSEs.' She turned to me. 'I suppose that's where he's met *you*? Cambridge?'

I nodded, not quite sure what else to do.

'Well, *I'm* not staying round here much longer either,' she sniffed defensively. 'I can't wait to escape this god-forsaken hole.'

'It's very pretty,' I countered. 'What I've seen of it, anyway.'

Jess pulled a face and snorted. 'Just another year of working behind my dad's bar and I'll have enough to set off travelling. Going to end up in Australia.'

'I've always fancied the Antipodes myself.' I smiled back in what I hoped was a friendly gesture to this girl who appeared to have a need to compete with me.

'The Antipodes?' Jess paused. 'Hmm, I'd thought about going on there once I've done Australia and New Zealand.'

Laurie laughed out loud at that and, gathering up our drinks, led me to a vacant table at the far end of the bar by the window.

'She's in love with you, isn't she?' I said, glancing back at Jess who was giving surreptitious looks in our direction under the pretence of hanging clean beer glasses on hooks above the bar.

'Yes.' Laurie was matter of fact. 'Ever since she was five and offering me her twopence...' Laurie broke off as the pub door opened and two attractive blondes in cycling shorts and helmets walked up to the bar.

'Offering you her *what*?'

'Her twopence bags of Kayli.'

'Kayli?'

'You know, coloured sugar crystals in a bag?' Laurie frowned. 'Oh, maybe it's a Yorkshire thing? Anyway, Jess always had sweets on her because her granny ran the village sweet shop.' Laurie moved so that his back was towards the bar area. 'Jennifer,' he took my hand. 'What's going to happen once we leave Cambridge?'

'In what sense?' I felt my pulse race. Was Laurie telling me there was no future? Was he planning to come back up north? To sort out the farm for his mum, whom he clearly adored?

'You know what sense. Jennifer, I want to be with you in London.'

'Really?'

'Of course, really. I don't want to be anywhere without you...' He broke off as Jess hovered at the next table, brandishing a yellow dishcloth at its already clean and polished surface. He waited until she'd sullenly retreated and was out of hearing. 'How about if you and I get a place together? You know, in London? You're obviously going to be working there. Or were you thinking of commuting from your parents' place?'

'I suppose that *was* the plan to begin with.' To be honest I'd not really given it much thought. 'Dad would be able to give me a lift most days and, if not, it's an hour or so commute up to Paddington.'

'And then another twenty minutes to your office.' Laurie was at his most persuasive. 'Think about it, Jennifer. I want to be with you.'

'But you haven't got a job yet. How on earth are you going to live in the most expensive city in the country without work?'

'I've got my Equity card. I can always do more photo shoots to make ends meet until I find the film work – I know I can make a success of it, if I can just get an inroad into it.'

'Is that what you really want to do?' I asked, feeling excited for him.

'I'm going to get to Hollywood. Listen, Jennifer, if Hugh Grant managed it, so can I. So, first job is to actually *get* a

First. I'm going to break my balls off to get a good degree. Once I know Mum is able to cope better up here – our Lorraine and Cheryl are just going to have to do their bit to help – I'm going straight back to Cambridge and going to lock myself in and work every damned minute of every sodding day for the next month until the exams. Then, I'll make sure I've enough photo shoot work to keep me off the breadline and able to pay the rent while I'm living in London. Then knock on every door of everyone I can think of in order to get myself known...' He broke off, downed his glass of wine and looked at me. 'And Jennifer, I really want you there with me.'

I took his hand and just gazed at him with what, on reflection, was probably a bloody silly soppy look. I came back down to earth as my Nokia rang out loud and clear, making the pair of us jump.

'Dad,' I said regretfully, not wanting to leave Laurie and return south. I stood up to take the call, giving Dad instructions as to where I was before turning back to Laurie. 'OK,' I said, taking a deep breath. 'Let's do it. We'll find a place together in London.'

ACT 2

7

September 2003

'Sweetheart, congratulations. I'm *so* proud of you.' Dad was already sat waiting – impatiently I could tell – at a table in Daphne's at Brompton Cross, but jumped up from his seat near the lofty continental windows which, on beautiful early September days such as this, were open onto the pavement and general bustle of South Kensington. He grabbed me in a huge bear hug, blocking the way of a diminutive waiter who was en route with pudding to the next table.

'Sorry, sorry.' Dad grinned at the waiter, pushing me down onto a chair. 'Could we have champagne when you're ready?'

'Dad, no,' I protested. 'I have to be back in the office in just over an hour.'

'Oh, come on, Jen, it's not every day my little girl becomes a published author. You do know I'll be constantly in Waterstone's rearranging the shelves so you're always on show?'

'You won't need to,' I laughed. 'I'll have already been there.'

'*Byron and the Women Who Loved Him.*' Dad smiled, almost dreamily, in my direction before turning to the same waiter who'd appeared with a bottle of Veuve Clicquot in a bucket of ice and was now twisting the bottle's metal cage. 'My daughter is a published author, you know; the hardback is in the window of Waterstone's on Kensington High Street…' He broke off, bending down to his bag and fishing out two copies of my book, published that morning.

'Dad!' I laughed at his paternal pride but, feeling pretty high myself, picked up one of them, stroking it like the newborn baby it was, transfixed as always by the sultry Byron glowering up at me out of the black and white cover.

'Sign it, sign it,' Dad urged. 'Both of them.' He thrust his best fountain pen in my direction and, without hesitation, I wrote:

To the loveliest, most supportive Dad in the world, relishing the feel of the rich, creamy vellum under the pen's nib.

'Ok, celebration now. You can't have a book published without champagne.'

'I think you poured enough down me when I actually got the deal,' I laughed, but nevertheless sipped at the fizzing liquid, loving the bubbles on my tongue and the sensation as it hit the back of my throat.

'So, Laurie was unable to make it?' Dad gave me one of his dad looks over the menu and, without waiting for my response, went on, 'What are you having, Jen? I had the calves' liver with smoked pancetta and cipollini last time I was here; totally ambrosial.'

'Linguine with surf clams, chilli and parsley, please. And, you know Laurie would have been here if he could.' I paused. 'Have you ever known him miss the chance of a celebratory meal?'

'Not like you, that, Jen.' Dad appeared still engrossed in the menu, but I knew he'd taken in and digested my last, not overly complimentary, words.

I sighed. 'He just can't seem to get the break he needs, Dad. He's having to do more and more of the awful photo shoots for catalogues that he hates. You know, beige polyester slacks and acrylic V-neck jumpers.'

'Well, I suppose he is getting on a bit now – you know, pushing thirty. He'll be suited to elasticated-waist trousers, camel-haired car coats and driving gloves.' Dad grinned, but I knew he wasn't a bit impressed with Laurie's inability to get the acting work he so craved.

'Come on, Dad, he's not twenty-five yet. Plenty of time to make it big.'

'Really? The pair of you have been in London over three years now.' Dad looked up from the menu, reading glasses perched on the end of his nose, and gave me yet another of his dad looks. '*You've* done it, Jen. You've got where you wanted to be.'

'Yes, with your support.'

'My support? I've not subbed you while you've been here. You've grafted and earned your wage – as well as the promotions you've been given – all without any help from your mum and me.'

'You don't think buying me a two-bedroom flat in Clapham constitutes a bit of a hand-out?'

'Your twenty-first birthday present, sweetheart. Good

financial planning – inheritance tax and all that. You know I didn't want you in some god-awful bedsit sharing a bathroom with other people's germs, wet pants and tights dripping on your head while you cleaned your teeth.'

'Yes, and I'm exceptionally grateful. You know that. Having somewhere of my own gave me the peace and quiet to let me get on with writing the book. But Laurie *hasn't* had the support and backing I've had.'

Dad raised an eyebrow. 'Living rent free in the flat? I think that's pretty supportive, don't you?'

'Oh, don't start that again, Dad. You know I love having Laurie in the flat. We're together; he's my partner. *And* he contributes what he can from the TV ads, voice-overs and photo shoot work he manages to get.'

'But all a bit thin on the ground at the moment?' Dad shook his head and downed his glass of champagne. 'Never understood why anyone thinks a broad Yorkshire accent sells beans and soup.'

'Dad, you only have to look at the actor Richard Armitage on TV to see the appeal of up-and-coming northern actors.' I didn't add that Laurie had almost prostrated himself at the producer's feet trying to get the role of John Standring, a Yorkshire farmer, in the BBC adaptation of *Sparkhouse*, only to be pipped to the post by Armitage. Laurie couldn't bear to watch it on the box, swearing and gesticulating wildly if ever he caught me drooling, like every other hot-blooded woman in the country, over Armitage's performance.

'A degree – albeit a Two-Two – from Cambridge and then two years at RADA and still nothing apart from debt? Time, don't you think, he gave up the dream and organised himself to putting that degree to good use?'

'Do *not* suggest he do a PGCE so that he can teach English or Drama, Dad, like you were hinting at when we came over for dinner on Mum's birthday.'

'I wouldn't dream of it,' Dad said a little huffily. 'I wouldn't suggest anyone end up at the chalk face. Although,' he went on, 'if he did, he might be in a better position to help out with the gas and electricity bills when they come in.'

'He helps out when he can, Dad. He'll get there. He'll be famous one day.'

'Is fame so important to him?' Dad asked mildly. 'You know, rather than buckling down to some career and working his way up.'

'Like you did, you mean?' I stopped talking as the ordered plate of linguine was put in front of me.

'Exactly like I did.' Dad sniffed, cutting his calves' liver with care. 'I didn't have the advantages you two have had from a Cambridge education. It opens so many doors, Jen. It should be far easier for Laurie, with his good looks, charm and education to land a plum role.'

'Apparently not in films or TV.'

'Well, I'm hoping Jeremy is going to come straight in with me once he's finished studying. I'm not having *him* fannying around trying to find himself.'

'Really?' I don't know why I was surprised. It had probably always been Dad's plan that my younger brother join Dad in his business. 'And Laurie, for your information, is *not* fannying around. You know as well as I do that breaking into acting isn't easy for anyone.'

'Too right I want Jeremy in,' Dad answered, ignoring my last comment re Laurie. 'I'd have been more than happy to give *you* a job too if I'd thought it was up your street. I want to hand over the reins to at least one of you once I'm able; you know, take early retirement and spend a lot more time with your mum, skiing and on the boat...' Dad trailed off as I gave a start of recognition and jumped up from my seat. 'Hang on, Dad.' I dropped my napkin into my half-eaten meal and inched my way around the table until I was through the open conservatory windows and out onto the actual street.

'Gudrun? Gudrun!'

Gudrun was crossing the road towards the restaurant, stopped when I called her name and, when she saw it was me, broke into a broad grin and continued walking until she was outside the restaurant, giving me a hug.

'You've finally arrived in London? Why on earth haven't you been in touch?'

'How very fortuitous,' Gudrun said almost grandly. 'I only landed a couple of days ago. Been up in the frozen north for the last eighteen months...'

'Iceland?' I grinned. 'I thought you were in Leeds? You were certainly still up there in your last email.'

'Leeds,' Gudrun agreed. 'Finished my time up there a couple of weeks ago, had two weeks back home in Sussex to recover and now about to do a stint at The Royal Marsden. Just getting my bearings seeing as how I'm finally back in civilisation.'

'Leeds wasn't civilised?'

'Actually, I loved it up there. I'd really like to end up back in the north.'

'You've changed your tune. You didn't even know where Yorkshire was a few years ago.'

'Thought you might have ended up there yourself.'

Gudrun smiled. 'You know, seeing as how your Byron is from there. I assume you and the Gorgeous One are still together?'

I nodded. 'I'm just in Daphne's with Dad. Only got half an hour left before I'm back at work. Come and say hello to Dad.'

Gudrun followed as I led the way back to Dad's table.

'Champagne?' she asked, eyebrow raised. 'On a Monday lunchtime? Are there celebrations afoot? A wedding in the offing? Patter of tiny feet...?'

'Bloody hell, I hope not,' Dad laughed, giving Gudrun a kiss and, when I glared at him, understanding he was plainly reiterating his reluctance to really welcome Laurie fully into the family amended with, 'I'm far too young to be a dad, let alone a grandad.'

'Come off it, Mr Baylis, you've adored every minute of this gorgeous girl here. So,' she went on, 'what's the big deal?' Gudrun sipped at the champagne Dad poured into a water glass for her.

'My daughter is a published author,' Dad said proudly, holding up one of the signed copies I'd just autographed and which he was openly flaunting to any customers walking past.

Gudrun reached into the huge satchel she'd planted beneath her chair. 'Snap,' she grinned.

'You *knew*?' I asked, slapping at her arm.

'Course I did, you daft thing. I've followed all the reviews in the Sunday papers.' She smiled at me. 'I knew you'd get there one day.'

'So totally *fortuitous* you just happened to be walking past?'

Gudrun started laughing. 'Totally. Well, with a bit of help. I rang your office and the girl on reception said you were out for a couple of hours celebrating here with your dad. She was very impressed you were *lunching at Daphne's*. I was going to surprise you and thrust your book under your nose, ready for an autograph, but you caught sight of me crossing the road...'

She broke off as Dad's phone rang. 'Sorry, girls,' he said, standing and going out into the street. 'I really must take this.'

'It's great you're in London,' I said. 'How long are you going to be here?'

'Six months at least. Maybe longer. I've really missed you, Jennifer.'

'Me too.' I looked at my watch. 'Hell, I know I've been given some leeway today, but I've a pile of manuscripts to look at from the slush pile as well as line edits to go through.'

'The slush pile?' Gudrun laughed. 'Sounds like that disgusting coloured ice stuff we used to drink as kids.'

'I'm going to have to go.' Dad had his city head back on and was already in a different world, champing at the bit. 'Really sorry, big deal coming in. You two stay,' Dad insisted, pulling on his dark suit jacket and adjusting his tie. 'I'll pay the bill, but add to it if you want. Have dessert.'

'Got to get back myself.' I pulled a face, knowing I'd have much preferred to while away the rest of the afternoon, drinking champagne and catching up with Gudrun. I'd been feeling horribly guilty that I'd let our friendship slide. I suppose living two hundred miles apart and both getting on with our busy lives hadn't helped, and we had emailed probably on a weekly basis to begin with, but that had waned as the years since we'd been together at Cambridge had become two, and then three.

'I'll walk back with you,' Gudrun said, getting up as Dad disappeared into the back of a black cab. 'And you can tell me everything.'

'How's your love life?' I glanced across at Gudrun as we walked purposefully up the King's Road (stopping only outside Waterstone's to grasp Gudrun's hand in delight and excitement at the display of my book in the window) across Sloane Square and towards Ebury Street where Wesley and Brown was situated at the very edge of Westminster itself.

'Oh, you know, not found The One yet...'

'And are you looking?' I didn't recall Gudrun ever being really involved with anyone apart from several drink-fuelled romps she invariably regretted in the cold light of day. She'd spent much of her free time either in *The Eagle* or the bar in Trinity or, much more likely, cloistered in the library, working her socks off.

'Aren't we all?'

'Well, I hope I've already found mine,' I smiled.

'And is everything OK, Jen?'

'OK?'

'Is he still your Byronic dream?'

'Well, even Byron has dirty socks and pants, morning breath and a predilection for leaving mugs half-full of cold coffee under the chair.'

'Right.' Gudrun glanced my way as we walked.

'The thing is, he just can't get the break he needs. He's done bits on *Hollyoaks* and *Emmerdale*...'

Gudrun laughed as I ushered her across the road towards the office. 'I'd have thought *Emmerdale* would have been right up Laurie's street – you know, with that Yorkshire accent and from a farming family to boot?'

'Hmm, playing a character on *Emmerdale* would be perfect, although it would mean him living back up in the north. And he really, really doesn't want that... Right, I'm here.' I looked up at the frontage of Wesley and Brown, one of the oldest publishers in the business, and for which I still got a thrill, three years on, every time I went through the shiny black door, knowing I actually worked there.

'Doesn't he go back up to Yorkshire at all? You know, to see his family?'

I shook my head. 'Not really. I've only been back up there with him a couple of times since that first bloody embarrassing time Dad and I were caught skulking outside their gate.' I laughed as I remembered. 'Jesus, what was I thinking of, letting Dad drive me up there?'

'I love your dad,' Gudrun grinned. 'He's a bit of a wide boy, isn't he?'

'Suppose he is, really.'

'But an absolutely brilliant dad...'

'And husband. Mum still adores him.'

'Right, better let you get back to work.' Gudrun smiled. 'I've got your phone number.' She was suddenly serious. 'I'm so proud of you, Jenny. You know, with the book and everything...'

'As I am of you too,' I laughed. 'Registrar at the Royal Marsden, for heaven's sake.'

Gudrun hugged me. 'Take care, don't put up with too

many dirty socks and pants,' she said, looking me straight in the eye. 'Famous writers have better things to do than clear up after other people.'

Gudrun's words came back to me as I let myself into the flat just off Clapham Common. The adrenalin of publication-day-fuelled excitement, together with the champagne drunk at lunchtime and then more champagne (cheap Cava) poured by my boss at work to celebrate Byron's outing into the world, had long worn off, leaving me with a banging head and a sense of anti-climax, as well as the need to close my eyes for ten minutes.

Laurie had promised he'd either take me out for a celebratory dinner, or shop for and cook something himself. I sniffed the air and, wanting nothing more than a mug of Earl Grey rather than spending huge amounts of money we didn't really have in an upmarket – latest place to be seen – top London restaurant, was hoping he'd decided on the second option. But there was no smell of cooking, none of the drama and swearing, crashing of plates and cutlery, coming from the kitchen which always heralded Laurie's time in there.

I pushed at the door which opened onto the tiny sitting room, shaking my head and swearing volubly at the mess that met my eyes. Used coffee mugs, some still more than half-full with the expensive filtered coffee Laurie loved so much, were sitting idly on every surface. Those surfaces that had escaped the deluge of empty cups were, instead, sporting several empty cans of Pilsner lager, one, obviously intended for the large wicker basket holding the previous Saturday's Guardian, TLS and some theatre review papers, missing its target and coming to rest, instead, at its base.

Walking through the door with as many mugs and cans I could collect at one go, I stopped and simply stared, taking in the devastation that was the kitchen. 'For fuck's sake. What is the *matter* with the man?' I shouted to the four walls (one splattered with either tomato soup or a badly-opened can of baked beans), real anger rising as I looked round my lovely apartment. 'Yes, Laurie,' I continued to shout out loud, '*my* apartment, not yours to leave in such a sodding mess.' The sink was piled high with unwashed dishes, while a bowl bearing a rim of superglued cereal, as well as the empty beans can, its half-sawn-off lid a dangerous mouth of jagged teeth, were testament to Laurie's choice for both breakfast and lunch.

The apartment door banged, and a few seconds later Laurie appeared in the doorway of the kitchen as I threw dirty dishcloths and wet stained tea towels towards the washing machine.

'Jen, I'm so sorry.' Laurie, dressed in his best casual interview clothes, held up both hands in surrender as if I were about to shoot him. If I'd had a gun, I'd have quite possibly blown his pretty little head *clean off*. When I didn't say a word, just glared in his direction, he came out fighting. 'I said I'm sorry, Jen.'

'This is publication day; my *big* day, and you can't even clear up after yourself.' I was really angry. 'You have *no* respect for this apartment, Laurie and I'm *not* the sodding maid either. I've been out at work all day.'

Laurie moved towards me, taking me in his arms. 'I

know it's your big day, Jennifer. And I'm so proud of you. You know that.' He kissed the top of my head and I began to relax. 'Oh Jen,' he went on and there was desperation in his voice, 'I've spent all afternoon out at Borehamwood. While you've been celebrating your success and drinking champagne with your dad, I've been acting my socks off for a new part in *EastEnders*.'

I glanced up at him. Was he having a bit of a dig at me and Dad?

'A fresh character they're bringing in,' Laurie went on. 'Some bloke – a really big permanent part – arriving in the Square.'

'And?' Hope flared that this might finally be it for Laurie.

'*And*, Leo just rang me as I got off the tube. They've given it to Daniel Morrison. Daniel fucking Morrison, for fuck's sake? That fucker can't act his way out of a paper bag.'

I winced at the plethora of F words. 'I'm sorry, Laurie. It *will* happen one day, you know.'

Laurie sighed in my direction, refusing to be placated.

'Come on,' I went on, 'I'm not really hungry after lunch out with Dad, so...'

'Good, was it?'

'You *were* invited, you know.'

'I know, I know.' Laurie moved his arms around me, caressing my hair with his chin. 'But the last thing your dad wanted was me – an out-of-work layabout – spoiling his lunch date with his clever, newly-published little girl.'

I laughed at that and eventually Laurie relaxed and I could sense him smile. 'Come on Laurence Lewis,' I went on into his chest. 'Get over yourself, you great big diva. Let's have a bath and a bottle of wine and drown your sorrows—'

I broke off as Laurie's mobile rang and he made to ignore it, exchanging his chin for his mouth on my forehead.

'You are a wonderful, clever, talented woman, Jennifer Baylis,' he said, hugging me tighter, 'and you'll never know just how much I love you...'

I reached for his phone in the back pocket of his jeans. 'Hello? Who? Oh, hi, Janice... hang on...' I handed the phone to Laurie, who frowned but listened as his eldest sister spoke.

'Is she there now...?' Laurie had the phone jammed to his ear, not speaking for a good forty seconds. 'OK,' he finally said, 'I'll get the next train straight up.'

Laurie shoved the phone back into the pocket of his pure wool navy jacket. 'It's my mum. I need to get up to Midhope General. She's had some sort of heart attack.'

8

September 2003

Laurie

The last thing he wanted was to leave Jennifer alone in the flat on this, her special day. How could he have left the flat in such an awful mess, too? He'd been going to give the place a good clean up and start on the preparations for a fabulous celebratory meal – not that he was much good as a cook, but he'd really wanted to show how proud he was of Jen. And then there'd come the unexpected shout to get himself down for this audition with all the excitement and hope that went with it. And once again, it had come to nothing. Laurie glanced out of the window; his own scowling face reflected back at him as the Leeds-headed train entered a long, seemingly never-ending dark tunnel.

Maybe this was what death was like: one long tunnel of blackness heading in the direction of a destination he didn't want to go. Perhaps he'd be better off dead. Laurie felt his throat constrict and a tear threaten with the thought of how life had treated him and he shook back his black hair, not unaware that two young girls in seats across the aisle – university students he guessed as he gave them the benefit of his crooked smile – were discussing him.

No one would miss him if he were dead: there would be no full-of-his-demise photographs in *The Sunday Times Review* magazine or *The Blazing Trail* arts magazine. Even Jennifer, lovely Jennifer who he adored, had looked at him this evening with something akin to dislike when he'd first walked in through the door. Well, she, cushioned as always from the real world by her protected, cosy upbringing and adoring daddy, had no idea how tough it was out there when everything had just fallen, almost unasked for, into *her* lap. She'd been given everything on a plate all her life – Laurie wasn't totally convinced this amazing book deal Jennifer had landed hadn't had something, somehow, to do with that father of hers. Though he'd never say as much to her, of course.

If only he'd had a father like Gerald Baylis: if he'd had Jennifer's father with him along the way, supporting, encouraging, throwing money at him, he'd more than likely be commanding zillions for every film he was being offered in Hollywood by now.

Laurie was now feeling utterly righteous, enjoying, even, the pain of being misunderstood when he was working so hard for both of them. For their future together. He sighed heavily and closed his eyes that he might more readily conjure up, on his death, a desolate Jennifer and her repentantly overcome father – as well as his agent, Leo, who would have to apologise to angry producers and directors that he'd not done enough to bring his, Laurie's, talent to the fore. 'But he was actually *free*?' Mike Newell, director of *Four Weddings and A Funeral* would yell down the phone at Leo, 'And you didn't think to put him up for (insert here brand new mythical and potential blockbuster written by Richard Curtis) and now he's *dead*? Taken his own life through your incompetence? A brilliant, shining new talent gone to waste because…'

'Excuse me.' One of the girls opposite was leaning across the aisle towards him.

'Yes?' Laurie offered her his half-smile, the one he'd constantly practised – eyes slightly closed, mouth just ever so slightly sardonic – in the mirror until Jennifer caught him at it and he'd had to pretend he had something in his eye.

'My friend was just wondering if you were the actor…?'

'*The* actor?' For all his assured self-importance, even Laurie was taken aback that someone should recognise him as an actor. *The* actor?

'Are you the actor that was in *Radical Blue* last week?'

Radical Blue. Hell, he'd almost forgotten that tiny bit part he'd had in the BBC2 drama aired last week. How could he have forgotten to watch it, or at least record it when it was on? Why hadn't Jennifer made a fuss of it? Proof, he thought grimly, if proof were needed, she wasn't really interested in helping him with *his* career.

'Yes,' he smiled, winningly. 'Just a tiny part – only thing, I'm afraid, I was able to fit in between all my other major filming schedules.'

Both girls leaned forwards eagerly and for one brief second Laurie wondered if he could have them both at once in the train loo. He dismissed the thought – hardly enough room to stand and take a slash in a Great Eastern train toilet, never mind convoluted sex. And, since meeting Jennifer, he hadn't looked at another woman. Not one. Hadn't wanted anyone else but her.

'You were so good in it,' the smaller, dark-haired girl was now saying. She was really quite gorgeous, very much, in fact, like Sophia who he'd been with for several months before being totally entranced by the first glimpse of Jennifer's auburn hair, that afternoon outside The Eagle. Jennifer, he thought somewhat sourly, didn't realise just what he'd given up to be with her. The girl continued to hold his eye and Laurie fished out one of the business cards he'd had printed several years earlier; a time when he'd felt so confident about his pathway to the success that he couldn't believe it hadn't actually come to fruition. 'Give me a ring if you're in London,' Laurie grinned. 'Anyone who recognises me, from one of my many TV parts I'd totally forgotten about, deserves to have a drink bought.'

The girl accepted it eagerly, placing it with reverence into the front of her wallet. Laurie grinned again but then settled back into the train seat and closed his eyes against the awful realisation that, not only was he flirting with another woman when he adored Jennifer but, more importantly, he might actually be too late to see his mum alive. His mum, Rita, who'd always been there for him, who'd recognised his talent from an early age and who'd refused to listen to his dad when he'd overheard them arguing, once he'd gone to bed, that Rita was spoiling him, trying to make him different from the other village kids and his own sisters. She had to be alright. She just had to be.

★

Janice was waiting for him at Wakefield Westgate and, concentrating on a Greggs sausage roll, didn't see him until he banged loudly on the off-side window of the battered lime-green Lada. Janice deigned to take her nose from the greasy blue and white paper bag in order to reach over and unlock the passenger side door before shoving the last bit of the flaky pastry into her mouth. Laurie had always – although he liked to disdainfully protest he was above such northern feasts – adored anything from Greggs and his stomach growled as he remembered he'd not eaten a thing since his early lunch of beans on toast back at the flat.

'Don't suppose you thought to bring one of those for me?' Laurie asked, as Janice screwed up the bag in one practised move, dropping it expertly into the well of the car where it met others like it, before wiping soiled fingers down her already dirty jeans.

'Too busy worrying about Mum,' Janice retorted, reversing at speed the wrong way out of the station car park.

'How is she? What do they think it is? Some sort of stroke?'

'Apparently. I'll take you to the hospital now.'

'Now? Isn't visiting time over?'

'Yes. Of course. It's…' Janice tutted, glancing at the car's clock which appeared frozen at 1.30. 'Bloody electrics in this car,' she muttered, taking both hands off the steering wheel as she struggled to pull up the sleeve of her anorak in order to find her watch. 'It's almost eleven o'clock, but the ward sister said we can visit at any time.'

'That serious?' Laurie felt his heart contract in fear.

'I don't know, Laurence. Possibly. They think maybe

she's had a stroke or heart attack. She's been getting a lot of strange symptoms lately.' Janice glanced his way. 'Doesn't help *you've* not been in touch.'

'Oh, it's my fault, is it?' Was he to be blamed for his mother's dying, now?

'You know what she's like with you. *Always* been like with you.' Janice paused. 'I think she's had enough of everything, to be honest. Dad's bloody hard work to live with, gets away with doing as little as he can and leaves it up to Mum and me to sort out when there's not enough feed for the hens, or one of the bullocks goes lame after it's wandered off-piste because Dad's too bloody idle to check the fences…'

'Bullocks?' Laurie stared. 'Since when's he gone back to keeping bullocks?'

'Bullocks? It's all *bollocks*!' Janice barked a mirthless laugh. 'Overnight, we had a field of five of them. Won't say where he got them but, as far as I can gather, he probably won them in a game of cribbage down at The Red Lion. And of course it's Mum who has to deal with them when Dad's had a skinful and is snoring it off on the settee in front of the racing. *I* can't always be there on hand…' Janice trailed off, '…especially now…'

'Especially now?' Laurie glanced across at his sister and realised, beneath the quilted anorak, she appeared to have put on weight.

'Due in five months,' she said grimly. 'Twins this time. The bloody man should have kept himself – and his sperm – safely with the travel agent tart, instead of coming back and bothering *me* again.'

There appeared to be no answer to that and Laurie

leaned back on the painfully uncomfortable seat, closing his eyes against the dark country lanes, now wet with late-September rain.

'She's come round quite a bit,' the nurse said, obviously put out at having to leave her station where she was catching up with admin and a packet of Custard Creams. 'I did speak to Mr Lewis an hour or so ago and told him this.'

'My dad?' Now that Janice was standing in front of him, rather than sitting driving him, Laurie could see the full extent of his sister's pregnancy as she quizzed the nurse.

'*I* don't know if Mr Lewis is your dad,' the nurse went on slightly irritably. 'I explained we've run a battery of tests and there's nothing untoward. So,' she went on, relenting slightly, 'your mum's fine. She'll be able to go home in the morning. You really needn't have come here at this time of night; I *told* Mr Lewis that.'

'But earlier you seemed to think she'd had a stroke? Or a heart attack?' Janice wasn't to be put off.

'She *was* having pains shooting down her arms as well as terrible palpitations…'

'Yes, and Dad found her on the floor in the kitchen…'

'And very sensibly rang 999. He did the right thing.'

Laurie hadn't said a word as Janice and the nurse – a rather attractive blonde, he now ascertained as worry about his mum began to recede – continued to spar.

'Are you sure? Dad said she was in a bad way?' Janice frowned, both hands shoved almost belligerently into her anorak pocket. One of them, Laurie noticed, was torn, the stitching coming away from the main body of her coat.

'Totally sure,' the nurse said, stroking at her already immaculate darkened eyebrows and running the tip of her tongue slightly across her top lip as she took in Laurie's devastatingly good looks.

'Can I see her?' Laurie reached out a gentle hand to the nurse. 'I've had to leave a very important audition in London – I'm an actor – and caught the next train north as soon as I heard she wasn't well.'

Janice snorted at that, but Nurse Brannagan, totally captivated by Laurie's smile, dimpled back at him. 'Of course. Of course, you can. Although she might be asleep...' She led the way down the ward to the end bed where Rita Lewis, looking pale, but very much awake, lay on a mound of starched white hospital pillows.

'Laurence? I thought it was your voice.' Rita suddenly looked afraid. 'You've come all the way up from London, Laurie? Have they said there's something seriously wrong then? Am I not getting out of here?'

'I'm here, Mum,' Laurie said, feeling close to tears. 'I'm here now.'

'Panic attack, Rita,' Nurse Brannagan said shortly, while giving covert little looks in Laurie's direction. 'Now, the doctor explained that to you, so don't you go looking for anything more sinister. Adrenalin overload probably,' she went on, addressing the other two and repeating, as if it were her own, the diagnosis the overworked registrar had come up with a couple of hours earlier.

'I'm so sorry to drag you up from London and your work, Laurence,' Rita said, trying to smile.

'Well at least a bit of passing out on the kitchen floor gets the Boy Wonder up here to see you.' Janice sniffed, pulling up the zip on her anorak. 'Do you want me to give you a lift home, Laurence? I'm absolutely bushed.'

'Do you mind if I stay here?' Laurie gave the nurse a beguiling smile. The thought of going back to the farm with just his dad in situ wasn't the most welcome of thoughts. 'I promise I'll be quiet and not disturb her and I'll be at her side if she has another attack.'

'I doubt she will,' Nurse Brannagan smiled condescendingly, her voice dripping saccharin. 'Doctor's given you plenty of medication to calm you down, hasn't he? We don't want this happening again, do we, Rita?'

Laurie spent the, not actually uncomfortable, night in the chair, dozing at Rita's side, holding her hand while praying to a god he didn't really believe in that his mum really was going to be alright. Nurse Brannagan – 'call me Tessa' – brought him blankets and numerous cups of revoltingly strong tea and even shared a couple of her cache of Custard Creams with him. Rita was obviously medicated up to the eyeballs and, apart from asking him about his work and Jennifer, slept through the night without stirring. He waited with her while the doctor in charge did her rounds of the wards and gave permission for Rita to be discharged and then, fed up of hanging around and starving hungry, ordered a taxi to take the pair of them the couple of miles back down the valley to Daisy Royd Farm.

9

September 2003

Laurie

The troops, Laurie saw, were out in force. Janice was already in the fields helping Bob Watson – who should very probably have been put out to grass himself years ago – with the bullocks, the sheep and the hens, while Lorraine, also notably very pregnant, was optimistically hanging out washing in the damp garden. Cheryl, who *didn't* appear to be with child – but who knew with this prolifically fertile lot? Laurie thought sourly – was washing up last night's supper plates as well as the morning's breakfast dishes. Terry Lewis, apparently having totally forgotten that a new complement of ten-week-old turkeys to be reared for Westenbury's Christmas dinners was about to arrive, was complaining vocally about the amount of work he was expected to do, while pulling on greasy overalls and heavy work boots. He nodded in Laurie's direction but said very little by way of welcome.

'You alright, Reet?' Terry asked. 'Gave us all a scare with that little turn you had yesterday. Doctor says it were a panic attack?' Terry sighed heavily, shaking his head. 'What've *you* got to panic about?'

'I'd have thought that was pretty obvious, living here with you, Dad,' Laurie said mildly, ushering his mother to a comfortable chair.

''ey, don't you start, lad, the minute you set foot in t'place after us not seeing 'ide nor 'air of you for almost a year. Your mother's been pining away, waiting for you to ring her. That's what's up with her.'

'Oh, don't talk so daft, Terry. Ignore him, Laurence.' Rita spoke with such contempt in her voice everyone, including Lorraine's one-year-old, in the process of pulling himself up with the help of a chair leg, turned to stare. 'Right,' she went on, 'breakfast, Laurence?'

'I see your Jennifer's in the paper,' Cheryl said, pushing Rita back into the chair before reaching for a large bowl of fresh eggs. 'Scrambled, poached or fried, Laurence?'

Laurie hadn't had a fried egg for years, and the thought of one now, swimming in lard and atop a piece of greasy, fried white sliced bread, had him salivating – but, remembering he was now a Londoner (did Londoners even know what fried bread was?), he replied, 'Poached would be great, thanks, Cheryl. Don't suppose you have wholemeal bread?'

While Terry Lewis snorted disparagingly in his direction and stomped out, slamming the door behind him, Cheryl grinned and for a moment, just one split-second moment, Laurie saw both himself and his mother reflected in her blue eyes. 'Of course,' she laughed. 'We're not total heathens up here. Some of us even read *The Guardian*.' She threw the previous day's paper, folded at the book review page, towards him and busied herself at the Aga while he read the glowing reviews of Jennifer's debut in the newspaper.

Pride at Jennifer's success fought with anger at the very obvious lack of his own and, after eating, and instructing Rita to remain resting in her chair by the Aga with the copy of Hardy's *The Woodlanders* she was re-reading, Laurie pulled on one of Terry's old coats his dad had worn when he still owned the herd of dairy cows he'd milked – usually grumbling – twice daily. He found a pair of Wellingtons from the plethora of outdoor footwear by the back door and, glad to be out in the open air, spent the day, much to Terry and Janice's raised eyebrows, helping out on the farm.

By nine o'clock that evening, despite being exhausted from the previous night's lack of sleep and a day spent in the chilly fresh air, Laurie was restless. While Terry lay, spent of all energy, on the sofa after ensuring the fledgling turkeys were settled in their new home, Laurie had spent the last couple of hours filling Rita in with where he was in regard to his acting work and opening up to his mother the despair he was feeling about his lack of success, while Jennifer appeared to be flying.

'You'll get there, Laurence,' Rita said almost fiercely. 'There's absolutely no reason why you wouldn't. Look how you were taken on for all those photo shoots when you were little.' She laughed as she remembered. 'Your dad said, no way was I taking any son of his off to stand all day in front of a camera. *He'll end up as a mincing faggot* were his words, as I recall.' She laughed again, pulling a face at the memory.

'A *faggot*? Oh, for God's sake...'

'It was the early eighties, Laurence. AIDS was everywhere and your dad said taking a six-year-old to that photography agency down near Canal Street in Manchester was as bad as entering Sodom and Gomorrah, and it would turn your head.'

They both laughed at that. 'I loved it,' Laurie said, remembering. 'Loved the attention; loved knowing my photo was up in the Marks and Spencer kids' department.'

'You don't think you missed out?' Rita asked, frowning. 'You know, playing football or something?'

'Football?' Laurie laughed. 'You know I've two left feet: certainly not. And all that hanging around waiting to be in front of the camera meant I could read. I can see the pair of us now, while we waited, me devouring all the Narnia books in turn and you into D. H. Lawrence.' Laurie turned to Rita. 'How *on earth* did you end up with Dad, Mum?'

'He was a very good-looking lad when he was your age.'

'Really?' Laurie's face was one of disbelief.

'All the girls were after him... and then, you know, the obvious...'

'Janice?'

'Yes.' Rita sighed. 'I was four months gone when we got married. Your gran and grandad Allen were furious. Thought I'd married beneath me. Had wanted me to go to teacher training college – university even, like your Auntie Sue. But there you go.' Rita smiled. 'Look, I've a few jobs to catch up with, Laurie. Why don't you pop down to The

Jolly Sailor and see if there's anyone from school having a drink?'

'I've lost touch with all the girls I was friends with.' Laurie frowned. 'And I never really had much to do with the other lads. Especially when I went on to sixth-form college and got into all the am-dram stuff and they were into football and beer.' He paused. 'Look, do you mind if I stay a few days, Mum?'

'Mind? Why should I mind? Of course, you can stay.' Rita gave him a quizzical look. 'Not getting on with Jennifer?'

'I just think she's disappointed in me. You know, that I haven't got where I intended by now.' Laurie sighed heavily. 'No, that's not fair of me – Jen is always supportive and encouraging. *I'm* the one who's disappointed in me.' Laurie sighed once more and glanced over at his father where loud snores from the sofa at the far end of the kitchen rose to a crescendo. 'Jesus,' Laurie frowned, 'he sounds like the Boston Strangler's got hold of him. Right, I'm going to wander down to the pub if that's OK?'

It was going up to ten by the time Laurie parked Rita's car. The Fiat of four years previously had been replaced by a non-descript beige Honda – the ubiquitous green amphibian still suckered to the windscreen, but losing the unequal battle in masking the pervading smell of damp and chicken feed.

'Jess? What *you* doing back?' Laurie leaned across the bar to give the landlord's daughter a kiss. 'I thought you were in Australia?'

'Well, I nearly got there.' Jess was obviously embarrassed. 'Got as far as Greece, grape picking, and then ran out of money – most of what I'd earned was pinched from my rucksack in a youth hostel in Heraklion – so I decided to come home, you know, just for a bit...' She trailed off, looking with some defiance at Laurie. 'And then, you know, things happen.'

'You're *married*?' Laurie spotted the wedding ring as Jess pulled a pint of the Tetley's bitter he'd ordered.

'Hmm. Got a little boy, Nathan.' Jess stared at Laurie and, as always, whenever he met up with her again, he was transported back to being five years old in Reception, feeling the connection once more between them.

Laurie took a long pull on his pint. He'd have preferred a white wine or even whisky – he always opted for a Southern Comfort when drinking with Jennifer's father – but thought Jess might laugh at that. And, for some reason, he didn't want to be laughed at by Jess. He'd much rather be kissing her, he thought as he downed a second pint and then thought, sod it, and ordered a Bell's.

'So,' Laurie eventually asked, once she was free to chat. 'Who did you marry then? Anyone I know?' He glanced round the bar as though a whole gang of potential husbands was about to manifest itself in his direction. He felt ridiculously put out that Jess hadn't waited for him. Had married *someone else*, for heaven's sake.

Jess leaned across the Heineken pump, giving it a slow suggestive up and down movement with her dishcloth. 'Karl.'

'Karl?'

'Karl Danvers.'

Karl 'Come and Feel my Biceps' Danvers? Laurie stared in disbelief. Karl Danvers, the year above them at Westenbury Comprehensive, had made his life a misery for six months, lying in wait for him in the bike shed, mocking Laurie's love of reading and his new glasses as well as his taking the main part in the school's production of *Joseph*. When Laurie had come home for the second time in a week with his glasses stamped on, Rita had had enough. Terry, fed up with Rita's badgering him to do something, had lay in wait after the village under-fifteen football practice one cold February evening, and threatened Karl Danvers with the slurry pit.

Jess nodded.

How could she have thrown herself away on Karl Danvers? And she had a child too? Laurie felt quite ill with the unfairness of it all – or possibly with the unaccustomed pint of Tetley's bitter he'd just downed. 'I thought you were going to wait for *me*?' Laurie teased, giving her the benefit of his lopsided grin.

'I did,' Jess said seriously. 'But you obviously had other ideas.' She crossed to the other side of the bar where a large woman in a strange pink hat was unceremoniously waving her empty glass.

'Hello, lad, back up for the week?' Len, Jess's father, appeared from the cellar where he'd been fitting a new barrel.

'Just a couple of days,' Laurie smiled. 'Mum's not been too good.'

Len nodded, apparently not overly interested in either Laurie or the state of Rita's health. 'Jess, you get off early; give Karl a break from babysitting.' He nodded once more in Laurie's direction and moved to talk to a couple of locals at the other end of the bar.

Five minutes later, Jess walked back through the bar, lifted the wooden flap and came through into the pub lounge. She was wearing a scarlet coat and black thigh-length boots, and had painted a fresh coat of scarlet lipstick onto her full mouth. For a split second, with her black hair, Laurie had the impression it was Rose Red – Snow White's sidekick in the Ladybird book Rita had read to him when he was tiny – standing in front of him. He'd adored Rose Red, sitting for hours in the big armchair in the kitchen just gazing at her picture.

Laurie's pulse raced.

'See you in another five years' time, Laurie.' Jess smiled and patted his arm as she walked past.

Laurie pushed his empty whisky glass away from him and, glancing towards Len Barrowclough who was now totally engrossed in the TV above the bar, stood and followed Jess out into the car park.

'Come and walk with me for five minutes.' Laurie caught up with her, taking her hand in his.

'Whatever for?'

'Old times' sake?'

'I need to get back. Karl will be waiting.'

'Your dad's let you out early,'

When she didn't argue the point, and kept her hand in his, Laurie felt the power of getting one over on his old nemesis, Karl Danvers. 'I can't drive, I'm over the limit. Come on, I'll walk you home and then walk home myself.'

'It's five miles at least back to your place.'

'Do me good.'

'I've got my car; I'll drop you off.' Jess led the way round the back of the pub where a smart little red MG stood waiting.

'Can't get a baby seat in that, I bet.' Laurie was impressed at the upmarket wheels.

'It's Karl's.'

'He's doing well.' How had Karl Danvers ended up with such a smart car – as well as *his* Jess – to go with the bulging bloody biceps?

Jess didn't say another word, but put the car into gear and drove carefully out towards Daisy Royd Farm. As she slowed, changing gear and dropping down into the valley at the edge of Sunny Bank Wood, she glanced across at him. Laurie smiled. 'Let's stop and stretch our legs for ten minutes.'

They did stop, but it was for a great deal longer than ten minutes and any guilt Laurie might have felt at his betrayal of Jennifer was swiftly assuaged, knowing he'd not only got his own back on Karl Danvers, but at the utter delight he felt at bringing pretty little Jess, his mate for years, to a juddering, quite explosive climax.

When Jess had dropped him off at Daisy Royd Farm, refusing to meet his eye and roaring off at speed, Laurie felt something akin to regret. As the night grew to a close, and his mother bid him goodnight, the feeling turned into an unsavoury lump in his chest which he soon recognised as downright guilt. The memory of Jess and what he'd done was now leaving nothing but a sour taste in his mouth and a terrible feeling of doom in his stomach. He felt exhausted, drained even, which, he supposed, he was. But more than anything he felt guilt. Guilt at betraying Jennifer.

He made the decision to ring Jennifer right that minute, although he wasn't convinced he could put on the act of a lifetime to tell her how much he loved and missed her

– after having sex with another woman. But it wouldn't *be* an act, would it? Because he *did* love her, he *did* miss her. He was suddenly aware of an almost crushing need to speak to Jen, not because of what he'd just done, but because he truly loved her, truly needed her. Laurie suddenly couldn't imagine life without her. He shivered slightly at the thought and went to find his phone.

There was one message from his agent, Leo:

Where the hell are you, Laurie? Jennifer says you're in Yorkshire? What the fuck are you doing up there? You are up for – and I mean seriously up for – the character of Ted Baxter in a new, potentially long-running, BBC series called A Better Life they've come up with to rival Emmerdale. Ted's a Yorkshire farmer who, after heartbreak, leaves home and finds work on a farm in Gloucestershire. Laurie, get your pretty little backside back down here, plaster that Yorkshire accent on full strength and do not let me down. Auditions are the day after tomorrow out at Elstree. I've said you'll be there...

10

December 2005

Dear Gudrun,

Merry Christmas! Massive apologies for not being in touch. How's life now that you're back in Leeds? I know we both lead such ridiculously busy lives – well you do, anyway – but that's absolutely no excuse for not emailing or phoning as often as we should. You do realise we've not seen you since the wedding? The silver photo frame you bought us has pride of place on my desk with an up-to-date photo of Ada in it. I'm sending you the same photo in this Christmas card so you can see your honorary goddaughter at nine months old. We're not actually having her christened, despite Mum constantly dropping hints that we should (she got her way with the big wedding do which, to be honest, I wasn't bothered about but, for once, she and Laurie were singing off the same hymn sheet as it were, with regards that), but, if we had, you were first on the list to be godmother. I do hope you'll accept the post, albeit an honorary one??!

So, at the end of yet another year – where do they go? – I'm sending you the photo of Ada, and a change of address card. Yes, we've sold the flat and have moved out to St Albans. I know, I know, all a bit *middle-class oasis*, but it's near the farm the studio use to film *A Better Life* which makes it so much easier for Laurie to get to work and it's so wonderful not to have to drag all the baby paraphernalia up those steps in the Clapham flat.

I miss the buzz of working and living in central London, but do enjoy, I think, living out in the country – if you can call St Albans the country – and I'm working part-time, mainly from home, for Wesley and Brown as commissioning editor. Any ambition I might have had of breaking through the glass ceiling of publishing and becoming Editorial Director appears to have gone into the ether. There's a whole new gang of frighteningly driven (and childless) young editors who are snapping at my heels and pipping me to the post at every turn. They're bloody good and I don't appear to have the energy or the wherewithal to compete with them. Poor old Percy Bysshe, published last year, totally bombed I'm afraid, and the hundreds of hardback copies are either quietly mouldering on library shelves – I know you'll have your signed copy somewhere in the house, even if it's being used as a doorstop – or are being mushed and recycled as we speak. When I try to analyse just why it failed – when Byron was such a spectacular success – I can only conclude that Shelley didn't ever have my heart and take over my life in the same way Byron always did (and still does!).

It does seem a bit strange that when I'm on the up and up with my books, Laurie appears to struggle. And the other way round. Now that he's a household name as Ted Baxter – rights to the soap have been sold globally and, apparently, Ted is a huge phenomenon in South Korea – and on the front of every magazine and invited onto every TV chat show going (did you catch him on Friday night's Jonathan Ross?) *I* don't seem to be able to string two words together. Maybe it's the after effects of giving birth? Don't they say every glass of wine knocks out a few hundred brain cells? Hell, if a glass of Merlot can do that, imagine what two days in labour and nine months without an unbroken night's sleep can do to the poor little suckers? If I'm sounding sorry for myself, I'm not. Really!

I digress. Do you remember my Great Aunt Agnes, Mum's aunt? She was at the wedding – you couldn't miss her in that very strange yellow hat she insisted on wearing – and I gather you spent a lot of time chatting with her? Anyway, she's been hinting for years she spent the war years, after Cambridge, at Bletchley Park as a fully-fledged cryptanalyst and has loved wrapping herself in the secrecy and mystery of it all – even though, I believe, after all these years, she can legally open up and tell all. It's just a matter of persuading her to let me write her story, but she's eighty-three now and not keen on crying babies, so I have to leave Ada with Mum and then drive on to Agnes's flat to make notes. All in between my commissioning work, Ada's feeds and cleaning the house of course.

Laurie is never at home. Not only is he filming every day – now that A Better Life is on TV three times a week – he's in demand once more for photo shoots. Michaud Saint-Jean are launching a new advertising campaign and Laurie is their face of 2006, on all their men's beauty products...

I broke off at this point. Was I coming over as being slightly envious of Laurie's phenomenal success? I went into the kitchen to make yet another cup of coffee to keep me awake and sent up a silent prayer to that great God in the sky nursery that Ada would manage another half hour at least before she started yelling. Once she was off on one, she reminded me uncannily of Laurie when *he* was tired and stressed, her navy blue eyes narrowing before she launched, and needing much persuasion and attention to calm her down. While the water boiled, I went to stand at the French window that looked over the large garden, watching myriad birds chattering and fighting for a place on the bird feeder station I'd hung on the one huge oak tree the previous week. If I could only get my brain together and make some sense of the copious notes I'd made sitting listening to Aunt Agnes, I might feel better. But I felt so tired all the time and yesterday I'd spent the morning weeping over a dead robin next door's cat had killed. I'd been too late to save it. But I had copy edits and proof reading for several of my authors, as well as a whole load of new submissions to wade through, and, while money was certainly coming in from Laurie's work, it was, it appeared, rolling out again at an alarming rate as the bills for the refurbishment of this house started to land on the doormat. I'd have liked to have resigned my post with Wesley and Brown. I'd had some promotions but while I was still only twenty-six, there were younger, more driven – childless – editors on their way up and, with a new baby in tow, as well as trying to make it myself as an author, it all seemed harder and harder somehow. While I poured boiling water on strong coffee, loving the smell of the stuff that was going to get me through the next few hours, and waited for it to brew, I watched the bank of grey, ominous clouds that had been building all morning turn a strange mustard yellow and felt my heart sink as the snow that had threatened all week finally began to fall and the notion of being trapped in my own home intensified. Telling myself not to be ridiculous, I picked up the cafetière and mug, as well as the biscuits I'd hidden from myself only hours earlier, and went to finish my letter to Gudrun.

Anyway, I digress once more. (It appears that's what motherhood does to you: the inability to concentrate on one particular point for any longer than a nanosecond.) It's all fascinating stuff with Aunt Agnes, and I'm really hoping I can get a book out of it at some point soon.

Do come and see us, Gudrun. We've three spare bedrooms (can you imagine!!) and I miss you. Come for the weekend. Bring any new man you might have in tow...

Much love, Jennifer xxxxx

ACT 3

II

November 2020

'Jen...? What do you think of the verdict, Jennifer? How does it feel to be married to a serial womaniser...?'

'Did you know about the other women, Jenny?'

'Will you stick by him, Jen? What do you think about it all...?'

I batted away the intruding mikes and cameras, blindly pushing my way towards the waiting car, while Neville Sanderson, Laurie's brief, urged me none too gently onwards. I needed no urging. I'd had enough: two days enough of argument and counter-argument, accusations and lies. Accusations that had led my husband to where he was now – defending his honour against *The Blazing Trail* arts magazine, which he claimed had libelled him when it published the defamatory article about his alleged extracurricular love life.

Neville took my arm once more as I tried to make my way to the waiting car, but eventually turned to speak to the media snapping at our heels, still doggedly determined to get a quote. 'A person wronged will too often give up the fight to prove their innocence in the certain knowledge they can't afford the risk of losing, and a settlement can be made out of court. I think it pretty obvious, to all those who have sat through this whole ridiculous pantomime and utter miscarriage of justice throughout the past week in court, Mr Lewis's determination to prove his innocence bears witness only to the truth: my client is innocent of the libellous accusations this smutty rag has had the temerity to publish. Furthermore, we shall be appealing the verdict at the highest level...'

'You're already at the highest level,' a female voice yelled derisively from the middle of the crowd. 'This is the crown court. You can't get much higher than this.'

Wrong, I wanted to retaliate. *You can go all the way to the Supreme Court*. But, instead, I kept my head down and carried on walking away. Despite both mine and Neville's commands to join us in the waiting car, Laurie had stopped at a large group of women who had gathered with banners, proclaiming their love and support for the long-running and highly successful *A Better Life* actor. My husband, Laurie Lewis, with his dark Byronic good looks, had captured female hearts from his very first appearance on their TVs and into their lives. They weren't prepared to give up on him now because of some completely denied accusations of philandering that had led to this much-publicised libel trial at Southwark Crown Court, and which I'd forced myself to sit through for the past two days.

Five minutes later, the media, still intent on their reward for sitting inside the courthouse, as well as out in the cold of a grey, damp November, turned and jostled when Laurie finally forced his way through them and took his place beside me on the back seat of the car. The driver pulled away from the kerb and Laurie attempted to pull my hand into his own.

'Don't even think about it,' I snarled furiously, pushing my hands deep into the pockets of my navy coat. I'd started out that morning with a pair of woollen gloves but had no idea, now, where they'd ended up. On the floor of the public gallery back in the court room, I supposed. Having watched Laurie give the acting performance of his career, repudiating every accusation thrown at him across that crowded court room, I was now finally forced to ask myself: was I, in fact, married to a womaniser as portrayed by the prosecution? But also, if that were the case, a liar as well? *Had* he lied in that court room? Had my husband lied to *me* as well? I no longer knew what to think. I no longer, I realised, knew my husband.

'Bloody magazine,' Laurie snapped as he made for the American fridge at the far end of the kitchen. 'They were just out to get me.' He opened the huge metallic door in a temper, snatching at a bottle of white from its chilly depths. 'Out to get me from the very start, Jen. Jealous. Jealous of my success. That's the media for you.'

'Laurie, I don't know what to believe anymore,' I hissed. 'So don't you go blaming that magazine. If they were publishing the truth.'

'The truth? The truth? You actually *believe* all that stuff the magazine printed?' Laurie poured himself a huge glass, but failed to offer one to me.

'Well, you managed a pretty good job of convincing me before the court case started that various women had it in for you for whatever reason. No, no...' I held up a hand in protest as Laurie lowered his voice and started to speak, 'don't you dare try to tell me now that those three women who were called to give evidence had all got together at some point in order to get their story straight just to get back at you.'

'Darling, Jenny. Jen...' Laurie turned on his most persuasive voice. 'How many more times do I have to explain how it was? We've been through all this time and time again: a little mild flirtation on set, totally expected of me. Avril Peterson was my love object for heaven's sake. We had to kiss; you know that.'

'Kiss? On set? Well yes, of course you had to; it was in the script. But now, apparently, full-blown sex *off* the set? And carrying on for weeks once her character had left?'

'You can't believe that, Jen? That I'd do that to *you*. To our marriage? It's a total miscarriage of justice...'

'Have you heard yourself?' I raged, reaching for the kettle and filling it with such force the water exploded from its depths and onto my hands. Oh, for the love of God. I slammed it down onto its usual hotplate on the Aga, wiped my hands and arms on a tea towel and glared at Laurie once again. 'You should hear yourself,' I repeated, banging cupboard doors in the search for an elusive box of teabags. 'You could be on set, spouting your lines. You know, Laurie, sometimes I don't think you know if you're you, a two-bit actor living in St Albans with his wife and kids, or if you've convinced yourself, after seventeen years of playing him, you're not actually Ted Baxter, the bachelor

Yorkshire farmer with an eye for the local women, who's found himself on a farm in Gloucestershire...'

'Two-bit actor? Two-bit...?' Laurie affected hurt. 'Can I just remind you of all the BAFTA awards that decorate this house for playing Ted? How many times *A Better Life* has trumped *Emmerdale* and *Coronation Street*?'

'Laurie, you don't need to damn well remind me; they're in my face every time I go to the lavatory. Only someone with an ego like yours would think it ironic putting them in the downstairs loo, where the world and his wife can see them every time they get called short, when, in truth, it's just bad form, bad manners and... and shows you up for the bloody show-off that you are.'

'Ted Baxter's paid the bills on this place, hasn't he?' Laurie drained his glass and reached for the wine bottle once more but, quailing somewhat as he saw my narrowed eyes, obviously thought better of it and, folding his arms, leaned against the Aga – seeking comfort from the warmth of the stove instead.

'Laurie, in order to pay off all the legal costs you've accrued in your arrogance that you just couldn't lose, you'll have to play your alter ego until he's a senile, mumbling old man, unable to get his leg over his tractor never mind the bevy of village women seemingly panting for him every minute of the day and night.' I actually felt my heart race at the thought of the thousands and thousands of pounds we must now owe in court costs. How much was in our bank account? Anywhere near enough to pay off those eye-watering Monopoly figures the judge had ordered at the end of the trial? And Neville didn't come cheap. Thank God, we'd known him years; he was a friend of Laurie's, and wouldn't be immediately banging on our door for his money.

'Your mother will help out. She won't see the kids turfed out of their school and into the local comp.' Laurie was obviously thinking along the same lines as me, his words breaking into my panic, his usual confidence – no, his bloody arrogance, I conceded – rising like cream on a bottle of milk.

When I didn't answer him, when I could only stare at this man I'd adored for over twenty years, Laurie went on somewhat hastily, 'But it won't come to that, Jennifer. We won't need to go, cap in hand, to your mother and that brother of yours. You know, I told you, only last week, Miriam had me in her office to tell me of the great new storyline they're thinking of for Ted. It's going to be mind-blowing. He's going to be arrested as a suspect for the murder of Judith Powell down in the village post office…' Laurie moved from the Aga, crossing the huge, newly extended and renovated kitchen to where I stood in a stance of abject defeat, still in my coat, hugging myself both for warmth and in the hope of some comfort. 'Jen,' he repeated, taking my arms from around my waist and moving them, instead, around his own, 'you know there's only ever been you. You *know* that.' Laurie bent to kiss my hair and I breathed in his familiar Laurie smell. Despite my fury at what had been alleged in court that afternoon, I felt my traitorous arms tighten around his waist and my head settle into the beat of his heart beneath the navy blue shirt that matched those amazing eyes of his.

'Honestly, Jen, we'll get through this. I'll pay off the court costs, I promise you. In fact, you know, it wouldn't surprise me if this court case doesn't work in our favour. The ratings for *A Better Life* have been going down a bit, I'll admit, but you know what they say: all publicity is good publicity. I'm in the news again, darling; the talking point of every coffee morning and ladies' lunch.' Laurie started to grin. 'Every granny in every care home, every teacher in every staff room, everyone standing in the rain in the bus queue will be discussing Ted Baxter and defending him...'

I stared. Was Laurie really unable to distinguish himself – Laurie Lewis, TV actor, husband and father living in St Albans – from his alter ego, Ted Baxter? I continued to stare at Laurie, willing him to at least show some remorse but he rambled on, an unstoppable train, '...and, apparently Graham Norton has already had a word with Miriam, when he happened to be at the next table to her in *Endo* the other day. We really should book a table there.'

'*Endo?*' I actually glared at Laurie. My husband was discussing upmarket restaurants when, quite possibly, because of his messing around with other women, my whole family was going to be out on the street?

'*Endo at Rotunda,*' Laurie smiled somewhat condescendingly. 'It's...'

'I know *exactly* what *Endo* is,' I snapped, stepping back and gazing up in silence at this man I'd loved unconditionally for so long. I was filled with a wild fury and continued to stare until Laurie, unnerved by the look and my silence, attempted to break it.

'What?' he smiled, his navy eyes crinkling in the way he knew had women, young and old – including his wife, usually – fall at his feet.

I shook his hand away from mine and stepped further

back. How had it all gone so terribly, horribly wrong? When had Laurie decided I wasn't enough for him? That he needed more?

He was saved from my actually saying these words out loud by the banging of the front door followed by hurried footsteps racing along the wooden floor of the hall. The glazed kitchen door was flung open at force, crashing back on its hinges away from its frame, the metal handle coming to a forced standstill in the kitchen's newly-painted cream wall.

'Mummy, is Daddy going to prison?' Seven-year-old George, his auburn hair standing up at right-angles where he'd run anxious fingers through its length, burst into the kitchen, my mother and his sister following behind.

'Oh, for God's sake, George. I've told him, Mum, and Granny's told him over and over again, Dad's not going to be ending up doing time in the cooler.' Ada, at fifteen, carried an air of world-weary exasperation.

'Of course Dad's not going to prison, you daft thing.' I made an attempt to flatten my son's hair as he flung himself into his father's arms. Fear of not finding Laurie at home once he'd been brought back from Berkshire, where the two of them had been staying with my mother, had rendered George tearful, myriad freckles standing out starkly on his deathly white face, his chocolate brown eyes – my own eyes – huge.

'Mind you,' Ada went on, refusing to look at Laurie, 'if he's been doing what the lunchtime news accused him of, incarceration is probably the best thing for him.'

'Ada!' My mother and I spoke – or rather hissed – as one, and I was gratified to see Laurie flush with embarrassment.

'Look, Ada…' Laurie held up his hands but didn't seem to

know what to say next. I supposed, being outed with your pants down on national TV wasn't something one would ever care to discuss with one's fifteen-year-old daughter.

I held up my own hand. 'Enough, Ada. You've had two days off school. I suggest you go upstairs and get yourself sorted for going back tomorrow. Check you've a clean shirt and you've done all your homework.'

'My homework is totally up to date.' Ada wasn't going anywhere. 'As it always is. And, how on earth you think I'm able to go back to school as normal in the morning to face all those girls now that my own father's been outed as a *serial womaniser* is beyond me.'

'Ada enough. You're far too young to understand…'

'Oh, don't be ridiculous, Mum. Lydia and Hermione and Martha Burrows will be all sympathetic to my face while totally stabbing me in the back behind my… behind my, well, behind my back. They'll be texting for Britain as we speak, loving every minute.' Ada's face was thunderous.

'You're over-reacting,' I soothed, even though I didn't blame her one bit for going on like this. 'Lydia's your best friend and would never talk about you behind your back. It'll all blow over and, you know, just because the magazine's been found not guilty of libel, doesn't mean that they *weren't* actually libellous.'

We all turned as Mum uttered a loud 'as if' snort, quickly turning it into an over-dramatic cough which fooled no one, particularly Ada who was, it appeared, determined to say her piece.

'You see,' she said, sullenly. 'Granny knows…'

'Enough Ada.' Laurie was cross now, embarrassment turning to anger. 'This really has nothing to do with you.'

'Well, I certainly think it will have something to do with me when the house has to be sold to pay the legal bills and George and I are thrown out of school.'

'Thrown out of school?' George looked hopeful. 'Don't I have to go to school anymore because of what Daddy's done?'

'Your father's done *nothing* wrong, George,' I soothed. 'It's the magazine that's been naughty and caused all this trouble for Daddy. It will be fine, you'll see. It will all be forgotten by next week.'

'I've got calls to make,' Laurie said stiffly, a martyred look on his handsome face. 'No one appears to want to listen to what *I* might have to say.' He crossed back over to the black granite-topped island (that piece of granite alone had cost thousands, I thought furiously) reaching for the bottle of Marlborough Sauvignon Blanc Reserve (almost thirty quid a bottle) as well as his glass. 'I'm too upset to eat supper. Please go ahead without me. Cynthia,' Laurie nodded in the direction of my mother, 'thank you for looking after the children in this, our time of trouble.' He walked slowly in the direction of his study, shoulders hunched and without a backwards glance at the rest of us watching him leave.

'Pillock,' Mum muttered under her breath. 'Utter pillock.'

'Darling, I don't want to pry into your financial affairs, but I have to ask: is Laurie in a position to be able to pay these horrendous court costs and legal fees?' Mum emerged from the fridge, where she'd been searching for ingredients to cobble together some sort of supper dish for us all. 'Have you Parmesan?' she added, placing bacon and mushrooms on the island. 'I'll do us some pasta.'

'I don't think I can eat a thing, Mum.' I actually wanted to cry. 'And yes, there is Parmesan – top shelf behind that Harrods' duck pâté Laurie insists he can't live without – and no, we haven't got any money *whatsoever* in the bank. This new kitchen,' I waved a despairing hand around the beautiful Renshaw and Forsyte designer kitchen fitted the previous summer, 'cost three times as much as we'd originally planned. I'd have gone with Ikea myself but...'

'But Laurie insisted on having the very best? It really is beautiful, darling, but at the end of the day your husband is a soap star, not a Hollywood film star. Or a city financier.'

'Like Dad was, you mean?'

'Exactly. And even then, your father would *never* have pushed the boat out to such an extent.' Mum sighed, remembering and missing my dad who'd died in a freak speedboat accident off the coast of Kefalonia two years earlier. She opened a large drawer in the island, obviously admiring its smooth-running motion before taking out a Swiss Diamond pan. 'So, all your savings have gone on this kitchen then?'

When I didn't say a word, couldn't face my mother and admit we'd never actually *had* any savings, she stopped chopping bacon and glanced across at me. 'Jennifer?'

'It doesn't matter, Mum. Not your problem. We'll sort it.'

'Please don't tell me you re-mortgaged this place?' Mum was understandably stunned.

I nodded, embarrassed.

'But your father was always worried about the massive

mortgage you'd taken on to buy this house? And now you've *re-mortgaged*?'

I sat down heavily on one of the Stafford padded-leather island stools in '*Aged Tobacco*' that Laurie had insisted the kitchen just had to have to complete the look. While, over the years, my dad had acquired a very healthy bank account, his business head had never allowed frivolity. His every purchase, whether the cars or the family homes, had been made with an eye to the future and its potential increase in value. Unfortunately, the 2008 financial crisis had not been good for either Dad or his business and, on his death, Mum had downsized from our large family house to a much smaller, but still rather lovely place in the neighbouring village of Hurley, although managed to keep the house on the Greek island of Kefalonia that had been in her family for years. While our family home in Sonning, Berkshire, had been incredibly beautiful, there was never anything flash or bling about Dad's acquisitions, nothing bought merely for their ostentatious, as opposed to their practical, value – and Mum knew my dad had had no time, and certainly no respect, for Laurie's apparent need for material, even pretentious, procurement.

'Mum, I hate to ask…'

'I know you do, darling.' Mum sighed and I could see she was having trouble meeting my eye. 'Over the years, your father helped you out of tight corners brought about by Laurie's poor business acumen.' My mum and I were equally embarrassed bringing up the subject of money, especially as Laurie and I had been bailed out on several occasions when Laurie's enthusiasm for a new business scheme had come to nothing. There'd been the share of a new restaurant in St Albans as well as the exciting new production company which Laurie had been assured would bring in huge profits. Both had failed dismally, as Dad had predicted they would, and, unable to see his only daughter in such financial dire straits, he'd once again stepped in to help us out. 'I'm sorry Jennifer,' Mum eventually said. 'I'm not actually in any position to help. Jeremy has taken over my financial affairs: he's tied up most of the capital in stocks and shares that give me an interest to live on and, as such, there's no big lump sum I can give you that will meet these court costs. Jeremy says it's the best way forward for me; something to do with inheritance tax or some such thing? There's the house in Greece, I suppose…' Mum trailed off, still unable to look me fully in the eye.

'Mum, there's no way you're selling the place in Kefalonia.'

'And I'm sorry sweetheart,' Mum now gazed directly across at me, 'even if I did have the huge amount of money this whole debacle has thrown up, I still wouldn't give it to you. Well, not to Laurie anyway. Darling, he's a philanderer. A womaniser. He's in love only with himself.'

'No, really, Mum, he loves *me*. He loves *the kids*…'

'Sell the house, Jennifer. Bring the kids back to Berkshire and live with me.'

'Berkshire's too far away for Laurie to travel back to the studios every day.'

Mum's eyes were unusually steely. 'Jen, Laurie isn't invited.'

'Mum, I could never…' I broke off as Laurie appeared at the kitchen door. His face was deathly white, his navy eyes glittering with emotion – I wasn't sure if it was fury or shock – and he seemed unable to speak.

'God, what's happened, Laurie? Has somebody died?' Seeing him in such a state, I jumped up from the kitchen table, knocking over my favourite Emma Bridgewater mug Dad had bought me just before *he* died.

'Worse.'

'Worse? Worse than someone dying?'

'He's not dead yet, but he *soon will be*,' Laurie snarled, throwing his mobile across the table.

'Oh Laurie, it's not your mother up in Yorkshire?'

'My mother?' For a second Laurie appeared genuinely shocked. 'My mother? No, *he*. I said *he*, not *she*!'

'Who is it who's dying but not dead yet, then?' I actually felt my pulse race as I racked my brains as to any friends or other relatives who might be on their way out.

'Me.'

'You?'

Laurie nodded. 'Me. I'm – going – to – die.' He put a hand in the general direction of his heart as he enunciated each word.

'Is he having a panic attack?' Mum glanced in my direction before addressing her son-in- law. 'I think you're having a panic attack, Laurie. Is your heart racing and you're feeling sweaty?' She gazed suspiciously at Laurie's forehead for any suggestion of moisture.

'No,' Laurie snapped irritably, 'I most certainly am not having a panic attack. And I don't *sweat* either. Never had a panic attack in my life and I don't intend starting now.' He took a dramatic pause. 'I've a month left to live.'

'A month?' My hand actually flew to my mouth in that

ridiculous way it says happens after the receipt of terrible news in particularly bad novels.

'They're killing me off. Next month. After seventeen years as Ted Baxter, I'm to be fucking well killed off.'

Mum snorted, coughed and then – as Laurie closed his eyes and added, through gritted teeth, 'drowned, drowned for heaven's sake, after falling into the fucking slurry pit,' – she started giggling uncontrollably, unable, it seemed, to actually stop.

13

March 2021

'I'm not going up there. I am NOT going to live on that farm up there. I refuse to go. It's nearly in Scotland, and you know Nicola Sturgeon doesn't want anything to do with the English. She doesn't want us there. Well, I don't want anything to do with *her*.'

'What *are* you talking about, Ada?' I snapped. I'd gone through every possible damned emotion with my now-sixteen-year-old with regards our potential – now confirmed – move up to Westenbury in West Yorkshire and I'd had enough. I'd reasoned, cajoled, pleaded and cried buckets with Ada and now I was *telling* her. Telling her, in no uncertain terms, we *were* moving north and she *was* coming with us, no argument. 'While your understanding of Scottish politics appears remarkably better informed than your geographical knowledge of the north of England, Ada, I'm telling you now, sweetheart, that this house is sold and, unless you intend on staying here with the Davidson family who are moving in...' I glanced at the 2021 calendar of *A Better Life* which had Laurie's character, Ted Baxter (RIP) on six out of the twelve months' photographs, and which I'd picked up in *Bargain Basement* for peanuts '...in exactly two weeks then, like us, you're out on the street and the only alternative is to take up Granny Lewis's offer to go and live on the farm for a while.'

'For *a while*?' Hope flared in Ada's eyes. 'How long is *a while*? A week? Are we going for a week's holiday until we find something back down here? A month?' The hope in her beautiful navy eyes – Laurie's eyes – died as she contemplated the possible awful reality. 'A year? More? What?'

'Ada, we've been through all this. I don't know...'

'Well, *why* don't you know? You've discussed it with Dad enough these last few months. Although,' she went on, 'I'm not convinced screaming and shouting at him constitutes discussion.' Very much her father's daughter, just occasionally I saw glimpses of my own teenaged self's assured handling of the English language when Ada spoke. 'And have you not given *any* consideration to my education? To George's education? Mum, I do my GCSEs this year: you're ruining my chances of getting any of them by taking me out of my own school and putting me into some bloody awful comprehensive up in that backwater. Do they even do GCSEs up there?'

'It's Dad's old school,' I protested. 'He went on to Cambridge from Westenbury Comprehensive.' I might actually have laughed at Ada's snobbish, ill-informed verbosity if I hadn't privately agreed with where she was coming from.

'Yes,' she hissed. 'Exactly. And look how *he's* ended up. Totally and utterly bankrupt and owing thousands.'

'Where've you got that from?' I asked, trying to calm the waters.

'From *you*,' she snapped. 'It was what *you* were shouting at him last night once we'd gone to bed.' My daughter and I stood at either side of the kitchen table, gladiatorial sparring partners, just waiting for the right opportunity to get in the next jibe. It wouldn't have surprised me to see Nero standing on the Aga, thumbs up, signifying I was the loser of this particular round and to get me out of there to fight another round another day.

I wasn't hanging around for any tyrannical Roman emperor to pass judgement: I was out of there on my own accord before I heard the sound of fiddling. 'I have things to do,' I said stiffly. 'I'm going to my room to start packing up my things and I suggest you do the same.' I headed for the door.

'Mum, don't walk out on me.' Ada's voice broke and the pent-up fury she'd been hurling both at Laurie and me – but mainly at me – turned to tears. 'Mum. Mum?' She lifted her face pitifully in my direction, her mascaraed eyes turning sooty as she rubbed at them. 'I *can't* go. I *can't* leave all my friends. It's not *fair*.' She paused to wipe at her nose with the back of her hand. 'Please let me go and live with Granny. She says I can...'

'Ada.' I went to put my arms round her as I'd done so many times in the last four months since the awful realisation of our predicament really hit home. 'We've been through this; you know we have. Granny lives fifty miles from here – fifty-five from your school. It would take an hour and a half driving down the M25 every morning. Probably more, knowing the M25. You can't expect Granny to spend four hours a day – because that's what it would amount to – driving you to school and back every day.'

'The train. I could get the train.'

'*Two* hours, by the time you've got trains and buses.' I'd already looked up the journey after Mum had offered to have the three of us live with her. She was still adamant, four months down the line, that Laurie wasn't included in that particular invitation – and a state of cold war was now in place between my mother and my husband. 'And,' I went on, closing my eyes against the hopelessness of the whole situation, 'you know there isn't a bus from the station out to Queen Margaret's and back again in the evening. In the dark. It's just not feasible.' I took a deep breath as Ada's protracted crying increased. 'But even if Granny lived near school it wouldn't help. Ada, we haven't got the money for your and George's school fees. They're nearly thirty thousand a year.'

'Granny said she'd pay mine.'

'Sorry?' I held Ada away from me. 'She said *what*?'

'That she'd pay the school fees. Until I've done my exams this summer. It's just for a few months, that's all.'

'She'd no right to say that without consulting me. Getting your hopes up…'

'So, can I?' Ada's sobs turned to little hiccupping cries.

I sat down at the kitchen table feeling totally defeated. 'I'll talk to Granny again,' I said, putting up my hand to my temple where a dull tattoo beat was heralding the start of yet another headache. The fury and utter misery I'd felt since first reading *The Blazing Trail* article that had accused Laurie of infidelity, of being a womaniser, had never gone away, had been doubly compounded by our losing our home and, now it seemed, the possibility of losing my daughter as well.

Ada picked up her history notes and, with the slight hope that she might yet escape the move *up bloody north* as she'd dubbed it ever since Laurie and I had told her that the house was up for sale, and the only way out was our temporarily leaving St Albans and going to live in Westenbury where at least the accommodation was free, left the kitchen for the sanctity of her bedroom, her phone and her mates.

I needed a mate. Gin and wine had probably been my go-to comfort the last six months or so, and I looked longingly towards the bottle of red beckoning beguilingly at the far end of the kitchen before looking at the huge designer clock Laurie had bought – at great expense – from some posh shop in Chelsea, and knew the last thing I should be doing at four o'clock on a Saturday afternoon was turning to alcohol. I wasn't a huge drinker, but a glass of the old vino did help to blur the edges of the reality of losing my home.

I didn't have the huge band of female friends that so many other women of my generation surrounded themselves with. From leaving Cambridge, I'd worked virtually full-time – whether writing my own, or commissioning and editing other people's efforts – and although I did know some of the school mums, I was too busy with work and bringing up my kids, with an often-absent father, to be one of those social playground-bunnies who organised playdates and took it in turn on the Saturday night Chez Nous supper circuit. The mild postnatal depression I'd experienced after having Ada – and which I'd not recognised as such, despite Mum and Dad urging me to get help – had resulted in my losing confidence in both my ability to socialise as well as in having another child. Until I found myself unexpectedly pregnant with George.

Laurie, of course, was always in demand as a dinner guest – I'd actually seen one of the mums in George's class giving the thumbs-up to her mates and, not realising I was standing nearby, had turned it into well-executed jazz hands with the explanation 'we've *got* him. We're having Laurie Lewis for dinner...' Very tempted to advise said host that Laurie was best cooked braised, with just a soupçon of sage and onion, the moment was lost when she went on, 'now, who do we invite to keep *Jennifer* entertained? It will have to be someone literary or worthy? Anyone got Salman Rushdie's number?'

I didn't really have, I felt almost ashamed of admitting, a coterie of friends to gossip and lunch with. I'd never really felt the need, to be honest. I'd always been fairly independent, shy, even, and apart from the lovely threesome of myself, Annabelle and Gudrun at university, was so busy with my writing, immersing myself totally in my poets' past lives, I'd not formed other close friendships. Laurie, I'd always thought, was my best friend as well as my husband. The realisation that this was not the case was as devastating as knowing Laurie had strayed.

Laurie was, that afternoon, in some meeting he'd asked for with his apparently reluctant-to-see-him agent, the scary Gillian Openshaw – Laurie had long since ditched Leo when the good times continued to escalate – and George was at a friend's house down the lane. I poured a small glass of wine and reached for my phone and then hesitated. What I really needed was my dad: I'd missed him every single day since Mum's awful hysterical phone call from Kefalonia telling me of the speedboat accident. Jeremy and I had immediately flown out to Greece to be with her and bring Dad's body back to the UK. It wasn't something I ever wanted to go through again, and it had taken me forever to get over not having him around. I'd felt I was just getting back on an even keel when all this had blown up with Laurie and the damned court case. If I couldn't have Dad, the next one in line was Gudrun.

'So, you're coming to join me in Yorkshire, then?' Gudrun phoned immediately after she read my text.

'Looks like it.'

'But you have the option of moving yourself and the kids in with your mum? She's actually suggested you do that?'

'Hmm. But not fair on her, really.'

'Probably fairer on her than knowing her only daughter is bent on resettling two hundred miles up the motorway with her grandchildren.' Gudrun paused before asking, 'What does Laurie think about living with your mum? I assume he'd prefer to be nearer London where any potential work is? I bet he'd far rather do that than go back north with his tail between his legs?'

'Laurie's not invited.'

There was a heartbeat of silence as Gudrun obviously mulled over the fact that my mother refused to have my husband living in her house. Eventually she said, 'You can't blame her, Jen.'

'Oh, I think I can.'

'Don't go falling out with Cynthia, Jennifer.'

'I don't want Ada and George to lose their father, Gudrun. George would be absolutely devastated if Laurie wasn't with us; you know what an anxious child he is at the best of times. I want to keep us together and, if Mum won't have him in her house, then we'll just have to move where we *can* all be together. I'm sure it'll only be a temporary move. Once all this has died down, there'll be offers of work…'

'*I'm a Celebrity, Get Me Out of Here?*' I could almost see Gudrun's raised eyebrows. 'Isn't that the elephants' graveyard of failed actors?'

'Gudrun, he hasn't *failed*. He's just…'

This time I actually heard Gudrun's derision as she gave a little, cynical snort of laughter. 'Why are you standing up for him, Jen?' Gudrun was impatient. 'Where's the strong woman I knew and loved at university? Who told that boring Beau bloke where to get off when he was following her around like a love-sick… a love-sick…?'

'Texan?'

'That'll be it.' There was a companionable silence as we both contemplated our glory days at Cambridge and then Gudrun said, 'But what the hell are you going to *do* in Yorkshire? How are you going to *live*? And, big question, how on earth are you going to cope with sharing a house with your mother-in-law, who'll be running after Laurie like there's no tomorrow?'

'Oh no. No.' I almost put up my hand in protest. 'No, Rita won't be there. She's already moved out.'

'What, you're throwing the poor woman out of her

home?' Gudrun sounded outraged and I actually laughed. Probably the first laugh I'd had in months.

'No, God, there's no way I would be moving in with someone else – that's the main reason I don't want to live with Mum – Rita's more than happy to be moving into a little council-owned bungalow in the village. She'd had her name down for one since Laurie's dad died, and had been planning to move out and sell up as soon as she was able. She's simply put the estate agent off on the sale of the farm for as long as we need somewhere to live.'

'I bet the Ugly Sisters aren't happy with that?'

'Don't call them that.' I laughed again, in spite of myself. 'Janice is always hard work but the other two, Lorraine and Cheryl, are OK.'

'And what do *they* think about you moving into the farm? Is it *still* a farm, for heaven's sake? Are you going to have to be up at four a.m. every morning to milk the cows?'

'No, there's not been cows as long as *I've* known Laurie. I think Rita's kept a few hens going and the dogs are probably still in situ…'

'Well, she can't take bloody hens to a council bungalow. Bet she's not allowed a dog either. And I bet the sisters aren't happy that they're not going to get a handout from the sale of the farm. They'll resent Laurie even more than you've always made out they already do.'

'George has always wanted a dog,' I protested. 'Look, Gudrun, it might be just for six months, just for a year or so until Laurie's got work and we can come back south and rent somewhere…'

'Renting in St Albans? In London? You won't get more than a garage for £1,000 a month.'

'And that's why we're moving north. We can live rent-free, the kids will go to the local schools, Laurie will find a new job and I'll put my all into coming up with a best seller: Samuel Coleridge is next on my list. There are several publishing houses interested after Aunt Agnes's memoirs from Bletchley Park did OK. And, I shall continue to commission and edit for Wesley and Brown from up there.'

There was a protracted silence as Gudrun took all this in and I drained my glass of wine and contemplated another to wash down the two paracetamol I knew was the only thing to get rid of my headache. Eventually she asked, 'Jeremy?'

'Jeremy?'

'He's your brother? Or had you forgotten? In charge now of your dad's business? Surely there's help – funds – there to help set you back up in London. A little terraced house in Watford? Hitchin, maybe?'

'I'm not really in touch with Jeremy.'

'Oh?'

'When Dad died and Jeremy took over fully at the helm, he was furious when he learned how much money Dad had ploughed into helping us out of yet another sticky situation. You know my dad: he might have been, as you once pointed out, a bit of a wide boy, a bit of an Essex lad, but he wouldn't see me out on the street.' I paused. 'He won't have to see me now...' I paused again, wanting to cry. 'And Jeremy, very cleverly being the financial expert that he is, has wrapped up Mum's money so that she has a good income, but no huge sums available to help us.'

'To help you *again*, you mean? You can't blame him, Jennifer.'

'It was Jeremy, I'm sure, who persuaded Mum that opening up her home to Laurie, as well as the three of us, just "wasn't to be entertained" as he put it. My little brother has become terribly stuffy and pompous over the years.'

'You're not telling me everything, Jen. What are you hiding?'

'Nothing.'

'Come on, Jen, why's Jeremy taken so against you? It wouldn't have been what your dad wanted. Or your mum, presumably?'

If I hadn't been drinking red wine, together with the added soothing effect of paracetamol hitting my bloodstream, I probably would have stayed schtum. But I needed someone to offload to. 'Miranda,' I said eventually, kicking myself as soon as I said her name.

'Miranda?'

'Jeremy's wife.'

'She doesn't like Laurie?'

'She obviously couldn't *get enough of him* when Jeremy found them "at it" as my little brother so eloquently put it when he discovered them in the cornfield behind their house at Miranda's birthday BBQ.'

'You are joking!'

'"Just having a bit of birthday fun," Laurie said to Jeremy, and reiterated to me afterwards along with, "Too much alcohol in the sun."' I paused, wishing I'd never started with all this, but wanting to explain. 'Look, Gudrun, I've seen Miranda when she's had too much to drink – do you remember what she was like at our wedding? All over the place, she was. She does appear to have a bit of a problem with alcohol – Jeremy actually once admitted that to Mum. Anyway, apparently, she'd come on to Laurie, big time, and not the other way round, as Jeremy so indignantly claimed. Even told Laurie she'd always had a thing about him. I didn't speak to him for several weeks after that.'

'Who? Jeremy?'

'No,' I tutted. 'Laurie. As far as I could see, both Laurie and my sister-in-law had fallen foul of Jeremy's Pimms. You know, you think you're drinking lemonade and then, suddenly wham, it hits you...'

'And were the pair of them engaged in full, you know, *full sex*, when Jeremy discovered them in and amongst the Fields of Gold?' Gudrun was shocked, I could tell.

'No, *of course not*.' I was equally shocked. 'It really was the Pimms, Gudrun. They'd had too much to drink and Miranda had gone in for a quick snog...'

'Oh, for heaven's sake, Jen. I'd have kicked the *quick snogger* back into the barley where Jeremy found them.' There was silence as we both digested Gudrun's response. And then she went on, 'Has he always, you know, messed around with other women?'

'No, absolutely *not*.' As I said it, the realisation hit me that I quite likely protested too much: the reality, after the alleged outing of Laurie by the magazine, that he *did* mess about with other women was, daily, becoming more real. He'd always flirted a bit – that was Laurie for you – but I'd never, for one minute, imagined him capable of out and out adultery. Until now. 'No,' I reiterated crossly, as much for my own benefit as Gudrun's. 'You don't think I'd have stayed with him if he had, do you Gudrun?'

'Well, maybe now is the time to reconsider, Jen. Much as I'd love you up in Yorkshire – you're only half an hour away from me down the M62 – I advise you, as your best and oldest friend, as honorary godmother to both your kids, to not even contemplate moving north. Go and take the kids and move back to Berkshire with your mum. Make it up with Jeremy and move the kids in with your mum. It'll do Laurie good to be without you for a while. Make him realise just how much he loves you. And misses you...'

'I've never actually doubted that he loves me, Gudrun,' I interrupted. 'It's just with him constantly being in the limelight. It sort of turns his head...'

'Jennifer, go and take the children to stay with your mum.' Gudrun was adamant.

And I might have done just that. Listening to Gudrun, who always talked sense, albeit somewhat bossily, was putting me firmly in the *move yourself and the kids in with Mum* camp. If just for a while, until we'd sorted ourselves and Laurie found work. I more than likely wouldn't have entertained moving north if Ada hadn't appeared in the kitchen, holding out her phone in a frenzy of excitement. 'Mum, Mum, talk to Lydia's mum. She says I can stay with *them* during the week when I'm at school. I can go to Granny's at the weekend and come and stay with you in Yorkshire during the holidays. There's only four months left at school until the summer break, and *then* I can come up to be with you. Please, please, Mum, don't make me leave school and everything here.'

And then, in the middle of all this pleading on the part of my daughter, and my being passed the phone to talk to Lydia's mum, seven-year-old George appeared in the kitchen after being dropped off by *his* friend Ethan's dad. George adored Ada and stood, white-faced, as the realisation hit him, she might no longer be living with us as a family unit.

'We're n...not leaving D...Daddy as well,' he shouted furiously, his stammer, which he'd worked so hard to overcome, back at full strength. 'If Ada's l...leaving us to l... live with Lydia and Granny, we're NOT leaving D...Daddy as well.' He burst into tears. 'He's *my* daddy and *I'm* going where *he's* going, even if *you two* aren't. I'm n...not bloody well leaving MY DAD.'

And with a hysterical sob, he ran upstairs crying to his room.

Unable to sleep that night, unable to make a decision about what I should do, I took my hand from Laurie's (ever since the very first night we'd slept together back in my room in Cambridge, Laurie had wanted my hand in his as he drifted off) and went downstairs to think. Ada needed the continuity of her own school if she were to excel in her GCSEs. OK, she was very bright and more than likely she'd get through them wherever she ended up. But was it fair when we'd been given this get-out-of-jail card for the next four months or so? Mum would pay the fees and Lydia's mum was more than happy to have Ada stay mid-week. Oh, but I couldn't bear not to have her with us, to leave her here while we packed up and moved – albeit temporarily – north. I gazed around at the huge, stylish, colour-supplement kitchen which didn't have my heart: it was just shiny surfaces and ridiculously over-the-top appliances we couldn't get our heads round. It was, I reflected, sitting there at two a.m. nursing a mug of Horlicks, as affected and shallow as my husband appeared to have become.

14

We arrived in Westenbury village on a miserably grey, extremely windy Saturday afternoon. George, always travel sick, had avoided throwing up into the green Harrods carrier bag on his knee all the way up the M1 but, once off the main road and hitting a veritable helter-skelter of twisting countryside lanes, his complexion paled and seeing the beads of sweat on his top lip – always a giveaway as to what was to come next – I urged Laurie to stop. I managed to get George out of the back seat and onto the verge where he stood, pale and trembling, while the sneaky cold wind, full of the promise of snow, proceeded to lift my abandoned *Telegraph* and its accompanying fliers for hearing aids, reading lamps and wine offers, sending them triumphantly into the air like demented kites.

'I hope you're going to pick that lot up?'

'I'm sorry?' With one eye on George, who was now dry heaving into a hawthorn hedge, I turned to see a tall, fair-haired farmer-ish type scowling at me from the other side of a five-bar gate.

'If you day-trippers must come here with all your accompanying can't-do-without chocolate wrappers and crisp packets, would you at least ensure your litter goes back with you?' He handed over the Mars bar wrapper and Walkers crisp packet I recognised as ours, the contents of which Laurie had eaten on the journey north and which had obviously made a bid for freedom along with my newspaper.

'I can assure you, we're *not* day trippers,' I snapped as George finally succumbed and vomited profusely. 'Would anyone in their right minds *trip* to this god-forsaken place for the *day*?' I handed George a wet wipe.

'Well, just make sure all that lot goes home with you...'

'The sick included?' I snapped once more, dabbing at George's jeans while glaring at the man.

'There's livestock in these fields,' the man went on, adopting a challenging tone. 'We've had problems with...'

'Finished, sweetie?' I cut the man off as I soothed George, whose cheeks appeared to have regained some colour. 'Not far now. Soon be there...'

'*You* were a lot of sodding help.' I gestured towards Laurie with the now rounded-up, mud-spattered newspaper.

'Never be confrontational with the natives,' Laurie said, his eyes closed. 'God, I'm knackered.' He turned to George. 'Nearly there, Georgio. Soon be at the top of this hill.'

'Not as high up as Chris,' I said mildly.

'Chris?' Laurie frowned and glanced across at me as he turned the car at the village church. 'Chris who?'

I indicated with a nod of my head the large wind-ravaged poster on the church notice board:

CHRIS IS RISEN

'Lucky Chris,' I scowled. 'Obviously got out of this place while he could...'

'Come on, George, let's go and survey our kingdom, shall we?' I threw George's thick school duffel coat, Wellingtons and scarf towards him before pulling on my own sheepskin jacket and gloves. We'd been here three days, and it appeared we'd arrived up in Westenbury in the middle of what appeared to be the coldest March on record, although Janice assured me I was just a southern softie and 'this is *nothing*, compared to what we've had in the past'. *Nothing* was a bank of grimy snow, clinging tenaciously along, and at the foot of, dry-stone walls, ice-covered swampy fields of tussocky yellowing grass and an evil east wind determined to permeate to the very core, everything – and everybody – it encountered.

'Can we take the dog?'

'Of course. He has got a name, you know, even if he does live outside in the kennel.'

'What is it again, Mummy?' George frowned as he tried to remember.

'Polonius.' At first, I'd thought it had been Laurie who'd christened the ancient black and white collie with such a literary handle but, although the dog was getting on, Laurie must have left home – been married to me – years prior to Terry Lewis getting the dog as a puppy. Terry had been dead a year or so now, and I'd probably only ever been in Laurie's dad's company a handful of times, but he'd never struck me as having any knowledge of Shakespeare's plays, but maybe this was where Laurie had acquired his dramatic bent – maybe Terry Lewis had been into amateur dramatics, and particularly Hamlet, in his younger days. I'd have to ask Rita because I knew Laurie would have no interest in either how the dog had acquired its theatrical name, or the now deceased Terry Lewis.

'We're not going far; just for a quick wander round. We need to go down into the village at some point to pick up a couple of sweatshirts for when you start your new school tomorrow.'

'Shall I wear my old school blazer and tie?' George asked doubtfully.

'No, not at all.' Not, I added silently, unless you want to be laughed at by the village kids for wearing a maroon striped blazer with the motif '*Altum Tendere*' emblazoned on its pocket. 'Your grey trousers and white school shirts are totally in keeping with the Little Acorns uniform,' I added. 'We just need the navy sweatshirt and you'll look like everybody else...'

I broke off as the back door leading into the tiny porch opened and slammed, bringing a blast of cold air into the kitchen. 'Blimey, you look as if you're off to Siberia, the pair of you.' Janice appeared at the kitchen door and, although I knew I shouldn't, I felt a tiny twinge of resentment that she was banging around, letting herself in as if she owned the place. Well, marking her territory like an old tom cat at least, I amended silently, as she went over to fill the kettle. 'Anyone would think it was cold out there.'

George thought that hugely funny and I said, looking at her dressed in just a bright orange hoody, 'You obviously don't feel the cold, Janice?'

'Flipping hot sweats,' she said cheerfully. 'They've been so bad lately I'm beginning to think I'm personally responsible for global warming. I had my bi-annual trip to the hairdresser last week – God I hate sitting there having some bloke prattling on about where I'm going for my holidays. "Nowhere," I told him. "Last time I went to the travel agent, they pinched my husband." Mind you, they should have damn well kept him. So, I'm sitting there, waiting, sweating like a pig under that black plastic shawl thingy, when the hair-washer girl comes up and says: "Oh I didn't realise you'd already been washed, Janice." "I haven't," I said.' Janice laughed to herself, pulled a somewhat grubby hand through her very short reddish hair. 'Right, I'm going to have a quick mug of tea and then I need to see to the sheep.'

'How many have you got, Auntie Janice?' George was wide-eyed at Janice's apparent confidence with livestock.

'Oh, just a small flock, now, George. They keep the wolf from the door, and the hens and pullets supply enough eggs that I can sell them to the butcher in the village.'

'Are you taking Polonius with you?' George asked.

'Polony? Hmm, he always tags along.'

'So why the Shakespearian name?' I asked, endeavouring to be friendly.

'Shakespeare?' Janice looked mystified, frowning as she audibly sucked at the strong Yorkshire tea before reaching for a ginger biscuit which she dipped into the hot liquid, shoving the whole thing wholesale into her mouth.

'Polonius?'

'Polony is from Shakespeare? I don't *think* so.' She shook her head and laughed, spluttering crumbs. 'The dog's named after that horrible red-skinned sausage my dad could never get enough of. Shakespeare? Duh!! The dogs at this house have always been named for things he loved and couldn't do without. There was Tetley at one point – that was the beer not the tea – and Hamlet...'

'Hamlet?'

'You know, those little brown cigars? Dad always smoked them on Sundays and at Christmas and if he'd had a win on the horses. He had to make do with his roll-ups the rest of the time. Couldn't afford anything else.' Janice laughed again and then, draining her cup, looked me in the eye. 'How are you going to manage here, Jen? I mean, you've been used to everything being done for you...'

'Hardly,' I protested.

'Oh, come on. I bet your mum always had a cleaner? I bet you did yourself?'

'Well,' I said, stung, 'I've been working virtually full-time ever since I left university. As well as bringing up Ada and George. It was a big house in St Albans to run.'

'Exactly.' Janice folded her arms. 'You were used to so much more. For a start, you're going to have a daily fight on your hands with this thing.' She indicated the cream, rusting Aga with her booted foot.

'Oh, I'm used to Agas. We had one in St Albans.'

'Oh? A shiny bright red, all-singing, electric thing you just switched on whenever you wanted it, I bet?'

'*Racing Green* actually,' I said, knowing the rest of her adjectives re my lovely Aga had been spot on.

'Aye, well, this one 'ere, as you can see, is Creeping Cream.' She laughed at her own wit. 'It'll sulk and stay in a mood unless you show it who's boss. Keep an eye on the oil level or it'll start smoking soot and go out and then you'll have to start all over again with it. Must admit, I'm amazed the Boy Wonder has remembered how to deal with it. Where is he, anyway?'

'Gone over to Manchester. Gone to see an agent over there who has something to do with Laurie's agent in London. He's determined to pick up work again.'

Janice nodded. 'So, how long do you reckon you're going to be here then?' She held my gaze, questioning.

'Who knows?' I smiled sweetly, determined not to let her get the upper hand. I'd always found Janice to be a bit of a bully and, like the kitchen Aga that was now resolutely pumping out warmth, you just had to know how to handle her correctly. Terry Lewis's daughter to a T in both looks and outlook, I'd never seen anything that indicated she was Rita's offspring as well. Janice was quite different from both Laurie and Cheryl – but especially the latter – who had inherited not only Rita's good looks, but her pleasant outlook on life as well.

'The thing is, you see, Jen,' Janice wasn't letting it go, 'Lorraine, Cheryl and me were all waiting for a bit of our share of the sale of this place once Mum moved out and put it on the market. You and Laurie have scuppered that, right good and proper.'

'Right.' I didn't quite know what else to say, and the terrible homesickness that had been building ever since

I'd hugged and kissed Mum and Ada goodbye three days previously, was now threatening to totally engulf me. I took a deep breath in order to calm myself and, glancing across at George who was stroking one of the elderly yard cats that had chanced its luck and followed Janice in, took comfort from knowing George was here with me. 'Look, Janice...'

'And I wouldn't have the cats inside. Dad always had them outside for the rats.'

Rats? Lovely! 'Yes,' I smiled once more, determined not to let Janice rattle me with talk of rats, 'and, according to Rita, she ignored your dad and had them inside. He's fine. George loves animals – always wanted a dog or a cat. Just Laurie who never wanted them in St Albans.'

'No, he wouldn't. It'd remind him too much of his life up here.' Janice scratched at dry skin on both hands and I wondered whether to offer her some of my hand cream. I decided against it.

'I really don't know how long we're going to be here, Janice. I don't particularly want to be here any more than *you* want us to be here. It'll be temporary, I'm sure, just until we decide where we're going to be once Laurie finds a job.'

'But you're putting George into school in the village?'

'Well, yes, he *has* to go to school, you know.'

'I *don't*, Mum.' George's North London clipped tones were a stark contrast to Janice's flattened vowels. 'I don't *have* to go to school. I can stay here and be a farmer with Auntie Janice.'

'Come on then, lad, come out with me and help with the sheep.' Janice glanced in my direction before moving to find and pull on a waterproof coat hanging on a hook in the porch.

'I'm really sorry you think we're stopping you getting hold of your inheritance...' I said to her back, and then wished I hadn't. It seemed a petulant, mean-spirited thing to say.

'Aye, well, we'll get it one day. Mum wouldn't see Laurie out on the street. Right, George?'

Once George had scampered off after his Aunt Janice without a backward glance in my direction, I unbuttoned my coat and went over to the Aga, seeking the warmth and comfort I was so badly in need of. Homesickness had never before featured in my life: I'd happily gone off to sleepovers as a kid, Guide camp, a week's exchange with a girl from Paris, university – but now it had me totally in its grip, its pernicious clammy hands reaching out for me until I felt I couldn't breathe. Panic descended. It was no good: before I took the step of putting George into the village school, I was off. Off back to Mum and Ada. What the hell had I been thinking of, uprooting the pair of us and coming two hundred miles north where we weren't wanted? Where, whenever I tried to talk to Laurie about how I felt, he just put his arms round me, assured me something was in the pipeline and the offers of work would soon be flooding in. He loved me, he constantly reiterated, and we'd get through all this.

I walked into the front room, as Rita had always called it – the chilly room where she'd first offered me the red foil-covered marshmallow teacake biscuits – now somewhat incongruously sporting a couple of our George Smith chairs, their stylish elegance standing out like sore thumbs against the red flock-covered wallpaper. Rita had taken what would fit into her new bungalow, the sisters had taken what *they'd* wanted from the house and we'd brought up what was needed to fill the gaps. The rest of our stuff was in storage, the expense incurred by that little necessity mounting weekly, as well as putting me in a spin every time I dared to think about it.

I went over to look out of the front room window. The weak mid-March sun was making a valiant effort to circumnavigate the bank of steel grey cloud and, as I stood watching, faint rays of sunlight managed to escape the gloom, putting out ghostly fingers of silver across the lawn. I hadn't realised how large the Lewises' front garden was and how much time and attention Rita – I assumed it was Rita – must have given the plants and the spring flowers which were now manfully ignoring the cold. I continued to gaze, admiring the manicured hedging which led, unfettered, down to the orchard of apple and pear trees overlooking the rolling meadows beyond.

I made a decision: I would think of Daisy Royd Farm as a stop-gap, a floating piece of wood to cling onto in the troubled waters we'd found ourselves. I liked that metaphorical analogy and found myself smiling slightly, the former panic beginning to slink back into its cave from where it had come. I knew it wouldn't take much for it to be out and at my throat once again, but I'd give our new home six months. Spring and the promise of summer was round the corner and I'd give it until the autumn to see where we were heading next. In six months' time, Laurie would surely have found work of some sort or other, Ada's GCSEs would have been taken and we could make some decision about where she was going next. And I would spend the time cracking on with Samuel Taylor Coleridge. And then we could return south and rent somewhere. If Laurie and I were to stay together in the future, that was; if the anger and resentment I continued to harbour – despite the continued protestations of his innocence as well as his being a victim of over-dramatization by the media – didn't continue to eat into me like caustic acid, then six months thrown together away from our former life would either make or break us.

I could see George, his red scarf a stark beacon against the grey and yellow hues of the winter valley, manfully climbing up into the cab of yet another knackered tractor, and nearly rushed down there to bring him back into the warmth and safety of the kitchen. I couldn't imagine Janice having much truck with health and safety. Stop being a helicopter mother, I chided myself; he's a Yorkshire farm kid now. Instead, I turned away, deciding I'd grab the opportunity to move more of our unpacked things into their final resting places.

There was little wardrobe space, and what there was already provided a haven for the clothes I'd unpacked. There were two huge boxes marked *Summer Stuff*: shorts and T-shirts belonging to George, swimsuits and bikinis (what, in God's name, had possessed me to bring those?) of mine and some rather lovely short-sleeved linen shirts of Laurie's. I didn't even bother stripping back the brown tape that held the boxes closed. I couldn't imagine it ever being warm enough again to warrant getting them out.

I looked around for somewhere to put them. The house had three bedrooms, Laurie and I taking what had been Terry and Rita's double bedroom, with George ensconced in the room across the landing that had once slept all three Lewis sisters. Laurie had, he informed me somewhat sourly, always been shoved into the little box room at the back. 'Where else did you *expect* to go?' I'd retorted equally acerbically and left him, still obviously disgruntled at the memory, to take all the best spaces in the one, utilitarian, heavy oak wardrobe which, if it hadn't come out of the ark, had certainly only just missed the boat.

I looked upwards and, spotting a loft trap door directly above my head, went back downstairs for the kitchen steps Rita always used to gain access to the large built-in kitchen cupboard in which she'd stored her treasure trove cache of tins of baked beans, pilchards in tomato sauce, tins of casserole stewed steak – I wanted to heave at the very thought – corned beef and rice pudding. Presumably in case of a nuclear holocaust.

The trap door went back on itself easily and, employing the gymnastic moves I'd last used probably at primary school, I was able to hoist myself up into its dark, somewhat fetid depths. There appeared to be no light, so I retraced my steps, found the huge torchlight Rita had used to go out to the hens at night if she felt there was a fox around, and went back up. If Rita had kept things up there during her almost fifty years of marriage, she'd obviously had a huge recent clear out. The space was devoid of anything: no rolls of unwanted carpet or wallpaper, no boxes of unwilling-to-pass-on baby clothes or toddler's first shoes. I'd cried over Ada's first pair of white leather sandals as I'd handed them to Mum for safe keeping, once I knew we actually had to get out of there.

Plenty of space, then, for my unopened boxes. It was quite possible, I realised, if I couldn't hack living up here with Laurie, I'd be bringing them back down unopened and heading with them and George, back down to Mum. I managed, somehow, to get the smaller of the boxes onto my shoulder and up into the gaping mouth of the loft, lying across its opening as I shoved the box forwards across the wooden slats that made up the loft floor.

There did appear to be something round to the left and behind me – a pile of books up against the wall. Ooh good, I'd had to pack up most of my library in St Albans, and was always happy to investigate other people's choice of reading materials. I was to be disappointed: a huge collection of Mills and Boon romantic novels which I'd never, in the past, deigned to pick up, let alone read. This must be Rita's secret stash – I'd only ever seen more literary novels: Hardy, Lawrence, Orwell, on the shelves downstairs. I knew she was a voracious reader but never imagined she'd be into this stuff, all Regency era, by the look of it.

I reached for the top one on the pile: *Some Day my Lord Will Come*, ready to disparage and abandon what was there after reading the first page: I did hope the poor serving wench wasn't going to have to wait days for the royal toff to get his rocks off. Instead, I was utterly entranced, hooked from the very beginning as I sat reading by the light of the powerful hen torch. Why had I never attempted to read this genre before? Because, I reminded myself, you were – are – a literary snob. I remembered Caroline Baker, who had the room next to mine at Cambridge and who, with a razor-sharp intellect, would hold forth *ad infinitum* on F.R. Leavis, arguing the toss on what constituted literary criticism. Having dropped my own copy of Wordsworth's *The Prelude* in the bath, I'd gone into Caroline's room to beg for a quick borrow of hers and found her totally engrossed in *Forever the Duke* or some such title. 'Guilty little secret,' she'd laughed, unembarrassed. 'You can knock back gin, or eat triple chocolate chip cookies or...' she indicated an arm towards a pile of Mills and Boon on the window sill... 'abandon reality with pure escapism. Much cheaper and not as fattening.' It hadn't occurred to me at the time that my obsession with Byron probably ran along the same escapist lines.

I laughed to myself as I remembered Caroline – where was she now? – and got stuck back in to m'lord and his antics. Bloody hell, it was good. Just what I needed. I must have sat there a good hour devouring the story, loving the characters, escaping from the true reality that I had no home of my own, that I'd abandoned my sixteen-year-old daughter and was married to a man who had almost definitely cheated on me. Eventually, my fingers numb with cold, and tired from holding the massive torch, as well as my backside that was aching from sitting on the edge of the loft mouth, I realised I'd better get on with unpacking my former life into this new one. Laurie – and probably Janice as well – would be scathing about my new choice of reading material, but I didn't care. I reached for the next couple of books on the pile and added them to the one I was almost halfway through. The very tip of a bookmark was peeking from the pages of the third paperback in my hand and I put the others back down to rescue it.

Except it wasn't a bookmark, but a newspaper cutting from the town's local paper, *The Midhope Examiner*. The newsprint that had escaped the protection of the book was torn, but the black and white photograph atop the review of a Midhope Polytechnic production of *Hamlet* was not. My eyes were immediately arrested by the very faded image of whom I assumed to be Laurie playing the main part of

Hamlet himself. *Alas, poor Yorick, I knew him...* I smiled, slightly indulgently, taking in the dark-haired image – as if for the first time – of this husband of mine.

Except it *wasn't* Laurie, of course. On closer examination, the man in the photo, although dark-haired and of a similar stature to my husband, could have been anyone. And yet, according to the list of actors' names printed underneath the photo, the man was certainly *called* Laurence. I peered at the newsprint more closely, scanning for clues. The cutting was dated February 1978, when the town's university was still a poly.

And the year before Laurie was actually born.

15

Laurie eventually returned from his foray over the border into Lancashire in even more of a foul temper than he'd been in when leaving the house that morning. Rather than wait for me to pick him up from Midhope station, where the TransPennine train called on its route from Manchester to Newcastle, Laurie had taken a taxi for the eight-mile journey back out to Daisy Royd farm and I went at him, berating him for the extravagance of spending the little money we had on a taxi, just because he couldn't be doing with waiting outside the cold station for me to pick him up.

We'd had to sell Laurie's prized little sporty number, and were both now dependent for transport on my Audi, the car into which we'd loaded up the belongings we'd not sent on ahead, and driven north from London, after taking Ada over to Mum's. I'd cried at leaving her, all the way up the M1 as far as Nottingham where Laurie had stopped at the service station to buy coffee and muffins, stating, somewhat sensibly, 'You can't cry *and* eat, Jennifer. I don't intend on staying up at Mum's place any longer than we have to, so come on, we'll soon be back in London once we've sorted out our finances.'

He was, I knew, being ridiculously optimistic. Once the house in St Albans was sold, and the remaining mortgage and the court case costs and other outstanding bills paid off, we had a small amount of money left. Despite Mum saying she wasn't able to help us, she told me she couldn't have me going up to Yorkshire without having something to fall back on and, if Dad had still been alive, she knew he'd have done the same. She had, she said, deposited some money into my personal bank account and I gained some comfort from knowing there was some money – something to fall back on – if I got desperate. I was *not* to tell Jeremy, she warned, and, if I had any sense, I wouldn't be telling Laurie either. She was more than happy, she insisted, to take care of all Ada's schooling, board and lodging until the summer when we'd review the situation and take it from there.

'Well, that was a bloody waste of time,' Laurie said sourly, once I'd tucked George up in bed, read him a story and was back in the kitchen carefully washing the supper dishes in the ancient Belfast sink. I'd already fallen foul of this great monstrosity, smashing one of my favourite Emma Bridgewater mugs on its hard fireclay base.

'No go?' I asked.

'Nothing. That little jumped-up nobody who was interviewing me had the temerity to suggest that not only was my face too well known to be considered for any of the northern soaps but, after the court case, he wasn't convinced anyone would want to touch me.'

'Your notoriety goes before you then?'

'I prefer infamy to notoriety, if you don't mind.'

'*Infamy, infamy, they've all got it in for me.*' I laughed as I recalled and quoted that wonderful line from one of the *Carry On* films.

Laurie didn't.

'Well,' I said in an effort to cheer him up, 'we've actually been invited for supper to one of the neighbours.'

'Oh? Well, it can't be from anyone of importance: supper to the locals round here is still a mug of Ovaltine and a Hobnob.'

'You can be such an unpleasant *snob* at times, Laurie.'

'Thanks for that.' Laurie glared in my direction, ignoring the tea towel I threw at him in the hope he'd come and help me with the supper dishes. 'So, who's invited us round for *tea*: Worzel Gummidge? Old MacDonald? Hannah Hauxwell? The Yorkshire shepherdess?'

'Imaginary; wrong country; dead; and you wish,' I replied. 'Try again.'

'No idea. Not overly interested.'

'Look, you got us into this mess, Laurie. I'm trying my best here.'

'Go on then, surprise me.' Laurie assumed a look of utter boredom and I wanted to thump him. Had he always been like this? I was sure he hadn't. I recalled the really lovely times when Laurie had sat for hours with Ada, reading to her, making her laugh as he acted out various characters from her favourite TV programmes, dressing up on more than one occasion as Bugs Bunny, Donald Duck and even that square yellow sponge whose handle I could never recall. 'I want a different, much better relationship with my kids than my dad had with me,' Laurie had said somewhat gruffly before crying uncontrollably as he held Ada in his arms for the first time and I knew, then, that my own dad had been so wrong when, even though I was already pregnant with Ada, he'd sat me down and asked me to think twice about actually marrying Laurie.

'You don't have to marry him, darling,' Dad had pleaded over a Starbucks on Kensington High Street. 'Have the baby, absolutely, but just wait a while. Don't tie yourself to Laurie. I don't know, Jen...' he trailed off when I glared at him and stood to leave, furious with him for trying, yet again, to persuade me Laurie wasn't right for me.

'Stop trying to run my life for me, Dad,' I spat. 'You're actually being really manipulative now. I am not your little girl any longer and you need to realise that.'

'I know, Jenny, I know,' Dad said miserably. 'It's just I don't know which is the real Laurie Lewis and what is an act he's putting on...'

'He's an *actor* for God's sake.'

'Exactly,' Dad had said, pulling me back down so I was facing him once more. He sighed heavily. 'OK, OK, I'll stop fighting you on this. I will welcome Laurie wholeheartedly into the family and...' he grinned sheepishly '...I can't wait, although I'm far too young and handsome, to be an actual grandad.'

'Who then?' Laurie repeated, glancing up at me. 'Who's invited us?'

'The headteacher at Little Acorns – the school in the village?' I answered, bringing myself back, somewhat grudgingly, to our present situation.

'Oh? Is this a new village tradition then? The headteacher inviting the parents of new children to the school round for supper? When I was a kid there, it was plain old Westenbury C of E and the only invitation you got from the sadistic sod who was headmaster then was to accompany him to his study for a damned good thrashing.'

'In the early Eighties? Don't be so ridiculous, Laurie. It was against the law to hit kids when we were at school.'

'You try telling *him* that. So, go on then, why are we invited to eat with the head? Did he fancy you or something?'

'He is a *she*. I drove George down there this afternoon so he could meet his new teacher. Lovely woman called Grace Stevens is the teacher in Year 3. George spent an hour in the class with her while I had a long chat with Cassie Beresford, the head. He came out of that classroom not only covered in paint, but more animated after one art lesson with this new teacher than I've ever seen him in the three years he was at St Bede's. Anyway, it turns out Mrs Beresford is one of our neighbours. She and her partner live about five miles down the lane, somewhere near Norman's Meadow? If that means anything to you? And, get this, they have a farm too.'

'Jennifer, there are *loads* of farms round here. All mainly on their last legs, especially now we're out of Europe and they won't be having the subsidies they've been used to.'

'So, what sort of farm do you think it is?'

'What sort? What do you mean what *sort*? Sheep? A few cows? Hens? Turkeys?'

'Have another go. Ask the audience.'

'Jennifer, I really can't be arsed playing Who Wants to be a Farmer?'

'Phone a friend then? *I'll* be your friend.' Laurie gave me such a withering look, I gave up. 'OK, OK – llamas,' I said, in some triumph.

'*Llamas?*' Laurie frowned, obviously totally bored with the whole conversation. 'I thought llamas lived in South

America, not West Yorkshire? So, why's this woman invited *us*?'

To be honest, I'd almost asked the same question. Was this new headteacher running true to form and inviting us for supper simply because of who Laurie was?

'She obviously wants to be first in the queue to have my feet under her table,' Laurie went on, giving a little smirk as he answered his own question. 'Well, we might as well make the effort. When is it?'

'She'd absolutely no idea who *you* were. Actually, knew more about me and *my* writing than you in *A Better Life*. Apparently, she's always been into poetry, especially eighteenth-century poetry, but also loved Aunt Agnes's Bletchley memoirs, which she said she'd actually done an assembly on. You know, strong, independent women? How about that, then?' I'd been absolutely over the moon when this new head had told me this little snippet. 'Anyway, once we'd sat and filled in contact details, she appeared more interested in welcoming *me* into the neighbourhood. So, stick that in your pipe, Laurie, you arrogant sod.'

Laurie stretched himself out on the battered old sofa Rita had left behind. The same sofa on which I'd seen Terry Lewis ensconced as he devoured his pork pie on my first visit to the farm. Rita had advised us to throw it out – she certainly wasn't planning on taking it with her – and, while Laurie had agreed, he'd not made any effort as such to get rid of it. 'What on earth are you doing reading *this* stuff?' Laurie pulled out the Mills and Boon I'd been reading, from behind one of the cushions where I'd left it before making supper.

'I think it's your mum's.'

'Mum would never read this. Despite her marrying Dad

– the most unintelligent thing I reckon she ever did – Mum was pretty bright.'

'Did she ever act?'

'Act? Mum?' Laurie shook his head. 'Acted up a bit when Dad drove her to distraction, that's about it. I don't think she had an acting bone in her body. Why?'

'Oh, I just wondered. You know, with your dad calling the dogs Polonius and Hamlet.'

'*She* called them that, not Dad. She once studied *Hamlet*.'

'Did she? Where?'

'At the university in town. Well, it was still the poly then, I think. She felt she'd wasted her education so, when the girls were little, before I was born, she did A-Levels at night school and then enrolled for a part-time BA in Humanities. It was one of those modular courses, apparently, that take forever to build up to a full degree.'

'And did she eventually get her degree?'

'No.' Laurie shook his head. 'Unfortunately, Dad got her pregnant again.' Laurie laughed. 'Well, obviously *not* unfortunately for me. I've always thought he got her pregnant so as to keep her at home on the farm and not carry on with her education. He was always jealous that she was so bright. You should see the stuff she used to read.'

'I have done. There's a whole pile of books up in the loft just like that one.' I indicated the Regency romance Laurie had tossed to one side.

'Well, it won't be anything to do with Mum; she wouldn't read this stuff. They must have belonged to Cheryl or Lorraine. I'm not convinced Janice *can* even read...'

'Where *do* you get such unpleasantness from?' I asked in some exasperation. 'Not from your mum, certainly.'

Laurie had switched off from what I was saying, fiddling around with the massive smart TV he'd insisted we bring with us. Unfortunately, the Wi-Fi was temperamental, prone to go off without notice, a bit like the Aga. Previously on the long cream wall of our huge open plan kitchen in St Albans, it looked ridiculous in this kitchen, sticking out like some sort of flat-screened space oddity amongst what was, in effect a 1980s – or even 1970s – time warp. Whilst I wished Terry and Rita had kept the farmhouse's original traditional open fire instead of blocking it up and replacing it with the now antediluvian purple gas fire, I actually wasn't averse to cosying up with a book in one of the two battered, but incredibly comfortable, armchairs pulled up in front of it that Rita had abandoned. I left Laurie swearing at the TV, the Wi-Fi and his life in general and went upstairs to our bedroom, where there was a better signal, in order to ring Ada.

Ada appeared animated and while I was pleased – utterly relieved that my daughter had apparently been able to switch so easily from her old life with us to this new life living between Lydia's house during the week and back with Mum in Berkshire for the long weekend – I also felt a mounting anger. Sitting there under our duvet, trying to keep warm in the chilly bedroom, I felt such helpless rage at Laurie – as well as at myself for staying with him – I could hardly breathe. Ada didn't appear to notice, so vitally excited was she with her new surroundings and what she'd been up to.

Ada spoke at length about the fabulous meals she was having at Lydia's house, the lovely bedrooms she'd be given both there and at Mum's place and how she'd auditioned for, and been given, the leading role in the school's summer production. Not only that, she went on, there was a local amateur dramatic society in Sonning that she was thinking of joining.

'Don't forget your studies.' I said, worried and, yes, a little hurt that she didn't appear to be missing me, happily getting on with life without us.

'Oh, Mum, I'm way ahead,' she boasted. 'I could take the exams *now* if they'd let me, and then I could concentrate on my acting.'

'I never thought…'

'That I wanted to follow in Dad's footsteps?' she interrupted. 'No, neither did I until this week. I can do it all, fit it all in. Which I couldn't if I'd come up there with you and Dad.'

'Right.' Where had I heard all this before? I felt an icy shiver run through me. Ada was so Laurie's daughter.

'And, listen to this…' Ada paused dramatically. 'Did *you* know?'

'Know what?'

'About Granny.'

'What about Granny?'

'She's got a boyfriend. Well, a *man* friend obviously.'

'Granny has?' I was shocked: Mum had never said a word to me. 'What sort of a boyfriend?'

'What *sort* of a boyfriend?' Ada tutted and I immediately heard the same impatient tone in her voice echoed in Laurie's when I'd asked him what sort of *farm* the headteacher at Little Acorns was living on. 'You know, a *boyfriend* sort of boyfriend.'

'Not just a friend then? Her neighbour, maybe?'

'I don't think Granny would have been snogging *her*

neighbour.' Ada giggled at this. 'Have you seen Mr Thomas, next door. He's ninety if he's a day.'

'And Granny was snogging him?'

'Who? The old man next door?' Ada laughed again, obviously thoroughly enjoying my apparent discomfort.

'This boyfriend,' I said, trying to keep calm.

'Snogging him? And *the rest*. She's well into him. He's lovely, actually, Mum. I think he's about five years younger than Granny. She's got a whole load of new clothes and is so *happy*. She's seriously thinking of turning that third bedroom of hers into a *proper* dressing room. You know, with shelves and places for her bags and shoes and everything? Part of me worries I might be in her way.' Ada didn't appear a bit worried. 'You know, now she's got a boyfriend. But I've told her just act as if I wasn't here.' Ada laughed at that. 'Bad enough *me* being here as a chaperone, but I bet she's *so* glad you decided not to bring yourself and George here as well. That would have been *really* getting in her way. To be honest, Mum, I think Granny quite likes having *me* here. I let her borrow some of my foundation and showed her how to do her eyes – that blue eyeshadow she's worn for years is a bit ageing you know. And now that she's got a *toy boy*, well…' Ada laughed again, before continuing non-stop, emphasising at least one word in every sentence, never once asking how we were doing up here in Yorkshire. That was sixteen-year-olds for you.

While I was so relieved Ada was happy and thriving, I was, I realised, feeling horribly left out. Like the kid who comes into school on a Monday morning to hear the rest of the class reliving the fabulous party they've all been to over the weekend when they themselves haven't been invited.

I wanted to be there with my mother and my daughter, discussing Mum's choice of clothes and makeup, eyeing up her new man and deciding if he was suitable. Again, while it appeared my mother was at last beginning to forge a new life for herself after taking Dad's sudden and unexpected death so badly – which I was so pleased about for her sake – I knew a huge part of me was hurting, somewhere deep inside, that he was being replaced.

'Mum's got a boyfriend, according to Ada.'

'Cynthia has?' Laurie looked up from fiddling with the TV as I went back downstairs. 'Has she?' Laurie gave what can only be described as a dirty laugh. 'Blimey, I always reckoned your mother was far too uptight to ever get her rocks off again.'

'Her rocks off? For God's sake, Laurie. That's my mother you're talking about.'

'Well, good for her. It'll do her good to have something else to think about rather than meddling in *our* lives.' Laurie was still holding a grudge that Mum hadn't seen fit to help bail us out of our debts as well as refusing to have *him* live with her when she'd offered a home to me, Ada and George. 'Mind you,' Laurie frowned, suddenly serious. 'You need to watch that. If Cynthia remarries, she could leave the house and that money of your dad's to a new husband. And *he* could then leave it to *his* kids. And *we'd* end up with nothing...'

I don't think I'd ever disliked Laurie more than at that moment.

'I'm going to bed,' I said, unable to even look at him,

reaching, instead, for my Regency romance. 'I'm seriously, *seriously* fed up with everything... but with you, with *you*, especially, you... you fuckwit.'

'What have I done now?' Laurie appeared genuinely puzzled. 'And will you stop calling me names? Even though that last one appears to be a new one in your repertoire...'

I slammed the kitchen door behind me and retreated up the revolting, thread-bare, patterned stair carpet to mine and Laurie's new bedroom.

16

And so, a cold sleety March morphed into an even colder rainy April, and my homesickness – and despair at the state of both my marriage and where I'd ended up – showed little sign of abating. George was happy, which was the one positive thing keeping me where I was when all I wanted to do was flee back south to Mum and Ada.

George was totally thriving up here. He'd always been a pale, anxious little boy, very bright and eager to please, but with a stammer and a slight tendency towards asthma, especially when forced out onto the rugby field at the all-boys private school, St Bede's, Laurie had insisted George attend. This was probably the only thing he and my dad had been in agreement over but, latterly, both Mum and I had seen George's reluctance to go to school every day and, even if the whole embarrassing court case, with its financial as well as its emotional impact on a seven-year-old in a school full of macho-encouraged rugger buggers, hadn't put us where we were today, I'd have been taking him out of that school.

'I love my teacher,' George stated every morning over his porridge and syrup ('it's treacle, Mum, we call it *treacle* up here') before impatiently waiting at the kitchen door until I found my car keys and drove him the five miles or so down into the village and Little Acorns. 'Mrs Stevens is really funny, Mum, and tells us funny stories, and we have art just about *every day*.' George would wax lyrical about this goddess who ruled his classroom – as well as seemingly his every waking moment – and I could only breathe a deep sigh of relief and thank God I'd got at least one thing right as George scampered off into the playground, unhampered by any blazer, tie or rugby kit, book bag whirling round his head, without a backward glance in my direction.

To be fair there were – several weeks into our exodus to the Frozen North, as Gudrun liked to call it – a number of things that were keeping me going in an otherwise bleak and worrying time in my life. I found that I really liked chickens. Rita had handed over the chicken reins totally to Janice. And now that she was free from the shackles of both Terry and the farm, she had embarked, at the age of seventy-two, not only on a degree course in Anthropology at Leeds University, but also what appeared to be a geographical catch-up of all the places she'd always wanted to visit but never felt able to. Janice had then passed on the care and well-being of the chucks to me, sniffing, in the way that she always did, that it would at least give me something to do with myself.

Unable – or perhaps unwilling – to take any reminder of her previous life at Daisy Royd Farm to the smart little bungalow with its tiny neat garden and total absence of mud, Rita had taken to her new life with gusto and, on the couple of occasions I'd called in to see her, wanting to know more about the books in the loft as well as the Hamlet production photograph, she'd not been at home. I hadn't shown the Hamlet photo with the man who I'd assumed to be Laurie actually *to* Laurie. I wasn't stupid: there were implications in that image – a big possibility that my coming across it, hidden in a Regency romance Rita must have assumed no one but herself would ever open, had the potential to open a total can of worms. I wanted to hand it over to Rita herself and let her do with it what she would.

Laurie and I now appeared to be in a state of cold war, particularly with regards our respective work. I needed office space: space for my laptop and all that went with working as a commissioning editor from home. The upset of the past four months meant I was horribly behind with my current authors as well as the reading through of a whole load of new manuscripts I'd been sent, and I needed to buckle down and get on with it. I'd set up my laptop in the box room bedroom but, on this Monday morning in April, it appeared Laurie had got in there first and was arguing the toss via a FaceTime meeting on *his* laptop with Gillian, his agent. He was stalking the room – as much as one can stalk a six-foot square box room – reminding me of images of those poor, anxious polar bears in London Zoo, back in the day. I had far more empathy with the poor old polar bear than Laurie and, unplugging *my* laptop and gathering all that went with it, exited with a well-aimed glare at the interloper before going downstairs and setting up a workspace at the kitchen table and then going to feed the hens. By the time I was back in the kitchen, Laurie too had descended and was watching a catch-up of *The Street*, volume set to high, on the TV monster dominating the kitchen.

'Do you mind?' I shouted over the TV noise, 'I'm trying to work here.'

'As am I.'

'Work?'

'Yes, I need to clinch a Lancashire rather than Yorkshire accent. There's possibly something for me on The Street.'

'And there's a difference, is there?'

'Of course, big difference. As there is between a true Lancashire and a Mancunian accent... not sure which one they're actually after.' Laurie frowned, talking to himself.

'Well, do you think you could possibly clinch it elsewhere and let me do some work that will actually pay the bills?'

'Can't you go upstairs?'

'Right.' I slammed the lid down on my laptop and did just that but, instead of reading and editing other novelists' manuscripts, sat back in my desk chair, reading the last few chapters of the last of the Regency romances I'd hoovered up ever since finding the pile in the loft. And then, once I'd finished, found myself opening a brand-new word document and going for it. I didn't write any notes, didn't plan anything, just hit the keyboard and wrote like a woman possessed for the next five hours... and then it was time to leave to pick George up from school.

Magnolia raised a hand to her chest, acknowledging the racing of her heart through the loosely-draped silk and lace of her robe as Lord Silverton, leather riding crop firmly to hand, appeared below her window and, without warning, came to an abrupt halt, looking directly up at her. She endeavoured to hide herself behind the gold brocade curtains in her chamber but it was too late; he'd already changed direction, a smile on his dark handsome face, and was heading towards the heavy wooden outer door to the house, his one intention only too clear...

'What in God's name are you reading?' Laurie had appeared at my side and so engrossed was I in Magnolia's heaving bosom, I didn't realise he was actually standing behind me, taking it all in as I read what I'd just written. 'Since when did Wesley and Brown publish this sort of rubbish?'

'Right,' I said, saving and closing the file without answering. 'I'm going to pick up George. Unless *you'd* like to go for a change?'

'Me?'

'You. You have to know, Laurie,' I said, emboldened by the taking on of my alter ego, Magnolia – who was, I'd realised, one hell of a feisty broad. 'George is the only reason I've followed you up here.'

'Are you trying to tell me you don't love me anymore, Jennifer?' Laurie sounded stricken and, for one moment, my resolve to keep him at arm's length as punishment for his messing around with other women wavered. We both had to work at our broken marriage if it were to mend, get back on an even keel and return it to the heady, glorious years at the start of our relationship. I turned to find Laurie grinning down at me. 'The only reason?' he asked, almost smirking. 'Surely not. Isn't *this* another reason? The *main* reason?' Laurie bent his head to my neck, licking the hollow beneath my collar bone, a movement that, even after all these years of marriage, still had the ability to send signals to where it mattered most. I looked up and saw that Laurie was watching not only my reaction, but also himself in the dressing table mirror opposite.

'Sorry, buster, you're way out of time.' The moment had passed and I stood, gave this man I used to adore a disparaging look through the mirror, and headed for the door. 'Keys to the Audi are on the kitchen table. *You* go and collect your son, and pick up some milk and bread and something for supper while you're at it. I'm going to walk down and see your mum and you can pick me up from there on the way back from the supermarket.' I went downstairs, grabbed my coat and left the house before Laurie had time to argue.

The journey down to Rita's place, a neat little bungalow on a small, well-kept estate of just five others, was a good three-quarters of an hour walk away from the farm, but I relished the fresh air and the pull in my muscles as I strode out after almost a full day at the keyboard. I knew I was going to have to catch up with my real work once George was in bed, but what I'd achieved today with Magnolia was putting a spring in my step.

Spring: there were definite signs she was just round the corner and I stood, just to admire, what must have been my first sight of the season's snowdrops, albeit now on their way out. I bent, taking in the miraculous, optimistic beauty of the pendulous white flower braving the elements from its shelter behind the dry-stone wall. Instead of sticking to the main road, I climbed stiles and crossed fields, keeping a wary eye for anything alive that might suddenly appear in my periphery. I was too much of a city girl to feel unconcerned about a possible random bull in my path, and wasn't overly happy with the trip of goats scrutinising me with what I could only think of as a satanic stare.

I made my way across acres of meadows and fields, as well as agricultural land sporting the beginnings of green shoots of something or other, while the overriding tang of muck-spreading played havoc with my olfactory senses.

I smiled at myself sporting such unnecessarily literary thoughts: after a day conjuring up early nineteenth-century jargon, I didn't appear to be able to simply say there was a constant stink of cow shit up my nose.

I came to a sudden standstill and actually said 'Oh!' out loud. What the hell were these creatures? A mixture of white, brown and piebald, there must have been twenty-five of them, all intent on gazing curiously in my direction. With a good-sized, sturdy wall between myself and them, I was brave enough to eyeball them back. They were huge things – a couple, I reckoned, taller than Laurie and he was six-foot-one (or so he liked to profess; I'd have said nearer six foot myself, but there you go). Llamas! Of course. Or were they alpacas? I'd no idea, but they held my attention for a good five minutes and I wished I had George with me. I took a photo on my phone and immediately sent it to Mum and Ada and carried on. To my right, acres of green dotted with what appeared to be several upmarket horses stretched into the distance, and I stopped to watch a few of them, either spooked by something, or running for the sheer joy of just being out in the promise of spring air. They belted at speed across the fields, necks stretched forwards, manes streaming – I was beginning to think I was in the middle of a Lloyds Bank advert – beautiful, magical creatures, coming to an abrupt standstill at the approach of two men who proceeded to put a halter on one of them, leading it towards a whole village of stabling ahead of him.

Beyond these meadows there appeared to be a long continuous line of green, and for a while I couldn't quite work out what it was. A cricket pitch? A jolly long one if that were the case. I knew Westenbury had a pitch down by

Little Acorns School and the village duck pond, but this one was the length of a runway at Luton Airport. And then, as I continued to stand and watch from my vantage point on the hill a mile or so away from the strip, the green became a hive of activity as a string of horses, presumably from the stables in front of me, were put at a gallop down the green. And then another string and then another. It was a glorious sight and I must have stood entranced for a good ten minutes, until I turned in the opposite direction and started walking once more.

By the time I was approaching Rita's place on the outskirts of Westenbury village, I was glowing with the exertion. This was what I must do to keep sane, I reckoned: walk and more walking. I might even take up running. Never having owned either a decent pair of walking boots or anywhere near a proper pair of running trainers, this was, perhaps, a wildly misplaced resolution brought about by the rush of fresh air to my brain and other vital organs.

Desperate for a mug of tea, I was glad to see Rita's car – now a sporty little yellow Mini – almost camouflaged in her drive of burgeoning yellow: forsythia, broom and enough daffs to make Wordsworth swoon. I made to dispose of my wellies (Rita's old ones, left in the porch at Daisy Royd) on the doorstep, knocked and went straight in just in my stockinged feet.

'Oh,' she laughed, 'I'm glad you've taken off your boots. After fifty years of traipsing in mud, I relish not having it on my floors and tiles anymore. Come on in, come on in. Lovely to see you. Have you walked? Is our Laurence with you? No? George?' Rita peered round the door, obviously disappointed I didn't have either or both of my two males with me. She urged me to sit, bustled off to the kitchen to fill the kettle and shouted back, over the sound of the water hitting metal, 'How's it going? You OK, love?'

'Oh, you know.' The rush of adrenalin from the walk in the fresh air was quickly dissipating and I didn't appear to be able to say anything more positive. 'It's fine,' I added, as Rita bent backwards to see me as well as hear me from the tiny but immaculate galley kitchen.

'I know, love, I know.' She threw me a sympathetic glance before heading for the fridge. 'It won't be forever, you know. Once our Laurence gets another job, and once you're back on your feet again, you'll be able to head back home. Back to London. Are you feeling a bit homesick? Missing Ada?'

I nodded, unable to speak, because her vocalising how I felt brought home to me just how miserable I was. Rita was so lovely, so kind and, looking up at her now, I once again marvelled at what a strikingly beautiful woman Laurie's mother was. She seemed to have blossomed further since leaving the farm without its constraints of husband, adult children and the hard work that went with the everyday chores of keeping house in a time warp. Now in her early seventies, Rita was tall and slim, her amazing navy eyes clear and intelligent. 'Here.' She pressed a mug of strong tea into my hands and placed the ubiquitous red-covered marshmallow teacakes onto the nest of tables in front of me. The sight of them made me smile. 'I don't know why I continue to buy these horrible things,' she laughed. 'Habit, I suppose.'

'I didn't realise there were stables and gallops on the outskirts of the village,' I said. 'I've just walked down and could see them in the distance,'

'Oh yes, the area round here has several. Clementine,

who runs *Clementine's* restaurant near the centre of the village, is married to Rafe Ahern who runs a small stable. But the big one, Mayhew's, is probably the one you spotted on the way down. Can't miss it really,' Rita laughed.

'Right. So, Rita, I've brought you something,' I said, suddenly nervous.

'Oh?'

I reached for my backpack. 'You left a pile of books behind.'

'Did I?' She frowned, indicating with a pink-painted fingernail the far wall of the sitting room, which was one unbroken bank of books. 'I thought I'd brought them all with me. I wouldn't leave books behind, even though I know probably both you and Laurie would have appreciated some of them?' She tutted. 'I'm sorry, I didn't think…'

'No, honestly it's fine. I found a pile of these up in the loft.' I brought out the book which had contained the newspaper cutting. It was still in there, waiting to be reunited with its rightful owner.

Rita frowned. 'Goodness. Are they mine?' She peered through the reading glasses she'd placed on her nose in order to investigate further. 'I don't think so, Jennifer. I don't… Oh, of course, I do remember now. As part of my A-Level English course, I took at night school, we were asked to evaluate a Mills and Boon Regency romance. I think it was an exercise in comparison with Jane Austen's *Emma*. Or some such thing.' She frowned and then laughed. 'I bought one as instructed and then became totally addicted.' She laughed again. 'As far as I remember, I ended up reading a whole load of them. Bit of a shameful secret really. That's probably why I hid them up in the loft. I remember Terry being totally sarcastic and saying something along the lines of, if I was able to get an A-Level in literature just by reading this slushy stuff, then he was going to get out his old Beano and Dandy annuals and sit the exam as well.' She made a grimace of derision as she remembered, and then smiled. 'And they were up in the loft?'

'Hmm, right at the back. You must have missed them when you moved everything out, in readiness for the sale of Daisy Royd.'

'Yes, possibly. More tea, love?'

I shook my head. 'There was a newspaper clipping in one.'

'Oh?' Rita smiled as I reached for it. 'What is it?'

'Laurie said you studied *Hamlet* when you were doing your degree in town?'

'Yes.' Rita's whole demeanour suddenly shifted. 'What about it?' she asked warily.

'It's just a photo of some production of *Hamlet*. I thought maybe...'

'What?'

'I thought maybe you'd had a part?'

'No,' she shook her head brusquely. 'Never once been on any stage. I've absolutely *no* idea where Laurie gets his acting ability from. From what I recall, Terry had an aunt who used to tread the boards.' Rita held my gaze, defying me to question her further. 'As far as I know she was part of ENSA – you know, entertaining the troops... Vera Lynn and all that...? You'll have to ask Terry about that. Oh no, but of course, you can't, can you?'

'Well,' I said, embarrassed at Rita's reaction, 'there you go, then. Oh,' I went on, with some relief as I heard a car pull up outside, 'here's Laurie and George now.' I made to pick up the book with its newspaper clipping but Rita got there before me. She took it, placed it behind a cushion on her sofa and, not meeting my eye, said, 'Well, I think I'll have another read of this then, Jennifer.' She turned as George ran through the door. 'Hello, lovie. Just in time for a chocolate marshmallow?'

17

'You look lovely, Mum. You've not had any lipstick on for ages. You look really pretty.'

'Thank you, sweetie.' George was right: in the six weeks we'd been up here in Yorkshire, I hadn't made much of an effort with myself. The chilly custard-yellow tiled bathroom at Daisy Royd Farm boasted one disintegrating cream medicine cabinet which had still housed tubes of Terry's now defunct haemorrhoid cream and a rusting Gillette razor and, while I'd emptied the cabinet of said treasure, I really hadn't fancied replacing it with my own stuff. Instead, I'd either tipped bottles and jars into the top drawer of the chest in our bedroom, or simply kept my makeup in its bag where I'd shoved it on leaving London. I also knew that, once those ridiculously expensive jars of mine were empty, I wouldn't be spending what little money we had on luxuries such as these. Apart from going through a shed-load of moisturiser to combat my dry skin – which had worsened tenfold in the raw east winds sweeping down and across from the Pennines – in the time we'd been here in Westenbury I hadn't been in any mood for general titivation. I really hadn't seen much point, since the only people we saw were Rita, as well as Janice and Cheryl and their families. Lorraine had moved over to Pontefract to be with her new online love, and we'd seen neither hide nor hair of her since moving up here.

With the supper invitation to the headteacher of Little Acorns, Cassie Beresford's, place eventually confirmed for the following Saturday evening, I'd pulled out my favourite brown suede trousers and a new top Mum had bought me for Christmas, and set to in order to make myself halfway presentable. My hair was still holding its style from its last cut in London, but it needed a trim and a few lowlights and pointing in the direction of a decent – but not too expensive – hairdresser. When I'd asked Janice who she usually went to, she'd laughed out loud and said she often cut her own and, if I wanted, she'd have a go at mine too. I declined her offer. Luckily Cheryl, who'd been round at the time and overheard this conversation, had suggested a friend of hers who was good, mobile and, as she didn't have the expensive overheads of a salon, relatively cheap.

I'd spent the previous afternoon with my head stuck under the kitchen tap while Chelsea – *My Hair Lady* – dug long purple nails into my scalp, removing foils and washing my trimmed hair in George's Kids' Sweet Strawberry Shampoo (I'd been too immersed in my laptop to break off to go shopping) with all the enthusiasm and vigour of a beaver on speed.

Ninety minutes after arriving, Chelsea was reversing back down the yard the way she'd come, and I was left spinning, but admiring one of the best – albeit Strawberry Mivvi smelling – hairdos I'd never achieved in the top salons in London.

The reason I'd not been out to buy my usual shampoo in

preparation for Chelsea's administrations was because I'd become a bit obsessed with Magnolia De Courcy and her antics with Lord Silverton, totally excited at getting Maggy – as I now fondly called her – and her story off the ground. Or, in truth, off the bed, where I'd left her, the previous day, about to be ravished by the stable lad – resembling a rather more muscular – but just as heavenly Zac Efron, whose thighs of steel... hang on, no, steel hadn't yet been invented had it...?

'And I like those trousers,' George brought me back into the twenty-first century, stroking the nap of the suede in different directions so that it resembled a newly-mown lawn. He suddenly looked up. 'Can I have a dog to stroke and brush?'

'Oh, George...'

'You can't really stroke Polony – his coat is full of bits of leaves and twigs and other things. And anyway, he only likes Auntie Janice. He'd rather be outside in his kennel than being on the sofa with me, I can tell.'

'I'll think about it.'

'You always say that. You said the reason we couldn't have a dog in St Albans was because Ada's allergic and we were too near roads and he might end up squished and I'd be devastated. But Ada's not here, and there aren't any *roads* round here. He won't get squished and so therefore I won't be devastated. QED – *Quod erat demonstrandum*.'

'Sorry?' I looked up as George continued to stroke at my suede trousers, the nearest thing, presumably, he could get to a Dachshund which, for some reason, appeared to be his mutt of choice.

'QED: it means *that has been proved*. Mrs Stevens told us

that yesterday. She knows everything. It's Latin, you know. Did I tell you Mrs Stevens…?'

'Yes, George, I believe you did.' To be honest, I was a bit fed up listening to what this paragon of virtue and creativity could do with a pot of poster paint and a cornflakes packet.

'*And,*' George wasn't letting it go. 'Mrs Stevens likes dogs. She *loves* dogs. And, *you* had a dog when you were my age. *And* you lived in London. So, can I have one?'

'Berkshire, actually.' I'd been more than happy for us to have a dog in St Albans, but Ada was so terribly allergic to dogs. We'd had a bit of a scare a couple of years ago when Ada, always slightly asthmatic like George, had been licked by a dog tied up outside the corner shop. Her face had rapidly turned scarlet, ballooning up to twice its size, and we'd ended up in A and E, where they'd administered adrenalin. She was supposed to carry an epi-pen with her at all times and I suddenly panicked that Ada's might no longer be in date. I needed to ring Mum and check. Laurie had always been dead against having a dog, saying he'd had enough of dogs when he was growing up and, if we must have *something*, why didn't we have a snake? He *liked* snakes; you knew where you were with a snake.

'George, are you ready to go and stay at Auntie Cheryl's? Clean pyjamas are in the airing cupboard.' Rita had offered to babysit on this, our first foray into Westenbury society, but Cheryl had said why not let George stay the night with her and Dean? It might toughen George up a bit by letting him play with his cousins, ten-year-old Imogen and eight-year-old Harrison. Whilst I wasn't convinced George needed any *toughening up*, of the three Lewis sisters, Cheryl, the youngest, was the one I liked most. Janice terrified me and Lorraine, having absconded to Pontefract, wasn't really in the picture, but Cheryl was great. Unlike her other siblings – Laurie included – Cheryl hadn't married until she was well into her thirties. Like Rita, she'd realised she'd missed out on her initial education – '*I was always messing around or into boys when I was at school*' – and had gone back to studying in her late twenties, ending up with an English degree and teaching the subject at Westenbury Comp. Much to the chagrin of her fifteen-year-old, Holly, who had to put up with the ignominy of seeing her mother in school every day and was, according to Cheryl, 'so bloody woke, she's never asleep'.

Half an hour before we were due to leave, Laurie rolled up looking slightly the worse for wear.

'Where the hell have you *been*?' I hissed, pointing towards the kitchen clock.

'Why? What's up? Are we going somewhere?'

'Well, *I* am. You can make up your own mind whether you're coming or not.' I was furious. The one time I was about to have some sort of social life and Laurie had totally forgotten. 'Have you been drinking?' Laurie's navy eyes were slightly out of focus and, as they say in all good police reports, *he was smelling of intoxicants*.

'Just had a couple.' Laurie was mulish.

'Where?'

'Down at the Jolly Sailor.'

'And you've driven back? Laurie, that's all we need, for the police to have stopped you and for you to lose your licence.'

Laurie went to lie down on the kitchen sofa, stretching

out fully on its battered length, closing his eyes against my interrogation. Was he turning into Terry?

'I was actually having a drink with a couple of police officers I was at school with. Nobody gives a toss about drinking and driving on these country lanes.' He laughed. 'Most of the farmers round here have probably been sniffing at the Red Diesel. You know, before putting it into their tractors in order to hold up the rest of the village with their insistence on driving at two miles an hour while aiming and splattering the cars behind with cow shit.'

'I didn't think you still knew any blokes from school?'

'Who said they were *blokes*?' Laurie opened one eye and raised an eyebrow. Not, particularly when you've had a couple of whiskies, an easy feat. Laurie, I could tell, was that way out, looking for a fight.

Well, I could be that way out, too. 'So, I suppose you were looking for Jess, the landlord's daughter?'

'Jennifer, Jennifer,' Laurie drawled. 'Whatever do you mean?'

'You know exactly what I mean.'

'For your information, and *I* didn't know this, Jess has been living in Australia for the last eight years or so. Divorced from that gorilla Karl Danvers and now living in marital bliss with some kangaroo in Tibooburraburra. Or some such place.'

'But I bet you went down there hoping to see her?'

'Give over, Jennifer, I've had enough.' Laurie opened his eyes and glared, obviously put out that Jess Barrowclough wasn't still hanging around for him as he'd anticipated. I could read him like a book. 'Right, mustn't keep my fans waiting. Give me five minutes if we really must go out to eat with some country bumpkins who want to meet me. I'm telling you now, Jennifer, it'll be one glass of warm Blue Nun, prawn cocktail in salad cream and ketchup and, *for afters*, a big wedge of frozen Black Forest gateau. Trust me.'

Trust him? I would rather, I was beginning to realise, trust Benito Mussolini.

Cassie Beresford and her partner, Xavier Balmforth, lived out beyond Norman's Meadow in a fabulous, newly-converted Yorkshire-stone barn with a view across the valley that was quite mind-blowing. I'd taken charge of the Audi and after dropping George off at Cheryl's place, followed Laurie's route as to where he thought the headteacher must live. We'd ended up down various dead-ends, as well as revisiting several Wesleyan chapels and pubs – the irony of which was lost on Laurie – as we went round in circles under his increasingly bad-tempered directions.

By the time we found the place, we were over half an hour late and, going by the number of cars pulled up in front of the barn, the last to arrive.

'This is such bad manners,' I tutted in Laurie's direction as we made our way up a newly-laid gravel path.

'We're in bloody Yorkshire, not London,' Laurie snapped back, pulling his scarf pointedly round his neck and pulling up his shoulders against the bitter wind that had continued to blow ever since we'd moved up here. 'They don't recognise manners, bad or otherwise, in this part of the world. Mind you, this is a fabulous place. Just look at it. What does this headteacher's husband do?'

'I've no idea, Laurie. Oh yes I do, I told you, he's a llama farmer.'

'Bloody hell, there's obviously money in llamas. Do they eat them?'

'Again, Laurie, I've no idea. You've got the farming genes; you tell me.'

Laurie was about to retort, no doubt something rude, when the front door – part of the now-glazed original barn door – opened and Cassie Beresford stood aside to usher us in and welcome us through.

'I'm so sorry we're late,' I apologised. 'Terribly bad-mannered of us – we got totally lost.'

'Oh, honestly, not a problem. No one can ever find us out here. Do come in.' Cassie led us through a rather magnificent dining hall, the table alive with cut glass and starched napkins, and into a sitting room where four other couples were already standing chatting and knocking back gin. 'We're trying out a whole load of different gins that my friend Fiona won in some raffle.' Cassie laughed almost apologetically. 'Would you like to join us or would you prefer something else? Let me introduce you to everyone, I'm so excited we have a real-life author with us.'

'Hi,' Laurie said softly, reaching out a hand in her direction, 'I'm Laurie Lewis.' He gave her the benefit of his lopsided smile.

'Hi, Laurie. Lovely to meet you. Sorry, I bet you get fed up of people rabbiting on about Jennifer's books all the time?' Cassie didn't appear a bit sorry. 'This is Jennifer Baylis-Lewis everyone, and her husband, Louis.' She frowned and then giggled, 'Oh gosh, that can't be right – Louis Lewis?

Hell, those gins of Fiona's must be stronger than I thought: I think we need to eat. I do apologise, erm…?'

'Laurie,' Laurie amended icily. 'Laurie Lewis?' He gave Cassie a withering look to which, as she now had her back to him and was intent on pushing me forward, she was totally oblivious.

'Right, OK,' Cassie took a deep breath as if to steady herself, 'my other half, Xavier; one of my best mates, Clare and her husband, Rageh.'

Hands were shaken, gin was poured and placed in our hands and then Cassie continued the introductions. 'I wanted you to meet Fiona – my other best mate – and Matthew, Jennifer, because they run a large farm not far from where you're staying at the moment. I'm dying to know why you've up-sticked – up-sticksed? Is that grammatically correct? – from London in order to hide out up here in Yorkshire. Is it for some special research, or simply for peace and quiet while you write your next book? The equivalent of the artist in the garret?'

Before I could get out a word in explanation, Fiona moved in, staring at Laurie and frowning. 'I'm sure I know your face? Have we met before?'

'Hello, Laurence.' Matthew Richardson gently elbowed his wife to one side. 'How're you doing? It's been a long time.'

I glanced across at Laurie, who seemed unsure as to who Matthew actually was.

Matthew grinned. 'I used to go out with your Cheryl: she was the year below me at Westenbury Comp. You must have been about ten or eleven when I used to call round for her on my motorbike. Your mum wasn't too pleased when I gave you a ride around your fields.'

'I really don't remember much about it,' Laurie answered.

'Well, no, you usually had your head stuck in a book, or you were off with your mum having your photo taken. Bit of a child prodigy as I remember.'

'Oh, for heaven's sake. It's Ted Baxter, isn't it?' Fiona grinned, moving in to give Laurie a big kiss. 'Let me snog someone *famous*.'

This obviously went some way towards placating Laurie, until Cassie tutted and informed Fiona that she'd got it wrong and Ted was actually Louis and it was Louis's wife, Jennifer Baylis-Lewis, who was the famous one.

Both Fiona and Matthew started laughing at Cassie, who was obviously more than half-cut. 'Cassandra,' Fiona said patiently as she held her own glass out for more gin. 'Laurie Lewis, here, is one of the most famous actors in the country. He's been playing his character, Ted Baxter for the last God-knows-how-many-years in *A Better Life*. Come on, you've heard of that, surely? You must have? He looks a bit different in real life, I grant you – maybe not quite as tall, a little less... you know...' Fiona broke off, frowning '... but just because you never watch TV, that's no excuse for not recognising him. He's the face of *Michaud Saint-Jean* as well... well, he used to be. He's Midhope's most famous son.'

When Cassie Beresford still didn't appear to know who Laurie was, Fiona said, in an aside, 'You know, Cassie, that big libel court case just before Christmas...?'

Xavier Balmforth appeared just in time, rescuing Laurie by taking his arm and leading him to where the man called

Rageh and another couple, who'd arrived five minutes after us and were now busy apologising and being introduced round, were standing.

'Right, Jennifer,' Cassie said, still apparently in the dark as to who Laurie was, 'I'm obviously totally out of the loop with all this somewhere. Do *not* have any of that gin of Fiona's. I tell you, it's lethal. She won three bottles of the stuff in a raffle down at the farmers' market at Christmas. It's probably moonshine, distilled from potato peelings or something. It's gone straight to my head and not only do I need you to see me as an upright village headmistress of some standing...' she swayed slightly '...but I also need to get some food down people or we'll *all* be under the table.'

I laughed at that. 'Can I help you?'

'Would you mind? Normally I'd ask Fi or Clare, but with Tod Mayhew just arrived, I'll *never* get them into the kitchen.'

'Tod Mayhew?'

'Hmm. Tod and Serena. They're always late to dos. I've never known a couple so busy.'

'Oh?'

'Tod owns and runs the stables half an hour from your place.'

'I've come across lots of fields with stables in when I've been out walking,' I said. 'And there are gallops down there. Are those his?'

Cassie nodded. 'Oh, these aren't just *any* stables... Hell, I sound like an M&S ad... these are top-notch, high-end *racing and stud* stables. Talking of M&S, where's that red cabbage?' Cassie paused to decant several packs of the burgundy-coloured vegetable into two serving dishes. 'I'm passing this off as my own, so don't grass me up. No,' she went on, 'you can't miss the Mayhew stables. Apparently, it's one of the best yards in the north of England; trains youngsters both for the flat and jumps season.'

'Youngsters?' I had a sudden vision of nursery-aged children being ordered across fields and over water jumps.

'Young *horses*,' Cassie giggled.

'I think I came across the place the other day. A couple of the horses were racing across the fields like they were in that Lloyds Bank ad.' I laughed as I remembered the beautiful creatures taking advantage of what was probably the first spring-like day as I walked down to Rita's bungalow. 'You seem to know a lot about it,' I smiled. 'Do you ride yourself?'

'Oh God, no. Xav and I've got into going along to the races though. Over at York mainly. We have a flutter with a fiver and bet on Tod's nags if he's racing them that day. Right, I think we're just about there. Shall we call everyone in?'

18

'We have actually met,' I said as Cassie brought the others through into the dining room and I was introduced to the horse man, Tod Mayhew.

The tall, blonde-haired man looked me up and down, frowning. 'We have? I'm sorry…?'

'A vomiting child? Amidst a mountain of escaped litter? About six weeks ago?'

'Ah, right, yes. Of course. How do you do?' Tod Mayhew held out his hand, shaking mine perfunctorily, before turning back to our host. 'Where do you want me, Cassie?'

I'd thought it would be lovely to be out and sociable again after the weeks following the court case, when I had been too embarrassed to be with other people if we were invited anywhere. And, in any case, the plethora of invitations – to openings, to suppers, to events – that had always racked up on the mantelpiece started to dwindle and eventually almost dried up completely.

When Ted Baxter finally met his untimely demise in that Gloucestershire slurry pit, going down and under with Ted's final cry of '*Will no one help me?*' accompanied by a desperately waving arm executed – in my humble opinion – somewhat over-dramatically by Laurie, we soon became, it appeared, social outcasts. Apart from the Sunday rags wanting to catch Laurie queuing down at the local job centre and the local radio station – Radio Verulam – asking him in for a chat as to his future plans, we were, it seemed, persona non grata. Particularly as, at the time, we had no idea what any future plans might be.

There'd been three or four months without a great deal of social intercourse apart from, latterly, my sisters-in-law and Rita – who, after confiscating that incriminating newspaper cutting, appeared to be avoiding being alone with me. The stress and strain that went along with not only finally accepting my dad had been right all along about Laurie, but being rendered homeless and separated from my daughter into the bargain, had resulted in my losing confidence as to how to actually interact with *any* people, but particularly new acquaintances who all knew each other and were totally at ease in each other's company. I sat ensconced at this lovely, friendly village headmistress's supper table surrounded by a load of equally warm and congenial – if gin-soaked – chattering strangers and felt terrified. I'd avoided the offer of gin – 'good move' Cassie had winked slightly haphazardly in my direction – in the sure knowledge it would be me driving us home but, without the prop of alcohol, I was beginning to fear I was putting a dampener on the whole evening: the spectre at the feast, no less.

Rescue came from the very attractive blonde, Clare, who was seated one to my right at the table and who – when Xavier Balmforth, Cassie's partner, jumped up to remove our starter (a totally delicious scallops and hazelnut picada, which blasted Laurie's anticipated prawn cocktail into oblivion) – immediately moved herself onto his vacated chair in order to chat.

'You OK?' she asked. 'Not easy when everyone else is half-cut and you're on tonic.' She held up her own glass. 'Without the gin.'

'You're driving?'

'I am. But, also pregnant.'

'Oh, how lovely. How many children do you have?'

'None. This'll be my first. My first at forty-three. I started late on setting out to meet the right one.' She smiled across at her husband, Rageh, who smiled back at Clare in a way Laurie had always used to smile at me – secure in my love for him, loving me back. I couldn't remember the last time we'd lost ourselves in each other like that, and had to shake myself slightly in an effort to shift what was surely an erroneous realisation and make myself concentrate, instead, on what Clare was asking me. 'Cassie tells me you have two children?'

'Hmm.' I found I was unable to speak, unable to admit I'd left Ada behind in order to follow Laurie up here.

'I know your son is with Cassie. Where's your other child?'

'Ada's still in the south,' I finally got out. 'She's staying with my mother until she's sat her GCSEs in the summer.'

'Very sensible of you.'

'Really? Do you think so? I've been totally beating myself up about abandoning her. You know, leaving her?'

'If she's anything like I was at sixteen,' Clare said, 'I couldn't wait for a bit of independence from my parents.

Bringing her up here where she would have had to leave her friends and start again at a new school in her final year? God, no, she'd have made your life an absolute hell.'

I didn't like to say living at Daisy Royd Farm was already pretty hellish. 'Do you know, you've made me feel so much better.' I shot her a grateful look.

'Not easy, even at our age, *especially* at our age, to suddenly find yourself maybe where you don't want to be?' Clare raised an eyebrow, said nothing further but patted my arm and I felt tears threaten.

'I should be grateful we've got somewhere to live,' I sniffed. 'You know, when there's people out on the street.'

She laughed. 'I can't see Laurie Lewis's adoring fans letting him sleep rough on the street in a sleeping bag. You've not had an easy time lately, have you, what with the trial and everything?'

'You followed it?'

'Didn't everyone?'

'Cassie obviously didn't.'

We both laughed at that. 'You know she really didn't realise who you were married to. Just said she'd invited this author who'd moved into the area and whose son was starting at the school. She's always had a bit of a thing about the Romantic poets, has Cassie. Now, if she'd said she'd invited Laurie Lewis for supper we'd have all been agog with anticipation... Actually, we probably wouldn't have believed her.' Cassie sipped at her tonic. 'Oh sorry, that came out wrong – it sounds like we weren't interested in meeting *you*.'

'Don't worry, I've got used to being in Laurie's shadow over the years.' I tried to laugh it off, but had a horrid feeling

I'd allowed some of the resentment that was churning away inside of me to seep out.

'Well, I don't know why you have been,' Clare said, glancing over at Laurie who was deep in conversation with Serena Mayhew. 'You're obviously a talented author in your own right. And bloody gorgeous to boot.' She laughed out loud as she said that. 'Gosh, and I've not even had a drink. Sorry, I don't usually go round telling other women how lovely they are. I think you just need a bit of a boost. You know, if you're a bit short on girlfriends up here – and, much as I adore Rageh, I still need a break from him and for female company – you can always join Cassie and Fi and me. We walk quite a lot and get together at the pub or a meal out. I'll give you my number before you leave.'

'Really?'

Clare looked momentarily puzzled. 'Really what?'

'That would be so lovely,' I amended. 'Thank you.' I felt so pleased I'd made a new friend and beamed across at her.

'No, thank *you*. It's always great to have someone new along. And Cassie, particularly, will be delighted to be able to have someone to discuss eighteenth-century poetry with when neither Fi or I have a clue about any of it.'

Cassie, slightly red in the face and giving an occasional swipe at her forehead with her pinny, was in the process of handing out plates of delicious looking duck breast with figs and rosemary, helped by Xavier and Fi.

'This looks fabulous, Cassie,' I smiled, suddenly feeling a bit more confident after my chat with Clare.

'All Xav's work,' she laughed. 'I can hold my own, but he's the real cook in this house.'

How lovely, a man who cooked. Had Laurie ever cooked? He professed to be something of a foodie, but surely real foodies got down and dirty in their own kitchen; were so interested in sourcing ingredients and scanning recipes they were always at it. A fried egg on beans on toast seemed to be the sum of what Laurie had produced for himself while up here. And, in St Albans, I didn't remember him ever really utilising the upmarket pans and knives he'd insisted on buying for the new kitchen that had cost so much money and, along with the court costs, just about bankrupted us. I winced at the recollection.

'You OK, Jennifer?' Cassie had seen me pulling a face as I remembered Laurie's tendency to spend any money he had. As well as any he hadn't. 'You're not vegetarian, are you? Oh bugger, sorry, forgot to ask.'

'Gosh no, this is absolutely delicious.' And it was.

'So, Jennifer, what are you writing at the moment?' Cassie put down her knife and fork and leaned across the table. She was so interested, so earnest, but with her pinny still on back-to-front and a smudge of flour down her nose, I wanted to laugh. I liked this woman very much, I realised. 'More on the Romantic poets?' she went on, encouraging me to speak out. 'Or code cracking? Your Aunt Agnes must have been a fascinating woman for you to write your book about Bletchley Park. You are so clever to be able to diversify in what you write.'

Mention of Bletchley Park and code breaking had obviously aroused interest, particularly from the men around the table. I often found this happened – whereas men didn't always appear overly interested in the Romantic poets, mention a code that needed cracking and they were all ears.

'Hey, don't forget the UK's Poet Laureate lives only five miles away from here,' Fi joined in. 'You could write about *him*. Blimey,' she went on, 'we really are a hotbed of talent in these parts. Must be the cold air up here – gets the creative juices flowing.'

'Or knackers them completely.' Laurie sniffed disparagingly.

'Simon Armitage?' I asked, ignoring Laurie. 'Of course, he's from Yorkshire, isn't he?'

'Matthew went to school with his cousin,' Fi said proudly. 'Lives over in the next valley.'

'So, what *are* you working on?' Cassie insisted. 'Or, sorry, is it a secret?'

'Actually,' I said, having a sudden need to get out into the open what I was actually writing, 'I've started a Regency romance.'

Nine pairs of eyes turned my way and I felt myself go slightly pink but held my ground as Laurie gave me a look of utter derision. 'I knew you'd been *reading* that rubbish,' he scoffed. 'I didn't realise you were actually writing one of your own. Whatever for…?'

'A Regency romance?' Fi's eyes sparkled, although Cassie looked doubtful. 'You mean like *Bridgerton*?'

'I don't know Bridgerton,' I smiled, shaking my head. 'Who's he?'

'What, not *who*.' Fi laughed. 'Oh, my goodness, where've you *been*?' Fi was almost swooning. 'More crikey moments in the space of an hour than I've experienced for a long time. Matt loves it, don't you, Matthew? Gets him right in the mood.' She gave a hoot of laughter. 'He gives the poor old cows their Ovaltine early on *Bridgerton* nights so he can watch it all from the very beginning.'

'You do exaggerate, Fiona.' Matthew laughed across at his wife but his neck was turning slightly red. He slid a finger into his collar and reached for the beer he'd turned to after the gin had run out.

'It's on Netflix, Jennifer,' Laurie sniffed. 'Seems to have gripped the nation by all accounts. I can see we're going to have to get a Netflix subscription again.'

Not on the money – or lack of it – that was coming in to *our* bank account, we weren't.

'Well, if you're writing something like that, or along the lines of the ever-wonderful *Pride and Prejudice*, I'll certainly buy a copy.' Clare smiled in my direction before glancing momentarily towards Laurie. The look she gave him spoke volumes.

'Do you not think stuff like this gives women an unrealistic notion of what sex is all about?' Serena Mayhew spoke directly to me for the first time that evening. She was a tall, slim blonde wearing a classically cut, obviously expensive, little black number. She abandoned her knife and fork, steepling her fingers and putting her head slightly to one side – waiting for, it seemed, a full political response. I felt as if I was being interviewed by Laura Kuenssberg for *BBC News at Ten*.

'Oh God, Serena, do you have to treat everyone as though they were in front of you in the dock?' Tod Mayhew frowned slightly, but didn't look across in my direction.

The dock? Was this woman a solicitor?

'Serena's a barrister,' Clare said at my side, as I floundered somewhat. Where was the intelligent woman I'd once been, who could give back as good as she got when faced with an opposing point of view.

'Possibly,' I replied, 'but probably no more than the Pornhub channels our teenage boys access daily...'

'Our *teenage boys*? We haven't *got* teenage boys. Have we?' Laurie looked slightly startled. 'George isn't even eight yet, for heaven's sake. He's not watching porn already, is he?'

'I was using the term *our teenage boys* generically,' I said, frowning across at Laurie. 'And yes, I'm sure you'll agree, Serena, that when our kids download porn, they're normalising the unusual if not the abnormal, so that girls are expected to orgasm with every single thrust of a penis and are seen as unkempt and sexually unliberated if they haven't followed the ridiculous notion of shaving off all their pubic hair...'

I felt myself redden as I realised the first real sentence I'd spoken over this lovely headmistress's starched linen and artistically arranged freesias included the words: penis, orgasm and pubic hair.

'Well said.' Clare clapped as Fi said, 'Bravo.'

'But,' Serena insisted, 'you don't think all these frilly white shirts women are sighing over...'

'... especially if coming out of a lake next to a great big house...' Fiona interrupted, sighing volubly herself.

'... are giving women a skewed view of what is real? Are we not retreating in the advancement of women's liberation from their being mere male playthings, if we insist on writing, reading and now watching rubbish like this?'

'Quite possibly,' I agreed. 'But I'd rather my sixteen-year-old daughter watch Colin Firth in his wet frilly shirt than my son – when he's that age – looking at stuff that gives him the notion women are constantly panting for it with numerous lovers, of either, or indeterminate, gender, in crotchless knickers barely covering their shaved pudenda.'

Bloody hell, now I'd added crotchless pants and pudenda to my maiden speech. Laurie and I – and possibly George as well – were going to be socially ostracised by Westenbury's chattering classes just six weeks after we'd arrived.

'Where's my *pudenda*, Clare?' Fiona hissed. 'Have I *got* one?' She made a show of loudly whispering behind her hand in Clare's direction and I started to laugh.

'That's my wife for you,' Laurie drawled. 'Says pudenda when fanny is more than adequate.'

'Right.' Cassie and Xav jumped up as one. 'Pudding anyone?'

The predicted – and much maligned – slice of Black Forest gateau (I'd actually been hopeful that we might be having such for pudding) was not on the menu. Instead, there was a fabulous sweet ricotta tart as well as a huge duvet of a pavlova filled with orange curd and roasted rhubarb.

'The rhubarb is off my grandad Norman's allotment,' Cassie announced.

'The famous Grandad Norman,' Clare added for my benefit. 'He's well over ninety now and has a whole meadow named after him.'

'Oh? Norman's Meadow? Yes, I've been instructed to walk out there.'

'I'd wait until the wildflowers are out,' Clare smiled. 'Wait until the summer.'

The summer? I felt my heart miss a beat. I didn't *want* to be up here in summer. I wasn't *going* to be up here in the summer. I was going to take George and go back to Mum. If she and this new man of hers were together and there was no room for us, well then, I'd just have to prostrate myself at her feet and ask her and Jeremy to help me out with the rent on a place down there. The homesickness, and my missing Ada that I'd managed to keep at bay over the past few weeks, suddenly threatened to overwhelm me and I lay down my spoon, unable to finish the delicious pudding as my throat constricted. I reached for my water, fought down the panicked realisation I really didn't want to be with Laurie any longer, and turned to Xavier, now sitting to my left.

'I believe you have llamas?' I asked, struggling to conjure up a bright and what I hoped was questioning smile when, in reality, my face felt as if I'd had a root canal at the dentist.

'You don't have *llamas*, do you, Xav, darling?' Serena drawled from across the table. 'I bet you can get something for that at the chemist.'

'Very funny, Serena.' Xav turned back to me. 'Yes, we've had the herd a couple of years. It's been an interesting time, project managing this place while starting out as a llama farmer.'

'You've obviously been able to make a good living from it, then?' Laurie was leaning across the table too, waiting intently for an answer, and I recognised the signs as he took in the beautiful interior of the barn.

'We get by,' Xavier smiled.

'How big is the herd?'

'One of the largest in the north,' Xavier went on. 'I fell in love with llamas on a backpacking holiday to Peru years ago.'

'Xav,' Fi added, joining in with the conversation, 'has a propensity for falling in love in South America. He fell in love with Cassie when she was sloshed and belting out – badly we hear – 'I Will Survive' during karaoke night in a hotel in Mexico.'

'I hope you're not suggesting I resemble a llama?' Cassie said pointedly. 'And, our famous literary author isn't going to take me a bit seriously if she thinks I'm always half-cut. I actually rarely drink, Jennifer. Honestly.'

'So, yes,' Xavier went on, 'we have around sixty domestic llamas – these are the woolliest of the species – which we farm for breeding as well as their high-quality fleece.'

As Xavier spoke at length about his llamas, I began to realise three things: Xavier Balmforth adored both Cassie and his llamas; Laurie had that look on his face which meant he was juggling some new – and probably foolhardy – idea; and, as I glanced up and across the table at Tod Mayhew, I realised out of all the lovely people around the table, he was the only one who had made little effort to speak to me or ask anything about why Laurie and I were living at Daisy Royd Farm. As I mulled this over, I looked over at him, taking in Tod Mayhew's almost battered features, the thick dirty-blonde hair, the tired but obviously intelligent brown eyes and the large mouth that was now, suddenly, made even larger as he yawned volubly, showing very white teeth. I couldn't quite work out what such a groomed, beautiful woman as Serena saw in him. He obviously realised he was under scrutiny and turned his gaze in my direction. He stared at me for some time and then, clearly uninterested, stood up. 'Sorry, Cassie and Xav, it's been a long day. I'm absolutely bushed. You ready, Serena?'

Serena pouted a little but drained her glass and stood. She waved her goodbyes to those of us across in the cheap seats, but made much of kissing the three most attractive men at the table – Xav, Rageh and Laurie – before taking the beautiful, obviously expensive, coat Tod held out for her and, after more – quite unnecessary – kissing and hugging, left the room with her husband.

'You came on a bit strong with Serena,' Laurie said almost crossly as I drove us back down to Daisy Royd Farm; I still couldn't think of it as driving *home*. 'You know, somewhat indignant, puritanical and full of yourself.'

'Just giving back as good as I got,' I replied tartly.

'And I can't believe you admitted to actually writing that rubbish you're obsessed with at the moment. You write literary, high-brow stuff…'

'Not anymore I don't.'

'Didn't think much of that Mayhew fellow,' Laurie yawned. 'Bit surly. Can't imagine how he's managed to net such a cracking wife as Serena.'

Net her? I turned to look at Laurie. Had Laurie actually said *net her*? As if Tod Mayhew had spent hours dipping his rod into a pond of potential marriage partners and had come up with a prize catch?

It wasn't very late – probably not even midnight – as

Laurie and I continued home in silence and I realised he'd fallen fast asleep. Luckily, there were certain landmarks I recognised – the old Victorian red pillar box, the Wesleyan chapel, the small Co-op on the corner – and then we were into the village itself with the church, The Jolly Sailor, Little Acorns and the fabulously upmarket dress shop which, a couple of weeks previously, I'd pressed my nose up against and sighed over. I knew my way back from there. Fifteen minutes later, I drove through the dilapidated farm gate tied back to its post with a piece of fraying rope, and pulled up into the yard. I made to nudge Laurie awake, but he'd obviously had too much to drink and didn't stir. I was just considering abandoning him in the car, relishing the idea of having the bed all to myself, when I realised there was another car pulled up towards the side of the house. I peered through the windscreen and shook Laurie awake. Did we have burglars? I couldn't imagine there was anything to nick unless someone in the village had got wind of the George Smith chairs or the TV monstrosity (which I'd have willingly handed over without the bother of anyone breaking in).

'Laurie,' I hissed. 'There's a man. Getting out of the car. Oh, dear God, it's not the bailiffs, is it? We don't owe more money?'

'Bailiffs? At midnight on a Saturday night? What the hell are you talking about, Jennifer?' Laurie hissed back but, nevertheless, made to lock the car doors. We both peered out through the windscreen as the figure, tall and dressed all in black, came towards us.

'Who is it? Do you know him?'

Laurie shook his head and then stopped as he obviously realised, he did. 'It's Len Barrowclough from The Jolly Sailor. What the hell does *he* want, lurking out here at this time of night?'

19

'Can I have a word, lad?' Len Barrowclough knocked tentatively on the offside window, pressing a large hairy face into the Audi as Laurie and I peered nervously back at him. My immediate thought was that something must have happened to George and for some reason this man was waiting here to tell us. Had Cheryl and Dean taken the kids down to The Jolly Sailor and there'd been an accident or something? They were all, at this moment, up at A and E, leaving the landlord to come and break the news?

'Is it George?' I asked, hurriedly getting out of the car and searching the man's face for clues. Polonius had started up a relentless barking staccato from his kennel by the porch and I had to run round the front of the car to hear Len's response.

'George?' Len Barrowclough frowned. 'No, it's our Saffron.'

'Sorry?'

'What's up, Len?' Laurie had exited the car now and the two of them faced each other.

'I've driven over from Mirfield,' Len said, shaking his head before stroking his large bushy black beard with one enormous hand. 'Been here a couple of hours waiting for you. I didn't want to drive back without seeing you. We need to get a few things sorted.'

'Oh?' Laurie frowned.

'Been staying with my sister this week. Before we get off.' Len gave us a look as if we were meant to know exactly what he was talking about. Maybe Laurie did?

'Right?' I glanced across at Laurie and it was obvious he didn't have a clue either.

'Bit parky out here, Laurence. Can we go in?' Len nodded towards the house where Polonius was straining on his chain and still making a racket. The dog might have been pretty long in the tooth, but he still knew his role in life. The three of us – I untethered old Polony to release him from guard duty – followed Laurie through the porch and into the kitchen where Aggie was belting out warmth into the room. I'd become somewhat attached to the cantankerous old boot of an Aga, her unpredictability reminding me of Aunt Agnes who could be warm and sunny one minute, eager to let me in on the secrets of Bletchley Park, or, on bad days, glowering at me from her chair by the window and refusing to cooperate with me on my research. Polonius gave Laurie a wary look before quietly sneaking in and settling himself on Terry's old sofa.

'Right, what is it, Len?' Laurie folded his arms defensively as I held up the kettle in their direction.

'Have you got anything a bit stronger, love? I'm perished after sitting out there for the last couple of hours.'

I stared, kettle held aloft in mid-air. Perished? Isn't that what knicker elastic eventually did?

'He's *cold*, Jennifer.' Laurie tutted in my direction. 'There's that bottle of Southern Comfort somewhere.'

Laurie pulled a questioning face, shrugging his shoulders, and I abandoned the kettle and hunted for glasses and alcohol. 'So,' Laurie went on, 'I didn't realise you'd left The Jolly Sailor until I was down there this afternoon and found totally new people in charge.'

'Been gone a week now. As I said, just staying with my sister over in Mirfield until we go.'

'Oh?' Laurie was still in the dark.

'Benidorm. That's been the plan all along, but the bar we were after five years ago fell through so we stayed put. Any road, another came up and we jumped at it. All been a bit quick, like, but bought a business in the Old Town and we're off to Spain next week.'

'Right. OK. Hope it works out for you, Len.'

'I don't suppose Mr Barrowclough has driven half an hour and sat outside for another two, just to say *bon voyage* to *you*, Laurie.' I folded my own arms. 'Who's Saffron, Mr Barrowclough?'

'Len, love, call me Len.' He sniffed and drained his glass. 'I keep thinking you're talking to my dad when you call me *Mr Barrowclough*.'

'Saffron?' I asked again. 'Who's Saffron?'

Len turned to Laurie. 'Are you honestly telling me, lad, you've had no notion of all this?'

Laurie stood stock-still, the actor in him executing his lines on cue: 'Of what, Len? What is it you're trying to appraise me of, exactly?'

'Praise you, lad? I'm not trying to *praise* you. I'm here to tell you you're going to have to take on the daughter you appear to know nowt about.'

If I'd known Laurie to be a classical, Shakespearian

actor, rather than a two-bit soap one, I'd have reckoned this to be his finest moment, but as, over the years, I'd come to realise it was probably Laurie's stunning good looks as opposed to his acting ability that had brought him success, I knew, standing there, against Aggie Aga, this was no act on Laurie's part and he genuinely had no knowledge of what Len was now telling him.

'Mr Barrowclough – Len,' I amended, 'are you trying to say that Saffron is Laurie's daughter?' I felt an icy trickle down my back and had to sit down, trying to take it all in.

'Aye, well, our Jess kept it all quiet. Never told a soul that Laurie here was Saffron's dad. Frightened, I suppose, of what Karl might do. And you couldn't have blamed him if he *had* done something. None of us had any idea what *these two...*' Len nodded towards Laurie and then towards the tiled floor in the general direction of where, presumably, he assumed was Australia '... had been up to. Anyhow, Jess and Karl and the kids – Nathan and Saffron – emigrated to Canberra ten years or so ago. We've been out there a couple of times to stay and, to be honest, Sharon and me might have ended up there ourselves instead of Benidorm, but then Karl started messing around with another woman and our Jess told him.'

'Told him?' I knew exactly what pretty little Jess, the black-haired landlord's daughter, had told her adulterous husband. That she'd been just as adulterous and, one upmanship here, she had proof of that adultery.

'Yes,' Len confirmed. 'Jess told Karl that he wasn't our Saffron's dad and that Laurence here...' Len nodded again (somewhat enthusiastically, I thought, given the circumstances) in my husband's direction '... was.'

'Was? Was *what*? I have a child – a daughter – that no one has thought to tell me about? And then you come here, sixteen years later...'

'I don't think anyone mentioned that Saffron is sixteen,' I hissed furiously. 'But *you* appear to know that, Laurie.' I was doing quick mathematical calculations in my head, trying to work out just when this daughter of Laurie's might have been conceived. Had there been numerous opportunities? Every time a guilty conscience at not seeing Terry and Rita and his sisters had us heading up to Daisy Royd Farm for a couple of days, had Laurie taken the opportunity for a quick – alliterative – jump with Jess? 'But we were *married* sixteen years ago, you bastard,' I finally said.

'It was just before we were married, Jennifer. We were on a break...'

'A break? You sound like some adolescent at school, Laurie. A break?' I repeated, ignoring Len who was, to be fair, now looking a tad uncomfortable. 'A tea-break? A coffee-break? What sort of sodding break, Laurie? Did you shoot up here one *lunch-break* and have sex and impregnate Len's married daughter?'

'Look, love,' Len interrupted, 'I'm going to leave you to sort your husband out in your own time. I don't want to get involved. All I need to know is whether you'll take Saffron?'

'What do you mean? Take her?' Laurie was looking a bit sick. 'Isn't she in Australia with Jess?'

Len shook his head. 'I'll be honest with you, Laurence, since she hit, you know...' Len lowered his voice '...that there *puberty*, she's been a bit, well, hard work like...'

'Hard work?' Laurie frowned. 'How do you mean hard work?'

'You know, teenage stuff. Our Jess was a bit the same at that age. Any road, apparently she was having massive fights with her mum. Karl had moved to Sydney with his new woman and didn't want to know, especially now that he knew Saffron wasn't his *biological* daughter, and so Jess came back to Westenbury with the kids and put them into school here.'

'So Jess is here?' For a split-second Laurie looked hopeful and then, when he saw my face, rearranged his own to one of mildly interested concern.

'No,' Len tutted. 'I told you. She's back Down Under. Some bloke she met online over there. Shacked up with him within a couple of months. Nathan was desperate to get back to Australia as well, but Saffron refused to go. Refused point blank to even get in the car taking Jess and Nathan back to the airport. So, she's been with us for our last year at the pub and carried on at the comp and then we hoped she'd go back to be with her mum when we moved to Spain. She's refusing to go. And refusing to come with us to Benidorm either. I've played her a couple of episodes of *Benidorm* – *you'll* know it, Laurence, Sharon reckoned you were in it at one time? – but Saffron says nothing on God's planet would get her there. She says she's big enough to stand on her own two feet.'

'Well, at sixteen, I suppose she is?' Laurie had on his hopeful face once more.

'No, she's just a kid. Anyway, she's one of those newts…'

'Newts?' Laurie looked horrified. 'What do you mean, she's a *newt*?'

'You *know*. Don't you read the Sunday colour supplements?' Len gave Laurie a superior look. 'And you an arty type as well? *You* know what I mean, love, don't you?' He went on, turning to me. 'Not in Education, Employment or Training – or summat like that.'

'That spells NEET,' Laurie said coldly.

'Aye well, you're the one that went to Cambridge,' Len said dismissively. 'Anyhow, Saffron is supposedly enrolled onto an animal care course at the tech...'

'Not actually a *newt* then?' Laurie snapped, interrupting Len.

'... but she's not going as regular as she should. Sharon says she won't move to Spain not knowing where our Saffron's going to be living, and carrying on with some sort of proper education or with a job. If we don't get over to Spain pretty quick, we're going to lose the lease. There's a lot of work to do before the season starts. It's May already and we need to be opening up this minute. Our Saffron's too young to be living in a flat by herself and, besides, not working, she hasn't got a penny. I want her to go to sixth-form college rather than this ridiculous animal course she's supposedly on, and then on to university. She's not daft – she got a whole raft of GCSEs last summer even though she'd just moved to a new school. Some of those brains of yours must have rubbed off on her somewhere.' Len narrowed his eyes and gazed at Laurie's head as if weighing up the size of his brain. 'Karl didn't have *any* brains of his own, but I reckon she must have some of yours, Laurence, somewhere in that cross little head of hers.'

'*Brains?* You think he's got *brains*, Mr Barrowclough?' An all-consuming explosive fury was mounting in my chest and I knew I was about to launch. I could almost picture the utter rage inside me as a malevolence, its personification into a furious, implacable being desperate to get out and attack this husband of mine, who was now standing, white-faced in front of the Aga. 'You fucking *brainless* moron,' I screeched. 'You had sex with another woman months before we were married? You were with *me*, you fucker.' I looked round for something to hurl at that empty head of his. When I could find nothing suitable, I advanced blindly on Laurie myself, intent on aiming my booted foot at any and every part of him. I found my mark several times on his ankle and calf, feeling a satisfying contact with flesh and bone until he moved away, his hands outstretched in my direction, and I kicked the rusting Aga instead. Hard.

'That's my fucking toe now,' I yelled, hitting out instead with my fists until Laurie took hold of my arms and forced me back onto a kitchen chair where I nursed my immediately pulsating big toe.

'I'm sorry, love.' Len Barrowclough didn't appear either overly sorry or taken aback by my actions and foul language. It occurred to me that women shouting and swearing in his pub was probably a regular occurrence, part of the job description that went with being a landlord. 'Look, I can see you've had a shock, love, but I need to get this sorted. Like I said. I can come back tomorrow...'

'The situation will *not* have changed in the morning, Mr Barrowclough. Apart from me not being here. My son and I will be on the first train out of this god-forsaken place, out of this... this Yorkshire den of iniquity tomorrow...' I took several deep, steadying breaths. I was going home to Mum. 'But, if I *were* here... and let me tell you now, I *won't* be... I wouldn't be taking on a sixteen-year-old girl I've never met. Why would I? Why? *And* there's no room... But, anyway,' I added, glaring across at Laurie, 'that's totally up to *him*, the brainless bastard cowering over by the Aga. If *he* wants to take on his other daughter now that he's abandoned his real daughter, then that's totally up to him…'

'But your own daughter would have been given a room if she'd come up here with you?' Len looked straight at me, but I held his gaze.

'You seem to know a lot about my family, Mr Barrowclough.'

'Not me, love. I've no great interest in any of you – apart from seeing Saffron settled with her real dad for a year at least and finishing her education. But our Jess seems to have kept tabs on Laurence's career. Knew you'd moved back into Laurence's old home. And then, when you weren't here when I arrived…' Len looked at his watch '… three hours ago, I did a bit of detective work and one of the neighbours up the road told me where your mum had gone to so I went and knocked on her door and spent an hour with her. Never met your mother before, Laurence. Very handsome woman, isn't she? Very pleasant, caring woman too. A lovely granny for Saffron.'

'Mum knows?' Laurie asked, some colour returning to his cheeks.

'Well, she does now. I couldn't just turn up on the doorstep of some woman I'd never met before and have a cup of tea and a chocolate marshmallow with her without telling her the whole story, could I? Anyway, she'd know soon enough when she came up here and saw our Saff, *in situ* as it were.' He said the words proudly, shaping and letting them loose in his broad Yorkshire accent. 'And that's when Rita said there's three bedrooms here…'

'As I said, Mr Barrowclough, there will be plenty of room here after tomorrow. George, my son, and I are leaving.'

'Leaving? Getting off on holiday?'

'No,' I said furiously. 'Getting on with the rest of my life and doing what I should have done weeks ago and returned home to my *own* sixteen-year-old daughter.' I glared at Laurie. 'Make sure you put the dog back out, *Laurence*, when you see Mr Barrowclough out.'

I spent the rest of the next few hours pacing, my throbbing, bruised toe having me hobbling from the kitchen and the warmth of the Aga to the front parlour, staring out down Rita's garden and to the rolling meadows beyond, and then back again. I tied a bag of frozen peas around my big toe with a tea towel and paced and hobbled some more. I was going home. Well, home to Mum. I didn't have a home of my own and that was the scary thing. How the hell had I got to the age of forty and not got my own bricks and mortar, my own mortgage? And Laurie had cheated on me. Sex, full-on *sex*, and not just *a bit of a snog*, the *bit of fun* he'd professed himself guilty of with my sister-in-law last year. I paced the rooms some more. He'd been with Jess when he was supposedly looking after his mum. So now I had actual *evidence* of his philandering. The *Blazing Trail* magazine had known all along it was in the right when it accused Laurie Lewis of being a womaniser. How many other women had he been with down the years?

Staring out of the window as a grey dawn slowly materialised from the rivet-coloured night, I knew Laurie and I were washed up. Finished. And this Saffron girl really wasn't my problem. Once it was light, I was going to ring Mum and tell her I was driving myself and George down to Berkshire. Beyond that, I didn't really have a plan.

Laurie, in typical Laurie style, had seen Len Barrowclough out, exchanging contact details and promising that we'd be over in the next few days so that he and Sharon could bring Saffron round to meet her biological father and see if she'd be prepared to move in with us.

'Stop threatening to leave, Jennifer,' he'd said drunkenly as he made his way up to bed after seeing off several more glasses of Southern Comfort. 'You know George is happy and settled here. And, OK, OK...' he ducked as I hurled his jacket and one abandoned shoe up the stairs after him '... I apologise for my transgression of sixteen years ago, I really do. I was young, for heaven's sake. You and I weren't married. Not even engaged...' Laurie grabbed hold of the banister as I looked for something else to throw at him. 'But it's all in the past. And, how good is this? I have another daughter...' I flung the other shoe, catching him neatly on the shoulder '... and she's Ada and George's sister, for heaven's sake. You can't deny...' I threw his mobile phone up the stairs – fear at having to shell out for a replacement screen had him instinctively reaching out, catching it and yelling *owzat* into the bargain – '...deny your children their new-found sibling. Come on, come to bed. I might not be able to totally rise to the occasion that you've come to expect from me, but...'

'Fuck off, *Laurence*. Go and fuck off, somewhere out of my life.' I slammed back into the kitchen, grabbing the bottle of Southern Comfort – in the hope that it might live up to its name – and draining what was left in several noisy gulps.

I knew Laurie was curious to see this daughter he'd never met, but also knew he was banking on the certainty – from what Len had told us about Saffron's refusal to go back to Australia or move with Len and Sharon to Benidorm – that she'd dismiss the idea out of hand of coming to live with this new-found father and his wife. I was in total agreement with him on this. Why on earth would a sixteen-year-old move into a somewhat isolated, time-warp farmhouse with people she didn't know?

Knowing I wouldn't sleep if I went to bed, and with the effects of the alcohol surging through every vein, I grabbed my laptop, pounding furiously at the keyboard and taking Magnolia to dizzy heights of fearless deeds, debauchery and what could only be described as softly pornographic antics.

I am a woman, a strong woman who will bow and acquiesce to no man's will, especially yours, Lord Silverton. I will lay with you, aye and have your strong, lithesome body, your tumescence inside me, pleasuring me until I may scream out loud, but you will never own me completely. Now, divest yourself of those breeches that have sat abreast your sweating sturdy stallion…

Excessive alliteration? I'd decide tomorrow on the drive back south. I replaced the lid of my laptop and, although now fully light, climbed the stairs to George's room and, wrapping my arms around Melvin Moose, slid beneath his duvet for a couple of hours' sleep.

*

I was wakened by an excruciating pain in my big toe as well as the sound of movement downstairs: the drawing back of curtains, the encouraging of the Aga back into life, followed by the filling of the kettle from the kitchen tap. It was almost eleven and George would be delivered home by Cheryl any minute.

George's bedroom door opened and I immediately plastered on my usual passive aggressive (as Laurie had once coined it) expression. I was ready for a fight, if that's what Laurie was about. Ready to reiterate I'd had enough – I was packing up the few things we'd need at Mum's, and George and I would soon be on our way heading back south. What Laurie would do without a car was his problem. There was always the tractor...

Instead of Laurie's dark tousled morning head, it was Rita's face that peered round the door, her startlingly navy eyes holding mine in a long searching look before sliding automatically down to my foot, now hanging out of the side of the bed to avoid the pressure of the bedcovers. 'I've brought you some tea, love.' She paused. 'What on earth have you done to your big toe? It's black.' Without waiting for any explanation, she went on, 'And then, before George comes home, I think it's about time that you, Laurie and I had a bit of a chat. Don't you?'

20

By the time I'd pulled on a pair of jeans and a sweatshirt, rubbed the previous night's mascara from underneath my eyes and pulled a brush through my tangled mass of hair, Rita was already sitting at the table nursing a pot of tea. Of Laurie, there was no sign. Something was amiss or, as they say round these parts, *summat were up*.

'Laurence is on the phone in the front room,' Rita said. 'Been on for ages, by the sound of it.' She refused to meet my eyes.

'What's the matter?' I sat down at the oilskin tablecloth and, although I found strong Yorkshire tea too blinking strong, I reached for the teapot Rita had left behind in the move to her bungalow and poured the orange liquid. I'd probably knocked back more of the whiskey last night than I'd realised and my mouth felt as though it had been slept in by a flock of pigeons, and not overly hygienic ones at that. It would be interesting to open my laptop and see what – and with whom – Magnolia had been up to.

'I think it pretty obvious what the matter is,' Laurie snapped, joining us at the table. 'After last night's visit from the Jolly Bearded Landlord.'

'It didn't appear to be a problem last night,' I hissed back. 'You were more than happy to be playing the part of daddy dearest, as I recall – ready to bring her into the bosom of your family. Have you just been on the phone to Len now? Arranging something? Planning for your daughter to move in? Without consulting me?'

'Just a spot of business.' Laurie refused to meet my eye.

I scowled back at him. Over the years I'd come to dread the words *just a spot of business, Jen...*'

'Never mind about a spot of business, Laurence. There's a young girl out there who's just found out the man she's always thought to be her father now *isn't*.' Rita was being particularly uppity and part of me wondered what it had to do with her. It was Laurie's problem. Not Rita's, and certainly not mine. I was off, and taking George with me as soon as I possibly could.

'I don't think she's *just* found out, Mum. I get the impression she knew Karl wasn't her dad before she left Australia two years ago or so.'

Instead of responding to Laurie, Rita turned in my direction. 'I suppose you've told Laurie, Jennifer?'

'Told him what exactly, Rita?'

'About this?' Rita pulled out the copy of *The Squire's Serving Wench* in which I'd found the newspaper cutting.

'Oh, I know all about Jen writing this stuff. Beyond me what's she up to when she should be bashing out another best-selling poet.' Laurie frowned. 'Why are *you* so upset about her reading and writing this sort of thing, Mum?'

'So, you haven't told him then, Jennifer?' Rita was pale, her blue eyes never once leaving mine.

I shook my head. 'And I wouldn't have done. I think that's up to you, Rita, don't you?'

'What *are* you two going on about?' Laurie leaned back in his chair until the front two legs were off the floor, its back resting against the kitchen wall. He folded his arms and held both our eyes.

Rita opened the book and withdrew the newspaper cutting. She took a deep breath and pushed it towards Laurie, who brought his chair back towards the table, pulling the cutting towards him as he did so.

'What? What am I supposed to be looking at? Hang on, I've not got my contacts in. Where are my glasses?' Laurie got up from the table, recovered his reading glasses from the bread bin and returned to his seat. 'Where's this come from?' he frowned. 'I've never been in a production of *Hamlet*. Have I? Bloody hell, I'm going daft if I can't remember…' He paused. 'This is before I was born, Mum. This isn't me…'

'No, it's your father.'

'Dad? Dad was in a production of Hamlet…?' Laurie trailed off as the implication of what was in front of him began to hit home. He studied the photograph intensely, not saying a word and then, surprisingly, began to laugh. 'So, Dad wasn't my dad? Terry Lewis wasn't my dad?'

'Yes, he was, Laurie.' Rita's mouth was set in a hard line as she held Laurie's eye. 'He was your father in every possible way.'

Laurie laughed again. 'Except the fairly crucial one of actually being there at my conception, you're now telling me?'

'Yes.'

'Did Terry know, Rita?' I asked gently. 'You know, that you were pregnant but it wasn't his?'

Rita shook her head as Laurie interrupted with, 'So who *is* this?' He shook the slip of faded paper none too gently in Rita's direction, and I could see the shock of such a revelation was beginning to have an impact.

Rita sighed. 'There have been so many times I was going to tell you the truth, Laurie, especially after your dad died…'

'Which dad, Mum? Which one are we talking here?'

'Your *dad*. Terry was your dad. When he died, I decided it was probably time to tell you about your biological father.'

'Dad died over a year ago, Mum.'

'Yes, and you've not exactly been up to visit since the funeral, Laurie. There's no way I was going to come down on the National Express Coach to St Albans with the sole intention of telling you the truth. And then, as time went on, I realised it really didn't matter – it was such a long time ago. I read an article the other day,' Rita went on, 'saying they reckon more than ten per cent of people are not actually fathered by the man they've grown up to believe *is* their father.'

'And that's your excuse, is it, Mum?' Laurie was at his most sarcastic. 'You've read some statistics on this course you're doing at Leeds, and that's salved your conscience?'

'Would you have been any better off knowing, Laurie?' I asked, feeling sorry for Rita.

'Depends who this bloke is?' Laurie looked at the photo once again. 'If he's an oil tycoon with millions, then yes, I'm going to be a lot better off. So, who is he then, Mum? Do I get to meet him now?'

'I heard he'd died about ten years ago. Brain tumour I believe.'

'Oh, great stuff,' Laurie snapped. 'Every time I get a headache from now on...' he put a somewhat dramatic hand to his forehead '... I've actually got a belter now....'

I picked up the empty bottle of Southern Comfort that was still on the kitchen table and upended it in his direction.

'I'm sure I didn't finish the bottle,' he said, looking at me with suspicion. 'Is it hereditary, Jen?'

'What, finishing a bottle of whiskey and not remembering?'

Laurie tutted. 'You know, brain tumours? Am I going to end up with one?'

A totally unrepentant hypochondriac, Laurie had, over the past five years, suffered both testicular and prostate cancer, ME, MS and, just a few weeks ago, a particularly bad dose of necrotising fasciitis. I'd had little sympathy with any of his symptoms but particularly the latter which, he'd initially informed me, on finding a suspicious large purple bruise, was indicative of *necrophilia*, to which I'd retorted he was indeed in a bad way if he was now being adulterous with dead bodies as well as extracurricular live ones.

'I probably still wouldn't have said anything,' Rita brought me back to the present, 'had you not found the photo in the book, Jennifer.'

'Oh, *you* knew?' Laurie was well into the drama of it all now. '*You* knew of my mother's past, my... my *heritage*... and yet you didn't think to share it with *me*? Your husband?'

'It wasn't my secret to tell, Laurie. Anyway, I only had my suspicions that the man in the photo was your dad. I mean, it's a pretty faded photo and, while he's very dark and does look something like you, it was the Laurence name that gave it away...'

'Shouldn't it be that I look like him?' Laurie interrupted crossly.

'I handed the photo back to your mum a week or so ago.' I turned to Rita and took her hand. 'Your reaction when you saw it, Rita, confirmed what I suspected. But, you know, I wouldn't have told Laurie. You obviously had your reasons for never telling him.'

'Stonking great reasons, I would have thought,' Laurie said sourly. 'OK, then, Mum,' Laurie glanced at the kitchen clock which was always running a bit slow, 'spill the beans before Cheryl arrives back with George. Tell all, and don't spare the horses.' Laurie swung back onto two legs of the chair once more and folded his arms.

'So,' Rita cleared her throat and seemed unable to start. 'So, when the girls were little, I'd had enough of just being a stay-at-home mum. I wanted to get a degree, maybe eventually train to be a teacher, which I would have done if I'd not got pregnant with Janice. Terry was a bit against it, didn't really like the idea of my having a life of my own and needed me for the farm. Anyway, I did A-Levels at night school. Oh, I loved all the English Literature and the Sociology. That's when I got into these Regency romances, Laurie, when we were asked to compare Jane Austen with modern Regency novels – don't let anyone tell you they're inferior to more literary stuff—'

'Alright, Mum, get on with it. We don't need an amateur belletrism-type literary critique of dastardly dukes and lascivious lords...'

'Shut up, Laurie, for God's sake.' I kicked out at him under the table, setting my toe throbbing once more. It actually felt broken. Would George and I be able to fit in a visit to A and E before we hit the motorway and headed south?

'Anyway, after doing exceptionally well with my A-Levels – much to both Terry's pride and consternation – I enrolled on a part-time modular degree at Midhope Poly. I loved it. Loved being a student.'

'A proper little *Educating Rita*.' Laurie was still sarcastic.

'Yes, it did feel a bit like that.' Rita wasn't to be put off. 'And I fell in love. I'd never felt anything like this before.'

'So, come on, get to the point, Mum. Who the fuck is he? My father?' Laurie picked up the photo once again and studied it intently before answering his own question. 'Laurence Reardon-Jones? Is this him? Laurence Reardon-Jones?' Laurie rolled the name around his tongue as if tasting a fine wine. Well, double-barrelled – that's something at least.' Then he frowned. 'Jones? I'm not Welsh, am I?'

'No more than Lewis is, I wouldn't have thought,' Rita said, eyebrows raised. 'Your father was from Hereford...'

'Nearly Wales,' Laurie said sagely.

'... and was lecturing...'

'Lechering...' Laurie interrupted.

'No doubt he's your father then...' I interrupted in turn.

'... was lecturing for a few years at the Poly when I was doing my English Literature module. He was a frustrated, if not failed, actor...'

'Definitely your father,' I sniffed, not looking at Laurie.

'... and was desperate to hit the big time. As you can

imagine, it didn't surprise me a bit when you got into am-dram, Laurence.' Rita sighed heavily. 'Anyway, we had a bit of a thing…'

'A *bit of a thing*? Are you saying I'm the result of a one-night stand?' Laurie was put out. 'I'd have hoped at least that he was the love of your life?'

'He was,' Rita said as tears formed and she brushed them away. 'But he was married, and *I* was married with three little girls who needed me. And I know this sounds like I was some sort of adulterous slut – which I suppose I was, I didn't know *who* your father actually was until you grew from a baby into a little boy. You had dark hair and blue eyes like me…'

'And Cheryl,' Laurie interrupted. 'Oh my god, Cheryl wasn't his as well?'

'No, no of course not.' Rita was cross. 'Your sisters were little girls when I met Laurence. The affair went on for several months. I helped backstage with the production of *Hamlet* – I was never into acting myself – and those months I spent down at the theatre were some of the best times of my life.'

'Did he know, Rita?' I asked. 'That you were pregnant?'

Rita shook her head. 'As I say, I didn't know which of them was the baby's father. No point telling my lover I was pregnant when more than likely it was my husband's.'

'Suppose it was confirmed when I didn't come out ginger and eating pork pies.' Laurie gave a short bark of laughter.

'There's no need to be disrespectful, Laurence.' Rita was still cross. 'I knew definitely you were Laurence's child when you were reading everything you could get your hands on by the time you were five, and you always wanted to have the main part in the school nativity.'

'So, didn't Terry suspect, Rita? You know, when Laurie didn't look anything like him?'

'I think he probably did have his suspicions – I think he probably knew, but the last thing Terry needed was me upping and leaving with Laurie to be with Laurence.'

'And was that ever on the cards?'

'No.' Rita was adamant, and emphasised her words by giving me a long, knowing look. 'Not only was Laurence Reardon-Jones married, you *don't* leave the father of your children, no matter what.' Rita gave me another questioning look and I realised she must have seen the suitcases I'd started pulling out before falling into bed. I glared back at her but she continued, 'No way would I have ever left my children just for some mad fling.'

'So how do you know he's no longer around?' Laurie asked.

'I get a newsletter from the university every now and again. There was a bit about him, must be ten years ago now, saying he'd been ill and gone to America for treatment. I rang someone who knew him, who confirmed he'd a brain tumour and heard he'd died out there.'

'Right.' Despite my contempt for Laurie following last night's little revelation, I was able feel some disappointment for him.

'Now, listen you two,' Rita said with a steely gaze across the table. 'This goes no further. I don't want the girls to know: there's absolutely no point in raking up old business. Janice especially took Terry's death hard. No good would come of her knowing he'd been, you know…'

'Cuckolded?' Laurie raised an eyebrow.

'If that's what you want to call it. You can keep the photo, Laurie.'

'You don't want it?' I asked.

Rita smiled a hard little smile. 'I've several, hidden away in various secret places... Oh, shhh...' she pushed the newspaper clipping towards Laurie, who had the sense to put it into his jeans' pocket. 'Is that George back?'

My heart lurched. Listening here to Rita's past story had taken me away from my present situation and my decision to leave it. I wasn't worried about telling Laurie – I felt little loyalty about staying after the revelation from Len Barrowclough last night. It was George I didn't relish telling. He was so happy here, already so settled in his new school and with his cousins.

'Where's George?' I stood up as Cheryl and Imogen, her ten-year-old, walked into the kitchen.

'He's coming.' Imogen was obviously excited. 'He's got a surprise for you, Auntie Jennifer.'

Couldn't be anything like the one I was about to land on George. My pulse raced as the open door slowly opened wider.

'Look, Mummy.' George's face was one big grin and my heart plummeted as I took in the look of utter happiness on his little face. Nestled in his arms was a tiny black and brown – and long – Dachshund.

'Oh, who does he belong to?' I asked, knowing the answer before Cheryl spoke.

'Now, don't panic, Jen. He wasn't wildly expensive – he's the runt of the litter and got something a little not quite right with his back...'

'Oh, dear God, a Dachshund with backache?' Laurie gave a bark of laughter. 'How much is that going to cost us at the vet every time he slips a disc?'

'Cheryl, you really had no right to raise George's hopes about having a dog. Ada is hugely allergic to dogs...'

'Yes, but Ada isn't *here*, Jennifer...' Laurie frowned.

But George and I are going back *there*, I said in silent fury.

'... And if she comes to visit, *when* she comes to visit, the dog can go to Mum's. Mum? Would that be alright?'

'No problem,' Rita smiled. 'Really, Jennifer, I've missed having a dog about the place. I've got so much on at the moment I certainly don't want a dog of my own, but I'm more than happy to look after this little chap and, I tell you what, George, I'll pay for him. My present for your birthday next week.' Rita looked across at me and I began to realise that, if not exactly manipulative, Rita Lewis got her own way when she wanted it. 'That OK with you, Jennifer? Does that make you feel a bit happier?'

The words *over*, *barrel* and *had me* sprung to mind but I came out fighting.

'I'm *sorry*, Rita,' I spat, 'but I've lost my home because of your spoilt, selfish, *brainless* son.' (I really liked Len's *brainless* handle.) 'I've been expected to *not* only move somewhere I don't want to be because of him, I'm *now* expected to welcome some stroppy teenager who *I* shall have to look after, and – to cap it all – a disabled puppy is thrust my way, who *I* shall have to clean up after and walk when George is at school and I'm trying to *work* to pay off our sodding *debts and bills*.'

There was an embarrassed silence as I stood up. 'I've so

had *enough* of all you lot with your little secrets and your manipulations and... and...' I could hear rising hysteria in my voice, and it was only catching sight of George's white face and trembling lip, as well as ten-year-old Imogen who was starting to nervously giggle, that had me pushing back the chair and hobbling from the room rather than continue with my ranting tirade.

'Hi, Mum, are you alright?' Ada's voice over the phone sounded slightly muffled.

'Is this a bad line, Ada? Can you hear me?'

'Oh sorry,' she laughed. 'I've still got a scarf around my mouth.'

'Why? Is it cold down there?'

'No, no.' She started to laugh. 'Phil and I are pulling out wardrobes.'

'Phil?'

'You know, Granny's boyfriend.'

Right. I took a deep breath. 'What do you mean, you're pulling out wardrobes? And on a Sunday?'

'What's Sunday got to do with it? You haven't gone all Wesleyan since you've been *oop north*, have you?' Ada laughed again and I felt a pang of envy. She sounded so happy down there with her new life. 'Phil's an interior designer. We're turning Granny's biggest spare bedroom – not the one I'm in, obvs – into a gorgeous dressing room for her. She had one in the other house with Grandpa and really misses it, so Phil has drawn up amazing plans for it. It's going to be all open wardrobes and shelving and a very fabulous – but totally functional – island sort of thing in the middle with more drawers. And then we're going to knock through into her bedroom, making it all en suite and absolutely massive. A bit like your old house with Grandpa I suppose, really. Phil said why didn't he give a head-start to his joiners by pulling out the old stuff and so that's what we're doing and I'm helping him. Do you know, Mum, I quite fancy being an interior designer? Phil says I've got a bit of a gift that way.'

'As well as acting?'

'I can do both.' Ada giggled happily. 'It's very cathartic bashing down doors,' she went on. 'Dusty though. Granny's cooking lunch for the three of us. Do you want a word?'

There appeared to be little point: there was obviously no room at the inn for George and me.

Not to mention a creaking, allergy-inducing Dachshund.

'It's fine, darling,' I managed to say. 'Tell Granny I rang and everything is fine up here.'

Fine? I closed my eyes at the totally ridiculous realisation that Laurie had acquired not only a new daughter, but a new father into the bargain. Both within the space of – I glanced at my phone – twelve hours. You couldn't make it up.

I walked slowly back to the kitchen and the others, where a tearful George was being patted and comforted by his relatives. A noisy truck, its broken exhaust emitting noxious fumes as well as angry growls competing manfully with the constant raucous barking from Polonius, was just pulling up in the yard and everyone turned from George and then to me and then to the open kitchen door where a flat-capped farmer-type now stood.

'Right. Mr Lewis? Here y'are lad, where d'you want 'em…?'

21

My first job here was to sort out my son.

'It's OK, George, really it is,' I soothed. Always terribly easily upset and prone to instant tears, my seven-year-old needed to know everything was going to be alright and that he'd done nothing wrong in proudly accepting and bringing home the dog. 'He's lovely.' I stroked the puppy's downy brown head and he yawned widely before fixing chocolate eyes on me – waiting, unwittingly, for my stay of execution. 'What's he called?'

'Can I keep him, Mummy? Daddy?'

Laurie appeared to have forgotten all about his son and the puppy and was, instead, in the process of reaching into his jeans' pocket for his wallet while ushering the farmer-type bloke out of the kitchen door and back into the yard. A few seconds later, the truck's knackered exhaust gave a couple of experimental throaty growls and then, with Laurie now in the passenger seat and obviously giving directions, the truck and attached horsebox bounced past the kitchen window, down the yard and towards the field where, years earlier, Terry Lewis had brought home and housed his bullocks.

'What's he called?' I asked again.

'Sausage,' Imogen said proudly. 'Can George keep him, Auntie Jennifer?'

I glanced across at Cheryl and Rita, who appeared to be holding their breath, awaiting my decision. 'Sausage,' I repeated. 'Well, what else could you call him?' I smiled, even though I knew that accepting this little mutt meant, for the time being, at least, there was going to be no going back home for me and George. 'I think he'll fit in pretty well here,' I added.

George managed to fling one arm around me, almost squashing Sausage into the bargain, before wiping at his tear-stained face with a grubby hand.

Cheryl handed over a carrier bag. 'Instructions,' she said, obviously still a little wary. 'You've clearly got enough on your plate with whatever Laurence has been up to now.' She glanced out of the window towards the empty yard. Little did she know just *what* Laurie had been up to *seventeen years* earlier. Or, for that matter, her mother, *forty years* earlier. Jesus.

Rita gave me a warning glance and shook her head before smiling at George and Cheryl. 'Instructions? Sounds like a flatpack from Ikea,' Rita said. 'Any of the other dogs we've ever had here have just arrived without any guidance or instructions. They went out into the kennel and knew their place from day one.'

'He doesn't have to sleep outside, does he, Mummy?' George's face had fallen once more.

'No, of course not. We can find him a cosy box in front of the Aga.'

'He's actually a lot older than the usual twelve weeks when dogs leave their mother,' Cheryl said. 'He's had all his jabs and can go out for a walk with other dogs. No one wanted him with his back problem. But, honestly, it's not that bad,' she added hurriedly when she saw my face. 'Here's the breeder's number. I suggest you ring and have a long chat with him. He'll be able to advise you on anything.'

I glanced at the paper where the name *Dermot O'Callaghan* was written, with an accompanying phone number.

'Dermot's brilliant with animals,' Cheryl said. 'He trains horses for Tod Mayhew down at the stables just out of the village. He'll always be on hand to give you any advice or help.'

'Tod Mayhew?' I interrupted. 'We met him last night.'

'Did you?' Both Cheryl and Rita's ears appeared to prick up at that. 'Was he at Cassie Beresford's place?'

'Hmm, we had dinner with him.'

'He's a bad-tempered bugger – sorry kids – didn't you find?' Cheryl frowned as she spoke.

'He certainly was on the day we arrived here,' I said, frowning. 'We stopped for George to be sick, down by the church, and he appeared over a fence giving me hell when papers flew out of the car.'

'That's Tod for you,' Cheryl grinned. 'Hates walkers and day trippers who leave gates open and don't take their rubbish home with them. I think there's something about him, though, don't you? Looks a bit like Robert Redford? In his younger days, obviously,' she added.

'To be honest,' I said, 'he didn't say a great deal last night. I had a bit of a run in with his wife though.'

'Did you? I didn't know he was married. He *was*, but I'm sure he's divorced now.'

'Oh, well, I *thought* it was his wife. Serena? A barrister?'

'Oh no, he's not married to someone called Serena.' Cheryl shook her head. 'Unless he's got shacked up again PDQ, I suppose. He was married to some Swedish woman, wasn't he, Mum? Beautiful woman, but she apparently couldn't stand the amount of time he spent with his horses and went back to Stockholm as far as I remember. Couple of years back now.'

'Right, Cheryl, you need to know...' Rita paused, lowering her voice and glancing across at George and Isobel who were in the process of digging out the large cardboard box that had been the repository of something Laurie, regardless of the fact that he was broke, had ordered from Amazon. '... Why don't you take Sausage out for a walk, you two? Let him meet Polony?'

'Are you sure Polonius won't think he's a tasty snack and eat him?' I asked, doubtfully.

'It's no wonder George is such a worrier with you for a mother,' Cheryl said, not unkindly. 'Let him get on with it, Jen. Right, what is it, Mum?' She turned back immediately to her mother once the kids had taken Sausage outside and Rita had closed the door behind them. 'Oh, hang on, someone else here.' Cheryl walked back over to the window. 'It's only Janice.'

'What the hell is that *thing* the kids have got out there?' Janice strode into the kitchen, bringing a blast of cold air and muddy boots into the kitchen, and I winced slightly: I'd spent several hours the previous morning cleaning and polishing the floor and had been pretty impressed with myself the way the kitchen tiles had come up.

'Right, Janice. Good you're here. I'd have rung you to tell you if you hadn't turned up.'

'Tell me what?' Both Janice and I stared. Was Rita going to come clean about Terry not being Laurie's biological father?

Obviously not. It was, it seemed, quite OK for Rita to spill the beans about Laurie's new daughter but not, apparently, about her own fling with the double-barrelled lecturer.

'Well, it doesn't surprise me,' Cheryl finally said, keeping one eye on the door. 'Our Laurence and Jess Barrowclough were always a bit of a pair. I'm amazed Jess kept it to herself all these years though.'

'Randy little sod,' Janice sniffed. 'He should have been castrated along with the spring lambs.' She laughed evilly. 'A couple of rubber bands around his balls until they dropped off would have done the trick.' She turned to me impatiently. 'What are you *doing*, still here, Jen? Have you learned nothing about the Boy Wonder after that court case exposed his constantly putting it about? And now this? Bloody hell, he'd shag a doughnut if there was one in the cake tin…'

'Enough, Janice. That really is uncalled for.' Both Rita and Cheryl looked with some distaste towards Janice.

'Just saying it as it is.' Janice shrugged. 'You two have always stood up for him, no matter what he's done. Maybe you should show a little thought and respect for Jennifer here instead.'

Goodness, was this Janice on my side for once?

'What's important is that Len Barrowclough wants Laurence to take his daughter.'

'Take her? Take her where?' Cheryl and Janice spoke as one.

'Take her *on*.' Rita tutted at her daughters' apparent inability to grasp her meaning. 'She's refusing to go back to Jess in Australia and is totally adamant she's not going to Benidorm with her grandparents.'

'Don't blame her,' Cheryl snorted. 'Benidorm's a dive. Do you remember that awful holiday me and Dean…?'

'Vaguely,' Rita interrupted, cutting Cheryl off mid-sentence. 'Len Barrowclough wants her to come and live *here*. Wants Laurie to finally accept responsibility for the daughter he fathered sixteen years ago.'

'Well, I can't see him doing *that*,' Janice sneered. 'And why the hell would this girl want to come *here*? I'd have thought it fell well below par of even Costa del Whotsit.'

'She's sixteen,' Rita said, and I could see she was struggling to be patient. 'Her parents still have a legal duty to protect, house and provide for her.'

'Put her back on the first plane to Australia then,' Janice said.

'Until she's eighteen,' Rita went on. 'Will you stop interrupting, Janice?'

'Unless she marries.' Cheryl started laughing. 'I know this because I looked it up when Holly was being at her most woke and I couldn't stand one minute longer of her telling me what a racist, sexist bigot I was. I knew if I could just get her married off as soon as she hit sixteen, my responsibility for her would end there and then.'

'You're the least racist, sexist bigot I know,' I said, smiling sympathetically at Cheryl.

'Oh, she said I was apparently using gender-biased language towards her when she was totally premenstrual and going off on one the other day. I tried to cheer her up and tease her a bit by asking if maybe she was *ovary acting* because of her hormones, and she flew off the handle, saying I wouldn't dream of making a comment like that if she was a boy.'

'What?' Janice shook her head in bemusement. 'Boys don't have ovaries and periods? Do they? Have I missed something somewhere...?'

'For heaven's sake, you two, will you shut up about hormones and help decide what to do with this girl?' Rita was beginning to lose her patience.

'Nothing to do with us, Mum,' Janice snapped. 'She's *Laurence's* responsibility. Not even yours, Jen.' She turned to me. 'So don't you go taking on more problems, because you know Laurence won't lift a hand to help. You'll have more cooking, more washing and ironing, more messy bedrooms and bathrooms...'

'We've only got *one* bathroom,' I reminded Janice.

'Exactly,' Janice replied. 'And she'll be in it every hour of the day. You won't get a look in. It won't be like being back in St Albans with Ada, you know, who, I suppose, had her own en suite?'

'Actually, she *isn't* Laurie's responsibility,' Rita sighed. 'I spent hours last night after Len left to come back here, Googling it all. While you might think, as her father, Laurie does share some responsibility, unless he was actually married to Jess – which of course, he wasn't – and unless he has entered into a parental responsibility agreement, or obtained a court order *granting* him parental responsibility – which, seeing as he only found out last night, we can rule out as well – then there is absolutely no reason for him to have anything to do with her.'

'Unless you consider it a *moral* responsibility,' I offered.

'To be fair to Laurie, he didn't know anything about Jess having his daughter,' Rita pleaded.

'Oh, don't start, Mum.' Janice snapped. 'Your precious son has always got away with everything. Where is he, anyway? Still in bed?'

'Outside,' Cheryl said. 'What was that bloke delivering? Something from Amazon?'

'Amazon? In a great truck like that? I doubt it very much.' I sighed. 'I would imagine your brother thinks he can rear llamas.'

'Llamas?' Janice snorted. 'For heaven's sake, Laurence can't even rear himself.' She started laughing uproariously. 'This will be one hell of a llama drama.'

Laurie and I spent the rest of that Sunday – once he and George and Sausage had finally come inside from settling the three llamas into their new home – circling each other in silence, putting off the moment until George was out of hearing in order to discuss Jess Barrowclough's daughter. Laurie wasn't stupid – apart from this latest daft idea that somehow three llamas were going to be the start of something big – and he knew I'd had enough.

'Do you need taking up to A and E, Jen?' Laurie eventually said. 'That toe looks painful. I'm sorry.'

'I Googled it,' I said crossly. 'Not much anyone can do for a broken toe apart from strapping it up and resting it. Your mother bandaged it up for me; I told her I'd stubbed it on the stair.'

'Sit down then, sit down,' Laurie was at his most solicitous. 'I'll do supper and get George to bed. And, you know, you shouldn't be even considering driving a long journey...' He broke off and glanced across at me. 'I suppose that was your mum you were on the phone to earlier?'

'Ada, actually.'

'She OK?'

'Perhaps you should ring her.'

'I don't think she's that bothered,' Laurie said glumly. 'Whenever I've texted her, she's taken ages to reply.'

'She's sixteen. Not overly interested in her parents, especially now that she's gained some independence from us.' I felt very sad at my own words.

'I bet you were still close to *your* dad at sixteen,' Laurie said.

'I miss him,' I said simply, absolutely longing for him at that moment. 'I miss him so much.' I felt tears start. 'He was always there for me. Always.'

'And neither of my dads were there for me.'

'Feeling sorry for yourself, Laurie?'

'Suppose.' He tried to give me his lopsided grin but failed. 'I've fucked up with everything, haven't I, Jen? Do you want to go back south?'

'Yes. I miss Ada. And I don't want to be here. I've given it a fair shot, Laurie.'

'Right. What are you going to do then? Are you off?'

'I rang Mum this morning to ask if George and I could go back and stay with her.'

'Right. I understand. I've nothing to offer you here.'

I glanced across at Laurie. I might have been married to him for almost seventeen years, but still wasn't always truly sure he wasn't putting on yet another act.

'I'm not trying to start a new business with the llamas,' Laurie smiled. 'I'm not that daft.'

'So why are three sodding great llamas now out in your field then?'

'You're still unable to say *our* field, aren't you?' Laurie said sadly, taking my hand.

'It's *not* my field,' I said, but let my hand remain in his. 'It's not even yours. It's your mother's.'

'The llamas will keep the grass down,' Laurie said. 'That's the plan.'

'Wouldn't the tractor and mower have done just as well?'

'I didn't pay much for them,' Laurie went on. 'Made a few phone calls to a friend of a friend of a friend of the people in the pub yesterday. The guy was glad to be rid of them.'

'Why, are they hot?'

'Hot?'

'Nicked,' I said impatiently.

'Oh shit, I hope not.'

'Well have they got certificates of ownership? Of health? Vaccinations? Deworming? *I* don't know, Laurie. I don't know anything about llamas.'

'Oh, they're just like donkeys: they're pretty hardy. You wouldn't think twice about having a couple of donkeys in

the field, would you? I bought them as pets for George.'
Laurie couldn't quite meet my eye. 'So,' he went on, draining
his mug and reaching for the pack of KitKats, 'what are
your plans then?'

'They've been temporarily scuppered.' I raised an
eyebrow at Laurie.

'Oh?' Laurie looked hopeful.

'Mum's in the middle of knocking her third bedroom
into her own to make a larger room for herself, as well as a
dressing room and much bigger en suite.'

'Hmm, that new boyfriend of hers getting his feet under
the table already? I tell you, Jen, you need to watch it. You
know, your dad's money?' Laurie patted at his jeans' back
pocket, like something from the Asda ad.

'Oh, for God's sake, Laurie.' I threw him a look of disgust.

'So, you and George would have to share that tiny box
room with its single bed?' Laurie looked even more relieved.

'And I would, I *would*,' I said fiercely. 'I could always
sleep in Ada's bed during the week when she's at Lydia's.
And then a put-up bed in Ada's room at the weekend...' I
trailed off.

'And Ada and your mum and the new man would just
love that, wouldn't they? Encroaching on their space.'

'You *know* the main reason we now can't go,' I said
furiously. 'And why *you* encouraged it. I'm not stupid, Laurie.'

'I don't know what you're talking about?'

'Sausage.'

'Sausage?' Laurie was all wide-eyed innocence.

'You know perfectly well how allergic to dogs Ada is.
And Mum was never that bothered about having a dog
around the place. We had one when I was a kid because

Jeremy and I both wanted one and Dad went ahead and brought Paddy home regardless.'

'What Jennifer wanted, Jennifer got,' Laurie said idly, attempting to fold the red KitKat wrapper as many times as possible before throwing the hard red dot towards the bin. 'Bingo. Of course, of course. Silly me, I'd totally forgotten about poor Ada's allergy to dogs. You'd have to leave Sausage here...'

'Exactly.'

'So, now we've established you're staying, I need to know what to say to Len Barrowclough when I ring him tomorrow.'

'I'm not having her here, Laurie. I'm *not* looking after some bolshy teenager that's suddenly come into your life. Anyway, you don't think, for one minute, this daughter of yours is going to want to come and live here? Why on earth would she?'

'Why not? I'm her dad. Apparently...'

'Exactly. I've been thinking about this, Laurie. How can you be sure she's yours?'

'Why would Jess lie?'

'How can she be sure? How can *you* be sure?'

Laurie pulled out his phone and scrolled down for a few seconds before handing it over to me. 'I'm sure,' he said.

I didn't need to study the photo in front of me. Saffron Danvers was the image of Laurie. And Ada. This was George and Ada's sister. I closed my eyes. Didn't I have some sort of moral responsibility to my own children's sibling?

'Fine, fine,' I snapped, watching Laurie get up to search in the fridge for something to concoct for supper.

'Omelettes?' Laurie offered, closing the fridge door and

turning to the bowl that was always full of the hens' prolific efforts.

'Fine,' I snapped once more.

'To the omelettes or to having Saffron here?' Laurie glanced over his shoulder at me while I continued to scowl at his back.

'Both,' I snapped. 'Let's meet her and see what she wants to do. But I'm telling you now, she won't want to come, and if she does, you, Laurie, can clear up after her, cook for her and wait up for her when she's out on the town and not in by midnight.'

I'd moved unwillingly to Yorkshire, but offset that by telling myself at least I'd be able to see Sylvia Plath's grave, be in the same town as the Poet Laureate and cross off a visit to Emily Brontë and her sisters' home over in Haworth from my bucket list.

It appeared instead of the promise of *Wuthering Heights*, it was *Mothering Heights* heading my way. Quite a different proposition altogether.

I picked up my phone from where I'd abandoned it earlier that afternoon once Rita, Cheryl and Janice had finally left and gone their different ways home. There was one voicemail and, as I dried my hands and moved to pick it up, I prayed it might be from Mum telling me to abandon ship regardless and get myself, George and the dog back down south pronto. It wasn't Mum – who had, I remembered, absolutely no knowledge of Sausage and who was, at this moment, more than likely wrapped around her new man on the sofa, drinking her favourite tipple of Cointreau on ice.

No, it wasn't Mum, but Janice who obviously thought it hugely funny to ring and leave the following message:

Jen, just to let you and that silly sod of a brother of mine know: those are *not* llamas in the back field. They're alpacas…

This, followed by hoots of hysterical laughter.

22

Monday morning, the first week in May, and with it came not only spring sunshine dappling the yard and the fields, but a determination to stop being a miserable spoiled brat and get on with my new life. Whatever it had thrown at me so far, and possibly what surprises it still had in store, it wasn't going to last forever.

The main thing, I continued to lecture myself, as I pulled the car back into the yard after dropping George off at school and vocalising aloud what was in the black credit column of my new life, was that my two children were *happy* – George much more so than when we lived in St Albans. And there were *billions* of people in this world who would kill for these four walls and a roof over their heads. I did a quick survey of the house, outbuildings and surrounding fields as I got out of the car, waiting for Sausage to take a momentous flying leap from the car. We had running water, a – sometimes malevolent – Aga to keep us warm, food in the fridge and a Belfast sink in which to wash – and break – the dishes.

Laurie was out in the yard, sorting feed and water for the llamas – sorry, the alpacas. The rather lovely notion of Laurie mucking in and getting on with his new life as an alpaca farmer was spoiled somewhat by his being attired in a black pinstriped suit, red tie and black polished brogues.

'So, is this what farmers round here wear then?' I asked, limping after Sausage who was bravely wandering off to investigate Polonius once more. A deep rumbling growl from the latter had the puppy skittering back towards me and safety.

'You wouldn't finish off here for me, would you, Jen? Been waiting for you to come back with the car so I could get off.'

'Finish off? With this toe? What exactly do I have to do?' I followed Laurie slowly, hobbling down to the field.

'Just take the hosepipe and fill their trough with water; they don't half seem to drink a lot...'

'Obviously take after you,' I sniffed, remembering the empty bottle of Southern Comfort. Oh, hang on, that was me, wasn't it? 'So where are you going, all dressed up?'

'To see the bank manager down in Midhope. Things aren't good, Jen.'

'I could have told you that,' I sighed. 'And don't tell me what you paid for those three...' I nodded towards the alpacas, who all stared back somewhat rudely, '... I really don't want to know.'

'And then,' Laurie went on, ignoring any mention of his spending, 'I'm going back over to Manchester. Gillian just rang. Wants me to get over to MediaCityUK in Trafford where they film *The Street*. The producer is really interested, apparently.'

'Well hallelujah and praise the lord for that.'

Sausage and I spent a good hour down on the back field with the alpacas. They were quite different from the llamas

I'd seen when walking over to Rita's place. In fact, they were really quite lovely. Smaller on the whole than their cousin, the llama, these three had rather pretty short faces with spear-shaped ears and a short triangular muzzle. All three apparently girls, George had named them Elsie, Heidi and Rosamund, for no other reason than he liked these names, he explained. Having previously been in an all-boys' school, George was loving having little girls as classmates and I reckoned, if I were to ask Cassie, there would be the same named girls in Year 3.

Once Janice had broken the – hilarious – news that we'd bought dud llamas and they were, in effect, alpacas, I'd done a bit of Googling on the creatures. You know, how to look after them, what they liked to eat. It appeared alpacas were amazingly hardy and rather easy to care for.

I was just contemplating this notion when I realised Sausage had scampered across the field and was now looking up at Elsie. Elsie lowered her head and then lay down, her legs encircling the dog even though I'd read alpacas rarely sit down. By the time I'd warily approached the pair she was making a sort of humming noise and appeared to be soothing Sausage rather than about to eat him. Sausage was quite happy and was actually on the point of falling asleep against Elsie's beautifully warm, hairy legs.

Being a bit of a towny, and not really into any sort of farm animal, it took all my nerve to reach out a hand and gently touch Elsie's forehead. She gazed at me with a mild expression and I realised she was used to being touched and petted. She was really lovely, her intelligent brown eyes weighing me up. Apparently, I passed muster. Heidi and Rosamund looked on benignly through the warm spring sunshine and, as I breathed in the beautifully fresh air devoid of petrol fumes and traffic noise, I knew I was at some sort of crossroads with my life. Did I still love Laurie? I didn't think I did. Could I spend the rest of my life without him? I wasn't totally convinced I couldn't. One can only be knocked down so many times before getting up, facing the world and fighting back.

I bent down to pick up Sausage – he was a baby and needed his morning nap – and, although Elsie hummed a bit louder and a bit longer, she allowed me to take him.

'I'll bring him back,' I smiled at her. 'You can be his nanny. But I'm his mummy.'

Oh, Christ on a bike, what was I doing, talking to a bloody alpaca like some sort of loon? Where was the bookish, animal-avoiding woman I used to be? I smiled at the thought and made my way back to the house for a well-earned strong coffee and a session with Lord Silverton and his sturdy stallion.

I'd got as far as downing half a mug of good strong coffee accompanied by not one, but two remaining KitKats, when my phone rang.

'Hello, Yorkshire neighbour.'

'Gudrun? Oh, I'm so glad you've rung.'

'How you doing?'

'Well, if you'd phoned yesterday, you'd have found me in the depths of despair and about to head back home to Mum.'

'Mum still always there as back-up?' Gudrun laughed, but not unkindly. 'Are you managing to stand on your own two feet at last? How's that feckless excuse for a husband of yours?'

'He's just gone over for an interview, and presumably audition, for a place on *The Street*.'

'Lock up your leading ladies then, if that's the case. He'll be like a fox in a hen coop with all that young totty they've got on there at the moment.'

'What, he'll be biting their heads off?' I said, slightly disgruntled as always when Gudrun was maligning Laurie. Which she invariably did whenever she got the chance. And *totty* for heaven's sake? Good job Holly, Cheryl's daughter, hadn't overheard that little derogatory sexist snippet.

'Yes, before spitting them out and crawling back to you.'

'Thanks, Gudrun.' There was no way I was going to admit to her that not only did Laurie have another daughter just several months older than Ada, but there was a strong possibility she was about to come and live with us.

'So, when can we meet up?' Gudrun asked. 'Do you fancy lunch in York at the weekend?'

'Gosh, yes I do. That would be fabulous. It's fifty minutes on the train from Midhope.'

'Well, you can tell me everything then,' she said. 'Oh, God, I'm late for a meeting. I'll text you where and when, as soon as I've thought where to meet.'

The day seemed to be getting better and better.

I spent the next couple of hours spiriting the headstrong – and impossibly lovely – Magnolia De Courcy down a secret priest passage in readiness for a swift gallop towards the white cliffs of Dover, before smuggling her aboard a ship to France where she was about to spy for the British government. Hang on, did Britain have a government in Regency times?

'Jove's beard,' the captain cried, backing Magnolia against the mast of the ship before pulling at her skirts, 'you are nothing better than an adventuress, my lady; a common whore suited for the best cathouse in Paris. You are but a cocktease, and these whirligigs, straining at my breeches, will soon be pumping their ballast...'

Hmm, was that final sentence a bit much?

I was just contemplating a better synonym for *whirligigs* when Polonius set up a cacophony of barking, accompanied, a few seconds later, by little inoffensive squeaks and woofs from Sausage laid on my feet. A black car had drawn up in the yard where Polonius was now in danger of garrotting himself, so eager was he to get at the newcomers.

I opened the kitchen door and Sausage legged it out, his comical asymmetrical waddle taking him with amazing speed across to Len Barrowclough and the diminutive, dark-haired girl who stood scowling at his side. I'd remembered Jess – *the landlord's black-eyed daughter* – being quite tiny, and her daughter, Saffron – *Laurie's* daughter too, I quickly reminded myself – was no different. I calculated that Sharon Barrowclough, Len's wife, must be the origin of the tiny genes pool because, compared to the quite massive Len, his daughter, and now his granddaughter, were simply tiny.

'Hello, Saffron, how lovely to meet you.' Being the well brought up girl I was, I walked towards the pair of them, hand outstretched. And, let's face it, it wasn't Saffron's fault she was the result of Laurie's inability to stay faithful to me. Should I kiss her? She *was* my step-daughter, for heaven's sake. And no mistaking that she was Ada's sister. No one could ever have denied their common heritage: they'd both inherited dark, curly hair, Rita and Laurie's quite amazing navy blue eyes and Laurie's beautiful dark skin tone. But whereas Ada had taken after my side of the family, being tall and large-breasted, Saffron was definitely Jess's daughter, no more than five foot tall and very slender. I'd bet anything her shoe size was no more than a three, so at least she wouldn't be up for nicking my shoes and trainers, which Ada did without compunction.

While we weighed each other up, Saffron totally ignored my welcoming hand and eventually, somewhat embarrassed, I pretended to scratch my nose before dropping it back down again. 'I'm afraid your father...' I hesitated and started again, 'I'm afraid Laurie has had to go over to Manchester. I'm really not sure what time he'll be back.'

Saffron shrugged, holding my gaze until I averted my eyes first. 'I'm glad you dropped the "dad" bit,' she eventually said, her accent, despite living back in Yorkshire for well over a year, still heavily Australian. 'My *dad* is in Australia.'

'Of course he is,' I said placatingly. 'I'm sorry.'

'Mind you, bloody waste of space he turned out to be. Buggering off to Sydney with another woman.'

'Alright, Saff, drop it now.' Len patted her arm and then turned to me. 'How about we show her where she'd be sleeping?'

Oh Jesus. I'd been so wrapped up in Magnolia and randy Captain Bligh (I'd not yet come up with a proper handle for the whirligig-whirling sea farer) as well as never actually believing Saffron would want to move in with us, I'd not done anything to prepare the tiny spare room for a new guest.

'Well,' Saffron sneered as she took one look at the untidy box room, still full of tottering piles of our empty cases and unpacked boxes, before turning and leaving it. 'I can see you've really gone out of your way to make me feel at home. Come on Grandad, let's go.'

'Hang on, love.' Len Barrowclough's huge bulk just about filled the tiny room. 'I know Jennifer here, and your dad – Laurence – are really happy to have you here.'

You know more than me then, I almost said. Laurie's daughter was a feisty little firecracker who was making it plain she didn't want to be here, any more, let's be honest, than I did.

'Look, love,' Len went on, taking Saffron's arm. 'You either come with us to Benidorm, go back to Australia to be with your mum or stay here with Laurence and Jennifer. Your gran and I can't get on that plane next week if we don't know you're settled somewhere nice. We've told you, right fair, we're not paying for you to be in a flat somewhere. You're not seventeen yet, and your gran would worry herself daft if she thought you were living by yourself in a bedsit. And anyhow, we can't afford it. All our savings have gone on this new place in Spain. Now, come on, we've been through all this, umpteen times. It'll just be for a year or so until you're eighteen...'

Len broke off as the sound of the kitchen door opening and banging came up the stairs, before George himself bounded up them, appearing at the top looking for Sausage. Rita liked to pick George up from school once or twice a week, and I'd gratefully accepted, knowing I could carry on writing for another good hour or so without breaking off. George stopped and stared in some confusion.

'I thought it was Ada,' he said finally, continuing to gaze at Saffron.

'This is Saffron, George. She's your... half-sister...' Oh hell, how did I explain to a nearly-eight-year-old just what his dad had been up to seventeen years previously? 'Saffron,' I went on, as George bent to pick up Sausage and Rita appeared on the landing, 'is Daddy's daughter. Just like Daddy is your daddy and Ada's daddy, Daddy is Saffron's daddy too.' Oh, bloody hell. Clear or what?

'Is she coming to live with us?' George asked, never once taking his eyes off Saffron.

'Yes,' Len and Rita spoke as one.

'No,' Saffron snapped.

I said nothing.

'Because if she *is*,' George went on, 'she's a *girl*, and girls need big bedrooms for all their clothes and makeup and stuff. So, if she is coming to live here, she can have my bedroom and Sausage and me can have the box room. Do you want to come and look at my room, Saffron?'

'Oh, Jesus.' Saffron tutted in exasperation, glaring first at Len and then at Rita who, apart from uttering the one word of encouragement in agreeing with Len, hadn't said another thing but simply continued to stare at the girl. Saffron tutted again, giving me, this time, the full extent of her displeasure but nevertheless following George and Sausage across the landing to his bedroom.

Len, Rita and I stood for the next five minutes until it became ten and the trio of George, Saffron and Sausage still hadn't come back to the box room.

'Do you think this is positive?' Len asked hopefully. 'I'm at my absolute wits' end. Sharon won't get on that plane unless she knows Saff has agreed to stay with you…'

He broke off as the three of them reappeared, Saffron now holding Sausage with a smiling George in tow. 'You've got alpacas?' she said, addressing me.

'We have. We actually thought they were llamas…'

'Did you? Why? I really like alpacas. We had a couple of roos just outside our backyard in Canberra.' Not waiting for any further response, Saffron turned to Len. 'OK, you win. I'll give it a go. But I'm not going to be treated like a kid here. I'm nearly seventeen and don't want to be stopped doing what I want to do. If I don't like it here, I'm off.' She frowned, and I could see she was already having second thoughts. 'I might not like this Laurence dude either, who's suddenly supposed to be my dad…'

'I'm sure you will, Saffron.' Rita smiled. 'He's your new father and I'm your new granny…'

Oh, for heaven's sake.

'Yes, but he's famous, isn't he? I bet he's full of himself? And how come he's living in this…' Saffron's eyes roamed the box room and then went across to the window where the rusting red tractor – unloved except when Janice deigned to put it through its paces – could just be seen, and I knew she'd been going to say *dump*. Jess and Len must have taught her some manners because, instead, she said '…place.' She stared at me before adding, 'Mum and me used to watch *A Better Life* together all the time in Canberra. It was our favourite programme because she said she used to go to school with him.' Saffron's eyes narrowed. 'I can't believe, all the years we used to watch it, she *knew* he was my real father and yet she never once let on. Not until she found out Dad was having it off with the woman from the chemist. He was always letting on he was feeling a bit crook just so's he could go down there to get something from her.'

There didn't seem to be much any of us could reply to that until Rita, who seemed unable to take her eyes from the glowering Saffron, eventually gave a little sigh and said, 'Goodness, you are the very spit of your father. Welcome, Saffron, welcome to your new family.'

23

Laurie didn't arrive back from Manchester until much later that evening. He was over-the-top cock-a-hoop, brandishing a bottle of fizz he'd apparently stopped off to purchase in the village.

'Don't look at me like that,' Laurie grinned, 'It's only the Co-op's cheap Prosecco, not Veuve Clicquot. More's the pity.'

'You got it?' I held my breath.

'Yep. You're now looking at Dr Christian Lund, new GP at The Street's health centre.'

'Well done.' Oh, thank the lord for that, we'd have some income coming in apart from mine. I might yet be able to go back home and rent somewhere for George, Ada and myself. 'Is it permanent?'

'As permanent as it can be. Of course, they wanted a BAME female doctor really, but Gillian persuaded them that my fans have been just *waiting* for the first opportunity to follow me from *A Better Life* – which apparently, I'm delighted to say, is going right down the toilet since I was kicked out – and my presence can only improve the ratings of *The Street*.' Laurie popped the cork from the Prosecco and poured the foaming liquid into two glasses. 'God, that's rough,' Laurie pulled a face. 'But don't worry, we'll soon be hitting the big time and have some decent stuff in the fridge once again.'

I stared at him. Had Laurie learnt nothing?

'And the brilliant thing about working for ITV rather than the BBC is that I'll be permitted to do more extracurricular stuff. The Beeb was always stuffy about their soap stars exploiting their onscreen persona, and I was constantly on a knife edge seeking permission to be the Face of Michaud Saint-Jean. I was never allowed to do TV advertising while working for the BBC, but now I'll be able to do just that – as well as all the magazine stuff...'

'I hate to remind you, Laurie, but you're no longer the face of Michaud Saint-Jean.'

'Oh, they'll have me back. They'll come begging, just you see. I'll be allowed to do voiceovers and personal appearances now and even the odd panto.' Laurie laughed out loud at that. 'Not that you'd ever get *me* doing Widow Wanky,' he guffawed.

Was there no end to the man's ego?

'Saffron Danvers has been here this afternoon,' I said.

'Who?' There was a pause. 'Oh, Jess's daughter?'

'Your daughter, Laurie. *Your* daughter as well.'

'Great. And?' Laurie had caught his reflection in Rita's mirror above the purple gas fire and I knew he was already trying out possible facial expressions for his new persona, Dr Christian Lund. Laurie sat down at the kitchen table, leaning back slightly and steepling his hands together as though listening to a patient across from him, rather than me telling him about Saffron.

'She's agreed to come and stay with us,' I said.

'Good, good, that's good.' Laurie moved his fingers to his lips as if to concentrate further. 'Tell me more.'

'For God's sake, Laurie, you're not this bloody doctor yet. Will you listen? *I've* had to agree to it as well as Saffron. *You* should have been here.'

'But Len didn't say he was bringing her round *today*, did he?' Laurie affected a hurt expression.

'No.' I had to concede the point.

'Well, there you go then. So, what's she like then, this new daughter of mine?'

'Angry, headstrong, obviously feels let down by the adults in her life. You can certainly see she's Ada's sister. And your daughter. And, from the way your mother was drinking her in, she presumably saw some resemblance to your biological father.'

Laurie raised an eyebrow at that, but made no relevant comment. 'So, when's she moving in?'

'In a couple of days. But don't be surprised if she moves out again. She doesn't really want to be here with us. I get the impression there's maybe a boy here she doesn't want to leave.'

'Right, well who can blame her if she's in love?' Laurie, I could tell, had already moved on and wasn't really listening, so wrapped up was he in his new role.

'Len says he can send over a single bed for the box room.'

'Good, good.'

'George has given up his own bed and bedroom for Saffron.'

'Good. Well, that's kind of him.'

'Laurie, are you listening to anything I'm saying?'

'Of course. Let's give it a few weeks and see if there's

some improvement.' Laurie nodded his head benignly in my direction. It wouldn't have surprised me if he'd started writing out a prescription.

'I'm telling you now, Laurie, I've work to do...'

'As have I.'

'And I can't be spending all my time and energy looking after this girl.'

'You would have done if Ada had come up here with us.'

'Ada's my *daughter*,' I hissed.

'Absolutely,' Laurie continued. 'As Saffron is too – well, your step-daughter. We need to open up our hearts and welcome her in.' Oh God, what role was Laurie playing now? He was beginning to sound like the Archbishop of sodding Canterbury.

'Right. Well tomorrow, *you* sort out the box room for George, shift his stuff and clean his room in readiness for Saffron. And then I suggest you go down to see Len and Sharon and actually meet your daughter. And while you're at it, go and do a huge supermarket shop. Teenage girls are either notoriously hungry or notoriously faddy.'

I spent the next few days chained to the kitchen table, my mornings taken up with editing manuscripts for my current authors at Wesley and Brown and then, after a short walk with Sausage around the fields and our daily visit to the alpacas, I turned back to Magnolia. Every afternoon, as soon as I dared relinquish my real, paid work, I got stuck into her, thrashing out page after page of her story like a woman possessed. Never having written a novel before, I'd no idea if what I'd created was any good. Most of my commissioning work at Wesley and Brown was concentrated on fairly heavy-going, non-fiction literary tomes – and I was having difficulty in being self-critical enough to know if Magnolia was at least readable. Once I'd fed George, dealt with any homework he might have and tucked him and Sausage up in the newly-restored box room, I'd spend my evenings immersed in any new work that had been sent to me, accepting or rejecting manuscripts in the manner of all good commissioning editors.

Laurie had been over with Rita to the tiny cottage in Mirfield – where Len, Sharon and Saffron Barrowclough had been staying ever since leaving The Jolly Sailor – in order to meet and get to know Saffron before she moved in with us the following weekend. That job apparently ticked off on his to-do list, he'd then felt able to immerse himself fully in his new character. '*I am a method actor, Jennifer*,' he constantly informed me, assuming a pair of black tortoiseshell glasses and a stethoscope he'd acquired from somewhere, slung casually around his neck. As long as he didn't want to be examining *my* chest, I let him get on with it. For the first time since I'd clapped eyes on him below my window at Cambridge, I realised I was feeling no physical desire whatsoever for Laurie. I actually sat one evening across from him while he watched TV, surreptitiously watching him while I pretended to read, trying to conjure up some feelings of lust, of desire, but it was a bit like looking at the pretty lid on a virtually empty chocolate box. Yes, on the surface all was lovely and full of promise but, delve deeper, go inside, and disappointingly there wasn't much left to write home about. What was that old saying of Aunt Agnes? *To thine own self be true.*

That was it. I knew Laurie had fallen in love with me in Cambridge, just as I had with him, but, while my love for him had only deepened as we'd had the children and set up home together, I now had to finally admit to myself that the past few years for Laurie had possibly been just another part to play. To act out. Maybe I'd been acting out my own part as well? You know, desperate to maintain the happy-ever-after marriage, perhaps I was blinded to what was real. And what no longer was. It made me very sad.

There was one commissioning editor, Catherine Barker, with whom I was friendly at a large established publisher – Alcidae House – across the road from Wesley and Brown, who I not only liked enormously, but knew would give me a fair assessment of Magnolia's antics. I spent a morning editing the chapters I'd written, wrote a fairly short synopsis and, before I changed my mind, emailed everything to Catherine. I had considered sending it to her under an assumed name, in order to lay it at her door from the usual level playing field as it were, but then accepted I probably needed all the help I could get to have it off the publishers' slush pile and into Catherine's hand itself.

She emailed me back immediately:

Woah, Jennifer Baylis-Lewis! Fancy you writing a Regency novel. Can't wait to get stuck into this one. Will get back to you asap. Hope all well up there with you in the north. Miss our coffee and chats in Tomtom's…

24

I spent the Friday before Saffron was due to move in, as well as my lunch date with Gudrun in York, blasting the house, not only because it needed a damned good bottoming (I was starting to get on board with Yorkshire parlance) and not only because it appeared I'd inherited my mother's inability to have guests without cleaning the house first (but *was* Saffron a guest? Or family? Or just a damned nuisance I really didn't want? Or all those things?) but also because I wanted to check out the durability of my stubbed toe. The bruising had gone down considerably but I wanted to see how it was bearing up, if, as I'd promised myself, I was going to really get into walking the countryside round Daisy Royd.

It was mid-May, and spring had totally sprung. I spent the whole morning with the doors and windows open to the warm sunshine, shaking rugs and throwing soapy water across the yard like Snow White on speed. And, all the time, I was creating conversations between Magnolia and various new characters I was conjuring up as I scrubbed; I was contemplating bringing in King George but thought, possibly, this might be a bit of madness.

Laughing to myself at my own little joke, I hunted for my

phone, which had just started ringing from under a pile of dusters and polish.

'Jennifer? It's Cassie Beresford.'

'Is George alright?' Helicopter mother immediately hovering into action once again.

'Absolutely. The last time I looked he was covered in paint and some sort of glue, but was giving a rather informative talk on alpacas to the rest of the kids in assembly.'

'Really?' Goodness, where was that shy, nervous, stammering child who'd burst into tears at the drop of a hat when asked to do anything that put him out of his comfort zone?

'Really.' Cassie laughed. 'We breed 'em tough up here.' She laughed again. 'No, it was you, I wanted. Clare – who you met at dinner the other week – has a hen party business...'

'Yes, she told me all about it. *Henotheism*, isn't it?'

'That's right, well remembered. She'd organised a trip to York Races tomorrow but the poor bride-to-be has gone down with glandular fever. Anyway, she's obviously got a number of tickets going free and decided we might as well make use of them ourselves. She asked if you'd like to join us? Should be a good do as they're corporate tickets – everything thrown in, as it were.'

'That sounds absolutely wonderful. How lovely. That is so kind... Oh hell, I can't, I've arranged to meet my friend from university for lunch. Funnily enough, also in York.'

'Well, change your lunch date and *both* of you come with us. I know Clare has more than enough tickets. Give you a chance to get to know us more. And realise we're not *always* half-cut on moonshine gin. God, I *was*, wasn't I? And how awful not to recognise the famous Laurie Lewis. Hell.'

I laughed at her embarrassment. 'Really? It's OK to bring Gudrun along?'

'Of course. Is it something your friend would like, do you think?'

'Do you know, I've no idea, but I don't see why not.'

Because Laurie had taken the car over to Manchester, Rita had promised to pick up George from school at 3.30. Giving my toe an experimental wiggle and finding it hugely improved, I found my trainers and made the decision to walk the five miles down to Little Acorns school and meet up with both Rita and George there before hitching a lift back to Daisy Royd with them. Most of it being downhill, I reckoned it would take me a good hour and three-quarters to cover the distance and set off, at a cracking pace, in the warm sunshine, sometimes following the road and, at other times, crossing fields and climbing the stiles I was now beginning to recognise.

By the time I reached the centre of the village, congratulating myself on not only the good time I'd made, but also on actually finding my way there, I was ready to murder a cold lager. Was it the done thing for a playground mum – and new to the area – to call in at The Jolly Sailor for a pint before walking across the village green to the school? As I skirted the perimeter of the pub heading, instead, for the post office and an ice-cold Coke, I found myself remembering my very first visit there with Laurie when he'd said he never wanted to be without me.

I was roused somewhat rudely from this bitter-sweet recollection by the sounds of shouting, doors banging and glass breaking. Two men were involved in a ferocious row, arguing, pushing each other, grabbing at the other's clothes and swearing volubly and profusely. The larger of the two had the smaller up against the wall of the pub, pinning his arms behind his back and then, when the other kicked out against this restraint, holding him in a headlock which, as the smaller man struggled further, had them both on the hard gravel, rolling over and over each other like something from an action film. Eventually the bigger, and obviously stronger, man had the upper hand once more, standing up, grabbing at the other's shirt collar and shaking him like a dog.

'Stop it,' I yelled furiously at the larger man over the hedge of the beer garden. 'What on earth is the matter with you? Pick on somebody your own size.' When the larger man ignored me, but carried on trying to manhandle the smaller, I shouted: 'Right, that's it – I'm calling 999,' searching every pocket for my phone which, as usual, it appeared, I'd left on the kitchen table.

'No, NO! Do NOT do that!' Momentarily distracted, the larger man turned towards me and, as he did so, the smaller man swung an arm. His aim was true, smashing a fist into both the man's right eye and nose. The larger man stumbled backwards onto the ground once more, blood spurting from his nose and giving the smaller man the chance to leg it, which he did through the car park and disappearing up the lane.

'You were assaulting him,' I yelled. 'ABH... GBH even... and you started it.' I broke off as the man attempted to stand while mopping at his face with his shirtsleeve.

'Mind your own sodding business,' the man spat, just

loud enough for me to hear, before turning and limping back into the pub.

The man, I could now see, was Tod Mayhew.

Rather than travel with Cassie, Clare and Fi on the late-morning train to York, I'd arranged to meet Gudrun – who was totally up for a day at the races – much earlier so we could have a coffee and a proper catch up before joining the others at the racecourse. It had seemed ages since I'd been with her and had a really good chat.

'Hey, you're looking good.' Gudrun was already sat out on the terrace of the Refectory Kitchen and Terrace near York station and immediately stood to give me a hug as I approached her.

'Cheap mobile hairdresser,' I laughed. 'Best cut and colour I've ever had.'

'Give me her number,' Gudrun smiled, running a hand through her short, un-styled hair. 'So, how's it going? How're you finding being a farmer's wife now you've had two months of it?'

'Hardly a farm,' I raised an eyebrow. 'Mind you, we have got a new sausage dog and three new alpacas.' I paused, not looking at Gudrun. 'Oh, and a new daughter moving in.'

'Ada's moving up after all?' Gudrun frowned. 'In the middle of her GCSEs? How come?'

'Not Ada.'

'You're pregnant?' Gudrun looked horrified.

'Oh, for heaven's sake, Gudrun.' I couldn't quite meet her eye. 'Pour me some of that champagne and…' I stopped stock-still '… Oh, Gudrun, it's your birthday, isn't it? Hence the champers? How *could* I have forgotten?' I pulled a face. 'I've *never* forgotten before.'

'Sounds like you've other things on your mind,' Gudrun said mildly, pouring me a glass. 'Anyway, I thought it was *de rigueur* to quaff this stuff when going to the races? Right, get that down your neck and tell all.' She paused again and grinned. 'And to be honest, you *were* second choice of who I was going to be spending my birthday with.'

'Oh, thanks for that. That makes me feel doubly bad. OK, who is he?'

Gudrun didn't quite meet my eye but, instead, reached for her sunglasses against the bright – and becoming steadily warmer – May sunshine before taking a sip from her champagne flute. 'You first. This daughter you appear to have acquired?'

'Laurie has another daughter. He's – we've – only just found out.'

'Is that supposed to make it all alright? How old is she?'

'About nine months older than Ada.'

'So conceived, presumably, when the pair of you were living in the flat in Clapham?'

I nodded before draining my glass and telling Gudrun the whole story as far as I knew it.

'I always knew you were slightly mad, Jen,' she retorted once she'd sat and been brought up to date, 'but now I know you're totally bonkers.'

'Oh, shut up, Gudrun. Please.' I was cross. 'At the moment, if I could be back at home with Mum and Ada, I would be. It's just not happening this minute.'

Gudrun wasn't taking any prisoners. 'You know, Jen, infidelity is such a serious breach of trust in a relationship, and continuing to condone it as you appear to be doing by accepting this Saffron girl, cannot be good for your mental health… And why,' Gudrun went on crossly, '*why* the hell you've followed him up here after the revelations that came out in that court case back in November is beyond me.'

'I didn't *follow* him, Gudrun. I *came* with him. I wanted to mend my marriage, didn't want to give up on it. I had to think of George; he was going through a bad time at school, wetting the bed once again, his stammer back…'

Gudrun tutted crossly. 'And bringing him up to Yorkshire away from Ada, with all the upheaval of a new home, a new school and now a new half-sister has stopped all that, has it?'

'Well actually yes. I've never seen George so happy.'

'And Ada?'

'Loving her life living part-time with her friend Lydia, and the long weekends with Mum.' I paused. 'She wants to be an actor.'

'Oh heavens. History repeating itself.'

'More than you know.'

'What do you mean?'

I put down my glass and closed my own eyes against the bright sunshine that was glancing off the metal tables and glassware and proceeded to tell Gudrun about Laurie's biological father.

'Ingrained then, all this adultery. George won't stand a chance.'

I smiled at that. 'I've already been thrown over *twice* by George. He's totally in love with his teacher, Mrs Stevens, and he gave up his bedroom for Saffron after five minutes of meeting her.'

'Your genes there, Jen. Too soft for words. And you?'

'Me?'

'I can't imagine *you're* as happy as your kids appear to be.'

'I have a certain acceptance of my life in Westenbury after two months of living it, up here. Laurie actually got the job on *The Street*…'

'Heaven help them.'

'… and once he's established there and has an income coming in again, I *will* go back to Berkshire with George and rent somewhere. I promise.'

'You don't have to promise *me* anything, Jennifer,' Gudrun said gently. 'It's yourself you have to promise. And, you know, *I'm* always here for you.'

I felt a tear threaten. Obviously, the effect of the champagne. 'Thanks, Gudrun. So, come on then, who were you *meant* to be spending your birthday with?'

Gudrun hesitated. 'Sam.'

'Sam? Ooh, tell all?'

'Sam's the chief executive officer at the hospital…'

'Ooh, good one. And?'

'And, for the very first time in my life – sorry the second – I'm totally in love.'

'You're hesitating?' I sensed there was something she wasn't telling me. 'Oh, Gudrun, he's not married, is he? Is that why he can't be with you on your birthday?'

Gudrun smiled. 'Oh, you're such a little innocent, aren't you, Jennifer? Sam is Samantha; we've been together six months. Unfortunately, she's been away for two weeks, speaking at a series of medical conferences in South Africa, and that's why you're second best and…' here Gudrun went slightly pink, '... and I asked her to marry me before she flew to Durban and, amazingly, she said yes.'

'Oh... Oh...'

Gudrun laughed. 'Close your mouth, Jen, there're a lot of flies about. You *must* have known, you *know*...'

'Well, no, to be honest. I just assumed you hadn't met the one.' I frowned. 'And you say you were in love with someone else? Before? Why didn't you ever tell me about this previous love of your life?'

'As I *said*, Jennifer...' Gudrun looked at me directly, laughing and shaking her head slightly, 'you always *were* such an innocent. Now, will you be my bridesmaid on the big day?'

25

'Jennifer? Over here, Jennifer.' Cassie Beresford beckoned Gudrun and me over to where she, Clare and Fiona were already ensconced in the County Stand. 'Isn't this lovely?' she went on. 'We've got the best tickets and the best view from here. And soon, we're going into the Melrose Club Lounge for lunch. Hope you're hungry – the food in there is supposed to be wonderful.'

'This is Gudrun, my friend from university.' I smiled, feeling something akin to happiness for the first time in months in that, not only was I with Gudrun, but in the company of these three new women friends as well. 'She's a consultant neurologist at Leeds General,' I added, proud to be introducing such an upmarket companion to the little group.

'Right,' Fi said, shaking Gudrun's hand. 'You must know my cousin's husband, Gerald? Specialist in the cardiac unit over there?'

'Oh, *Gerry and the Pacemakers*?' Gudrun laughed along with Fi. 'I know him well, he's a good friend of mine.'

'So, I'll talk to you later about my many ailments, Gudrun, if I may,' Fi grinned. 'Until then, we're already stuck into the champagne.'

'Not me,' said Clare, holding up her glass of mineral water.

'Or me,' said Cassie. 'I swore off all alcohol for ever the other night.'

'Just you, me and Gudrun then.' Fiona grinned, pouring out three full glasses of the stuff before upending the empty bottle in the ice bucket on the table in front of her. 'Now, I accept Clare, as a mum-to-be, has an excuse not to drink, as has Cassandra here as Westenbury's Drunk of the Week, but you, Jennifer, did not have a drink the other night... You're not driving, are you? No? Good. OK, bottoms up then, and lots of luck on the gee-gees.'

Gudrun and Clare were soon engrossed in conversation about a mutual colleague of Gudrun's and Clare's husband, Rageh, a paediatrician in Sheffield, and Cassie, Fi and I wandered over to the front of the stand to watch owners, trainers and jockeys assembling on the pre-parade ring in front of us.

'We always try to get over to York at least a couple of times in the season,' Fi said. 'Never been to First Saturday before, though. This is always special apparently, being the first of its eighteen-day season. The total prize money today is over £225,000 for the seven-race card, and there's a brand-new feature race worth £90,000.'

'What, we can win all that? A bit like the Lottery?' Was this going to be the answer to my financial prayers? Should I stick the fiver I'd allowed myself to gamble and hope to win nearly a quarter of a million pounds? I could be back in Berkshire this time next week.

'No, you daft thing.' Fiona laughed. 'I guess you'd have to stick thousands on the one with the lowest odds and hope it came in first in order to win that sort of money. No, the big bucks are won by the horse owners themselves, although I suppose the jockeys, especially if you're famous like Frankie Dettori, will get some of that. Dermot O'Callaghan who trains horses at Tod Mayhew's yard once explained it all to me.'

'Oh, Dermot O'Callaghan? We've just inherited one of his puppies. Or at least George, my son, has.'

'A Dachshund?'

I nodded. 'Sausage,' I grinned apologetically.

'Original,' Fiona laughed. 'Dermot's always bred Dachshunds for some reason. Look, there he is now.' Fiona pointed across to where a small, dark-haired man was running over to a beautiful black horse whose jockey appeared to be having some trouble controlling his mount. 'Gosh, look at that. *He* obviously knows what he's doing.'

'Who, Dermot?'

'No, Tod Mayhew. *He's* attempting to take charge now. Must be one of the horses he trains. Here,' Fiona handed me her binoculars and I raised them to watch what was going on over in the pre-parade ring.

I continued to watch the black horse stepping sideways as if intent on learning some intricate new dance step, tossing its head and prancing wildly, refusing to behave for either the yellow silk-attired jockey or Dermot O'Callaghan who had the horse's head. Tod, however, appeared to be having some success in calming the nervous animal. I narrowed my eyes, wondering whether to give an account to Fiona of the totally different Tod Mayhew I'd seen fighting in the Jolly Sailor beer garden the day before. I decided against it.

'Blimey, you can see all the horse's five legs really going for it,' Fiona said, wide-eyed.

'It's a horse with five legs? Bit of an advantage that, isn't it? You know, an extra leg?' I stared at Fi.

'A racehorse's tail is acknowledged as its fifth leg,' Cassie said knowledgably, laughing at my face. 'Oh, look he's off again. If they can't get the horse into the stalls, they're snookered. The owner's looking a bit worried.'

'So, does Tod own them all?' I asked.

'No, no, of course not. Tod just stables and trains them,' Cassie explained. 'Got quite a reputation…'

'A reputation?' I lowered the binoculars and stared at Cassie before lowering my voice. 'For what? For being drunk and fighting?'

'Drunk? Fighting?' Cassie stared back and frowned. 'Tod's got a bit of a temper – hates litter louts and day trippers who let their dogs off the lead in the sheep. But fighting…?' Cassie turned back to the crowd. 'The actual owner's down there, see? Dressed in a suit with a yellow tie and cravat the same colour as the jockey's shirt?'

'Tod's a bit of a horse-whisperer by all accounts,' Fiona said in obvious admiration. 'Gosh look at that, he's brought the horse to heel…'

'Can you bring a horse *to heel*?' I laughed, thinking of the training George was doing with Sausage.

'Tod Mayhew appears to be able to.' Fiona glanced my way. 'What did you think of him? You know, the other night at Cassie's place?'

'Not much, really. I don't think he said a civil word to me. In fact, I think he's arrogant and foul-tempered.'

'Foul-tempered? Tod? No.' Fiona shook her head. 'He

can be a bit surly if he's that way out.' She grinned. 'But I don't think there's any horse – or woman, come to that – what do you reckon, Cassie?' Fi laughed loudly '… who wouldn't like the chance to have Tod Mayhew's hands on them. There you go, brought to heel; quiet as a mouse. Look at that.'

I continued to direct the binoculars onto Tod Mayhew, whose dark blond hair was escaping from some sort of trilby hat.

'Why's he wearing a trilby?' I asked, passing back the binoculars somewhat reluctantly. 'I remember my Great-Uncle Arthur always wearing one whenever he went out.'

'I think Tod's is more of a fedora,' Fi frowned. 'It's the thing to wear for horse trainers at the races, apparently,' she added sagely. 'You know, together with the three-piece loud tweedy suit – it distinguishes them from the owners and other staff down there.' She sighed. 'Whatever hat it is, he looks bloody good in it, don't you think?'

'Come on, let's go for lunch.' Clare and Gudrun joined us, before I could agree with Fi that, yes, Tod Mayhew looked bloody good in it, only just acknowledging, even to myself, that since first setting eyes on the man a couple of weeks earlier, my thoughts had returned again and again to him. But now, not in a good way after yesterday's little performance in the Jolly Sailor. 'And if I don't have a wee soon,' Clare went on, 'I'm in danger of wet pants. You never warned me of this constant need to pee, you two.' Clare tucked a hand into one each of Cassie and Fiona's arms and went ahead of us down to the Melrose Club Lounge, Gudrun and I bringing up the rear.

★

'Blimey,' Fiona breathed. 'BTF.'

'BTF?' I laughed as Fi smiled in contentment over the remains of lunch, folding her napkin neatly and replacing it on the table.

'Bottom Teeth Floating,' she grinned, loosening the pink leather belt on her pretty pink and yellow floral dress. 'Full to the top. Gorgeous lunch, Clare. Obviously put a few pounds on as well since I wore this frock last summer. Hang on, I'll have to take this bloody fascinator thing off as well.' She reached up to remove the bit of pink froth from her dark hair. 'What is the point of these things? Will somebody explain it to me?'

We'd just demolished an array of canapes including a York Racecourse special of apple and lardo black pudding, followed by a totally delicious selection of both cold and hot tapas. There'd been Yorkshire-ale-battered fish and chips ('no mushy peas?' I'd laughingly asked) and a pulled shoulder ('whose shoulder? Fi had frowned. 'I pulled mine badly last year trying to stand on my head and have every sympathy for whoever's we're now scoffing') accompanied by an apple compote and mini wedges. This was followed by a choice of a strawberry and cream meringue nest or a dark chocolate orange pot. Unable to make that choice, we all ended up having both, Fiona encouraging Clare to 'eat for two', Gudrun because she deserved 'birthday treats' and myself who 'obviously needs fattening up a bit'.

I was delighted that Gudrun seemed to be really enjoying herself. Not always the easiest person to get along with, she appeared relaxed and happy in the company of these three lovely new friends who had welcomed both of us in, but particularly Clare with whom she'd never stopped talking. I caught bits of their conversation, and it was mainly about the medical profession, but also centred on women having their first child in their early to mid-forties. It suddenly occurred to me that Gudrun was quite possibly considering a baby herself. I did hope so.

'Now, don't forget you have afternoon tea as well to get through in a couple of hours,' Clare warned us, as though she were ticking off one of the twelve tasks of Hercules. 'I think we ought to wander and do what we came for.'

'What's that? Drink more champagne?' Cassie looked slightly worried.

'No, a bet on the horses.' Clare grinned. 'Come on, you can't come to the races without a bit of a flutter.'

I did hope the others weren't about to flutter hundreds of pounds on the donkeys. My two five-pound notes were going to be a bit on their lonesome if that were the case.

'Now, I promised Matt I wouldn't throw more than £20 of the housekeeping on the horses,' Fi said, 'so I won't spend more than £40. That's probably a good compromise.'

'It's my birthday, so I'm allowed to spend £50,' Gudrun laughed. 'My mum sent me a £20 note with my card – she's been doing that since I was fifteen – so I'm going to include that.'

'Cassie and I are spending £25 each,' Clare said. 'We've made a deal to stop each other spending any more than that. Right come on, let's go and look at the bookies' stands and see which are the favourites and which we should be avoiding.'

'What's he doing?' I asked Clare, pointing to a man who, with a gathered crowd around him, was doing all sorts of tapping on his fingers and arms. 'Some sort of sign language for the deaf?'

'The tic-tac guy,' Clare explained. 'When I first started organising stag parties at the races, years ago, there were lots of them standing here giving out the constantly changing odds. It's a dying art unfortunately, everything's computerised now.' She pointed to the myriad bookmakers' stands, with their brightly coloured LED-lit charts of horses' names and the accompanying racing odds.

For the next hour or so, I just watched, trying to work it all out, trying to decide where to place a bet with my £10. Fiona was whooping with joy, having won £50, Cassie had spent up and lost the lot, but both Gudrun and Clare had done some homework and were also in the black.

'Come on, Jen, make a decision.'

'Oh, I can't, I mean I really like this one's name – Poetry Pie – but I don't know if it's any good. Shall I put £5 on one horse and £5 on another or blow the whole tenner on a rank outsider?'

'Rank outsider? Hey, Jen, you're getting the hang of it.' The others were standing watching, laughing at me and I started to giggle. 'Hell, it's not like I'm gambling my life's savings away, is it?' Little did they know that, apart from my current account used for everyday expenses, I no longer *had* any savings. No, I tell a lie: there was still the money Mum had given me for absolute emergencies, that Laurie knew nothing about.

'Oh, I can't decide. A fiver on *this* and a fiver on *this one*?'

'How about *this one*?' A hand was placed on my arm as I continued to laugh and dither. I turned in surprise to find Tod Mayhew at my side, and my heart gave a little thump as I glared at him. I'd actually finally admitted to myself that I found something quite compelling about the man. That there was something about him I really admired. That I'd begun to weave little fantasies about him. OK, let's admit it, I'd begun to have a bit of a thing about Tod Mayhew. Right up until the previous afternoon when I'd seen him thumping the poor little guy in the pub garden. And now I was embarrassed, cross even, that my little fantasies about this man had turned to dust. I was still, it appeared, a bloody awful judge of character when it came to men. I turned away, unable to meet his eye.

'Blimey, Tod…' Fiona stared and the others turned in his direction. 'Who the hell thumped you?'

'Horse's head came up unexpectedly as I was grooming him and made contact with my nose,' Tod said easily. Too easily. I could feel his gaze on my back as I put all my energy into studying the odds for the next race.

'Thought you hired grooms to do all your dirty work?' Fiona laughed, accepting his explanation without further question.

'We all muck in together.' He smiled down at Fiona and as I turned back towards him, taking in the black eye and swollen nose, I couldn't believe this act he was now assuming of gentle, good humour. He was obviously as good an actor as Laurie, a total Jekyll and Hyde character, because gone were all aspects of the angry man I'd seen pinning the poor little chap up against the pub wall. Tod raised an eyebrow in my direction but his smile was gone.

Clare reached up to give Tod a kiss and stroke his damaged face, frowning in sympathy as he winced slightly. 'Are all your horses done? A good day?'

Tod nodded. 'Not the best, but not the worst. We live to race another day.'

'You OK, Jen?' Gudrun was looking at me strangely.

'Oh, sorry. Gudrun, this is a neighbour of ours, Mr Mayhew. We met at Cassie's house a couple of weeks ago. And,' I added, looking straight at him, 'as well as the day we actually arrived in the village when he wasn't overly sympathetic to poor old George throwing up in his hedge.' I paused. 'And I believe that was you, Mr Mayhew, I saw yesterday?' I turned to the others. 'I think I spotted him as I walked past the Jolly Sailor yesterday afternoon.'

'Tod, please.' Ignoring me, he held out a hand to Gudrun and smiled and was soon engrossed in conversation with the other four about the racecourse here at York, his horses, the trainers, the owners and anything and everything else remotely equine. He eventually turned back, looking down at me from his over six-foot height.

'Made your mind up yet?' Tod stared at me.

'About what?' I stared back and he placed his hand on my arm once more, turning me slightly, back towards the bookmaker's stand to the right. '*Take a Chance on Me*,' he said, nodding towards the board.

'Sounds like something from Abba,' I replied, moving away from him.

'Rank outsider, but there you go. Stick a fiver on that one and a fiver on the favourite, *Harry's Lad*, and you might have a few pennies to take home.'

Because the race was about to start, I reluctantly did as

Tod suggested and we all moved over to watch the trainers and owners giving their jockeys a leg up before the riders cantered down the track to the stalls.

'Come on Jen, they're off.' Gudrun pulled me in front of her, Fi jumping up and down (every now and again landing on my already aching toes in their unaccustomed high heels) and shouting in glee as *Harry's Lad* set off like a bullet, immediately and effortlessly pulling ahead of the other horses. Fi grabbed hold of me and we jumped together like kids in the playground, shouting Harry on to the winning line.

'Oh no, who's that comer-inner on his tail?' Fi stopped jumping and clutched at my hand, disappointed as the horse behind *Harry's Lad* drew level and then nosed forward. The jockey in scarlet and white silks – leaning so far off of his seat the whole vista ahead of him could be seen through his straddled white-clad legs as he raced past us – was urging the interloper on and on and the crowd was cheering and then I couldn't see a thing as people surged forwards.

'Well done.' Tod was back at my side.

'But *Harry's Lad* didn't win, did he?' I didn't understand this racing malarkey one bit.

'No, but *Take A Chance on Me* did. With your fiver on him, you should come out with...' Tod did a quick calculation, '...around £250.'

'*What?* Really?'

'Really.' We just stood there, our eyes locked together until I had to look away. 'Well, thank you,' I manage to eventually get out. 'I feel I should give you half my winnings.'

'You can buy me a drink, next time you – and your

husband, of course…' he trailed off as a cross-looking figure marched through the crowd towards us.

'Come on, Tod, what the hell are you playing at? We're supposed to be at Mummy and Daddy's in an hour's time.' Serena, dressed from head to toe in floaty white linen (for heaven's sake it was only May, not mid-summer, and – now that the afternoon was drawing to a close – quite chilly), looked me up and down, trying, I imagine, to recall where she knew me from. When Clare, Cassie and Fi pushed their way through the crowd, looking for me, the penny must have dropped. 'Ah, Gemma? Lovely to see you again. Where's that ravishing husband of yours?'

'It's Jennifer actually, and my husband is more than likely dressed up in a white coat and a stethoscope playing doctors – and, knowing him, nurses too…' but Serena had gone, melting back into the crowd and air kissing several people she obviously *did* recognise, before turning and barking a command at Tod once more.

Tod Mayhew frowned and, before I knew what was happening, had bent to kiss my cheek. 'Good to see you *again*, Jennifer. Don't spend your winnings all at once.' And with that, he followed the general direction of Serena through the crowd. I stood there for a while, gazing after him until I could no longer see the brown fedora moving through the now-dispersing race-goers.

'Come on.' Gudrun took my arm. 'Let's go and get your winnings.' She stopped as I continued to look into the crowd. 'Oh, heaven help us,' she sighed. 'I've seen that look on your face before.'

26

The following week, on the Sunday, I woke to a morning utterly ravishing in its painted, brand-new dawn. It was only 5 a.m., but I needed to be out there in its unmarred beauty and simplicity. Not stopping even to clean my teeth, I pulled Rita's abandoned old Wellingtons on over my pyjamas and unlocked the back door to the farm, wanting to smell, and feel and be at one with this incredible feat of nature. How clever was old Mother Nature to start afresh: a new beginning every twenty-four hours? I grinned to myself – I was beginning to sound like the Romantic poets I'd tried so hard – and latterly failed – to write about.

I walked across the dew-laden grass, heading for the broken-down gate and the path through the fields towards the woods whose native trees had now completely unfurled their finery in acid-green. An unvarnished wilderness of yellow stretched as far as the eye could see, and I stopped to marvel that the humble dandelion, en masse and framed by a patchwork of dry-stone walls, could create such an extravaganza. I closed my eyes to better take in the sounds and smells: the distant call of an early-morning cuckoo; a growing tumult of birdsong from the woods in front of me; the damp, sexy reek of wild garlic. I turned, like Maria on those damned hills, and, almost before I knew it, I was singing and turning, arms stretched out wide, wellingtons gathering grass and dew as I spun and sang, 'Oh what a beautiful morning...'

Grinning foolishly at my own little private exhibition, my little homage to nature, I opened my eyes to take in the rays of sunshine appearing over the trees to the east, my arms raised in supplication to its power and beauty. And stopped short. A large, utterly beautiful chestnut-coloured horse stood just ten metres in my path, its rider staring across at me with such intensity I floundered, bringing my arms in their pyjama-ed sleeves back down to my side. Tod Mayhew continued to stare at the spectacle in front of him and then, without either of us uttering a word, turned his mount in the opposite direction and took off across the fields.

Unsettled, my pulse racing for some reason, I turned myself and made my way back to Daisy Royd Farm.

That afternoon, Len and Sharon Barrowclough brought Saffron and all her things over. I say all her things but, in fact, for a girl of sixteen, she had surprisingly little – just one suitcase of clothes and toiletries and a case of books.

'You like reading?' I asked, pleased, as I led Saffron and Sharon up the stairs to George's newly vacated bedroom. George had been into the front garden that Rita had tended so well, picking a huge bunch of the last of the tulips – red, yellow and white – arranging them in an old jam jar when there didn't appear to be a single vase in the house, before placing them carefully on the pine chest of drawers next to the single bed. I'd exchanged George's Spiderman Ultimate Metropolis duvet cover and pillowcase for one of Ada's pink ones she'd abandoned several years earlier but which I'd brought with us, not knowing what the state of play re bed linen was going to be up here on the farm.

'Now, isn't this *nice*, Saffron?' Sharon Barrowclough stroked the pink frills almost in reverence. 'Isn't this *lovely*?'

'It's a bit *pink*, isn't it?' were the only words Saffron deigned to speak, while Sharon continued to extol the virtues of everything in the room with a non-stop litany of: 'Isn't this *nice*, Saffron?'

I'd been right in my assumption that both Jess and Saffron must have inherited Sharon's miniature genes. She was tiny: I couldn't imagine how Sharon had ever managed to reach the beer pumps behind the bar at The Jolly Sailor. Or how Len and she had ever, you know, *fitted together*. Hair blacker than tar (that surely couldn't have been her natural colour?), a long, full fringe almost obscuring her large grey eyes, Sharon Barrowclough wouldn't have made five foot even in heels. She reminded me of a more diminutive Cher in her early days when she'd been with Sonny Bono. (I knew of these two Sixties icons only because Dad, at the age of fifteen, had apparently loved their big hit '*I got you, Babe*', and years later, not only got the DJ to play it at their wedding reception, but insisted on playing the single to Mum on every wedding anniversary that followed.)

Thinking of Dad and how much he'd adored Mum always made me want to cry. Now, with this step-daughter of mine who looked uncannily like Ada – but wasn't Ada – standing mulishly in front of me instead of my own daughter, I was in great danger of having a bit of a meltdown. Instead, I pasted a great smile on my face and made a big thing of showing Saffron where the towels and spare loo rolls were kept, how to turn the hot water on and off, as well as advising her that the lavatory needed *two* good flushes in order to clear the bowl efficiently.

'Well, make sure you don't forget that, Saffron,' Sharon beamed anxiously. I knew she still wasn't convinced Saffron would actually stay with us even one night and she and Len might not, even yet, be getting on that flight to Spain from Leeds Bradford airport.

'So, you like reading, Saffron?' I asked once again, turning to smile at her.

'Nose never out of a book,' Sharon said when Saffron didn't reply. 'Anything with animals in it and she's lost to the real world.'

'Oh?'

'What's that book with rabbits you like so much, Saffron?'

'Beatrix Potter?' I asked.

'Is that supposed to be funny?' Saffron gave me a look of utter disdain. '*Watership Down* actually.'

Well and truly chastised, I replied, 'Oh, that was one of my favourites too when I was your age.'

'Well, there you go,' Sharon beamed gratefully. 'You two are going to get along right well; you've something in common already. I'm afraid I was never a reader. I can read a page and haven't a clue what I've just read. Prefer the telly myself. And we've just been hearing your dad's going to be on *The Street*...'

News travelled fast in these parts.

'I'm *not* calling him Dad,' Saffron tutted.

'Call him Laurie,' I suggested. 'Everyone else does.'

Everyone except me, who now prefers wanker, pillock, bighead…

'Even George?' Sharon looked surprised.

'Well, no, not George. Or Ada. *They* obviously call him *Dad*.'

There was a bit of a pregnant pause at that juncture and Sharon leapt in with, 'Yes, our Saffron loves reading.' She tutted slightly through her fringe. 'We don't know *why* she's insisted on doing this animal care course at the Tech when she could have gone to sixth-form college to do her A-Levels. She could have ended up at Cambridge like her dad.'

'He's not my *dad*, Gran, I keep telling you. Anyway, I like animals. I like them better than most people. The only reason I've agreed to come here is because you've got the alpacas and hens and dogs. I wouldn't have come otherwise.'

There was another pause as we all digested this bit of information. 'Why don't you go and see the alpacas now, Saffron?' I smiled. 'And your gran and I can sort out anything else that needs sorting.'

'Jeez, I'm not six years old, Jennifer. No wonder your daughter refused to come up here with you if you insist on suggesting she goes to stroke the pets every time you want to talk about her. Right, Gran,' Saffron turned to Sharon. 'You need to get off or you'll miss that plane. I know you've left it as late as possible before setting off, just so you can be sure I'm here and I'm not going anywhere. I'm here…' She threw up her arms. '… Go on. Go.'

'I'll leave you to say your goodbyes then, both of you,' I smiled, heading for the bedroom door. 'You'll be able to go out and visit your gran and grandad in Spain in the summer holidays, Saffron. It's only a couple of months off.'

'If I'd wanted to go to *Spain*, I'd be on that plane with them right now,' Saffron snapped.

'Right. OK.' I went slowly back downstairs, well and truly put in my place once more.

Once Len and Sharon had left, driving slowly out of the drive in their rental car, heading back to Mirfield to pick up their cases before departing for the airport and their new life in Benidorm, I wandered down to feed the hens. I could hear voices over by the alpacas and shaded my eyes against the early evening sunshine. Was Laurie back already? Even though it was the weekend, I'd seen little of him as he'd said they were doing extra filming in order to get Dr Christian Lund fully established on *The Street*. I was rather enjoying my time without him, and felt irritation that he was back. Laurie was sitting on the wall, his back towards me, chatting to an animated George who appeared to be pointing out various things to his father. I glanced back at the drive. There was no Audi parked in its usual spot by the gate, and walking towards the two of them I soon realised it wasn't Laurie, after all, talking to George.

'Mum, Mr Mayhew's got *loads* of horses over there.' George pointed an excited finger somewhere in the general direction of the gallops. 'He says I can go down sometime and watch them train.'

'Right.'

Tod turned to me. 'If that's alright with your mum, George?'

'George, why don't you go and help Saffron unpack? I think she could do with a bit of help?'

'Oh, has she arrived?' George jumped off the fence, shouting for Sausage who was sniffing at something exciting in the hedgerow. 'Goody.'

'I thought I owed you some sort of explanation,' Tod ventured as George raced off in the direction of the house.

'Did you? Why?'

'It wasn't what it seemed. You know, the other afternoon down at the Jolly Sailor?'

'Well, what it seemed, was you beating up a defenceless, much smaller man.'

'Defenceless?' Tod shook his head, tutting and frowning as he did so.

'Well,' I said again, 'you weren't taking any prisoners. He didn't stand a chance against you, whatever you thought he'd done.'

'Are you always this judgemental?'

'I know what I saw.'

'Right.' Tod gazed into the distance, saying nothing further.

'So, what was it all about?' I eventually said. 'You said I needed some sort of explanation.'

'I didn't want you to think I spent my Friday afternoons boozing, getting drunk and beating people up.'

'It's what it looked like.' I gave a little laugh.

'I know exactly what it looked like.' Tod sighed again. 'That was my brother.'

'Your *brother*?'

Tod nodded. 'He's an alcoholic with various mental health issues. If it's not booze, then it's drugs. He started going off the rails when he was a kid – you know, thrown out of the boarding school we'd both been sent to when he was fifteen for every misdemeanour going. Came back home and drove my parents mad with worry. He stays at the stables sometimes when he's been thrown out of wherever he's been sofa surfing. Or Mum has him back to stay until he nicks all her money or her jewellery again and is back on the booze...'

'Oh.' I didn't know what else to say.

'He's on several court orders and restraining orders not to enter the premises of a whole load of pubs in the area. The new landlord at The Jolly Sailor is a good bloke. He could have rung the police and they'd have hauled him off to the cells for *failure to comply*.'

'Failure to comply?'

'Oh, I know all the jargon.' Tod gave a rueful smile. 'Anyway, Brad at the pub rang me to come down and remove Ashton or he'd have to ring the police. And then he'd have been back in the cells once more, waiting to appear before the magistrates.'

'And that's what you were doing? Removing him?'

'Attempting to. When he's drunk, there's no reasoning with him. He just lashes out and ends up in more trouble.'

'I'm sorry, I thought *you* were assaulting him. Thought it was *you* that was drunk.'

'I know you did.' Tod exhaled deeply. 'And I didn't want that...' He broke off. 'Where's your husband?'

I shrugged. 'Doing what he does best: acting out his alter ego and charming people, I would imagine...'

Neither of us spoke but, sitting on that fence, breathing in the beautiful evening fresh air, the first of the swallows swooping towards their nest in the dilapidated barn, I felt a connection between us. I gave a surreptitious glance sideways.

How on earth had I ever thought this man unattractive? Certainly, he had none of Laurie's superficial beauty, but his face was lived-in, lined and somewhat weather-beaten, I guessed from spending all his days outside, whatever the elements might throw at him.

We must have sat there a good five minutes not speaking until eventually Tod jumped down from the wall, dusting off his jeans with his hands. 'Friends?' he asked, smiling.

'I hope so,' I smiled back and, leaning down from my seat on top of the wall, briefly stroked the now barely visible bruise and then, before I had time to think better of it, moved my mouth to his eye and kissed it better.

Tod stared up at me as I leant back, scarlet with embarrassment. Jesus, what was the matter with me? 'God, I'm sorry...' I gave a nervous laugh. 'I must have been thinking you were George's age and it needed kissing better... sorry... so sorry...'

'Don't be. It was lovely.' Tod was obviously as embarrassed as me. He turned and set off back down the meadow towards home and then, as if an afterthought, turned once more. 'Really lovely, Jennifer.'

And so, before I knew it, we were coming to the end of June and we'd been up here in Westenbury almost four months. Laurie spent more and more time at the studios, filming *The Street*, often not even coming home but staying, he said, in one of the studio apartments that were available for the cast when filming had gone on late into the evening or for those, like him, who lived a long distance from work. I didn't question it, didn't even Google to ascertain whether these *studio apartments* even existed or were rather, as I imagined, a figment of Laurie's creativity in not telling the truth. I didn't, I realised, much care anymore. The tabloids, and those garish magazines much loved on every supermarket and corner shop shelves – *Gossip*, *Tell All*, *Disclose*, *Expose* et al – were once more determined to have Laurie Lewis on their front covers. Ted Baxter, the Yorkshire farmer living and working on a Gloucestershire farm for the past sixteen years or so, appeared to have morphed seamlessly into Dr Christian Lund, the gorgeous new, caring GP based on a northern street. George took it all in his stride: he'd grown up seeing his dad peering down at him from the newsagents' shelves and, now that Laurie was back on TV three times a week, accepted it as a matter of course. Mum was constantly on the phone, questioning why, now that Laurie appeared to be potentially earning once more, I wasn't immediately heading back down the M1 and should she be looking out for somewhere small for me to rent, near her, with the kids? I hadn't actually told her about Saffron being Laurie's daughter, bending the truth somewhat by telling her we had a friend of the Lewis family staying with us temporarily in order that she be able to finish college here while her father had taken up a post in Australia earlier than anticipated. A lodger helped with the bills, I added, once I heard Mum squawking in some indignation down the phone.

We were in the middle of a glorious summer. The days were beautifully warm and sunny and the whole of the countryside, stretching out seemingly for ever in front of me, was alive with green. The woodlands surrounding the farm thrummed with a continuous birdsong that drifted in through the open bedroom windows even before the first rays of light appeared in the east, ending the short, never quite totally black, northern summer nights. I loved it. All we'd ever heard from our bedroom windows in St Albans was the continual hum of traffic from both the A5183 and the busy North Circular. I was growing to appreciate and love these new sounds, as well as the tang of the countryside emanating not only from the many neighbouring farms and pastureland, but also from the very countryside itself, decked now, as she was, in her wedding finery of white blossom and cow parsley.

Laurie and I had spent most of the weeks since the commencement of his new job squabbling about who should have control of the Audi. While I acknowledged that, without a car, the journey over to the studios in Old Trafford from Daisy Royd Farm wasn't easy, Laurie could also see I had to have wheels to get George down to the village school five miles or so away, as well as drop Saffron off at the bus stop where, every morning, she waited for the bus which took her into the town centre and her college course.

Mum, always concerned about my being marooned out in the wilds (I was never quite sure exactly what picture both she and Ada had in their heads despite me sending myriad photos of the glorious countryside now that summer had arrived), eventually conceded that this transport problem did indeed constitute an emergency and suggested I be the keeper of the Audi while purchasing a second car to enable Laurie to drive himself over the Pennines to Manchester. I was to use the funds she'd placed in my bank account when we left London. She made it abundantly clear that

Laurie should pay this money back once his salary started to come through, as well as being adamant that it should be Laurie who inherit the little second-hand Citroën that Dean, Cheryl's husband, helped me to find, while I keep the Audi for my own use. However, even I could see that negotiating the notorious westbound M62 from Yorkshire into Lancashire – arguably the highest and windiest stretch of road in England – was best done in the more solid Audi, and so it was that there was one more thing to keep secret from Mum.

Those summer days in Yorkshire took on their own pattern. Laurie would be off over to Old Trafford in Greater Manchester – if he'd come home at all – before it was light and, happy to welcome yet another glorious morning, I'd be up, Sausage paddling manfully down the stairs after me, George, always eager to get to school, following a couple of minutes later. The same couldn't be said for the step-daughter I'd inherited.

Despite my doing everything I could to make Saffron feel welcome and a part of our little family – and with Laurie away more and more of the time, it was, indeed, just George, Saffron and myself – I knew Saffron viewed herself as the unwelcome lodger, foisted on Laurie and me at this late stage of her life because of her mother's untimely revelation of her actual parentage. Persuading her out of bed each morning, despite the sunshine pouring in through the thin, ill-fitting curtains, was a daily Herculean task and more often than not I had to send in the troops – George, Sausage and, once, even Polonius – to persuade her to get up and ready for college. There were mornings when, despite my encouraging, pleading and downright harassing, I just had to leave her in the fug of her teenage bedroom while I set off to take George to school and, on more than one occasion, returned to find her gone. She would never tell me how she'd managed to get to the bus stop if, indeed, that had been her destination. She was a closed book and wouldn't open up to me – and certainly not to Laurie on the couple of occasions he'd tried to find out what she was up to. I think she knew, as did I, he wasn't really interested in where she went and with whom, viewing his apparent concern as caring father as just one more role he was intent on acting out.

I'd often find her down in the main field behind the house with both Sausage and Polonius – and occasionally George when she relented and allowed him to trail along with her – talking to the alpacas, stroking their foreheads and once, when she didn't realise I'd followed her down, actually crying into Rosamund's woolly shoulder.

'I'm sorry, Saffron,' I said, patting her arm and wondering if I dare give this prickly almost-seventeen-year-old a big hug. 'This really isn't easy for you at all, is it?'

'What isn't?' She rubbed at her eyes and glared at me.

'You know, all this. Having to stay with us; with people you don't know.'

'You don't know *anything*,' she spat crossly, sniffing and wiping at her nose on her bare arm like a little girl. She reminded me then so much of Ada, who'd cried and cried when she was told she'd have to leave her school, her friends and her home and move north with us in order to have a roof over our heads.

'Try me,' I said. 'Tell me. I've been through all this with Ada...'

'With Ada?' Saffron gave a disdainful snort. 'With spoilt kid Ada? Who gets her own way and gets to stay just where she wants? She sounds exactly like Laurie to me: spoilt brats the pair of them.'

I smiled at that. 'I think both you and Ada have managed to get your own way, don't you? You know, Ada refusing to come up here with us and you refusing to go back to live in Australia with your mum?'

'I reckon Ada's got more of what *she* wanted than I have,' Saffron said sulkily.

'What do *you* know about Ada?' I asked mildly.

'Janice told me all about her. You know, about her refusing to come north with you.'

'Well Janice had absolutely no right to be telling you that,' I said. 'And once Ada's finished all her GCSEs next month, she'll get on the train and come north. Or my mum will bring her up...'

'Are you sure about that?' Saffron gazed at me frankly. 'Where's she going to sleep? In my bed? With me? You'll need me to go, won't you? I should never have come in the first place.'

'Oh, we'll work something out,' I said airily, not wanting Saffron to see I'd been grappling with this whole conundrum ever since Laurie's daughter had moved in. The different permutations of where I could shuffle bodies and beds around the three-bedroomed farmhouse – once Ada came up for the summer break – had had me, on numerous occasions, still awake as the first dawn patrol's soprano uttered her solo note, almost immediately joined by the full chorus, eager to greet the coming day. 'Laurie and I have discussed,' I lied, 'that we could turn the front room – you know, Rita's parlour – into a sort of bedsit for you? There's plenty of room for your bed and wardrobe in there and we could find a microwave and kettle. There's shelves for your books,' I added, warming to my theme. 'What do you think?'

Saffron shrugged and turned back to Rosamund, burying her nose into the creature's warmth once again. 'Why don't you wait and see if Ada actually arrives?' she asked from the depths of the alpaca's neck. 'From what Janice was saying, I would imagine it unlikely. Anyway, why don't you and George go back down there for a visit? To see Ada? And your mum?'

'We very possibly will do,' I agreed. 'Once George breaks up for the six-week holiday, I think we'll be heading south for a week or so...'

'But you don't want to leave me alone by myself? Out here, in this house?' Saffron held my gaze and I knew she was putting into words my own thoughts on the matter.

'You wouldn't be alone.' I smiled. 'Laurie would be here...'

'Really?' Saffron raised an eyebrow and I could see this girl knew a lot more than she was letting on.

'Well, I'm sure you could go and stay with Rita. She is your granny, after all. Or Janice? She's your aunt and you seem to get on with her...' I trailed off. 'Look, Saffron, I know this isn't easy for you, as I said, but we want you here.' It suddenly seemed really important that she should know she was wanted. Wasn't in the way. I could feel her unhappiness coming off her in waves. 'Saffron, why didn't you want to go back to Australia? You know, to be with your mum?'

Saffron said nothing for a while and then she appeared to want to talk. 'Mum and I hadn't been getting on for a while.'

'Well, mums and teenage daughters often do argue and fall out. It's what they do.'

'I suppose it came as such a shock to find out Dad – you know, Karl – *wasn't* actually my dad. That my real dad – my birth dad – was the bloke off the telly. You know, we'd sat there, together, Mum and me, watching *A Better Life* for years. And she *knew*, she knew all along he was my dad. My dad! How could she do that to me?'

'Well, I don't suppose your mum could suddenly come out and say, *Hey, Saff, that guy there, you know, Ted Baxter on the TV, is actually your dad. What do you think about that, then?* I mean, she just couldn't, could she?'

'Well, the way she did actually tell me wasn't much better. And my dad – Karl – was as bad as her. Always messing about with other women. And then Mum used me, *used me*, to get back at Karl when she found out he was knocking off the woman from the chemist. How do you think it feels...' Saffron paused to glare at me as though it were my fault, 'to be sitting at the tea table, eating pie and chips, and then Mum just comes out with it?'

'Over your pie and chips?' I was horrified.

'And peas. I can't eat pie, chips and peas ever again.'

'Well, maybe not that combination of three?' I soothed.

'Any bloody combination,' she growled, and I mentally replaced the chicken pie I'd been about to retrieve from the freezer once I was back in the kitchen.

'And then Mum and Dad – Karl – divorced and we had

to sell the house so Dad could have his share to buy a flat in Sydney with the chemist woman and then we didn't have a brass razoo…'

'A brass razoo?'

'You know,' Saffron tutted. 'We were *broke*. So, Mum decides to come back here. And I had to leave the roos in the backyard. And Billy and Bertie and Bobby.'

'Billy and Bertie and Bobby? You had pet kangaroos?'

'No, don't be such a drongo.' Saffron tutted and pulled a face in my direction. 'The roos weren't *pets*. They were just *there*. You know, like the squirrels and the… the magpies here?'

'Right? So, Billy and Bertie and Booby?'

'Bobby, not Booby! Jeez.' Saffron sighed heavily. 'Billy was my German Shepherd and Bertie and Bobby my horses.'

'You had horses?'

'Yep. But they were expensive to keep. Mum couldn't afford it all. She made me sell them.'

'Well, I suppose she had no choice,' I said sympathetically. 'You know, she couldn't ship them to the UK, could she?' I smiled at Saffron, who continued to glare at what life had thrown up at her.

'Anyway, that's why I agreed to come here to live with you on the farm. Thought you might let me have a horse?'

'A horse? What sort of horse?' I asked nervously. 'A big one?'

'Well, a little one's not much good to ride on, is it? I'm used to handling and riding a good sixteen-hander.'

'Right.' I paused. 'Is that big then?'

'Pretty big.'

'But you're so tiny.'

'Doesn't stop me being able to control a seriously big horse.' Saffron glanced my way. 'Thought you might have horses out here. Or wouldn't mind having one?'

'We have alpacas.'

'I can see that,' she scoffed, winding Rosamund's wool around her fingers. 'So, no chance of a horse then?'

'You've obviously got the Lewis farming genes in your veins,' I smiled, avoiding the question.

'Hmm. Janice had horses and rode when she was young.'

'Janice did?'

'Hmm. Terry Lewis was big into horses as well.'

'I never knew that.'

'I reckon there's a lot you don't know, Jennifer.' And with that, Saffron picked up the bucket she'd brought down to feed the alpacas and stalked off back to the house.

27

'Jen, what are you going to do about these girls?' Janice was leaning over the gate that led into the large field where the alpacas appeared to be grazing happily. I handed her the mug of strong sweet tea she'd asked for and a couple of shortbread biscuits, one of which she shoved into her mouth wholesale and chewed thoughtfully as she continued to gaze at the creatures.

'What do you mean, what am I going to *do*? They're not a problem, are they?'

'Well, they would be if Saffron and I weren't keeping an eye on them.'

'I keep an eye on them,' I said, stung. 'I make sure they have water and the feed that Laurie bought. And I've read up on them – they're one of the easiest livestock animals to care for, apparently.'

'Jennifer, they need shearing. They should have been done a couple of months ago – you imagine wearing a cashmere sweater every day in this heat. And they could probably do with being looked at by the vet.'

'Why, do you think they're not well?' I asked, worried.

'No, I think they're absolutely fine, although they should

be checked for TB and worms. Alpacas are susceptible to gastro-intestinal worms such as Barber's Pole...'

'God, I hate worms,' I shuddered. 'Red and white, are they? Erlack!'

'You're such a city girl, Jen. The sheep have worms, the dogs will have worms – have you wormed that excuse for a dog yet?' Janice glanced across at Sausage who, as usual, was cosying up to Elsie. 'My horses had to be checked for red worm, round worm and lung worm. *George* has probably got worms – all kids get them at some point...'

'Alright. Alright.' I put up my hands. 'Enough already with the sodding worms.'

Janice grinned. 'I'll get Graham Maddison, the local vet, to come over and give them the once over and then ask Dermot O'Callaghan what to do about shearing them. He keeps a couple of alpacas himself over at Tod Mayhew's place. And, have you thought ahead to the winter?'

'The winter?' I lived very much in the moment here (except when I was putting Magnolia through her paces when, obviously, I was back in time three hundred years) and had always assumed, especially now that Laurie was earning once again, my time up here in Yorkshire would come to an end and we'd return to the south without my having to face a cold winter in Westenbury.

'They *can* sleep out here in winter, even in the snow, but there's the old barn that's got the tractor in. You could tidy that up a bit. Roof needs mending – more expense – but they'd be OK in there. You'd obviously have to get in hay and pellet supplements and muck them out every day.'

'Me? Muck them out? Oh, I don't think so, Janice. I

mean, I bring them apples – Heidi loves apples and Elsie isn't averse to a raw Brussels sprout...'

'It'll all be different in winter.' Janice warned, looked directly at me. 'And I don't suppose the Boy Wonder will be doing anything to help? You've ended up with this place, three bloody alpacas you don't know how to look after and now his cross-patch daughter as well.'

'He's thankfully earning again,' I protested.

'Still wearing those blinkers, Jen?' Janice shook her head but said nothing further about Laurie, apart from adding, 'So, any idea why that daft brother of mine actually bought these three?'

I started to laugh. 'To be honest, I don't think he actually shelled out any money for them. He'd been down in The Jolly Sailor, heard that some old bloke's Petting Zoo and Animal Sanctuary over near Holmfirth was folding and the guy needed to rehome his donkeys, llamas and alpacas. Laurie's ears pricked up, especially when he'd been hearing about how well Xavier Balmforth was doing with *his* herd of llamas. So, he got the bloke's number, rang him and said he'd take the llamas. Apparently, the llamas had already been taken – don't ask, could have been for dog food – and so the old bloke decided to pull a stroke and send the alpacas instead and hope Laurie wouldn't notice the difference. Which, if you remember, the idiot didn't.' I laughed again at the memory.

'He always was such a pillock,' Janice said comfortably, shoving the remaining biscuit into her mouth and draining the remains of the tea alongside it, a feat of engineering I found fascinating if not exactly admirable.

'You know, it's very trendy in Berkshire and Surrey to take alpacas out for a walk. Apparently very soothing and good for anxiety or depression. Mum was telling me...'

Janice stared. 'Oh, for God's sake, don't go all Berkshire on me, Jen. If you're depressed get down to the bloody pub for a pint. Or get on the Valium like the rest of the poor farmers round here.' She snorted with derision. 'Alpaca walking... duhh.' She paused, obviously thinking. 'Now, you might be able to sell some of the fleece. As I say, Dermot will know.' She jumped down from the fence with an 'oof' as she landed in the field.

'You OK?'

'Leg giving me a bit of gip at the moment.' Janice stretched out her jean-clad left leg, massaging the thigh.

'What did you do to it?' Janice had always walked with a slight limp, usually indiscernible, but at times, like now, I could see she was in pain.

'Laurence never told you?'

I shook my head, feeling guilty that I'd never asked further when Laurie had said she'd broken her leg badly in an accident. 'What happened?'

'Horse.'

'Oh, Saffron did say you were into horses at one point.'

Janice pulled a face. 'Bit more than into them. Dad had been a pretty good show jumper in his day.'

'Really? Your dad had?'

'Hmm, he started off working as a stable lad when he was just fourteen over at the stables which Tod Mayhew eventually bought and totally developed into the successful racing and stud stables they are now. In those days it was livery and eventing stables. Anyway, Dad appeared to have the knack of getting horses successfully over high jumps. Could have possibly gone international. I'm sure that's what Mum probably saw in him; quite dashing he was, if you look at the photos of him in his red and black jackets. His aim was to have a small yard out here on the farm, but there wasn't the money of course. *His* dad wanted him here on the farm looking after the dairy cattle and the milking twice a day, *every* day, as well as actually delivering the milk daily. And, of course, there's always been the sheep. And then Mum got pregnant with me and all his dreams went down the drain together with the beer he pissed up against the wall...'

'Right. I'd no idea.'

'No, you wouldn't have.' Janice sniffed disparagingly. 'Laurie never showed any interest in anyone other than himself. He's never really known what Dad once achieved.' She looked me straight in the eye. 'I sometimes wonder how on earth Dad ever produced a son like Laurie.' Janice continued to hold my eye until, feeling myself turn hot under her sharply questioning regard, I turned away.

'So,' I said, taking a few steps forwards to fetch Sausage from his alpaca nanny, 'Saffron tells me you were a pretty good rider yourself?'

'I was. One of the best. Dad trained me up, putting all his shattered dreams of international stardom onto me. We had jumps and a menage across there, in the fields we used to own.' Janice pointed into the distance. 'All sold off now, of course, to pay for four kids and a farm producing stuff no one wanted. Why buy a pint of milk from the farmer, when you can get four pints in a plastic bottle from Tesco for the same price? Anyway, all was going well with my riding; I had to join the pony club of course – which Dad thought ridiculous, but Mum loved – and I was on track, winning various one-day events in Yorkshire and Lancashire. We were looking at three-day events: you know, Bramham, Bolesworth, Liverpool?'

I didn't know, but let Janice carry on. 'Until I came off, going over a too-high practice jump over there when I was fourteen.' Janice pointed once more to the distant fields. 'And with half-a-ton of horse on top of me. Spent the next three months in hospital on traction and never really rode again. Dad sold the fields and the horses and he and the farm began to go downhill after that. I don't think he ever forgave himself for putting that jump too high.'

'I'm sorry.' I patted Janice's arm, not sure what else to say.

'Don't be,' she said, in typical Janice style. 'All in the past. You have to take what life throws at you. But,' she added, looking straight at me, 'that doesn't mean you can't throw it right back where it came from and go and live your own, much better, life.'

I'd always found Janice daunting. In fact, I'd go so far as to say I was a bit frightened of her. But after the morning's chat, I felt I was beginning to understand her a little more, warm to her even. It was too ravishing a day to be cooped up inside writing. I could, I supposed, sit outside in a shady spot in Rita's garden with my laptop and hope the sunshine didn't obliterate the screen, but I was feeling restless. Catherine Barker hadn't got back to me in any shape or form since that original enthusiastic email re Magnolia. But then, I suppose her enthusiasm was more centred in surprise at me daring to think I could write a Regency romance rather than for what lay within those initial twenty chapters I'd sent her. I checked my emails searching for any response from her, as I did at least five times an hour, but there was nothing.

Feeling deflated, I decided to abandon Magnolia and Lord Silverton and, instead, take Sausage down to Tod Mayhew's stables where Janice told me I'd almost certainly find Dermot O'Callaghan, and not only show him how well Sausage was doing, but pick his brain re the alpacas. 'Who the hell do you think you're kidding?' I asked my reflection in the ornate mirror above the gas fire in the kitchen. 'Don't give me the *looking for Dermot O'Callaghan* tale. You want to bump into Tod Mayhew.' And I did. It had been a week or so since I'd kissed him – aghh, total mortification every time I thought of it which, to be honest, was constantly – and several since he'd laid his hand on mine at York Races and laughingly suggested *Take a Chance on Me*. Had it meant anything? Or was I just behaving like a love-struck teenager, seeking some meaning when there was none to be had except in my imagination. He was with Serena, another scary female, who no doubt guarded him jealously. Hands off, Jennifer Baylis-Lewis.

I'd Googled him, of course, finding image after image of him with his horses, with trainers and with groups of stable hands and, unfortunately, with a plethora of rather lovely women as well. One, Annika Mayhew, a gorgeous blonde whom I assumed to be his ex-wife, was the stereotype of every lusty male's dream of a beautiful Swede. And every night in bed, even when Laurie deigned to come home and lay breathing loudly at my side, I had lovely little daydreams that all involved Tod Mayhew, his fedora and galloping horses. In one little scenario I'd actually morphed into Jane Eyre, with Tod Mayhew as Mr Rochester and where his horse – a big black stallion – having slipped on ice, had thrown Tod off and I had to hold the sweating, soaring stallion (oh God, cut the alliteration, woman) while Mr Rochester – sorry, Tod – assessed his sprained ankle from where he lay on the road.

I went to fetch Sausage's lead. I knew I'd have to more than likely carry the dog most of the way, but he was a good excuse to be arriving, uninvited at the stables. The lead was not on its usual hook and, tutting in irritation, I spent the next five minutes hunting for it amongst the various coats, Wellingtons, trainers and sacks of dog and alpaca food in the untidy and overloaded porch. I ran up the stairs to George's box room but it wasn't there. Then I remembered Saffron had taken Sausage out for a walk the previous evening and went to look for the missing lead in her room. Saffron was incredibly tidy for an almost-seventeen-year-old teenager. She had few clothes and toiletries, but what she had was neatly put away or arranged on the pine bedside chest of drawers. I smiled when I saw she was reading *Jane Eyre*, and approved of the pile of D. H. Lawrence novels – *The Rainbow*, *Women in Love*, *Kangaroo* – wondering if she'd thought the latter was about her beloved roos, rather than the fictional nickname of Lawrence's Benjamin Cooley. The dog lead was nowhere to be seen and I dropped down the side of the bed and lay on the floor to look under the old-fashioned brass bedstead that had previously been slept in by one or all of the Lewis girls. Nothing except a rather sagging mattress on even more saggy springs and I felt guilt that I'd thought it alright for first George and then Saffron to sleep on this bed. I determined I'd get Ada's lovely bed we'd packed up and left in storage in St Albans, and pay for a man with a van to bring it up here for Saffron. I heaved myself up off the floor with the help of the brass knob on the foot of the bed, but immediately fell back onto the floor as the knob came away in my hand.

Stuffed into the hollow of the brass knob were at least twenty small plastic bags of white powder together with several more of miniscule white pills. I pulled each one out in turn, each one a shockingly gruesome labour, giving birth on the revolting purple carpet to what must have been a drug dealers' paradise. A parallel amount was revealed in two more of the four brass bed knobs.

I sat back down on the carpet, my pulse racing, Sausage sniffing at the pile of plastic bags. Uncertain what else to do, I gathered up the whole cache and took them into my bedroom, locking the lot in a drawer before putting the key in my jeans' pocket.

The dog lead I found over the bannister on the way back down. Whistling for Sausage, my brain trying to work out the best way forward re Saffron and what I'd found hidden in the bed knobs, I set off across the fields in the direction of Tod Mayhew's racing stables.

As I walked and grappled with this new problem Saffron had thrown my way, the glorious fields and woodland spread out below me in a seemingly never-ending green quilt, giving a superior alternative to the unpalatably unsavoury one Saffron appeared caught up in. All the way there, on the forty-minute walk through unspoiled, sleepily rustic countryside and then across agricultural land made ripe and fertile through the labour of farm workers, I tried to think what to do. How was I going to approach her? Every mother's nightmare to find *gear* in their kid's bedroom. But I *wasn't* her mother, I argued with myself, talking out loud so that Sausage, glancing back at me in surprise, came back to walk to heel. If that stuff was for her own use, she had one hell of a habit. If she was pushing it, she was in great danger. I'd read the Sunday supplements; knew all about the grooming of kids and county lines.

As I approached Mayhew's Yard, I saw there were several beautiful horses grazing in the fields, tails swishing at clouds of flies, but otherwise undisturbed by the sultry afternoon's heat. I climbed stiles, avoiding the fields which held the horses and found myself at the entrance to the stables. It was immaculately kept, not a stray piece of straw, hay or horse feed to mar the cobbled yard and, apart from the sound of horses moving in their boxes, the only noise was that of a phone ringing in what I assumed to be the office to my left.

'Jennifer?' Tod appeared at the office door, phone receiver in one hand. 'Hang on, just let me take this and then I'll be with you.' He was in jeans and a white T-shirt, both doing nothing to disguise the incredible physique below them. Standing outside in the yard, my pulse racing at the nearness of this man, I supposed it mandatory to have thighs of steel in order to stay on sweating, soaring stallions...

'I recognise this little fellow.' A laughing, heavily Irish-accented voice broke into my increasingly erotic fantasy of just what else those strong muscular thighs were capable of, and I jumped guiltily.

'You must be Jennifer?' Dermot O'Callaghan thrust a hand in my direction. 'How's the little one doing?' He hunkered down to Sausage, feeling at the dog's legs and along his spine before turning him over and tickling at his pink-speckled tummy until Sausage was a quivering mass of ecstasy. 'He's seems to be doing well. Thank you for that. To be honest, I don't usually allow any of my dogs to go to homes I've not inspected, but I know Cheryl and Dean well and Janice of course. Your wean was so desperate to take him home immediately. And no one else seemed to want him.'

'George just adores him.' I laughed. 'In fact, they gaze at each other in mutual adoration.'

'That's grand, that is. Just the way it should be. Now, Janice rang me half an hour ago. Says you need help with your girls? Shearing and the like?'

'That would be wonderful.'

'Well, they need doing annually, particularly when we're having a good summer like this one. A male can become sterile if suffering heat stress; luckily yours are all girls. I'll come over this evening with my shears. If the wool's any good – and I'm not promising it will be, knowing where your three have come from – you might get something for it. But shearing will make them much cooler and that's important. Janice says you're looking after them well...'

'Really? Janice said that?' I felt ridiculously pleased at the compliment.

Dermot laughed. 'Her bark's worse than her bite. She's a bit of an awl softy under all that Yorkshire bluffness she likes to wear...' He broke off as Tod walked towards us. 'Right, I'll see you this evening, Jennifer.' He turned to Tod, grinning. 'OK, you win, you were absolutely right.'

'Have you been betting?' I asked as Tod bent down to stroke Sausage. Two other dogs of indeterminate breed joined Tod, lying down at his bare feet as, once more, Sausage rolled in delight. Lucky dog, I thought wistfully.

'Something like that.' Tod replied, not quite meeting my eye. And then, when he did look me fully in the face, he stopped mid-stroke. 'You OK?'

'Just had a bit of a shock actually.'

'Oh?'

I hesitated. 'It's nothing.' Why on earth was I thinking of telling this man, who I knew nothing much about, what Saffron appeared to have been up to?

'That husband of yours again, is it?' Tod searched my face.

'I'm sorry?' I stared at him.

There was a long pause and, obviously embarrassed, Tod stood up. 'Oh, nothing. Come on, let me get something on my feet and I'll show you round the stables.' He smiled at me. 'Have you spent your winnings yet?'

'Saving it up for a rainy day,' I laughed. 'Although,' I went on, suddenly feeling ridiculously brave, 'I owe you that drink sometime...'

'I'll look forward to that, Jennifer.' Tod turned to me and I found I couldn't tear my eyes away from his. Eventually, I looked away first but, as he gave me a tour of the stables, I was conscious of every part of him – his bare arm tantalisingly close, occasionally touching my own, his well-muscled jean-clad thighs, the turn of his blond head, his large hands unlocking stable doors, before reaching in to explain, appraise or simply pat and caress the horse within.

'So, Jennifer,' Tod asked as he handed me a large mug of tea back in the office, 'are you happy?' It was cool and dark in there after the mid-afternoon heat and glare of the sun and, as I leaned against the whitewashed wall of the office, his eyes never left my face.

'Happy?'

'I don't think you have been?'

'That obvious?'

Tod smiled. 'Not easy uprooting yourself from your home and all your family.'

I took a deep breath, taking even myself by surprise as I vocalised what I knew to be true. 'Laurie and I are washed up. I should have left him years ago; certainly shouldn't have come up here with him.'

'And why didn't you? Leave him, I mean?'

'Oh, trying to salvage what was left of my marriage. You know, not wanting my kids to lose their father.'

Tod nodded, understanding. He reached out a hand and stroked my arm. I turned towards him and his hands moved from my arm to my face, his fingers touching my cheek, his thumb moving slowly and ridiculously sensuously across my open mouth. One simple movement of a thumb across my lips and I felt more alive than I'd done for years, every bit of me wanting more. As though they had a life of their own, my hands moved up to his arms and Tod smiled before moving his mouth to mine. 'I hope, Jennifer... I'm...' he broke off as one of the grooms, a young lad of around Ada's age, popped his head round the office door.

'Vet's here, Tod.'

'Sorry, Jenny,' Tod frowned. 'Going to have to go. I'd much rather stay here with you,' he went on as the boy set off back down the yard. 'You've... you're...' he bent down and kissed my lips, first the top before moving slowly to my lower, '... you've done something to me...'

28

'Jennifer?'

'Yes?' Despite my worry about having it out with Saffron once I returned back to Daisy Royd Farm, I fairly floated back home, Sausage managing half the return journey before he sat down mulishly, giving me a mutinous look and refusing to go further.

'Yes?' I said again as I lost contact with whoever was ringing me.

'Jennifer, it's Len Barrowclough. I've just had our Saffron's college on the phone to me.'

'Oh?'

'Wanting to know why she's not been to any of her lectures for the past three weeks. Why haven't you been sending her? Is she poorly?' Len, I could hear, was angry and upset. 'I tried Laurence – I mean she is his daughter after all – but he's not picking up. I left a message with him. Did you know she's not been going? Have you let her stay at home? Is she poorly?'

'Hang on, hang on, Len.' I put Sausage down and found somewhere to sit on the grass. 'Right, I'd absolutely no idea she's not been going to college. I get her up every morning

– sometimes with great difficulty – and take her to the bus stop. Some days she says she doesn't have to be in until the afternoon...' I trailed off. I didn't know much about technical college courses. I'd assumed, now she was almost seventeen, college kids were treated more like university students than schoolkids.

'Well, that's probably a lie. It's up to *you* to make sure she goes in.'

'To be honest, Len,' I said patiently, 'I don't really feel it *is* up to me. I'm certainly not letting her stay in bed or stay at home when she's supposed to be at college, but other than escorting her all the way to her classroom, I can only trust her when she tells me she's been where she should. Have you spoken to her yourself recently?'

'Yes. Me and Sharon ring her two or three times a week. We thought she'd settled with you and was happy. You said as much when we rang you last week. Settled, you said, you know, with the dogs and them there llamas...?'

Alpacas, I corrected, mentally. And the crack cocaine and ecstasy tablets? I bit my tongue. Now was not the time to be telling Len this.

'Look, Len, hopefully Laurie's home this evening. He's been so busy filming this week I've only seen him briefly. Passing ships and all that?'

'This is a very bad line, Jennifer. Ships? He's filming on a ship? No wonder he doesn't know what our Saffron's up to if he's on some cruise.'

'No honestly, Len, he's in Manchester...'

'Manilla?'

'Manchester,' I shouted down the phone, Sausage giving

me a world-weary look. 'Look, I'll ring you back as soon as I've spoken to her.'

So, two things I was going to have to have out with her now. I picked up a complaining, wriggling Sausage and strode off at full speed, the wonderful feeling of happiness I'd felt during the past hour in Tod's company beginning to fade into the ether.

By the time I reached the top of the hill from which Daisy Royd Farm surveyed all before her, I was puffing and panting. Need to get fit, I reminded myself. Need to get this body of mine in tip-top condition. For what – or whom – I wasn't admitting, even to myself. Rita's yellow Mini – it was one of her days for meeting and picking up George from school – was pulled up in the yard and George ran out to meet me, a piece of bread and jam in both hands.

'I'm so hungry, Mum. We've been practising for Sports Day all afternoon. Mrs Stevens says…' And he was off again, extolling the virtues of Saint Grace Stevens once again. I smiled. At least I didn't have to worry about my son's happiness. He shoved a piece of bread into his mouth, scooped up Sausage and they set off down the field to see to the alpacas.

Rita was wiping down the kitchen tops, replacing the bread in the bin and the jam in the cupboard. 'Saffron's not been going to college,' I said.

'I know. Len's just rung me.'

'You as well?'

'He's worried, Jennifer.'

'He'll be more so if he knows what I found hidden in the bed knobs this morning.'

'The bed knobs?' Rita stared.

'Drugs.'

'*Drugs?* What kind of drugs?' Rita sat down, dishcloth still to hand.

'Looks like crack cocaine to me. And some sort of pills. I don't know what kids take these days.'

'Right, she needs sitting down and talking to. Do you think she's using or pushing?'

'You seem to know all the correct terminology, Rita.'

'Why wouldn't I? I might be in my seventies, but I read the papers.'

'Right. Well, I suppose I'm just going to have to wait till she comes in and face her with it.'

'Laurence should be here.'

'You're right. He should.' I stared at Rita and she had the grace to look away first.

'Do you want me to stay?' she asked eventually. 'You know, until she comes back?'

I looked at the kitchen clock. 'She's usually home on the five o'clock bus. The one that stops down the road. I wouldn't mind some back-up if you don't mind staying.'

Desperate for the loo, I went upstairs. Saffron's bedroom door was wide open, the brass bed knobs lying brazenly on the pink duvet cover where they'd obviously been dropped and left. I knew I'd not only replaced the knobs on the bedstead but had closed the door carefully behind me. I crossed over to our bedroom and pulled at the locked drawer: still locked, the drugs presumably safe inside. Something was different. The top drawer where I kept the little jewellery I possessed, passports and any spare coins, wasn't closed properly and the envelope that had contained my £250 winnings from the races was on the bed. Empty. Written on the front were the obviously hastily scrawled words:

Sorry, Jen. Sorry. Just borrowing this. Will pay it all back, I promise.

'She's taken my money.' Rita looked up as I went back into the kitchen.

'Pinched it?' Rita was shocked.

'Borrowed it, according to the note she's left on my bed.'

'Have you any idea where she might be? Why she needs money?'

I shook my head. 'I've an awful feeling she's got herself mixed up in something she can't get out of.'

'Do we get the police?'

'What, with a great stash of drugs in the house? I wonder if Janice knows anything? She seemed to think there might be some boy Saffron's got herself involved with.'

'There usually is.' Rita raised an eyebrow. 'I raised three daughters, remember. Both Janice and Lorraine – especially Lorraine – went off the rails when they were sixteen and didn't know what to do with themselves. Lorraine got herself into a bit of trouble...' Rita trailed off.

'What sort of trouble?'

'Oh, you know, smoking dope, hanging round one of the rough estates; the police coming round.'

'Drugs?'

Rita nodded, embarrassed. 'She ended up in the juvenile court. Terry went mad with her – arguments day and night, threatening to leave home. You *know*, the usual thing...' Rita glanced at me. 'No, I don't suppose you *do* know.

Anyway, Lorraine turned out alright in the end. Just a phase you have to get through.'

'Rita, I think a whole stash of drugs locked up in a bedroom drawer is a bit more than a phase you *just have to get through*. For heaven's sake, if Len rings again, don't answer until Saffron comes back and we can work out what to do.'

My phone rang and we both jumped nervously. 'It's Janice,' I said, reading the screen.

'Just wondering if you managed to get in touch with Dermot about the shearing?' Janice spoke as soon as I pressed the green button.

'Yes, I did, thank you. Listen, Janice, has Saffron said anything to you?'

There was a pause. 'About what?'

'Is there some boy she's been seeing?' I hesitated, glanced at Rita who nodded. 'We're worried about her.'

'I warned her off,' Janice said. 'I should probably have said something to you but she said she'd stopped seeing him. She said she hadn't seen him since she'd moved in with you, so I assumed she'd learned some sense.'

'Who?'

'Hang on, I'll drive round.' And with that she switched off.

Janice arrived within minutes, speeding up through the yard and coming into the kitchen with not only George and Sausage in tow, but Fiona as well.

'Just out for a walk,' Fiona smiled. 'Thought I'd call in and see how you're doing?' She hesitated. 'Sorry, is this a bad time? Tea time?' She made to retrace her steps.

'I'll phone you, Jennifer. Just wondering if you fancied meeting up with us at the Jolly Sailor tomorrow evening.' She paused, obviously uncomfortable when no one else spoke. 'Mind you, it's not the same since Len and Sharon left...'

'Saffron, their granddaughter is staying with us,' I finally said, smiling at Fiona.

'Yes, I know. Small place like this – can't keep people from a bit of juicy gossip... Oh sorry, that came out wrong... didn't mean to say that...' Fiona trailed off, embarrassed. 'Look,' she said, 'I didn't call in to be a nosey parker... it's just something, maybe, I mean, I'd want to know if it was one of my girls...'

'Are we talking hens, alpacas or actual daughters here?' Janice asked slightly irritably and, if the situation hadn't been so serious, I'd have laughed.

Rita took charge. 'Right, George, help me make these ladies some tea and then we can take it out to them in the garden...' Rita indicated with a nod towards the open door that we should leave '... and then you and me can finish that jigsaw we started last week.'

Once seated on the garden bench in the late afternoon sunshine, I turned to Fiona. 'You said something about you'd want to know if it was one of your girls?'

'Look, Len and Sharon are friends of Matthew's mum. Sharon told me the whole story about, you know, about Laurie Lewis being Saffron's dad and that's why she was staying with you. Beatrice – Bea, my nineteen-year-old – has just started as a PCSO...'

'PCSO?'

'Police Community Support Officer.' Fiona broke off as George brought out a tray of tea things and then, once he'd gone back into the house, added, 'She's desperate to be a detective – been watching too much *Line of Duty*, if you ask me – and this seems to be the way forwards. Volunteer as a PCSO, train as a PC and then apply to be a DC...'

'And?' Janice was becoming more irritable. 'Any more abbreviations? Is this just a *CV* of Bea's career path or is there something we should know?'

'Bea was down patrolling the Sunny Mede estate the other day...'

'Bloody hell,' Janice interrupted. 'I hope she had a few Alsatians with her.'

'... and saw Saffron down there. She was with one of the Da Silva boys.'

Janice nodded. 'Yes, I knew she'd fallen for one of them. I warned her off and she said she'd ended it.'

'The Da Silva boys?' I stared. 'Sounds like the mafia.'

'As good as,' Fiona said.

'Better than,' Janice added, pulling an imaginary knife across her throat. 'They're one of the most notorious families in Midhope. Tony Da Silva – that's grandad – has been banged up in Wakefield prison for years, but still controls his patch from inside. Dino, the father, is out at the moment I think, probably helping launder drug money. And then there are the boys.'

'How come you know so much about them, Janice?'

She looked embarrassed. 'Had a thing about Dino when I was Saffron's age. When there was no future for me with eventing anymore, you know, after my accident, I drifted a bit. Of course, Dino didn't really look at me twice – I had red hair and a limp – but I suppose I was a bit feisty in those days...'

'In *those days*?' I snorted.

'... and Dino liked having me round,' Janice went on, ignoring my interruption. 'They're a bad lot. And this new generation of boys won't be any better: there are three of them, all dark-haired, brown-eyed and devastatingly good looking. Anyway, where's Laurence?' Janice snapped crossly. 'Saffron's *his* daughter. *He* should be sorting this out. Going down to Sunny Mede and hauling her back home. Like my dad did with me.'

'Oh, I can really see Laurie doing that, can't you?' I said. 'I mean, he's not exactly Popeye, is he?'

'Popeye?' Fiona and Janice frowned.

'You know, a can of spinach and he's off, fighting for good against the evil Bluebeard.'

'Laurence'd be too worried he'd muss his hair or get blood on his silk shirts.' Janice sniffed.

'Right then,' Fiona said, eyes gleaming. 'Up to us then. Come on.' She stood up, brushing Bourbon biscuit crumbs from her shorts.

'Come on where?' Janice frowned once more.

'She's obviously down there on the estate. Let's go and drive down and get her. If necessary, I'll get Bea to rustle up a few of her PCSOs...'

'Rustle up a few PCSOs?' Janice snorted. 'They're not bloody ham sandwiches you rustle up after a night at the pub, Fiona. And it's dangerous down there.'

'It's light until 10 p.m. at least.'

'Have we no men to go with us?' I asked. 'Your Matthew?' I turned hopefully to Fiona, remembering her large, steady-looking husband with his huge farmer's hands, from Cassie's supper evening.

'Haymaking,' Fiona said. 'You can't disturb Matthew when he's haymaking.'

'No, you can't.' Janice shook her head. 'And, to be honest, I think it's better we're all women.'

'Do these Da Silva's actually live on the estate?' I asked, as Janice drove Fiona and me into a maze of red-bricked council houses. Some – those that had been privately purchased, presumably at Margaret Thatcher's behest – were immaculate, neatly fenced off and awash with an abundance of summer flowers: dahlias, marigolds and nasturtiums. But as we drove further into the heart of the complex array of streets (Wordsworth Fold, Shelley Close, Coleridge Way and, yes, even Byron Crescent) my heart sank at the deprivation, the choice graffiti (*Asilum Seakers, Fuck Off Home*) and the sturdy metal grilles on the doors and windows of the Sunny Mede Community and Health Centres.

'Live here?' Janice asked as she negotiated a pile of black bin bags, a mattress and a rusting fridge at the side of the road. 'They did when I hung out with Dino. Hell, he was handsome in those days. I used to come down here to his place just over there.' She pointed to one of the larger houses on Bluebell Grove. 'As far as I know they've moved on now, living off their drug money. Having said that, there's nothing sophisticated about them: any money they do get their hands on, they'll probably lose again. Dino ended up a heroin addict – probably still is.'

'Can you *be* a heroin addict for thirty years?' I frowned. 'Wouldn't he have overdosed and be dead by now?'

'He's big into breaking and entering to feed his habit. The police nick him and put him inside and he comes off the drugs. Two years later he's out and gets sucked into it all again. Tony, his dad, is much more sophisticated, even though he must be seventy and doing a long stretch for armed robbery. I hear one of the boys Saffron has got herself involved with is more like his grandad than Dino.'

'I'm not sure this is doing any good, Janice,' I said, after we'd been circling the estate for what seemed ages. 'Those kids over there are watching, wondering why we're going round and round every fifteen minutes.'

'They're only little kids. Hang on.' She stopped the car and wound down the window before shouting: 'Oi, kids, over here.'

'You the feds?' one shouted back. He couldn't have been more than nine or ten.

'Might be,' Janice agreed.

'Well fuck off, if you are.' And then, his curiosity obviously getting the better of him, added, 'Nah, you don't smell like bacon...'

'*Bacon?*' I whispered to Fiona.

'You know, pigs,' she offered, knowledgably.

'What you after?' the kid asked.

'Need to score some stash,' Janice said.

'Score?' I whispered at her side. 'Do they still say *score*?'

'Show us where we can get some stuff, kid,' Janice went on, 'and I'll give you a fiver.'

'A tenner and I'll take you,' he shouted back, arms folded.

'Robbing little devil,' Fiona hissed from the back. She produced a five-pound note from her shorts' pocket and thrust it through the open window.

'Tight arse,' the kid sneered, but nevertheless took the money and said, 'Follow me.' He jumped on his bike, pedalling and doing wheelies through various rat runs on the estate until we ended up back outside the house Janice had pointed out earlier.

'God, he must still live here,' Janice said, looking quite shocked. 'Crime obviously *doesn't* pay.'

'What do we do now?' I asked. 'Just go and knock on the door and see if Saffron is in there?'

'You stay here. Lock the doors,' Janice warned. I could see she was nervous, something I'd never seen in my sister-in-law before. 'Saffron's my niece. If she's in there...'

Janice got out slowly and deliberately and, much as I wanted to reassure her by telling her, *actually, Janice, only your half-niece, since your mum had sex with a lecherous lecturer, and produced Laurie, making him your half-brother*, I conceded this was not the time or place to be offering up family secrets.

Fiona and I sat waiting nervously. Rita and Len rang a couple of times but I cut them dead and eventually turned off my phone.

'I probably shouldn't be telling you this,' Fiona suddenly said. 'And I *am* only telling you because I'm a bit frightened and need to talk...' she was shivering slightly... 'and if I end up dead, I won't have told you. And if *you* end up dead, you'll die not knowing...'

'Knowing what?' I turned from the front seat to stare at her.

Fiona said nothing further for a few seconds.

'What *are* you on about, Fiona?'

'OK. Here goes.' She breathed heavily. 'Tod Mayhew has got a bit of a thing about you. There, I've said it now. And I know I sound like a thirteen-year-old, you know, passing it on down the line in assembly at school, and I've no idea about the state of your marriage... although, from where I'm looking, it doesn't appear overly healthy... and Matthew will go ballistic with me for telling you. Because Tod told him in confidence and Matthew told me in confidence and Tod is so lovely and...'

'Oh, Fiona, I've got a bit of a thing for Tod too.' Despite being in the middle of a rough estate with Janice – and presumably Saffron – still in the den of iniquity that Janice had been swallowed up into, I felt something akin to utter delight. 'Laurie and I are totally washed up, you know. I suppose it's been obvious to everyone, except me... But what about Serena...?'

'Oh, jeez, look...' Fiona interrupted me, grabbing hold of my arm and pointing.

I swivelled back round from where I'd been facing Fiona as she imparted that wonderful little bit of information, and my heart lurched as Janice and Saffron exited the house together, but with two youths and an older man jostling them down the path towards the car.

'Right, you two bitches in there, listen up.' The taller and darker of the two boys, who must have been in his early twenties, had his face right up to the car's offside window and was making an angry winding down action with his hand.

'Don't open it,' Fiona hissed.

'Don't be stupid. I have to.' I'd seen the glint of the knife blade in the boy's other hand, as well as taken in both Janice and Saffron's white, frightened faces.

29

The car window went all the way down and immediately the boy thrust the knife towards my own face. He drew it slowly and meaningfully down my cheek to my neck, the cold blade making contact but not actually cutting into my flesh, before retrieving it and holding it against Saffron's neck. My heart raced with terror.

'Right, you drive Saffron back down with the stuff she says you've nicked from her...'

'Leave her alone, Kyle.' The smaller, and obviously younger, of the two boys hissed crossly. 'She'll bring it back tomorrow, once she gets it. She said.'

The older man spoke for the first time. 'He's right, Kyle. Janice has said – she'll drive the girl back down tomorrow...'

'Tonight. I swear down, bro, I'm 'aving the stuff back tonight – there's over two grand's worth. I don't trust any of this lot. Who's to say they won't bring Plod back down?'

Plod? Ye Gods. If I hadn't been so frightened, I'd probably have laughed out loud at the ridiculously antediluvian language this kid was coming out with.

Janice took control. 'We're going to drive back, pick up the stuff and then I'll bring it straight back here. Dino knows that, don't you? Dino?'

We all turned to the older man standing behind the others. Older? He looked ancient. If this was the once devastatingly handsome Dino who had so enthralled Janice as a teenager, then he was testament to what a life on drugs could do to a body. His face was lined and sunk in on itself and what remained of his black hair was wispy, greasy and grey. When he spoke, any teeth still in situ were brown. He appeared to be rotting away in front of us.

'She's alright is Janice. She'll do as she says,' Dino confirmed with a nod towards the older boy. During this stand-off, Saffron had said nothing, her face white in its frame of untidy black curls.

'I'll give you...' the older boy broke off to pull out his phone '... an hour. I want the gear back here in an hour.'

'OK, OK, we *hear* you.' Janice's feisty head was obviously firmly back in place once more. 'Open the door, Jennifer.'

I did so and Saffron made to get into the back seat.

'Oi, you, you're staying here.' Kyle Da Silva pulled at Saffron's green hoody. 'In case *she* doesn't come back.' He nodded towards Janice who was now at the wheel of the car.

'No, she's coming back with *us*. Now.' A sudden fury at this cocky little toe-rag had me leaping out of the car, shoving Saffron roughly into the back seat next to Fiona, who pulled her towards her, before jumping back in and slamming the door closed. 'You'll get your stuff tonight,' I shouted through the closed window. 'Now eff off and let us go and get it.'

Janice glanced my way and I like to think I'd perhaps gone some way up in her estimation, but she didn't say anything, just started the car and set off at speed, scattering

Da Silva's as Kyle gave a final warning bang on the boot with his fist.

'He had a bloody machete down his jeans,' Janice breathed as she drove far too quickly out of the estate. 'If he sneezes, he'll slice his donger off.' She exhaled a couple more times then said, 'Right, back to Daisy Royd and pick up the stuff – hope for God's sake I'm not stopped by the police on the way back. How the hell would I explain that?' She turned slightly to address Saffron. 'And you, lady, think yourself lucky. We'll sort this and then you have nothing more to do with the Da Silva's. D'y'hear, Saffron?'

Saffron nodded dumbly, her navy eyes huge in her drained, pallid face. 'I've *been* trying...' she eventually managed to get out.

'Trying what?' Janice snapped.

'To have nothing more to do with them. I was taking the stuff – you know, the drugs back to them today. I was only *looking after it* for Kyle. His grandad told him to get it all out of the house for a few days – he'd had a tip-off the Thompson Firm were after it – so Kyle split it all up – he had a lot – and asked – no told – different people to look after it. Kyle was really nice. Said he'd get me a horse once I brought it back.'

'A horse?' Fiona, Janice and I turned as one. 'What sort of a horse?' Fiona asked.

'Presumably one with four legs,' Janice said dryly.

'I want a horse again.' Saffron was sobbing now. 'I've not got my grandad and gran, my mum, or my dad, or my *new* dad – he's as interested in me as my *old* one. I'm living with people who don't really want me there and doing a bloody rubbish college course I shouldn't have picked. It's so bloody boring learning how to feed fish and rabbits. I should have done A-Levels so I can go and be a vet, but it's *all too late* now.' Saffron was almost incoherent. '*And* I've started my period and nobody in that house had anything. I'm stuffed full of toilet paper and I've got a headache and period pain. And I'm a good rider. No, I'm a *brilliant* rider. Like you were, Auntie Janice. And your dad. My *grandad*.'

I didn't feel it the right time to put both Janice and Saffron in the picture with regards the cuckolding of Terry Lewis by Laurence Double-Barrel. We'd had enough drama for one night.

Janice put her foot on the accelerator and sped down country lanes hung with bowers of horse-chestnut, their candles that had waxed so beautifully all through May and early June, now brown and on the wane. We pulled up into the farm yard where Rita's yellow Mini, a black Defender (for one mad, heart-stopping moment I thought it was my dad's ancient one) and Laurie's Audi were parked in a line next to my little Citroen.

'Boy Wonder's back,' Janice sniffed.

'Get him to go back down with you,' I urged. 'You know, for protection.'

'Protection?' Janice laughed hollowly. 'Laurie couldn't protect the skin on a rice pudding.' She laughed again. 'I know that because *I* always managed to get it when we were kids. Mind you, the Da Silva's would take one look at Laurie Lewis and probably kidnap him. Hold him to ransom for all the money they think a famous actor should have.'

'They'd have him forever then,' I said and Janice and I both tittered, if somewhat nervously.

'Ok, Jen, give me the key to unlock your drawer and I'll get straight off.' Janice and I stepped out of the car.

'You can't go by yourself,' I protested. 'Let me come with you.'

'Saffron needs you here,' she said bossily. 'Find her some Tampax and paracetamol, make her some hot chocolate and put her to bed. If she's suffering as much as I used to every month – thank God for the menopause – she'll be feeling pretty rough. I think she's very depressed, Jen. Go easy on her.'

'What are *you* still doing up?' I asked, as George, barefoot and in pyjamas, came bounding down the path towards us, Sausage waddling behind. 'You should be in bed and asleep now.'

'Daddy's back,' George said happily. 'And I've been helping Dermot – you know, Sausage's dad – shear the alpacas. He's got loads of wool off them. Says it should make us a bit of cash.' George nodded sagely as if he were Farmer Giles himself. 'I've been making a PowerPoint all about it on your laptop,' he went on, confirming that Grace Stevens and Year 3 appeared to be in for yet another presentation. 'Where've you been Mummy? Why's Saffron crying?'

'Oh, we've just been for a bit of a run out,' I lied. 'OK, bed. Where's Daddy now?' I broke off as Dermot O'Callaghan appeared at the door, drying his hands on a tea towel.

'Right, I've loaded up the fleece, Jennifer. Not bad stuff, actually. I'll let you have what I get for it.'

'Make sure you take some for doing the shearing,' I protested, but Dermot wasn't listening, his eyes narrowing slightly as Fiona ushered a red-eyed Saffron past him into the house.

'I'll be with you in a minute, Fi,' I called as I turned back to Dermot who was frowning, his eyes following Saffron.

'Is that the girl you've got staying with you?'

'Saffron? Yes, she's my husband's daughter. My step-daughter.'

'Well, you tell her from me to keep away from the sodding horses. She's always down at the paddocks, hanging around, making a nuisance of herself. Tod and I are constantly telling her to get off home or we'll call the police. She actually had her arms round the neck of one of our best racehorses last week. Never seen anything like it. She'll be trampled one of these days and then it'll be the yard's fault. They can be dangerous creatures. And,' Dermot paused, 'she was down there not long ago with a couple of lads. Didn't look particularly horsey types to me.' Dermot was growing really angry. 'We'd no idea she was anything to do with *you*.'

'I'm sorry, Dermot, I didn't realise…'

'Well, you do now.' And with that he strode off, jumped into the Defender and set off at speed out of the yard.

Without another word, Janice appeared back outside and followed Dermot across the yard, holding up the white Aldi carrier, which she'd obviously transferred the drugs into, to show me she'd got them and then, like Dermot, drove out of the broken-down gate and roared off in the opposite direction.

'What the hell's going on?' Laurie demanded, once I'd climbed the stairs to find him. 'Sounds like the Grand Prix down there. And Janice has just barged in, shoved me out of the way, unlocked a drawer and emptied whatever was in it into a carrier bag. I'd been trying to unlock that drawer. Thought my passport must be in there.'

'Your passport?' I stared.

'Got to go, Jen. Dr Christian's becoming so popular, the writers have got him having some love tryst in Paris.'

'Paris?'

Laurie nodded. 'Hmm, flying out there on the last flight from Manchester. Need to go, sweetheart.'

'Paris?' I repeated. 'For an episode of *The Street*?'

'It's a lot more sophisticated now than when that character fell under a tram in Blackpool.' Laurie was slightly indignant. 'They've filmed in Mexico and Barbados before now, you know.'

'No, Laurie, I don't know,' I snapped. 'And maybe you could have suggested they film *you* next to Blackpool Tower, instead of the Eiffel one, and then you could be home at night to see to your children.'

'Oh, I don't think *that* would work, Jennifer,' Laurie said seriously, and I wanted to hit him.

'Do you *realise* just what's been going on this evening?' I snarled. 'Saffron is *your* daughter, not mine. You've left her here for me to look after, and we've been down on the Sunny Mede estate…'

'Well, I'd keep right away from there if I were you.' Laurie stared. 'It was bad enough when *I* was a kid. It must be a hotbed of drugs and depravity now.'

'Exactly. Janice, Fiona and I have been down there all evening rescuing Saffron from the machete-manipulating Midhope mafia…' Oh God, too much alliteration again. 'She's in great danger, Laurie.'

'They're not in the garden, are they?' Laurie visibly paled. 'Ring the police.' He paused. 'Mind you, it'd all end up in the papers again and I really can't afford any more bad publicity just as everything is going so well with the new job. Ring Janice and get her to stay with you – she'd frighten anyone away, would Janice. Make sure the doors are locked and if Polonius barks, ring the police.'

I suddenly felt total defeat. The anxiety of the whole evening was making me feel shaky, especially when I remembered the cold blade of that knife against my throat. Maybe I *should* be ringing the police, having them here for protection. But wouldn't they be questioning Saffron then, and hauling her off to the station? And would the Da Silva's then be arrested and we'd be seen as grassing them up? I'd read my Martina Cole – I knew what happened next if you crossed the bad boys.

'Jen?' Janice was calling from downstairs and I ran down to where she was stood in the kitchen with Rita. 'I've taken the stuff back but I don't imagine you'll see your £250 again. Dino's *promised* me there won't be any reprisals.'

'Did he actually use that word?' I asked, walking down the stairs to meet her.

'Reprisals?' Janice pulled a face. 'I know. I was impressed he said it, and even more I understood it! Mind you, he probably uses it a lot knowing his father, Tony, and now seeing the next generation in action. Little sods,' she added. 'You'll feel safer – well, a bit – now Laurie's home.'

'He's off again,' I said as Laurie appeared in the kitchen, a small smart case in hand.

'I'll stay.' Rita offered. 'You can swap George in with you and I'll have his bed.' She didn't look at Laurie, who was bobbing down at the mirror in the kitchen, examining his hair and teeth.

Janice shook her head in disbelief. 'Go back down to your own family, Jen. Pack Saffron off to Spain – she might go more willingly now she isn't seeing Jamie Da Silva anymore – or she can come and stay with me. I've a spare room now there's only one of the twins left at home. You don't owe anyone anything here, you know.'

'Stop encouraging Jennifer to leave me,' Laurie said, almost mildly. 'She's happy here. George is *more* than happy here. Give it another six months and we'll be able to look for somewhere to live over Manchester way. Cheshire maybe – there's Alderley Edge and Wilmslow. We'd be mixing with the top brass there, Jen. You know, Man United players. Won't be long now. Dr Christian is in for the long haul.' He laughed and kissed my cheek and then Rita's. 'Must fly. Literally.' He laughed once more – a pantomime character – and was gone in a dramatic swirl of his new black Christian Dior jacket.

'Go back to your mum, Jen,' Janice advised as she moved to the door, car keys in hand. 'I don't *want* you to go – I've kind of got used to you being round, love – but there's nothing for you here.'

Rita stayed the night in George's bed and was there for Saffron while I took George to school the next morning. I felt absolutely shattered: I'd forgotten how George actually had conversations with himself while sleeping. I was just dropping off when I either awoke with a jolt remembering the knife at my neck, awoke while George had a one-way conversation with his teacher, Mrs Stevens, about the alpacas or turned over to find Sausage squashed against my nose. By six a.m. I'd had enough and got up and made coffee, which I took out into the garden. It was the most beautiful morning – each new summer day, it seemed, repainted with an unbroken cerulean sky; lush green meadows as far as the eye could see and an almost vulgar abundance of frothy white cow parsley on every verge.

When I returned from the school run, my mother-in-law and step-daughter were sitting in Rita's garden – now giddy with summer flowers – at the back of the house, drinking tea but seemingly making little inroad into the pile of toast that sat on the table in front of them.

'I suppose you want me to leave and go to Spain now?' Saffron asked. Black mascara smudges morphed into the dark rings of tiredness beneath her eyes and her long curly hair was unbrushed and probably in need of a good wash. She reminded me so much of Ada in a lot of ways, and my heart went out to her.

'Not at all,' I said, reaching for a slice of toast and buttering it thickly. And it was true, I didn't want her to go. I was getting used to her being round, even though we needed to sit her down and discuss her options re schooling or work. 'Maybe you can fly out to Benidorm for the holidays and then, when you come back at the end of August, enrol at college to do A-Levels. I know you'll be a year behind, but that doesn't matter a bit. You'll have to study maths and the sciences if you're serious about becoming a vet?'

Saffron said nothing for ages, her face hidden in Sausage's warm brown fur on her knee. 'That wouldn't be a problem,' she said finally. 'My GCSEs were all at Grade 9. Grandad and Gran and my teachers were furious when I decided to do the animal care course. I just wanted to be near animals every day.'

'Takes after Laurie,' Rita said proudly. 'Not about the animals – Laurie never liked them – the brains I mean. Do they do veterinary at Cambridge, do you think?' She pronounced it *vitnary*, like the Yorkshire farmers from *All Creatures Great and Small*, and I wanted to laugh.

'But *you're* going back south. Or moving to Cheshire,' Saffron said in a small voice. 'I heard Laurie talking last night. Everybody bloody moves and leaves me. Mum, Dad – my real dad, I mean,' (and I knew she wasn't talking about Laurie) '... my brother, Nathan, Grandad, Granny... No one really wants me...'

'Now, you're just being a drama queen,' I laughed. 'Have you ever thought about taking up acting, like Laurie?'

'Get *lost*,' she snapped and then started laughing herself, Rita and I joining in until we were really quite giggly. And then I remembered Dermot O'Callaghan's fury at Saffron hanging round Tod Mayhew's yard, and nothing was funny anymore.

'Look, Saffron, Dermot O'Callaghan was here last night.' I held her eye.

'Who?'

'Dermot O'Callaghan. He trains the horses over at Tod Mayhew's place.' I only had to speak Tod's name and I felt the beginning of lust starting right down where it mattered most.

'Right?' Saffron looked wary and wouldn't meet my eye.

'He says you've been hanging round down there, actually *handling* the horses in the paddock.'

'So?' Saffron was a mutinous adolescent once again.

'Oh Saffron, you can't do that, love.' Rita was horrified. 'You'll get yourself into trouble.'

'They're pussycats.'

'I thought they were horses,' I said mildly.

'You know what I mean,' Saffron scoffed. 'Compared to the horses I rode in Oz. I even broke in a brumby...'

'A brumby?' Rita and I leaned in.

'Brumbies – they're the feral horses that roam in the Northern Territory and also in the Australian Alps. I took part in the Brumby Challenge before we left Oz.'

'Brumby Challenge?' Rita and I leaned in even further.

Saffron nodded. 'You have a hundred-and-fifty days to tame a feral brumby, passively trapped from the wild. Horse and trainer are judged in Victoria. I worked with Sid, one of our neighbours, and absolutely loved it.'

'Weren't you frightened?' I asked. The thought of going near any horse, let alone a feral, Australian one (I'd seen Crocodile Dundee so knew what a native Australian creature was capable of), was terrifying. Unless I had to hold Tod Mayhew's stallion when he'd fallen off and sprained his ankle of course...

'Frightened? What of?' Saffron's scoffing brought me back from my lovely little Tod Mayhew dream. 'We didn't win that year, but I was determined to do it by myself next time, when I could. And then Dad buggered off and we came back to the UK.'

'I'm surprised you don't want to go back to Australia then,' I smiled.

'Trying to get rid of me?' Saffron raised an eyebrow and then relented. 'Not many brumbies or roos in Sydney. That's where Dad's living now. Or where Mum is with her new man in Perth.'

'I'm sorry,' I said. 'And no, of course I'm not trying to get rid of you. But if you were to take a flight out to Benidorm for a month or so, it would get you away from the Da Silva's and let you see Len and Sharon, and then…'

'And then Ada could have my bed for the summer?' Saffron shot me one of her looks.

'…and then,' I said patiently, 'you could sort yourself out and come back knowing what you want to do in September.'

'And if *you've* gone to Cheshire?' I could see fear of abandonment once more in Saffron's eyes. I was beginning to understand this step-daughter of mine.

'George and I are *not* going to Cheshire, Saffron,' I said firmly. And I knew that we absolutely weren't, despite Rita's raised eyebrows to the contrary.

'Back to Berkshire then? To your mum and Ada?' Saffron refused to look at me. 'With Laurie working again, he'd have to pay you maintenance…'

'You seem to know a lot about these things?' I smiled.

'Obviously. I heard all the arguments with Mum and Dad over who should pay what for me. In the end, Grandad ended up paying for it all. They didn't have to fork out for Nathan because he was over eighteen and had gone to live with his mates back in Canberra. So, as I was saying, Laurie would have to pay maintenance and you and George and Ada – and Sausage – could go and rent somewhere near your mum.'

'If that were to happen then you could lodge with your Aunt Janice. Just until you went off to uni—'

'To Cambridge to be a *vitnary*,' Rita interrupted, nodding sagely.

'—to train to be a vet,' I concluded.

'I'll think about it,' Saffron said, reaching for the toast. 'This stuff's cold; I'll make some more. Don't suppose you've got any Vegemite?'

30

It was really quite lovely sitting out there in the warmth of an English summer's garden and, while Rita dug around with a trowel, weeding the flowerbeds I'd been too busy to give any attention to, Saffron and I stretched out in the sunshine, the birdsong and the soporific murmur of bees, our eyes closing as the mellifluous sounds of the countryside lulled us to sleep.

'Oh,' Rita suddenly said, waving her trowel in my direction. 'I'm so sorry, Jennifer. Totally forgot. Someone called Catherine rang both your mobile and the landline while you were out. I told her you'd forgotten to take your phone and you'd ring her when you got back from taking George. Really sorry. She said it was important as well...'

At once fully awake, I dashed inside to find my phone where I'd left it in the kitchen and rang Catherine Barker straight back.

'Ah, Jen, where've you been? Been ringing you all morning.'

'Sorry, missed your calls.'

'You need a better secretary,' she laughed. 'OK. Sit down.'

'I'm sitting,' I said, clutching the phone with a sweaty hand.

'They love it.'

'Who loves it?'

'The team here at Alcidae House.'

'Really?' I felt my pulse race with excitement.

'Now, as your friend, I'm going to suggest you get an agent...'

'I've got an agent – Marcia – you know I have.'

'Yes, and she deals with worthy literary stuff like your Byron and your Aunt Agnes's Bletchley Diaries.'

'I know Marcia. She'd be up for this as well.' I wasn't actually convinced: Marcia was old-school literary stuff and would more than likely think Magnolia and her gang totally beyond the pale. And her consideration.

'Well, you need to get her on board; I bet you've not told her you've been writing this, have you?'

Catherine laughed when I didn't answer. As far as Marcia knew, I was well entrenched into my research on the life and times of Samuel T. Coleridge. I wasn't.

'Speak to Marcia, Jen, and send the rest of it to us through her. We're all a bit excited here – you know, with people still on a Bridgerton high, we're convinced this might just be the next big thing.'

'Right. Are you sure?'

'Absolutely.' Catherine laughed again. 'And obviously with you married to Laurie Lewis... you know after the court case... well, the press and readers won't be able to wait to get their mitts on it. It's a bit hot in places, Jennifer. Mind you, since you're married to a Sex God, it's not surprising. You're a dark horse, you are, Jennifer Baylis-Lewis...'

'Right,' I said, when I finally manged to get a word out. Or a word in. Was it in or out?

'Are you there, Jen? You're not saying anything?'

'I'm here, I'm here,' I said slowly. A black cloud that Magnolia might only be seeing the light of day because I was married to Laurie Lewis was starting to descend. 'If you take it on, Catherine, maybe I should assume a pen name? I mean, it's nothing like my literary non-fiction stuff, is it...?'

'I wouldn't know, Jennifer, I've always found them a bit hard going to be honest.' She laughed once more.

'The thing is, I don't want people to get the wrong idea that my other stuff is also full of, you know, heaving bosoms and whirling testicles...'

'Yes, we *really* liked that bit.' Catherine giggled. 'Now, don't worry about details such as pen names at this stage – although I think you'd be mad not to jump on the Laurie Lewis bandwagon...'

But I'm in the process of finding a way to jump right off it.

'... What you need to do now is 'fess up to Marcia what you've been up to, finish those final chapters and then we can all work together on it. Must dash, Jen – I bet you've forgotten how mad life down here in London can get when nothing at all happens up there in the countryside?'

I've had a stash of drugs in my pants drawer... I've had a knife held against my throat... I've fallen in love with a man who isn't my husband... I'm going to leave my husband...

I put down the phone and made a decision.

With an overwhelming need to see Tod, I left Rita and Saffron in the garden and set off in the direction of the stables. I didn't even take Sausage with me, just dashed on some lipstick and mascara, sprayed perfume and ran fingers through my hair before walking quickly down the lanes and across the fields towards the yard. As I descended into the valley, becoming hotter and sweatier by the minute in the late-morning sunshine, I shielded my eyes against the bright light in order to make out a figure climbing a stile before making its way up towards me.

'Jennifer?' Tod walked quickly towards me.

'I was just coming to see you.'

'Me to you too.' He wasn't smiling. He'd obviously come straight from the gallops as he was wearing jodhpurs and black riding boots. A black T-shirt, its underarms ringed with sweat, was tucked into the jodhpurs and kept in place with a black leather belt. 'Sorry, a bit sweaty,' he apologised. 'I wouldn't come too near…'

Not come too near? It was all I could do not to reach out a hand to the lock of blond hair he constantly and impatiently pushed back. All I could do not to jump on him there and then in that daisy-strewn meadow, push my face into his black T-shirt-covered chest and breathe him in.

'Look Jennifer, Dermot's just told me. I've been out with the horses since five a.m. and he found me a few minutes ago to tell me.'

'Told you what?' As if I didn't know.

'About your husband's daughter.'

'Right, I'm sorry, I really am.'

'You *have* to tell her to keep away. The horse Dermot said she was just about to jump on is one of the best in the yard. I don't know how the hell she got into the paddock.'

'Is it worth a lot?' I asked, for something to say. Tod, I could see, was angry.

'Just a *bit*,' he said. 'At least a couple of hundred.'

'A couple of hundred pounds? Goodness, is that all? I'd have thought…' I trailed off when I saw Tod's arched eyebrow. 'A couple of hundred *thousand*? Pounds?'

He nodded. 'They're not my horses, Jennifer. They mainly belong to racing syndicates and big businesses. I merely handle and train them, but they're my responsibility. That husband of yours *has* to have a word with her. It's my reputation and the reputation of the yard at stake here.'

'I'm sorry,' I said, turning away. 'I can see that.' I suddenly had an awful need to cry. To sob and yell. To let out all the pent-up worry and emotion of the last nine months – losing my home, having to leave Ada, being with a man I didn't love anymore, never mind even like much… The knife at my throat… I wanted my dad.

'Jennifer?'

'I'm really really sorry,' I repeated stiffly. 'I'll make sure I know where she is all the time… I need to get back…' *Don't cry and make a fool of yourself, Jennifer. Do not.* I knew if I started, I'd never stop.

I turned and quickly started back up the wildflower-covered sloping meadow in front of me.

'Jennifer… What is it?' Tod was at my side, his hand on my arm. 'Look, I'm sorry if I came over a bit heavy but she has to understand…? Surely you see that… Jennifer…?'

I couldn't stop the great racking sobs that were tearing out of me. There were tears, snot, running mascara and incoherent explanations all trying to get out at once, but amalgamating only in one great mess and making a total exhibition of myself. I was now at that stage of trying to gulp down air and muttering that I wanted my dad. Like the little girl I'd once been.

'Your dad? Can I ring him for you?'

'He's died.'

'Oh no. I'm so sorry, Jennifer. When?'

'Two years ago. And I... And I didn't cry for him then. Why didn't I cry for him? Probably because I knew if I started, I'd never stop. And, you know, he never wanted me to marry Laurie Lewis. And I wouldn't listen. And I should have done. But I was pregnant with Ada. I *wanted* to be pregnant with Ada. And over the years we eventually fell out about Laurie. He never ever said, but I think my dad probably *knew* he'd been messing around with other women. In fact, things are beginning to fall into place more now... You know, *none so blind as those who will not see*? I didn't know. I really didn't. I never thought Laurie would do that to me. But it's just something Mum said to me after Dad died. She didn't come outright with it, but I think Dad knew something – possibly he'd seen Laurie with some other woman. Dad never even told Mum, well I don't think he did, but it's just little things Mum has intimated. I think Dad had got himself worked up about Laurie – didn't know whether to tell me and Mum. And he went out on the boat. He always knew what he was doing, always did go too fast. But he wasn't concentrating, obviously had other things on his mind... And we... we hadn't been speaking for a couple of weeks before he was killed in Kefalonia. And I never... I never... I never saw him again... And it's all my fault.'

'Jennifer. Come on, come and sit down.' Tod took my

hand and pushed me gently onto the grass behind me. He found a pristine white hanky in the pocket of his jodhpurs and passed it over. I blew loudly into it and saw it was now covered in pink lipstick and mascara.

'Sorry,' I said, handing it back.

'It'll wash.'

'No, I mean sorry for laying this all on you.'

'You obviously needed to let it all out,' he said, stroking my arm. 'I've been there,' he said seriously.

'Been where? Kefalonia?' I looked across at him.

'No!' he actually laughed out loud at that. 'No, I mean I've been in a relationship when it's turned toxic and those who love you try to warn you and you end up falling out with those who're trying to make you see sense, rather than the one you should be booting out.'

'Oh? Serena?'

'Serena?' He pulled a face. 'No, there's never really been anything serious between Serena and me.'

'Your wife then?'

Tod nodded. 'You knew I'd been married?'

'Cheryl, my sister-in-law told me. Where is she now?'

'Back in Sweden. But not before I ended up falling out with Dermot for telling me the truth.'

'It must have hurt.'

'What? Me falling out with Dermot? Yes, yes it did.'

'No,' I tutted. 'Losing your wife.'

'Hurt like hell. And then, out of the blue, after years of it hurting like hell, someone appears in your life who you feel a connection with for whatever reason, who has you smiling into the mirror when you're shaving, who you really want to get to know more. But who you daren't even begin to hope they're no longer in love with the man they're married to…' Tod broke off, embarrassed.

I brought a tentative hand up to the recalcitrant lock of hair, pushing it back into place and he smiled, wiping away mascara from my face with the ball of his thumb.

And then he bent his head to mine, kissing the corner of my mouth and then the other corner and that lock of hair kept coming between us and I said something about finding a scrunchy but then found I was kissing him back with so much fervour that I think I surprised both of us. We came up for air and sort of looked at each other and then I reached out for him once more and my face was in that black T-shirt of his and, with an overhead lark yelling its heart out and the smell of newly mown hay drifting across the dry-stone walls, pervading all my senses, it was, I think, the most wonderfully erotic experience of my life.

'I need to get off,' Tod eventually said, looking at his watch. 'I'm driving up to Edinburgh with Dermot. I don't like leaving the stable in the grooms' hands, even for one night, but there's a young horse I'm looking at. I want to train her up for myself and need Dermot's opinion. 'Come on, much as I'd rather stay here, kissing you, I need to go.'

Tod walked back with me across the meadows towards Daisy Royd, holding my hand while he explained how the yard was run, how dependent he was on Dermot O'Callaghan and how delighted he was that the Mayhew Racing Stable was gaining both national as well as international recognition amongst the racing fraternity. He was so busy, he said, he'd had to take on new staff, new stable hands, training up a couple of new jockeys he'd poached from stables in Ireland on Dermot's recommendation. Tod wanted to know all about my writing, what I was involved with and I told him about the morning's phone call from Catherine Barker at Alcidae House. Obviously remembering the debate I'd had with Serena at Cassie Beresford's place, Tod laughed delightedly about my writing Regency romance instead of researching Coleridge, and told me to go for it. He left me at a stile several fields from the farm, kissing me so deeply I wasn't convinced I'd be able to get up and over it.

'You are the best kisser I've ever kissed,' I smiled dreamily, sounding like that thirteen-year-old in the school assembly once again.

'I aim to please,' he grinned, kissing me some more and then, looking me in the eye as he stroked my face, adding, 'Jennifer, you're going to have to decide what you want. With your marriage, I mean? I've never been into having affairs with other men's wives… I'll see you soon.' He patted my arm and, with that, set off back down the fields while I stood and watched until he was a black and cream dot on the horizon and then disappeared. I floated home. And yes, I'd called Daisy Royd Farm *home*.

'Why don't you ever take your phone with you, Jennifer?' Rita thrust my phone towards me. 'Your mum's been ringing. It's your auntie. Your great-auntie?'

'Aunt Agnes?'

'I think that's who your mum said. Sorry, love, but she's not well, *not well at all*.' Rita emphasised the last words and I wondered if this was a Yorkshire euphemism for Aunt Agnes actually having died.

'Has she died?' I asked, staring at Rita, my heart sinking. Please say she hadn't gone before I'd had a chance to say goodbye. Not like with Dad.

'No, but your mum wants you to get down there. Your auntie's in hospital – had a fall – and she keeps asking for *you*. You'd better go, love. Is she getting on?'

'She's ninety-eight.'

'Goodness,' Rita looked at her watch. 'Every second counts when you're that age. Right, love, you get off. Shame Laurence has got the Audi. Will you be OK in that little car?'

'Hang on, hang on. I need to think. I might be better going down by train. Which hospital is she in? Let me ring Mum.'

'Don't you worry about George. I'll fetch him back from school, go and get a few of my own things from the bungalow and stay with him until you get back.'

'What about the hens? The alpacas? Sausage? Saffron? Where *is* Saffron?'

'Jennifer!' Rita gave me such a look. 'I've looked after dogs, hens and kids all my life. If there's a problem with the alpacas, I'll get Janice over.'

'Saffron? Where is she?'

'She's gone out – I gave her a lift down to the bus. She's had Len on the phone all afternoon and he's told her to go down to college and sort things out there. It's good she's going to start with her A-Levels in September.'

'Right, yes, that is good. Did she seem OK? You know, after last night?'

'She's a little toughie, that one – there's a lot of her Auntie Janice in her. Now, come on, go ring your mum.'

I wasn't convinced Saffron was the little toughie Rita appeared to think she was, but I needed to get off. I loved Aunt Agnes. We'd necessarily spent a lot of time together when we were working on her Bletchley diaries, and what had started as work had soon morphed into a total pleasure at being in her company as she recounted her past to me. It was obvious to anyone that, at ninety-eight, Agnes didn't have many years left – although *she* really was an old toughie and I'd always assumed she'd be around for that telegram from the Queen. Assumed that, once I'd returned down south to live, she'd still be around, pottering away in that untidy Berkshire flat of hers, its shelves overflowing with books and documents, Mahler's Symphony Number 5 (Adagietto) blasting out at full volume as she mixed her lunchtime gin and tonic.

I rang Mum.

'Oh, you're *there*, Jennifer.' Mum sounded stressed. 'Now, do you want me to pick you up from King's Cross? Drive you straight to the hospital? She's in the Royal Berkshire in Reading and is doing nothing but asking where you are. When you're going to get here.'

'I was going to drive.'

'You'll get stuck in the rush hour traffic. There's a train from Wakefield at four-ten. I looked it up. We can be at the hospital just after seven-thirty if you get your skates on.'

'Right, OK,'

'Just keep your phone on. Tell me what's happening.'

The 16.10 Great Eastern from Wakefield pulled into King's Cross two hours later and I spotted Ada immediately as she waited under the spectacular new steel structure on the western concourse.

'Darling, you've grown,' I said, hugging her to me, not wanting to let her go. 'And your hair? Goodness, it's quite different.' The black curls were gone, replaced by a sort of aubergine-coloured, very straight, choppy – and asymmetrical – bob.

'Do you like it?'

'Well, it's different. But, yes, I do.' I hugged her again. 'Where's Granny?'

'Circling.' Ada laughed. 'A bit like a plane at Heathrow that can't land. We'd no idea where to park so she's just driving around. If we've missed her, she'll be another twenty minutes… oh we're in luck, she's over there. Come on…' Ada grabbed my hand and, taking no notice of the hooting black cabs, Ubers, great big red London buses, cars and myriad bikes, plunged me into the early evening traffic of the Euston Road.

'Jesus,' I breathed. 'The only traffic I see at home is your Aunt Janice's tractor. And that only comes out now on heydays and holidays.' I actually felt quite scared, the noise of people, traffic and London in general totally overpowering my senses. Had London always been like this?

'Save your breath, Mum,' Ada ordered as she grabbed my hand once more and set off from the safety of the refuge in the middle of the road. 'Get in,' she added as Mum, kerb crawling despite the furious onslaught of gesticulations and hooting, pulled up in front of us and we jumped in and roared off at speed, Mum pulling out and overtaking into the main lane like she was in a James Bond movie.

'Bloody hell, Mum.'

I fell back onto the front passenger seat and she grinned across at me. 'Phil persuaded me to do one of those skid-pan courses in the car.'

'Dad would have been proud,' I said, not looking at her.

'Right,' she said, indicating left. 'Let's get out on to the A40. 'How are you darling? We've missed you so much, haven't we Ada?'

'Totally,' Ada said from the back seat, already concentrating on her phone.

'New boyfriend,' Mum mouthed.

I'd rung Ada every evening after each GCSE exam and had received the same replies: *No problem; A doddle; Easy peasy.*

'So, school all finished now, Ada?' I turned to the back seat. 'How does that feel?'

'Well, for the summer, obviously...'

I knew I needed the big chat with Ada as to what was going to happen next with her schooling and where she was going to be in September but, catching the glance between Mum and Ada through the mirror, and with her fingers back texting for Britain, I realised now was not the moment. Half an hour into a car journey down the M4, with Mum confidently speeding along like some deranged roadrunner, I decided to hold my tongue and turned, instead, to Aunt Agnes.

'She's not so good, Jennifer,' Mum frowned. 'A possible stroke or heart attack. That's why she fell, apparently. I've been with her this morning and the hospital told me to expect the worst. She just kept asking where you were and saying she wanted to see you before she, you know...'

'Right OK.' I felt tears start.

'You always were her favourite. Don't expect too much, will you?' Mum took her hand from the wheel and patted my knee before overtaking an Eddie Stobart lorry and continuing towards Reading in the fast lane.

31

'Jennifer?' Aunt Agnes clutched at my hand with dry, papery fingers, but she managed a small smile. 'I knew you'd get here. I wanted to tell you something myself.'

'I'm here.' I pulled a chair towards the bed, and sitting down reached for her hand once more. The blue veins stood out on her yellowish hands, a veritable motorway map, going nowhere but to their final destination.

'How's that husband of yours? Have you left him yet?'

I glanced across the single-bedded room towards the open door where Mum and Ada were being brought up to date by the nurse in charge. 'I'm working on it, Aunt Agnes. I'm not going to be with him much longer.'

'Good, good. That's good. The thing is, Jennifer, I don't want that little popinjay getting his hands on any of it.'

If it hadn't taken so much out of Agnes to speak, I'd probably have laughed at her description of Laurie. Instead, I smiled and said, 'Actually, Agnes, I'm in love with someone else.'

'Decent, is he?'

'Very. You'd like him; he trains top racehorses.'

'The gee-gees?' Her eyes widened slightly. 'Good girl.' She paused, obviously taking this in before asking: 'Who won the seven-thirty at Epsom last night? Any idea? Had an either way bet on something last night... until I fell...' She trailed off and her eyes began to close. 'Can't remember the name of it...'

'I'll look into it for you,' I promised. 'Get your winnings from the bookies if there are any.'

'Listen, Jennifer. Everything I have is yours... Cynthia's to have the jewellery... there's some money each for Ada and George and Jeremy's little ones... but the flat and the rest of the money is yours.' Agnes's eyes opened and she cackled slightly. 'There's enough, once you sell the flat, for you to have some independence.'

'Right. OK.' As far as I knew, Agnes had had enough to live on, enough to pay for her gin, some decent bottles of wine and a flutter on the horses, but apart from that she'd lived pretty frugally and within, what I assumed were, her means.

'Listen, come here.' Agnes pulled me closer. 'Been playing the market for donkeys...' She broke off, unable to continue.

'Which market? Newmarket?'

'The *market*,' she tutted. 'The *stock* markets. Donkeys' years.' Her eyes opened and she became quite animated. 'I love it; just like being back codebreaking, working out where to go next. Anyway, it's all yours. I know I should probably have let you have some of it when the house in St Albans was taken away from you...' Agnes's eyes fluttered and then closed and for a good twenty seconds she didn't carry on, but then her eyes opened wide once more '... but no way was I letting *him* getting any of it...' She grabbed at my hands once more and whispered gleefully into my ear: 'Listen, Jennifer, there's enough for you to come back south.'

'Oh?'

'You heard. Now, spend it well with this lovely new horse man of yours and don't let that other bugger near it...' She trailed off. 'Jennifer...' she clutched at my hand once more, '... the will's with my solicitor... what's he called...?' she trailed off. 'Anyway, there's a copy in the top drawer...' Her hand went limp as her eyes closed and her breathing became laboured. Mum and Ada joined me and the three of us sat with her for another ten minutes. Eventually an awful gurgling sound replaced the heavy breathing and, frightened, I went for the nurse.

'Could you all leave the room?' she asked.

'I'd like to be with her,' I pleaded. 'Is this it?'

'Just give me a few minutes,' the nurse replied.

Five minutes later we trooped back in, and sat at Aunt Agnes's bedside for the next two hours, me stroking one hand, Mum the other while Ada went for endless cups of coffee. Just once, Agnes opened her eyes slightly, turned and winked in my direction, but around ten p.m. she took the last breath of her ninety-eight years.

Mum, Ada and I drove back to Mum's house in Hurley in silence. This had all happened so quickly and none of us had been prepared for it. One minute Agnes was still pretty much on the ball: reading, conducting music with a ruler, eating her way through tins of corned beef and M&S scotch eggs to accompany her favourite *Domaine Serge Laporte* Sancerre. As well as, apparently, gambling both on the horses and the stock exchange.

And then she was gone.

The three of us ate shepherd's pie, raising a somewhat

tearful glass of Sancerre that Mum managed to find in the cellar, and thus paid tribute to my great aunt's almost-century. Then, after admiring Mum's new dressing room and en suite, and absolutely shattered from the previous sleepless night, as well as the emotion of losing Agnes, I squeezed into the single bed in the spare room and slept ten hours undisturbed.

I woke in the tiny box room to find Mum sitting on the edge of the bed while a mug of tea steamed in her hand. She handed me the mug as I sat up.

'When were you going to tell me?' Mum, I could tell, wasn't happy. In fact, she appeared downright angry.

'I don't know. Today I suppose. It's still sinking in. Did *you* know?'

'How would *I* know?'

'I thought she might have told you what she was planning.'

'What who was planning?' Mum stared.

'Aunt Agnes.' I stared back.

'Jennifer, I'm not talking about Agnes. I'm talking about *this*.' Mum almost threw the folded newspaper at me. 'Are you telling me you didn't know?'

One of the more garish tabloids, its front page screaming the accusatory headline:

LOVE RAT LAURIE LEWIS IN ROMP WITH STREET'S PATSY

lay on the cream counterpane in front of me.

'Not your usual *Telegraph* read, Mum?' I glanced at the first couple of lines and handed it back to her.

'I wouldn't dream of buying this normally,' she said indignantly, giving it a little shake between finger and thumb as if, simply by touching it, she'd be infected by its content. 'I just walked down to the corner shop to get milk and it was there, shouting out at me, loud and clear.'

'No,' I said calmly, 'I didn't know. And Mum, apart from the kids having to see this and go through it all once again, I really, really, *really* don't give a flying fuck.'

'Language, Jennifer.' Mum was shocked. But whether it was at my use of profanity, or at the content of the newspaper, or that, at last, I appeared oblivious to anything Laurie was still apparently capable of throwing at me, or all three, I wasn't quite sure.

Eventually, she took my hand and said, 'Please don't tell me, darling, you don't give a...' Mum hesitated '... a flying... *wotsit* because you knew all about this and you're *still* happy to go along with it? Prepared to carry on as you are with him, yet again?'

I started to laugh at Mum's inability to swear, even while the garish headline continued to scream its indignation into the room. 'No, Mum, I don't give a *flying wotsit* because I'm totally and utterly free of any love I once had for Laurie.' I paused and held Mum's eye, 'And now that Aunt Agnes has left me her flat and some money, I'm financially able to be just where *I* want to be with my two children.'

'Left you some money? Oh?' Mum stared. 'Oh, darling, don't be disappointed, will you? Apart from the flat – which is wonderful now that it's yours, of course – she really didn't have much, you know.'

'She told me there's *some*.' I repeated word for word what Aunt Agnes had told me.

'Oh no, Jennifer, I don't think so – you just had to look at those old cardigans she used to wear to see she had very little. She always lived pretty frugally, although I think possibly there's always been some family money in there somewhere. I never knew she played the stock market. Mind you, she was always on that computer of hers, spent hours on it – I did sometimes wonder if she wasn't into a bit of, you know, *porn...*'

'Mum!' I tutted, laughing.

'Sorry, sorry. It's reading *this stuff...*' She picked up the paper, looking for somewhere to hide it. 'Don't want Ada to see it, just yet.' Mum suddenly appeared to have second thoughts and handed it back to me. 'You've not read it all, Jen.'

'And I don't intend on doing so.' I smiled, feeling such a glorious sense of freedom; of finally knowing and realising there was nothing Laurie could do to hurt me anymore.

'So,' Mum was saying, as she continued to looked at me worriedly, searching my face for clues that my reaction was genuine and I wasn't just trying to appease her, 'you'll come back south.' It was a statement rather than a question. 'No reason not to now. And while you're here you can look for somewhere to rent, can't you? Although, I suppose you could live temporarily in Agnes's flat? I don't think it's really a permanent place for you and the children. Having said that,' she went on, shivering slightly, 'I'd be a bit frightened of Aunt Agnes coming back...'

'Mum, she's died, not just popped out for a pint of milk.'

'You know what I mean. There are two bedrooms for

you and George to stay there until you sell it and find somewhere that you really want to buy. Mind you, house prices round here are extortionate.'

'You have a key to the flat?'

'Yes, of course. We can drive over there later, if you want. Need to turn the water off and empty the fridge and things, I suppose.'

I picked up the newspaper and made to get out of bed. 'I need to talk to Ada first. And then ring Rita to try and keep this from George as best she can.'

'Are you not going to ring Laurie?' Mum raised an eyebrow. 'You know, to ask him what's been going on?'

'I think it's pretty obvious what's been going on,' I smiled. 'And no, I have no intention of speaking to him. It's all over, Mum, and apart from sorting out what's best for Ada and George, I really don't care.'

'Dad been up to his old tricks again, Mum?' Ada was at the kitchen table eating toast dripping in honey.

'You know?'

'Mum, I'm on social media; I've got "*friends*…"' Ada drew speech marks in the air, 'only too happy to ask if I'm OK and is there anything they can do to help.' Ada snorted disparagingly. 'You know, Mum, apart from not wanting to leave my friends and school, as well as not wanting to live in that farmhouse up there…' Ada pointed northwards with her slice of toast, honey running onto her hand, 'I didn't want to come with you and George because I didn't want to see you go through all this again.'

'Oh?'

'Well, that's what he's like, isn't he?' Ada licked at the splodge of honey on her wrist. 'A leopard doesn't change its spots,' she added sagely, sounding more like my granny than my sixteen-year-old. 'And I'm fine about it. And now, hopefully, you and George will come back home. I *would* like that, you know. I *have* missed you both.'

'Have you, darling?' I went to hug her.

'Of course. Mind you, I'm not going to fall out with Laurie.'

'Laurie?' I stared.

'I think from now on, I shall call him Laurie. I mean he's not been much of a *dad*, has he? You know, lately? Really? Not like *your* dad was with you. I know Dad was always there for me when I was little, but he just seems to have changed these past two or three years. Too busy doing his own thing to always be available for me and George. I've been looking at all the photos of you with Grandpa. *He* was there for every occasion: every holiday, every school sports day, all your speech days. Now, he really *was* a dad, wasn't he? How many photos are there of me with *Laurie* after my thirteenth birthday?' She emphasised his name, obviously trying it out for size. 'But I'm fine, Mum, honest. I won't fall out with him, because I *am* going to be an actor, you know, and that will be one thing he'll be able to help me with.'

'Right,' I said faintly, not quite knowing how else to answer this confident, clever, beautiful daughter of mine. 'OK.'

'Phone, Jen.' Mum held out the house phone from its place in the hallway. 'Rita,' she whispered.

'Jennifer…? I don't know what to say.' Rita was obviously distressed. 'I've been trying to ring your mobile all morning, well, since I found out. You've turned it off,' she said, almost accusingly and then immediately added, 'but I don't blame you, love.'

'Out of charge, actually. You don't read the tabloids, do you?' I laughed.

'Are you OK? Are you laughing? And no, I don't read them, but Janice does. She came round to tell me. She was furious. And I don't blame her, Jennifer. We're all so sorry. So sorry you're being put through this all over again.'

'I'd already made the decision to leave him, Rita. This is just the icing on the cake, if you like.'

'Icing on the cake?'

'Sorry, probably wrong choice of words. Look, Rita, my only concern now is George. Where is he?'

'At school. Obviously. I dropped him off before Janice told me. To be honest, Jennifer, I did feel some of the playground mums were looking at me a bit strangely. I didn't realise why at the time.'

'Hell. Right, I'll ring Cassie Beresford and make sure he's OK.'

'When are you coming back, Jennifer?'

'Rita, if it wasn't for George, I wouldn't be coming back at all.'

Yes, you would, you big fat fibber: You're desperate to get back to see Tod. And to make sure Saffron is OK…

'Look, Rita, are you OK hanging on to George for a couple of days?'

'Of course I am,' she said indignantly. 'I'm his granny.'

'Thank you. I have so much to help sort out here – the funeral and everything and Agnes's flat.'

'Will you be able to live *there*?' Rita's voice was small. 'You and George, I mean?'

'Yes.'

'I'll miss George so much.'

'I know. I'm sorry. Listen, Rita, can you make sure Saffron is going to be alright? She's not getting mixed up with the Da Silva's again? Get Janice involved, will you? She knows what's going on and she said Saffron can lodge with her once she comes back from Spain.'

'Comes back from Spain?'

'That's the plan. She goes to stay with Len and Sharon until September, and then Janice has offered to have her stay with her while she does her A-Levels.'

'Right. Goodness me, what a flipping to-do all this is. I am *not* happy with Laurence.'

She obviously wasn't if she was giving her darling son his full Sunday-best handle.

'Tell George I'll ring him this afternoon, after school, Rita.' I rang off, immediately dialling Little Acorns school and was put through to Cassie Beresford by the school secretary.

'Oh, Jennifer? You alright? Where are you?'

'With my mum in Berkshire. My great-aunt has died.'

'Oh, I'm so sorry. George said she was poorly.'

'Is he OK?'

'Bit tearful. I've had him in here with me for an hour. You know, on the pretext of helping me with a couple of jobs? I thought at first it was because you'd gone to London and he was missing you and worried about this aunt of yours...?' Cassie trailed off.

'George hardly knows her, Cassie. I'm assuming you know the real reason?'

'I do now. Some of the older kids were teasing him at playtime about it; I've totally blasted them out. Look, I'm sorry, Jennifer. If it helps, I know pretty much how you're feeling.'

'I doubt it, Cassie.'

'My husband was outed at a charity auction. I had to go through all the gossip and sympathy and gloating...'

'No, I'm sure you went through hell. And I understand that. What I *am* saying is I'm really *not* going through any emotional turmoil with regards Laurie. Because I no longer love him and certainly don't want to be with him anymore. I was on the point of leaving him.'

'Tod?'

'I beg your pardon?'

'Oh god, Jennifer, I'm so sorry. I'm just being an agony aunt here instead of a headteacher. I should learn to shut up...'

'Cassie, all I'm bothered about now is George.'

'Of course, of course. God, me and my big mouth...'

I actually smiled at that. 'Cassie, stop beating yourself up. And yes, it's Tod...'

'Really? Is it?' I could almost see Cassie's big grin.

'I think so. I hope so. But, as I say, George is my only consideration at the moment.'

'Yes of course.' Cassie's headmistress head was firmly back in place. 'I'll make all the staff aware of the situation. We'll do everything that's necessary here to help George.'

'Has he been in touch?' Mum pulled out of her drive and turned left, heading in the direction of Agnes's flat.

'Who?' My immediate thought was Tod, who hadn't.

'Who do you think?' Mum tutted. '*Laurie.*'

'I think he's probably gone to ground. He's in Paris, filming.'

'So, who is this Pasty?'

I actually laughed at that. '*Patsy*, Mum. Patsy Pilkington. Barmaid on *The Street*.'

'Pasty Pilkington?' Mum sucked her teeth once more. 'Made-up name, obviously.'

'Well, you've just made it up. Pasty! Yes, we'll call her Pasty from now on. No, he'll have gone to ground in a lurrrve nest. Not sure how it's going to affect this new role of his.' I tutted myself. 'God, just when I thought he might be having the means for some financial solubility – stability even – the stupid pillock goes and does this.'

'Pillock,' Mum agreed comfortably. 'Always was.'

It seemed strange, rude almost, unlocking and entering Agnes's flat without knocking. Agnes had apparently banged on the wall of the neighbouring flat and the young woman there not only had a key but had rung 999 and then Mum. She'd obviously missed the glass of wine, presumably upended as Agnes fell, and there was a tiny, colourless puddle on the coffee table. Her computer was still on, but I had no idea of any password to be able to save anything and turn it off. Instead, I switched it off at the mains.

'Agnes said the will was in a top drawer somewhere,' I frowned. 'I don't know if she meant in here or her bedroom.' I hesitated. 'You don't think it's all a bit money-grubbing? You know, coming here the day after she's died to find the will?'

'You have to find the will, Jen, in order to see what her

instructions were regarding her body.' Mum was already pulling open top drawers.

I stared. 'What do you mean?'

'Jen, she'll have left instructions about her funeral. You know, cremation or burial.'

'Did you never discuss it with her?'

'No, I always assumed she'd go on for ever.' Mum pulled the top drawer of a beautiful Queen Anne bureau. 'Right got it.' She pulled out a stiff white bulky envelope and perused the first page of the contents in silence. 'Right. She doesn't want to be buried.'

'Don't blame her. Can I just inform you now, Mum, with my horror of worms, *I* want to be cremated…?'

'She doesn't want to be cremated, either.'

'There's a third option?' I stared.

'She's donated her body to science. She wants to go back to Cambridge University.'

'What? You're having me on?'

Mum passed me the will without another word.

'Do you think they'll want such an old one?' We caught each other's eye and I could see, like me, she didn't know whether to laugh or cry.

'Well, that's one way to go back to her beloved college,' Mum said, beginning to giggle. 'As a sodding cadaver. Good for her.'

'Right, here's the name of the solicitor who has the original will. Shall I ring them?'

'Yes, I did this when Dad died.' That thought sobered us both up somewhat and I pushed the numbers on my mobile and got through to a receptionist who immediately put us through to Agnes's solicitor.

'Oh, I'm so sorry to hear this. So sorry for your loss,' Rodney Castle at Castle, Denton and Ali said, once I'd explained who I was and that Aunt Agnes had died. 'I was only with her last week. She was a game old bird, wasn't she? I've spent many an evening round at the flat discussing her time at Cambridge and then at Bletchley Park. So, you must be her great-niece, Mrs Baylis-Lewis? The editor of her memoirs?'

'Yes, that's right.'

'I'm sure you've seen a copy of the will?'

'Yes,' I agreed. 'That's how we knew to ring you.'

'And you know you're the main beneficiary, Mrs Baylis-Lewis?'

'Yes. She told me this before she died last night.'

He hesitated. 'I obviously can't really discuss this with you over the phone. I'll make an appointment for you to come in to the office.'

'Thank you. Can you make it sooner rather than later? I have to get back up to Yorkshire... my little boy...'

'I can see you early tomorrow morning?'

'Lovely. Look, Mr Castle, I'll be blunt. Agnes intimated she'd left me some money as well as the flat?'

There was silence from the solicitor's end and I wondered if the line had gone dead. 'Mr Castle?'

'Sorry, Mrs Baylis-Lewis. I think Agnes has been having you on...'

'Oh.' I felt a jolt of disappointment.

'Definitely having you on.' Rodney Castle laughed. 'It's not just *some* money.'

'Oh?'

'Look, suffice it to say at this stage, I was able to have

a conversation with her only last week about how much was accrued in her estate and portfolio. Now, my lips are sealed – I'm saying nothing more until I'm with you face-to-face. But yes, my dear, there's quite a bit more than *some* money…'

32

With the pair of us in a bit of a daze after the news imparted by Rodney Castle, Mum and I locked up the flat and walked into nearby Whitchurch-on-Thames to find coffee.

'Millionaire's shortbread, Jen?' Mum asked from the counter where she stood, ordering lattes. Her eyes widened as she realised what she'd said, and I started to giggle almost hysterically.

'Shh,' Mum hissed, starting to laugh herself. 'If you carry on like this, I'll have to slap your face. Oh Jen, how fortuitous – the day you really accept what a cheat that husband of yours is, it sounds like you may have been given enough money to do something about it.'

'Mum, I don't need money to *do something about it*. I told you, I was already leaving Laurie. I just need to sort out a few things in my mind...'

'What is there to sort out, for heaven's sake? Get back up to that god-forsaken place, pack up your things, pack up George and get back down here where you both belong.'

'Mum, there's Saffron...'

'Nothing to do with you,' Mum snorted. 'She's Laurie's *love child...*' Mum almost spat the words '... after cheating on *you*. You know,' Mum went on, scowling, 'from what you've told me, you and this barmaid must have been pregnant around the same time.'

'Saffron is Ada's and George's *sister*, Mum.'

'Not really, surely?' Mum took a sip of her coffee. 'Anyway, thank goodness your father never knew about all this carry on. I reckon he'd have gone after him with a gun, if he had.'

'Don't be so bloody dramatic, Mum.' Any reminder of how I'd ignored Dad's advice – his almost pleading – that I didn't marry Laurie, always brought guilt crashing down on my head.

'It would have broken his heart to see what you've put up with these past couple of years,' Mum sniffed, before dabbing at the remaining crumbs of her shortbread with a finger.

'Mum, a lot of the time my life with Laurie was lovely. Really, really lovely. He was a good husband and father. He was always there for the kids. He adored them; you know he did. He was determined to have a different relationship with them than he'd had with Terry Lewis.'

'Yes, alright, alright, Jen.' Mum held up both hands, relenting. 'Your father, particularly, felt maybe we'd misjudged Laurie. You know, once the kids came along. When you went through that depression and anxiety after you'd had Ada, and it seemed to go on for such a long time, we couldn't fault Laurie then. He was there for you…' Mum sighed. 'But then he wasn't. These last few years have not been good…' She held my gaze, her eyes steely and determined. 'Now then, what are you going to do?'

'As I say, there's Saffron; I can't just abandon her. And George adores his life in Westenbury. Honestly, Mum, you wouldn't recognise him: his stutter's almost gone, he's filled out and he's actually become quite sporty. He's just started training with Westenbury Cricket Club Juniors.'

'George? Playing cricket?' Mum's eyes widened. 'Well, that's my father's genes for you. He was a brilliant cricketer...'

'And there's Sausage...'

'Oh Sausage, schmausage,' Mum said dismissively, throwing up her hands like the Jewish mama she wasn't. 'Leave the damned dog with Rita. Or, if you insist on bringing it back down here, it'll be fine in Agnes's flat until you find somewhere to buy. Oh, Jen, shall we go and take a peek in the estate agents' windows?'

'And the girls...'

'Laurie's sisters? Since when have you been bothered about leaving *them*? That Janice sounds a real pain in the neck. I remember her at your wedding, didn't even bother with a hat as I recall.'

'Mum!' I shook my head at Mum's nit-picking. 'Janice is really great. No, I actually meant *my* girls – Heidi, Elsie and Rosamund.'

'Oh for heaven's sake, Jennifer. They're damned llamas.'

'Alpacas.'

'Is there a difference? Really?'

And Tod? I don't want to leave Tod. I'm in love with Tod Mayhew and I don't want to leave him. I need to see him, to smell him, to know that he wants me as much as I want him. Was it only yesterday, not even twenty-four hours ago, that I was kissing the life out of him like something out of Tess of the D'Urbervilles down in the long meadow?

'Mum, I'm going to take the train back to Yorkshire tomorrow. I need to get a few things sorted out. George's term finishes next week. We'll both come back then for the funeral, so don't arrange it until we're back... Hang on, will there be a funeral? You know, if we have to give Agnes to science as she says we have to? *Do* we have to? I hate the idea of kids just out of school looking at her and... you know...' It didn't bear thinking about.

'It's what she wanted, Jen. She'd obviously thought it through.'

I didn't say anything, just nibbled at the somewhat cloying shortbread while I tried to think things through. 'So,' I said eventually, 'this afternoon, now I'm here, I'm going back up to London.'

'Are you? What for?' Mum frowned and then laughed. 'Ah ha! Harvey Nicks? Liberty's? Spend some of that money? Now, be careful, Jen, you don't know how much there is. And you'll need all of it for a three-bed house down here. Mind you,' she looked me up and down, 'you look as if you could do with some new clothes. I'll come with you...'

'No, I'm not interested in new clothes. I've gone so long without anything new to wear, I can't say I'm bothered. Bit like having sex – you know, the more you have, the more you want.'

'I really wouldn't know, Jennifer,' Mum said, going pink.

'I believe you,' I laughed, elbowing her in the ribs. 'Anyway, believe *me*,' I said, thinking of those heart-stopping kisses with Tod, 'it's all true. Right, can you drop me off at the station? I'm going to see Marcia and tell her all about what I've been up to.'

'Oh, *Jennifer*? Regency *romance*? Really? Oh, I don't *think* so.' Marcia peered at me over her spectacles, emphasising every other word in her derisive response to what I'd just told her.

'Well, I'm sorry, Marcia, but I *do* think so.' I folded my arms and smiled across at her.

'But what about poor old Coleridge?' Marcia frowned. 'The publishers are waiting for the first drafts. I've already said you need a bit more time... you know, under the circumstances? What you've been through since the court case?'

'I won't abandon Samuel completely, Marcia. But I am going ahead with this. Alcidae House are already very interested.'

'Alcidae House? You've gone to them directly? Bypassing *me*?'

'Well actually, yes. Now, more than happy for you to be my agent with *Magnolia and the Lord...*'

Marcia pulled a pained expression, '*Magnolia and The Lord?*'

'... but if it's not your cup of tea, I'll look elsewhere for representation.'

'I didn't say I wouldn't. How much of this, this *romance*, have you written?'

'Just about all of it. I can send it to you this afternoon when I get back to Mum's. I'll tell Catherine Barker at Alcidae House we can go ahead then?'

'I think that's up to me to tell them, don't you?'

'Absolutely, Marcia. I'll leave it all in your hands – I have every faith that you will do all in your power to negotiate the very best deal for me.'

And with that, I made the decision that, instead of calling in to see my publishing colleagues at Wesley and Brown, before then crossing the road to see Catherine at Alcidae House, I would, instead, treat myself to an Earl Grey tea and a bun in Pret A Manger and indulge myself in a little bit of window shopping in Harrods.

After less than an hour of negotiating the exceptionally busy Brompton Road and its surrounding streets in Belgravia, I'd had enough. There were just *so* many people. Where had they all come from? I'd always adored just gazing longingly at the deliciously sumptuous goods on offer in the food hall in Harrods, but today there were so many people aimlessly milling around me, not only did I struggle to get a glimpse of the rainbow-hued pile of macarons, but I actually realised I didn't even want to. So many shoppers, tourists, more shoppers. Where *had* they all come from? What the hell did they all think they were doing, squeezing and squashing and spending money on ridiculously overpriced fripperies?

I wanted to get back to Mum's to have a long chat with Ada, learn more about this new boyfriend of hers, discuss where she wanted to be in September. But I also wanted the peace and quiet of Daisy Royd Farm. I was missing George and Sausage, the girls and Saffron – needed to know that Saffron hadn't slipped out to meet the Da Silva boy, that there weren't more drugs in the bed knob.

But most of all I wanted to see Tod.

My phone rang while I was desperately trying to exit Harrods and, hopeful that it was Tod ringing from Edinburgh, I scrabbled in my bag for it, unintentionally knocking into the woman in front of me.

'Excuse *me*,' she snapped, rubbing at her arm and giving me such a filthy look, it almost floored me. Jesus, just let me get out of these crowds.

'Jennifer?' The voice from the phone was drearily familiar.

'Laurie.'

'Look, Jennifer, what's in the paper is all made-up lies. Just lies. Full of lies. People out to get me once again. I'm here in Paris, *working*. Working my socks off for you and the children. I don't know where on earth they've got all this, this, *gossip* from...'

'Laurie?'

'Yes?'

'Bye, Laurie.' I put the phone back in my bag and headed for the tube in Knightsbridge where rush hour commuters were already spilling out of the exit like ants, as well as congregating at the entrance before rushing down the escalators into the bowels of the earth towards the trains.

I'd often wondered how my marriage would actually end. What would be its death knell: my parting shot to the almost seventeen years tied to Laurie Lewis? *Bye, Laurie* seemed short, succinct and wholly appropriate. I removed my wedding ring, tipped it into the bin at the entrance to the underground and descended into the melee.

I felt such an amazing sense of freedom, such an excitement and anticipation of a whole load of new beginnings just waiting in the wings for me, I was almost giddy with frustration at not being able to get on with it.

Tipping my wedding ring into the nearest bin had been a jolly good start. I actually laughed out loud to myself as I stood at Paddington waiting for the train out to Berkshire and when, unable to curb the occasional recalcitrant squeak and titter, and several commuters not only glanced my way but actually *moved away*, I decided to ring home. Home? There, I'd said it again: Daisy Royd Farm was home. That sobered me up slightly, but then as realisation hit me, I giggled further. Who would have thought it? It's probably delayed shock at being told you're about to inherit some money, I told myself, tittering like a mad woman while reaching for my phone and ringing the farm's landline.

'Jennifer? Are you OK? Oh, love, I'm so sorry, don't cry...' Rita soothed. 'That son of mine. I'm so *sorry*...'

'No, I'm not... crying, Rita...' More laughter from my end. Jesus, I needed to get a grip.

'What *are* you doing then? Jennifer...? Is your mum there? I think you're in shock, love...'

'I think I probably am, Rita. But not for the reason you think.' I giggled once more, took a deep breath and endeavoured to control myself. 'Is everything OK your end, Rita? Is George there? Is he OK?'

'He's absolutely fine. Honestly. Cheryl took him down to cricket practice and then she and Dean and Imogen are taking him off for a pizza. He's staying the night there.'

'Has he said anything about, you know, about Laurie?'

'Cheryl and I told him the newspapers are saying unkind things about Daddy and he wasn't to worry. He just said, "Oh? Again? Seems par for the course."'

'Par for the course?' I almost stared at my mobile in that

daft way they do in films. 'George said *par for the course*? He's eight years old, Rita!'

'Tell me about it. Apparently, Mrs Stevens, his teacher, has been explaining certain, you know, *sayings* in their English lessons. We've also had *letting the cat out of the bag* and *the last straw*. He's just like Laurie was at his age – used to drive Terry mad. Anyway, don't worry about George, he's fine.'

'And Saffron?'

'Good too. Been on the phone with Len and Sharon trying to organise a flight to Benidorm in the next couple of weeks.'

'Oh great.' I breathed a sigh of relief. 'Is she there? Can I have a word?'

'She's taken Sausage out for a walk.'

'I'll be back soon.'

'Right, love.' There was a long pause and then she said. 'Jennifer, what about Laurie? What are we going to do about Laurie?'

'*We?*'

'Well, I probably have to take some of the blame for how he's turned out. You know…' Rita lowered her voice, although, from what I gathered, she was in the house alone, '… you know, me having an affair, hiding who his real father was, probably spoiling him…?'

'More than likely, Rita,' I said tartly and then, realising how unkind that was, I added, 'I'm probably just as much to blame for putting up with his behaviour these last few years. How about we stop blaming ourselves, Rita, and let Laurie take responsibility for his own actions?'

'I wish I could.' Rita gave a little sniff.

'Got to go, Rita, train's here.' And I rang off.

I'd lied. The train hadn't arrived. But a text from Tod had:

'Just seen the paper, Jenny. You OK?'

'Reading the tabloids now, are you?' I texted back.

'Stopped for fuel and coffee at the service station. Couldn't miss it.'

'Am actually in Berkshire with Mum. My great-aunt has died.'

'I'm so sorry. But are you OK?'

'Absolutely fine. Honestly. Will be home tomorrow or the day after.'

'Can't stop thinking about you, Jenny.'

'And me, you.'

'Got to go. Dermot peeping the horn. Have to drive pretty slowly with a horse trailer.'

'You got the horse you wanted?'

'She's a beauty. Going to call her Jenny. Spent the day looking and negotiating. Home in a few hours. Let me know when you're back in Yorkshire. Xxxxxx'

I counted the kisses: six. That must surely mean something? My train pulled in to the station and I found a seat before indulging myself rereading Tod's texts.

It was going up to nine p.m. by the time Mum picked me up from the station and drove me back to her place. Ada had seemingly spent the whole of the afternoon making a broccoli and stilton tart as well as lemon posset with a lemon shortbread and I was totally impressed that, not only did she remember these two were my absolute go-to favourites, but she had the skill and knowhow to actually make them.

'Wow, this is wonderful, Ada.' She ushered me into the dining room where the table was set with Mum's best starched cloth, napkins and cut glass. 'What's all this in aid of?'

'Well,' she said, bringing in a green salad, 'you deserve it. You've been through a lot. And I've missed you, Mum.' Ada avoided my eye as she poured wine for the three of us. 'And I wanted you to know I'm still your daughter and love you, even though I really didn't want to come up to Granny Rita's place with you back in March.'

'Oh, and you *do* now?' I smiled, gratefully taking a good glug of the cold white Sauvignon Blanc. 'Lovely wine,' I added.

'What? Live in Yorkshire? God, no. Anyway, you'll be coming back to Berkshire now, won't you? You and George? Go and pack up your things and then come back to Aunt Agnes's flat until you buy somewhere? For you, me and George?'

I glanced across at Mum who had the grace to look a tad guilty. She busied herself with the salad, not meeting my eye. 'You've told Ada?' I said pointedly.

'Oh sorry, darling, I couldn't help it. I was so pleased, it just sort of slipped out.'

'Mum,' Ada went on, 'I don't want you to think I've made a celebratory meal just because… well, you know, suddenly you're coming into a bit of money. I'd planned to do this anyway to show you how I'd learned to cook – Granny's been teaching me every weekend. And,' she added, 'to remind you you've still got *another* daughter down here…' Ada trailed off, embarrassed, something, I realised, that was as surprising as the newly-found cooking skills. My daughter was growing up.

'*Another* daughter?'

'Your *real* daughter. To be honest, Mum, you've done nothing but go on about this Saffron girl ever since you found out about her – Saffron this, Saffron that… every text, every phone call…' Ada trailed off once again and I was totally floored to see tears start, before running unheeded down her cheeks. She brushed them away angrily.

'I'm so sorry, Ada, I didn't realise…'

'Mum, I've *missed* you. I've missed George and I've missed Dad too. It's not easy living at your friend's house during the week, especially when you realise you've not that much in common with them anymore. Lydia was horrible to me when I told her about Dad having another daughter. She said it didn't surprise her one bit, and she also wouldn't be surprised if there was a *whole load* of half-sisters and brothers around the country, knowing what Dad was like. And she really put me down, you know, when I said I wanted to be an actor like Dad. She and her mum kept giving each other knowing looks whenever I mentioned him.'

'Oh, Ada, I really thought you'd been happy these last few months.' I moved to hug her but, instead, she came to sit on my lap, something she'd not done for at least ten years.

'I *was* happy to begin with. It felt great. You know,' she sniffed, 'sort of being independent. Sort of being grown up. But then I wanted to be with you all, but I had to stay and finish all my exams. And then seeing all that stuff in the papers this morning. He *is* still my dad.'

'Not *Laurie* anymore?' I stroked her new aubergine hairdo.

'Oh, I'm definitely going start to call him *Laurie*.' Ada picked up her glass of wine, but almost immediately replaced it back on the starched white tablecloth, reaching, instead for her glass of coke. 'Can't bear wine,' she sniffed. 'And no, Dad is *Laurie*. He doesn't deserve to be called Dad again. Not just yet, anyway...'

'Sorry, darling, phone.' I moved Ada away from my lap where she'd been sitting on my jeans' pocket.

Tod.

'Sorry you two, I won't be a minute.' I stood to move away – I wasn't ready to share Tod with anyone just yet.

'*Mum*...? Food's ready.' My daughter gave me the same look I'd been bestowing on her ever since we'd bought Ada her own phone when she was twelve.

'Hang on, two secs...'

'If it's that Saffron girl again, tell her we're eating... And you're *my* mum, not hers...'

I took my phone into the kitchen, over the moon that Tod was ringing me again so soon after our earlier texting.

'Jennifer?' Tod didn't wait for an answer. 'You just tell

that *husband* of yours to tell that *daughter* of his, enough is enough.' He appeared incoherent with rage. 'I've rung the police this time.'

'Oh, Jesus, what's she done?' My pulse was racing.

'Done? What's she *done*? She and that gang of yobs she hangs round with have bloody well taken *Gallant Gourmet*. That's why she's been hanging round the stables: casing the joint, waiting for the right opportunity. Your husband's daughter, as well as the best horse in the north of England, will be halfway to Ireland by now. You tell that feckless husband of yours, Jennifer, to sort that thief of a daughter of his. Got to go... Police are here...'

And with that, he rang off.

33

I got straight on to Rita who was, apparently, out in the gardening watering her perennials. before it got too dark.

'Rita, where's Saffron?'

'Out somewhere, love. She brought Sausage back from his walk and said she was going off to see a friend.'

'What friend?'

'*I* don't know, love. She just said she was going out and would be back later. I let her take the Mini. It's insured for anyone to drive – I did that so Janice and her kids can drive it if needs be. There's no bus up here after eight.'

'You're joking?'

'Joking? No, I thought you knew there were no buses in the evening?'

'No,' I hissed. 'I know about the damned buses, Rita. I didn't even know Saffron could *drive*.'

'She said she'd been driving in Australia since she was fourteen.'

'Illegally, more than likely. Probably in the bush out there, rather than on the road.'

'Is Canberra *in the bush*? My geography was never wonderful.' I could almost see Rita weighing this up at her end of the phone. 'I was always far more into English, as you know...'

'For heaven's sake, Rita, there's no country lets its kids drive legally at fourteen. And I've no idea whether the Australian outback stretches out to where Saffron lived.' My geography was as bad as my mother-in-law's. 'Listen Rita, this is important, I've just had Tod Mayhew on the phone...'

'Is the bush the same as the outback...? Tod Mayhew? I didn't know you were friendly with... Oh... oh... oh my goodness...' Rita broke off our geography lesson in a volley of exclamations.

'What? What is it? Rita?'

'Hang on... Goodness me...'

'*What?*'

'There's the most beautiful black horse in with the alpacas... What a beauty... Oh, hang on... Saffron? Saffron, what the hell are you *doing*? You haven't bought a horse, Saffron? Saffron? Where are you *going*? Oh...?'

'*What?*'

Rita had obviously made her way down to the alpacas, and I could hear Polonius hysterically barking, drowning out whoever Rita was now in conversation with. 'Janice?' Rita shouted. 'Janice! What are you *doing*? Is this *your* horse? Whose damned horse *is it*?'

'Rita, what's going on?' I was shouting myself now, while Mum and Ada were at the kitchen door, arms folded, obviously trying to work out what was going on themselves.

'Well, there *was* a horse in the field,' Rita finally answered, seemingly out of breath. 'But it's gone now.'

'What do you mean, it's *gone*? Rita?'

There was silence for a good five seconds. 'Right, Jennifer, there *was* a horse in the field, and now Saffron has jumped on its back and Janice was shouting, *it's not safe here*, and now they've both gone...'

'Gone *where*?'

'I don't know *where*, Jennifer?' Rita was cross. 'Nobody tells me anything. It's always been the same with those girls of mine. Laurie now, well, Laurie was different. He'd tell me everything...'

'Rita, this is no time to be extolling the virtues of that son of yours. Especially at the moment. And especially to *me*.' I tried to stay calm, but my heart was pounding. I took a deep breath. 'There's something going on with one of Tod's best horses. He says Saffron has pinched it.'

'It would appear so.' Rita, I could tell, was going off into sulking mode. 'Well, if she has, it would also appear Janice is in on it too. That's all we need – the pair of them up in front of the judge. I really thought Janice – especially now she's in the menopause – had finally learned some sense.'

'What? What's the menopause got to do with it?'

'I told you they're all bonkers up there, Granny.' Ada, obviously deciding she rather liked wine after all, was working her way down one of Mum's cut-glass flutes and started to giggle as she tried to work out what was going on from my one-ended conversation with Rita up at Daisy Royd.

'I really don't know what's going on, Jennifer,' Rita snapped crossly. 'First, it's Laurie in the papers once again, and now Saffron and Janice are horse rustling.'

'Right, if Janice is with Saffron, that's good. I'm going to ring Tod...'

'Tod?' I could almost hear Rita's eyes narrow. 'Is there something going on with you and Tod Mayhew?'

'After tonight, Rita,' I snapped, 'I doubt it very much.'

'And does Laurie know about this... this *fraternisation*?'

'Rita, I'm going. I'm coming back up north tomorrow. And,' I added, staring meaningfully across at my daughter, 'bringing Ada back up with me.'

While I really was too pent up to eat, the last thing Ada needed was for me not to enjoy and comment on the delicious food she'd spent all afternoon preparing. Once we'd eaten, I rang Tod's number constantly, but he was either on another call or deliberately shutting me out.

Laurie was obviously in the process of doing the same with *my* number, ringing it every ten minutes until, fed up with the constant repetitive jangle of Vivaldi's 'Spring', I not only cut him off, but eventually blocked his number as well.

Something I should have done months ago.

The next morning, once I'd kept my appointment with Aunt Agnes's solicitor, Mum drove Ada and me back to King's Cross station. We then had two full hours on the train together where Ada talked non-stop, bringing me fully up to date with her now depleted friendship with Lydia as well as the previous week's audition down at the Sonning Amateur Dramatic Society for the production of *Romeo and Juliet*, where Ada was after the plum role of Juliet herself.

'And how fortuitous, Mum, that Ethan Bradbury, who I've fancied like mad, like *for ever* was auditioning for Romeo? Can you *imagine*, Mum?'

I could. While my stomach was one big anxious knot with what had been going on up at Daisy Royd the previous evening, I concentrated wholeheartedly, instead, on Ada, catching up with her life, letting her talk, telling me everything. It was so lovely, sitting there on the train, drinking our Costa coffee, watching the mid-summer green and gold flash by, all my attention on my gorgeous girl while she opened up fully to me, perhaps for the first time in years. I felt I'd regained a daughter. Which, I suppose, I had.

I tried not to think about the step-daughter I'd possibly lost, not wanting to rain on Ada's parade as it were. I'd rung and texted Saffron, Rita and Janice constantly before we boarded the train, but none of them was deigning to answer.

'Is your car in the car park, Mum?' Ada asked, as we came down the escalator at Wakefield Westgate and onto the concourse. She broke off, suddenly standing stock-still and staring as we drew level with WH Smith. 'Mum...' Ada grabbed at my arm, dragging me backwards. 'Mum, there's a photo of *me* in the paper. Of me and George.'

'What?' I turned sharply to where Ada was indicating the display of newspapers at the front of the store. 'Oh, I don't *believe* it,' I hissed, sounding like a particularly vicious Victor Meldrew. I marched over, grabbing a copy of *The Daily Clarion*, scanning the headline...

JEN VOWS TO STAND BY CHEATING LEWIS

... as well as the accompanying family group photo of Laurie, me and the kids. It was the photo Mum had insisted on us posing for, and her paying for, as our Christmas present the year before last.

'You wanting that, love?' The assistant glared in our direction as Ada and I continued to read, both holding a corner each of the tabloid.

Ignoring him, we scanned the front page together in silence until, with a snort of derision, I read out loud:

My darling wife, Jennifer, and my two wonderful children, Ada and George, all mean the world to me. Jennifer has already vowed to stand by me, despite what was printed about me yesterday…

'Not actually denying it then, is he?' Ada remarked, turning to the centre pages while the rest of the paper fell, unheeded, to the shop floor.

'Are you buying that, or what?'

More family photos – as well as, I have to say, a particularly nice one of me in a yellow bikini on a beach in Barbados, laughing at something Laurie had just said – and, of course, another resurrected churning-out of the lost libel court case from last November.

I felt physically sick and, thrusting a five-pound note in the assistant's direction, I took Ada's arm, shepherding her out to the adjacent car park where I'd left the car two days earlier.

'Mum, look, the police are here.' Ada craned her head backwards as I pulled up at the top end of the yard, away from the police car parked towards the bottom.

'It'll be Saffron.' I felt my stomach lurch as I pulled our overnight cases out of the boot.

'Sausage? Is this George's dog?' Ada bent to stroke Sausage who'd run out to greet us.

'Don't, Ada, *don't touch him*. Oh hell, I'd totally forgotten all about your allergy.'

'Oh, I'll just sneeze,' Ada said breezily. 'I was allergic to Lydia's cats...'

'You are joking? Oh, for heaven's sake, Ada. Why didn't you tell me?' Guilt reared its ugly head once more.

'Because you wouldn't have let me stay there. And, to be quite honest, I'm not half as bad as I was when I was younger. I don't get hay fever as bad as I did either.'

'Oh, really?' More guilt that I hadn't known that. What sort of mother was I? 'Well, just wash your hands and take a Piriton and don't get too near him. He'll have to go back with Granny Rita when she goes home this afternoon.'

Ada followed me through the porch and into the kitchen. All was neat and tidy: the dishcloth draped over the taps, the tea towels drying on the Aga.

'I'd forgotten how pretty Granny's farmhouse is,' Ada said almost reverentially, gazing round the kitchen and to the parlour beyond. 'Mind you, that great big TV looks totally out of place up there.' She pulled a disparaging face as she spoke, and then her face lit up as Rita came through the open parlour French window with a tea tray.

'Ah, Ada! How lovely. Goodness, you've grown. Look at that hair. How gorgeous you are...' Rita held out her arms. 'Don't you forget you've another granny, young lady.'

'What's going on, Rita?' I indicated with a nod the police car that could just be seen through the kitchen window.

'Go and see for yourself. They're all out there having tea and scones.' She smiled. 'Not a chocolate marshmallow teacake in sight.'

Ada and I made our way through the parlour and exited the French window, breathing in the heady smell of newly mown grass, and the last of the white and purple, distinctive cone-shaped lilac. The sweet citrus fragrance of mock-orange mingled with the more subtle gardenia, iris and honeysuckle, but my attention was all on Saffron, sat at the rattan garden table between two uniformed police officers and Janice who, for once, didn't appear overly vocal. Janice nodded in my direction and Saffron glanced across at me, but said nothing by way of welcome, all her concentration focused on Ada. The two of them stared at one another.

'Well, you two must be sisters,' the woman sergeant smiled. 'Goodness, you do look alike.'

'Half-sisters,' Saffron said pointedly, burying her face in Rita's best bone-china teacup. 'We were sired by the same male.'

'Sired?' Rita had reappeared with a fresh pot of tea. '*Sired*, you daft thing? What a thing to say.' Rita laughed uncertainly.

'OK,' I said, addressing the two officers and Janice. 'Come on, tell me everything. How much trouble is she in?'

'Possibly quite a lot.' The young PC spoke first and then reddened as the woman officer raised an eyebrow in his direction.

'All depends on Mr Mayhew,' she said calmly. 'On whether he wants to prosecute. There's theft of an extremely valuable horse and kidnapping of said horse. And then we shall be prosecuting the driving without a licence...'

'... and therefore, without insurance,' the young PC interrupted proudly. He'd obviously been listening on the day they did driving offences at police training school.

'But we've been through all this,' Janice said crossly. 'Saffron was *rescuing*, not pinching Gallant Gourmet.'

'She rode off at full pelt with him,' the sergeant said mildly.

'Could have broken his leg,' the constable added officiously.

'Or killed *herself*.' Janice snapped. 'Mind you, I thought I was pretty good with horses – this girl's a genius. Obviously takes after me. And my dad.'

Don't *think so*, Janice.

'Anyway,' she went on, 'Saffron was coerced, groomed even – isn't that the word they all use these days? If she hadn't pretended to go along with the bloody Da Silva's – and I bet *you* wouldn't argue with that lot...' Janice raised an eyebrow at Constable Baker, who went very red and looked away '... that horse would be on its way to Ireland by now. Saffron went along with them, did as they'd ordered and took the horse from its stable, but instead of taking it in the horsebox to the hiding place they'd organised up on the moors, she jumped on its back – without a saddle for heaven's sake – and galloped off across the fields back to Daisy Royd farm.'

'Blimey.' Ada, who'd never so much as sat on a donkey on the beach at Brighton, was impressed.

'Blimey indeed,' Janice agreed, nodding. 'It was just like something out of *Bunty*.'

'*Bunty?*' Ada, Saffron and Constable Baker stared at Janice, no idea what she was talking about, but Sergeant

White and I smiled and nodded in agreement, totally getting where Janice was coming from.

'*Bunty* comic,' Janice explained to the girls. 'I almost expected the Four Marys to be in there somewhere, coming to the rescue. The Four Marys,' she went on, almost dreamily. 'Talk about Girl Power – they probably influenced the Spice Girls.' She laughed at that. 'What were they all called?' Janice closed her eyes and frowned, thinking. 'Mary Cotter, Mary Radleigh…'

'She was the posh one,' the sergeant put in. 'The earl's daughter. Then there was Mary Field…'

'And Mary Simpson,' I concluded. 'I always felt a bit sorry for her. You know, from the poor end of town but at that posh boarding school for some reason.'

'Anyway, it was like something out of a comic strip seeing Saffron gallop across the fields in the dark,' Janice went on. 'She…'

'Hang on,' I interrupted. 'You can't just kidnap a racehorse from upmarket stables like Tod Mayhew's.' Just saying his name made my heart race. 'There's CCTV, security, horses locked up for the night. I've been there. Several times,' I added, ignoring Rita's raised eyebrow. 'You can't just go in there and nick a quarter of a million-pound racehorse, like they do in a comic.'

'No,' Saffron spoke for the first time. 'You absolutely can't, unless the owner and trainer are away for the night and it's an inside job.'

'Now you sound like something off *Midsomer Murders*,' Rita sniffed.

'No one was *murdered*, were they?' Ada leaned forwards,

obviously fascinated by the goings on in a quiet Yorkshire village.

'No, of course not,' Saffron snapped. 'But one of the grooms was in on it – he did something to the CCTV and unlocked the stable and gates in readiness.'

'A groom had access to all that?'

Saffron hesitated. 'Liam. He's Dermot's cousin's son – I met him a couple of times down at the stables.'

'When you weren't supposed to *be* there, Saffron.' I shook my head. 'When you should have been at college. Tod told me.'

More raised eyebrows from Rita, which I ignored.

'Apparently, Liam had only been sent over from Ireland as a favour to Dermot's cousin,' Saffron explained. 'Liam doesn't even like horses much, for God's sake. But he'd got into drugs in a big way in Dublin and his dad wanted him out of there. Assumed a village in the Yorkshire countryside, where he'd be surrounded by everything horsey and under the strict eye of Dermot O'Callaghan, would get him clean.'

'And it didn't?' I asked.

Saffron gave a little snort. 'Hardly. Just the opposite. He was bored – hated all the mucking out, having to be up at five a.m. to get the horses ready for the gallops. He's a city boy – like you and Ada are city girls, Jennifer. Put you out of your comfort zone, where you don't want to be, and you'll turn to something – or *someone* – to help you through it,' Saffron looked at me knowingly and both Rita and Janice exchanged a look. She hesitated. 'Look, I don't know if you know, but Tod Mayhew has a brother.' She hesitated again. 'Nothing at all like Tod. Anyway, he's often hanging round at the stables when he's got nowhere else to go. Tod takes him in, feeds him, gives him money. Waste of space he is. If I was Tod, I wouldn't have anything to do with him. Anyway, it was this brother – Ashton, he's called – that got Liam in touch with the local pushers,' Saffron went on, 'who just happen to be the Da Silva's. They got him hooked again on H, and when they knew he worked at Tod Mayhew's place, came up with the daft plan to kidnap Gourmet. With some help from Tod's brother as well – I saw him skulking around the back of the stables. They were all in on it. I reckon Kyle Da Silva had been reading all about Shergar.'

'Shergar? Who's Shergar?' Ada frowned. 'Someone else in this *Bunty* comic?'

Both Janice and Saffron tutted in derision, united once more in their love for, and knowledge about, horses. I patted Ada's knee in sympathy.

'Shergar,' Saffron explained, 'was a brilliant racehorse who was retired to stud in County Kildare in the early eighties. He was stolen from the stud, and a ransom of £2 million was demanded. It wasn't paid, and basically the poor horse was never seen again.'

'Possibly the IRA,' Janice put in, knowingly.

'Oh, Saffron, you've not got yourself mixed up with the IRA, love?' Rita was horrified. 'What on earth will Len and Sharon say?'

'For heaven's sake, Mum, for an intelligent woman, you don't half come out with some bloody daft things sometimes.' Janice tutted again. 'The Da Silva's are small-time crooks. I doubt they'd even thought about how they were going to get the horse actually out of the country. Mind you, if Tony Da Silva, from his prison cell, was in on it…'

'Nah, nothing so organised,' Saffron said, folding her arms and leaning back in her chair. 'It was Kyle's idea and he's not the brightest star in the sky. It was doomed from the start. It was only at the last minute that Liam and Kyle panicked when they couldn't get Gourmet into the horsebox. Kyle rang me and demanded I get over there or he'd kneecap the horse.'

'Kneecap the horse?' I frowned. 'Can you *kneecap* a horse?' But then, remembering Kyle Da Silva's knife at my throat, and the alleged machete down his undercrackers, I realised you probably could.

'I was terrified for Gourmet. I love him,' Saffron scowled. 'I rang Janice for help and then I borrowed Rita's Mini, drove over there at a rate of knots...'

'Speeding as well then,' PC Baker said accusingly.

'... and instead of riding him into the box like they said I had to, turned him round and galloped him here.'

'Mother o' God.' PC Baker shook his head.

Ada and Saffron's eyes met and the pair of them started giggling as Sergeant White raised an eyebrow towards the young PC – who couldn't have been much older than the girls – and said, 'Don't think you've quite made superintendent yet, Joe,' before turning back to Janice.

'I followed her here on the road while she came across the fields,' Janice explained. 'I knew the horse and Saffron wouldn't be safe here, so I got her to turn round and take him to my place. There's the old barn down the meadow. We put him in there and calmed him down and rang you lot.' Janice nodded towards Sergeant White. 'Saffron didn't want to ring the police...'

Saffron shrugged, looking mutinous. 'I thought we could

eventually just return him. You know, put him back, return him...'

'Like a flipping library book?' I snapped. 'For heaven's sake, Saffron.'

'But Tod and Dermot had returned from wherever they'd been and had seen me just as I was galloping off.' Saffron pulled a face. 'The Da Silva's had done a runner and Tod obviously thought I was nicking Gourmet and rang the police themselves.'

'Right,' I said faintly.

'We're going to need a full statement down at the station, Saffron...' Sergeant White suddenly broke off, her mouth an 'O' of surprise as she gazed at the open French windows. 'Oh, sorry,' she went on, flicking her hair back and running her tongue around her lips, 'always had a bit of a thing for Ted Baxter...'

We turned as one.

'Ada,' George shouted in utter delight as he ran towards her.

'George,' Ada shouted back, meeting him halfway and giving him a huge hug before putting him down and racing towards Laurie.

34

'I'm actually surprised Cassie Beresford let you pick George up from school,' I said as Laurie and I sat on the dry-stone wall together, taking in the last of the evening sunshine and the glorious view down the meadow.

'Why wouldn't she?' Laurie frowned. 'I am his father, for heaven's sake.'

'She's on my side,' I said, mildly. 'And you might be his *father*, but you've not been the best dad in the world lately, have you?'

'Or the best husband?'

'Or the best husband,' I agreed.

We both mulled this over for a while.

'Ada's looking good,' Laurie said, lifting a hand to shade his eyes against the evening rays in order to make her out down at the edge of the woods where George and Sausage were proudly taking her round their stomping ground. 'I've missed her,' he added.

'Me too. She's changed, I think. You know, grown up a bit,' I smiled. 'Not as self-centred as she once was.'

'Aren't we all self-centred at sixteen?' Laurie said, almost sadly. 'I know I was.'

I didn't reply to that.

'Any idea what she's going to do in September?' Laurie went on. 'She can't carry on between Lydia's and your mum's for another two years while she does A-Levels.'

'There are two options, I reckon: the local sixth-form college, wherever we're going to be living…'

'You'll move to Cheshire with me then? There are some fabulous places out near Wilmslow. Or Prestbury? Or Alderley Edge?' Laurie became quite animated.

'… or she goes away to school for sixth form. You know she's always wanted to do that, but whether that's still on the cards after six months of her being away from home, I don't know. I get the impression she'd rather be back living with me. I've not discussed it with her – been a bit like the elephant in the room, we haven't got round to talking about it yet.'

'Jen, I may be doing OK at work at the moment – and luckily this latest little blip doesn't appear to have altered that – but…'

'This *little blip*?' I interrupted. 'God, you don't change, Laurie.'

'Yes, and I apologise for that and it won't happen again.'

I actually started laughing at that and found I couldn't stop.

'As I was saying, Jen, work is going well, I have the Michaud Saint-Jean contract back again…'

'Are you sure about that, Laurie? After this "*little blip*"?' I was really laughing now.

'I don't know what's so *funny*, Jennifer – I don't think this is a laughing matter. We need to be seriously thinking about our relationship. You know, what it is that's made me behave this way…?'

'What?' I stopped laughing and just stared. Was this man for real?

'Alright, alright,' Laurie held up his hands, crossly. 'I'm to blame. As always.'

'Yes, you are. No one else to blame.'

'It's that father of mine who I never met: Laurence Reardon-Jones.' Laurie was mulish. 'It's obviously *his* genes I've inherited. If I'd had a father like yours to keep me on the straight and narrow—'

'Oh, for heaven's sake, Laurie.' I looked at him in disbelief.

'As I was *trying* to say,' Laurie went on, 'work *may* be going well, but if we're going to be buying a new place in Cheshire, with the huge mortgage we'll have to take out, then boarding school for Ada is out of the question. There'll be a good sixth-form college in Wilmslow, or wherever we end up.'

'If Ada wants to go away to boarding school, she can.' I didn't elicit further.

Laurie stared and then smiled. 'Oh, of course, your Aunt Agnes's place?' He nodded, understanding. 'Sell that and we'll have enough to pay the two years' fees. And, Jennifer, that will also really help with the deposit on a place in Cheshire. Good old Aunt Aggy, coming up trumps.' Laurie grinned and reached for my hand. 'OK, that's Ada sorted. What about Saffron? Will she come to Cheshire with us?'

Saffron had left with Janice, following the two police officers down to the station in Midhope town centre. They'd been gone ever since and I was beginning to get worried. What if they'd locked her up in a cell overnight? What if the Da Silva brothers were lying in wait to do her in for grassing them up on their bungled horsenap attempt?

'Once she knows what's happening with the police, whether Tod Mayhew is going to prosecute, the best place for her is Benidorm for six weeks or so.'

'Like the Great Train Robbers?' Laurie asked. 'Didn't *they* all scarper to Spain?'

'South America, wasn't it?' I mused, not really listening. I was getting worried about Saffron being away so long.

'Somewhere they speak Spanish, anyway,' Laurie said sagely. 'Mind you, I think villains ever since have always hopped it to Spain.'

'Saffron is not a *villain*,' I snapped. 'She's a lovely, brave girl, who has just saved an expensive horse from ending up in Ireland. She'll need a good solicitor if it all goes to court.'

'Expensive.' Laurie shook his head.

'Irrelevant,' I snapped.

'You're not wearing your wedding ring.' Laurie turned to me, taking my hand and lifting it to his chest where he held it between his own two in the warmth of his navy sweater.

'In a rubbish bin at the top of the underground in Knightsbridge.' I left my hand in Laurie's, enjoying the closeness, breathing him in, remembering that very first time down in Berkshire when he'd kissed me and held me close. When I knew, then, that I would love this man for ever.

'I'll buy you another – you know, a new start. Although,' Laurie whispered into my hair, his hands now burying beneath my shirt in the direction of my own chest, 'we have so many mammaries to hold on to.'

'Mammaries?'

'*Memories*,' Laurie tutted, hastily correcting himself

while pulling me in closer. '*Memories* of the good times we've had together.'

I wrapped my arms around Laurie, closing my eyes and breathing him in, remembering all the good times. All the love we'd shared. Our falling in love at university; the heady days in London. The two children we'd created and brought up together.

Laurie Lewis, the love of my life.

Breathing in my Byron: *mad, bad and dangerous to know.*

For the final time.

There was absolutely nothing there.

'No, you won't buy me another ring, Laurie,' I whispered. 'The memories are there, but the marriage is dead. It died a long time ago.'

I opened my eyes and saw deep regret, fear, in Laurie's eyes.

And then, something else. Someone else...

Telling Laurie to make sure George was in bed by nine and that Ada was going to be sharing my bed with me and *he'd* have to go to his mother's, I jumped up and ran back to the house – as quickly as humanly possible in flip-flops. Trainers? Where the hell was my other trainer? After a feverish search in every room, I finally found it, half chewed and full of tacky saliva in Sausage's bed, pulled it on to match the other, and set off at speed after Tod who, from what I'd observed, had just ridden across the fields and, after witnessing me with my arms around Laurie, had hurriedly turned his horse and retreated back in the same direction.

'Where the hell are you going?' Laurie shouted as I sped past him, jumped over a fence – which quite possibly put paid to my ever having any future sex life – and flew down the fields in the direction of Tod's place. He must have had a good ten minutes on me and I eventually stopped, bending over to alleviate the stitch in my side before feverishly scanning the hedges and copses, stiles and fields of cattle trying to spot a rider on a chestnut-coloured horse. He appeared to have vanished into thin air.

Breathing heavily from the exertion of running a good mile in an ill-fitting, half-chewed trainer, I turned towards a rocky outcrop a quarter of a mile or so away where a movement of brown had caught my eye. The evening light was dimming and I had to really strain my eyes to make it out as it moved slowly and then disappeared behind a high, dry-stone wall. Tod's horse! I stood there for a good minute, dithering, not sure what to do and then the brown appeared beyond the broken wall once more, grazing nonchalantly before once again moving out of view. It looked suspiciously like a riderless horse to me, but without my glasses I couldn't be sure. Tod must have been thrown and was lying at the other side of the wall: it was *Jane Eyre* revisited.

It was getting really quite dark now – although, up here in the north, in July, there was never the fully dark night of a later season. I set off towards the wall; Tod obviously needed help.

I made my way cautiously over the rough grass, little hillocks and molehills impeding my progress in my sloppy trainer. I could no longer see anything that looked remotely like a horse and I was beginning to wonder if I'd imagined the whole thing. Why the hell hadn't I brought my phone with me?

And why the hell, as I scrambled over the broken wall, was I now eyeball to eyeball with Bronson – the prized brown Limousin bull belonging to Ian, the farmer down the road – that terrorised the area like a present-day Hound of the Baskervilles? Bad enough coming across this bad boy during the day, never mind in the now almost non-existent light.

The blood roared in my ears as I stood, petrified, unable to move. Bronson looked at me. I looked at Bronson. He lowered his head and snorted, the same nasal, guttural hawking sound made by a dirty old man before he spits. I closed my eyes…

'What the fuck are you doing, Jennifer? Get the fuck out of there.' Tod, his backside still very much attached to his chestnut mount, was at my side while another horse – a smaller black one this time – cantered up and drew level with him.

'Jesus, Jennifer, just back out slowly,' Saffron instructed from atop the black horse.

And then Tod had hold of me, hauling me up from underneath my arms and somehow getting me seated messily in front of him. He turned the horse, checked to see Saffron was OK and then the three of us cantered down the valley like – as I recounted to Gudrun later – amateur ride-on parts in Calamity Jane.

'But how did you know where I was?' I asked, once I'd stopped shaking – as much from the gallop down and across the field to Tod's place, as from coming face-to-face with Bronson – and was sipping at the brandy Tod had poured for me.

'I rang your mobile to let you know I was here,' Saffron

frowned. 'Janice had dropped me off earlier, after being at the police station, saying I had to apologise to Tod and explain what had really happened, and then to ring you and you'd come and pick me up.'

'Saffron and I had had a good chat for an hour or so.' Tod took up the story. 'We sorted a lot out, made progress. I totally understand what she was up to when she took Gourmet last night.' He paused. 'My brother appears to have been in on it too – he knows where I keep all the keys.'

'And then I suggested *you* might want to see Tod, Jennifer.' She looked at me from under her lashes. 'He set off while I stayed here, but soon came back after seeing you with your arms wrapped round Laurie…' Saffron tutted, shaking her head, '… just as Ada answered your phone. She told me you'd run off after some bloke on a horse and now she didn't know where you were and was worried. I told Tod this and he saddled up Dermot's horse for me and we set off to look for you. As we rode back up the hill, we could see you in the distance wandering in the other direction, obviously lost…'

'I wasn't *lost*,' I snapped, the realisation of the danger I'd been in making me speak more sharply than I'd intended. 'I was on my way to rescue Tod.'

'Rescue me?' Tod took a good swallow of his own brandy and raised an eyebrow. 'From what? Bronson?'

'I saw a brown… thing…'

'A brown *thing*? That was a ton of solid angry bull you were facing, Jennifer.'

'I thought it was your chestnut-coloured horse.'

'Did you? Why?'

'I obviously *should have gone to Specsavers*,' I said

crossly. I sighed, embarrassed at my romantic idea that a brilliant horseman like Tod could have been thrown by his horse. 'I thought you'd come off your horse. You know, like Mr Rochester?'

'The fishmonger in the village?' Tod frowned. 'I didn't know Brian Rochester had taken up riding? And he's come off, you say?'

I glanced across at Saffron, who was giggling. 'Ring Ada,' she instructed, holding out her mobile once she'd stopped laughing. 'She's worried about you.'

'I need to get back,' I said, looking at the clock in Tod's sitting room. It was cosy here, a fire dancing in the grate against the now chilly evening. 'It's Ada's first evening up here in Yorkshire with me. I can't just abandon her.'

'I'll drive you back up, Jen. Saffron can stay here for the night if she wants. I don't know where else she's going to sleep with a houseful at Daisy Royd Farm.'

'Really? Can I?' Saffron breathed, obviously delighted at the thought of staying the night among the horses.

'We've a couple of rooms at the top of the yard for the grooms. I'm sure one of them will have toothpaste and makeup remover.' Tod smiled. 'As long as you help muck out in the morning to earn your breakfast.' He smiled again in her direction, and my heart lurched. What a totally lovely, kind man.

Tod drove me the three miles back along the country lanes to Daisy Royd farm in silence, pulling up in the yard, the engine still running. He turned to me. 'I hated seeing you back with your husband, Jennifer. I wanted to throw him off that wall, pummel him into the ground and have you all for myself.'

'You have me,' I said simply. 'You had me at: *I hope you're going to pick all that lot up*.' I smiled, remembering my very first sight of Tod Mayhew when he was ordering me to pick up my litter down by the village church.

Tod closed his eyes and smiled. 'Pompous, or what?'

'Pompous,' I agreed.

He laughed loudly. 'Sorry.' And then he sobered up and reached for my hand. 'What about your husband, Jenny?'

'No longer my husband,' I replied, holding up my left hand. 'Wedding ring is in the bin, where my marriage is about to follow. All that stuff in the paper about me standing by him was utter rubbish. I was telling Laurie goodbye when you saw us together, on the point of telling him I was in love with someone else…'

'Anyone I know?' Tod asked, nuzzling my neck.

'I think you're acquainted,' I smiled, kissing this wonderful, kind, unassuming, strong man right back where it mattered.

THE FINAL ACT

35

September 2021

It was Janice who told me about the house. Ada and I had earlier come across the most ravishing cottages when we were out on one of our walks following the footpaths around an area called Holly Close Farm. There were two cottages several yards from the farm, and one had a To Let board newly posted in its garden. The pair of us had walked down there, still in summer T-shirts, breathing in the warm air that, nevertheless, carried the heady smell of autumn, harbinger of the new season to come. The whole vista in front of us was turning golden, and two huge combine harvesters were already at work, intent on bringing in the wheat and barley that had yielded to the glorious sunshine of the past summer months.

'Oh, Mum, look.' Ada was ecstatic. 'What about this? It's a fairy-tale cottage.'

We walked right up to the cottage, taking in the mellow stone, the garden with its two apple trees almost bent double with their bounty of red fruit, the glorious views across the valley.

'Too small,' I frowned, disappointed. 'It's only two bedrooms. Look.' I pointed out the information on the estate agent board. 'And,' I added, 'I don't want to rent, even for a short while. I want to buy somewhere for us.'

'Big commitment,' Ada said, looking at me. 'You know, buying.'

'*You've* made that commitment to stay up here and go to sixth-form college in Midhope, Ada. I think the least I can do is find somewhere suitable for you to live and study while you're here. I want a place that's going to be home for you and George. That you'll continue to come back to even when you're off to university in two years' time.'

'Or drama school.' Ada was adamant.

'Or drama school. Although you know both Dad and I want you to go to university first. You know, like Dad did.'

'Do you think I'll get into Oxford or Cambridge?'

'If you want it enough. Midhope sixth-form college has an enviable reputation for getting their students places at Oxbridge. I'm not convinced it's the be all and end all though, you know...'

'Well,' Ada laughed, 'if Leeds Uni is as good as their festival, I'm going *there*.' Ada and two of her friends from school (not Lydia, I hasten to add, who had become somewhat persona non grata) had spent three days after GCSE results were out (Ada had achieved ten Grade 9 passes to my utter relief that abandoning her to follow Laurie up north had not affected her grades) at Leeds Festival, a rite of passage after GCSEs, Cheryl had informed me, particularly for kids in the north.

'We need at least four bedrooms,' I pointed out as we walked on, abandoning any idea of renting the Holly Close Cottage.

'Four?'

'Me, you, George and Saffron.'

'Does Saffron *need* her own room? Isn't she spending most of the time over at Tod's place now she's working for him, training to be a jockey?'

'Yes, she's over there eighty percent of the time. But I want her to know she has a home with us too. You know, her own room where she can come and stay when she's had enough of Tod putting her through her paces.' I glanced across at Ada. 'You're alright with that, aren't you? You don't feel I'm putting your nose out of joint?' I wanted Ada with me, didn't want her heading off back to Mum's.

'Of course I'm OK with it; we get on really well now. Saffron and I are hugely different – she's obviously inherited Grandad Terry and Auntie Janice's horsey genes...'

Now was not the time to inform Ada she and Saffron might share the same father, but Saffron's *horsey genes* certainly didn't come from the cuckolded Terry Lewis. Rita and I had made a silent pact that the spectre of Laurence Reardon-Jones should not be resurrected, but laid peacefully to rest without further discussion.

'... and I'm as frightened of horses – and bulls...' (Ada poked me in the ribs, laughing as we walked down the hill towards Norman's Meadow) '... as you are, Mum.'

'Len and Sharon Barrowclough still want Saffron to do

her A-Levels. And I'm with them on that. She's taking a lot on, as well as working with Tod, but she's got the idea of being a vet eventually. You know, if being a top female jockey doesn't pan out.'

'Knowing Saffron, she'll think she can do both.' Ada smiled. 'She's incredibly sassy, isn't she?'

I nodded, and we walked on, a comfortable silence between us.

'Do you think Dad's going to end up properly with this Pasta woman?' Ada asked eventually.

'Patsy Pilkington?' I smiled. Patsy had become Pasty and, sometimes, even *Pasta*. 'Possibly.' I smiled, knowing no regret, whatsoever, that Laurie was now living a bachelor life in a rented studio flat over in Manchester city centre. How much he was involved with his fellow actor on *The Street*, I didn't know. And didn't particularly care. 'And, again, you OK with that, Ada?'

'Well, I'd obviously prefer that my parents were still together?' Ada looked at me hopefully, but I shook my head.

'Sorry, darling, the divorce will come through pretty quickly. No reason not to.'

'And are you actually going ahead with a divorce because you want to marry Tod?'

'No, I'm going ahead with a divorce because I no longer want to be married to Laurie Lewis.'

'I don't blame you, Mum. It's OK, honestly.'

'George does.'

'Does what?'

'Blame me.'

'He's eight,' Ada said. 'He'll get over it. He'd have blamed you more if you'd made the decision to go back down south and he'd have had to leave Saint Grace of Primary Education.' Ada started laughing. 'He's over the moon that this teacher is moving up with them to take Year 4.'

I smiled, remembering George's ecstatic face as he recounted Cassie Beresford's announcement in assembly that Grace Stevens would be taking Year 4 from September. 'I do worry about George though. You know, not having your dad around all the time.'

'Was Dad *ever* around all the time?' Ada glanced my way. 'George will be able to go over to Manchester at weekends. He's met Pasta and rather likes her. Especially as she has a Dachshund of her own. He'll be fine. He's happy, Mum, that's all that matters.'

'That's George for you: sunny natured. And, unbelievably, he's getting into Tod's horses. There's a small rescue pony at the stables that George appears to have teamed up with. He had his first riding lesson last week with Dermot.'

'More of the Lewis *horsey genes* coming through, then.'

I didn't reply to that.

'And, er, you don't feel that having me around is going to be holding you back?' Ada finally asked.

'In what sense?'

'In the Tod Mayhew sense?'

'How do you mean, holding me back? It didn't seem to hold your Granny Cynthia back with Phil when you were living with her,' I replied.

'Yes, but don't forget I was only there for long weekends. I think Granny is going to end up marrying him, you know.'

'So do I.'

'And are you going to marry Tod?'

'He hasn't asked me.'

'And would you?'

'What? Marry him if he asked?' I laughed at Ada's question. 'Do you know, Ada, once I can find a house round here that I can put my own stamp on, I'm going to enjoy my life just as it is. I've you two and Saffron, and I have Tod as well. We've both *been* married. I'm not going to have any more children. Why should I want to marry?'

'I think Magnolia has influenced you,' Ada smiled.

'I think she probably has. I've fallen in love with Tod, want to be with him as much as I can, but I also want to be with you kids. And write as well. And travel. I want to spend more time in Kefalonia – I'm planning on taking Tod, if I can ever get him away from the stables. But meanwhile, I have a hell of a lot of writing to do for Alcidae House.'

'A four-book deal with them is fantastic.' Ada patted my arm in a congratulatory fashion as we arrived back at the gate of Daisy Royd Farm, which Rita was planning to put straight on the market as soon as I found somewhere we wanted to live. 'Well, just need to find that dream house now and we're sorted.' Ada stopped as her phone rang. 'Ethan,' she mouthed, excitedly. 'Coming up this weekend to look at the halls of residence he's been allocated in Leeds…'

'Fabulous place just outside Westenbury village itself,' Janice said, later that afternoon when she popped in for the sole purpose of bringing round the brochure she'd picked up from the estate agent. 'It's just come on the market, today. There'll be loads after it,' she warned. 'Great position, five bedrooms, huge garden with orchard and paddock – you can take the alpacas, Jen – and amazing views. Perfect for you and the kids. Pricey, but there you go.'

So, there I was, the next morning, having made an appointment to be shown round by someone from Kennedy's, the upmarket estate agent down in Midhope town centre, just as they closed the previous evening. I'd fallen in love with the picture in the brochure, driven Ada, George and Janice down there immediately, and we'd spent a good half an hour peering excitedly through windows, and exploring the paddock and orchard. All three of us knew it was just where we wanted to be.

Here I was, alone this time, ten minutes early for my appointment, feverish with excitement and ready to sign on the dotted line. I reckoned I must be in a good position – no house of my own to sell and Aunt Agnes's legacy, after probate, ready to go in my bank account.

A saloon car pulled up on the drive and a tall, smart looking man, probably in his early seventies, got out and, seeing me in the garden, walked towards me, briefcase and phone to hand. He put down the case, moved the phone to his left hand and held out his right. 'Ms Baylis? Laurence Reardon-Jones from Kennedy's.'

'Sorry?' I stared.

'Laurence Reardon-Jones?' He smiled, obviously slightly taken aback by my reaction. 'From the estate agent?'

'Laurence?' I repeated. 'Reardon-Jones?'

'Er, yes, that's right. Ms Baylis? You made an appointment to see the house?'

'You're an estate agent?' I felt my legs buckle slightly. Was this man Ada and George's –and Saffron's – biological grandfather? I stared at his face, taking in every feature, the dark hair, now greying, the faded blue eyes.

'No, not an estate agent as such. I'm from the agency, but I just show people round. Bit of a part-time job. You know, keep me out of mischief?'

'You're not dead then?'

'Er, no. Well, I wasn't when I looked in the mirror this morning.' He put a hand to his chest. 'Heart still going... look, have we met before? Do I know you?'

Maybe there was another Laurence Reardon-Jones? I peered closely at him. 'Were you an English lecturer at the university in Midhope? When it was still the Poly?'

'Ah.' He broke into a smile. 'Did I use to teach you?'

'No, I think quite probably you were long before my time. Not that I ever went to the Poly,' I added. 'I was at Cambridge. Met my husband, Laurence Lewis, there.'

'Right.' Reardon-Jones smiled, not really understanding. 'Great place to be, Cambridge.'

'No,' I reiterated. 'You didn't teach *me*. You taught my mother-in-law, Rita. Rita Lewis?'

'Right.' No light bulb moments. No pennies dropping. 'So, do you want to see the house...?' He jangled keys in his pocket and indicated the front door with his phone.

'Yes, yes, of course. In fact, I'm almost certain I'm going to buy this place.'

'You've not seen it yet,' he frowned. 'Come on...'

'Look, before we go in, can I ask you a question?'

'About the house? Are they willing to come down in price? Is that it? I doubt it very much, there's so much interest.'

'No, no, nothing to do with the house. I'll pay whatever

they want. And more, if necessary. Look,' I took a deep breath, 'Did you go and live in America? Were you ill?'

'That's two questions,' he said, looking at me strangely. 'But yes, my wife and I moved back down to Hereford and then across the pond to Texas and lived in the States for many years. I became ill, but, against all odds, pulled through and eventually we decided to retire back here in Yorkshire... I'm sorry, what is this?' He looked at his watch. 'I have five more people with appointments here... We really need to get on.'

'OK.' I took another deep breath. 'I think, Mr Reardon-Jones, you are my children's biological grandfather.' When he didn't say anything, but just stared at me, I went on, hurriedly, 'You became friendly – well, *very friendly*, if you get my meaning – with my mother-in-law, Rita Lewis, in the late seventies? She was one of your part-time mature students and helped backstage in a production of *Hamlet*?' The man in front of me went slightly pale and then flushed a deep red. 'Rita had Laurence – Laurie – and, while her husband *could* have been the true father, she has always accepted that *you*, Laurence, are my husband, Laurence's, biological father. She'd kept it secret all these years. In fact, only just recently revealed all this to my husband. You know, told him who his biological father is...? You were an actor, like my husband?' I was gabbling now, trying to get it all out. 'Well, soon to be *ex-husband*...'

'Laurie Lewis, the actor? Are you trying to tell me I'm Laurie Lewis's father?'

I nodded enthusiastically. Just wait until I told Rita. Until I told Laurie I'd found his father. That he was still alive.

Laurence Reardon-Jones smiled a sort of sneery, superior

smile and I realised I wasn't keen on this man. Didn't like him at all. 'I'm sorry, m'dear,' (I hated being addressed *m'dear*) 'I can tell you categorically, there is absolutely no way I am Laurie Lewis's father. *Anyone's* father.'

'Oh?'

'Since my thirties, when my wife and I were trying to conceive a child, I was made aware that I have a genetic disorder called Klinefelter Syndrome. The symptoms in my case were subtle. What I'm trying to say is, I had no idea at the time. What I'm also saying – and you'll have to excuse my telling you this in the middle of a showing round of a house – as a result of this genetic problem, I have no, and never have had any... shall we say *capacity*... to father a child. Alas, m'dear, the fantasy that Rita Lewis has woven, believing me to be the father of her child, remains just that – a fantasy. Now, shall we?' Reardon-Jones jangled keys in my direction once more and, embarrassed, I slowly followed him down the garden and into the house.

The revelation that Terry Lewis was, and had been all along, Laurie's actual father, was totally unexpected, leaving me, as I followed Laurence Reardon-Jones through the front door of the cottage, utterly stunned. Had Rita wanted this man to be the father of her child so much that she'd convinced herself he actually was? I knew I was going to have to make some decisions about just how I'd tell Rita and Laurie what I'd uncovered, but that was for later.

Much later.

Now, all I wanted was to take in every single aspect of the house I was determined to make into a home for myself, Ada, George and Saffron. The south-facing kitchen that I was already knocking into the dining room and extending outwards in order to house my new navy Aga; the traditional Sanderson-covered sofas and curtains that would grace the sitting room; the beautiful beamed room overlooking the woods at the rear which would become my writing room, books on every shelf and surface.

'I want it,' I told Reardon-Jones. 'I'll take it this minute. Do *not* sell it to anyone else... Just let me sign on the dotted line...'

'It's not *quite* as simple as that, Ms Baylis.' Laurence Reardon Jones' voice dripped condescension. I reckon he'd already marked me out as a mad woman.

'No, I mean it. Let me telephone Kennedy's now... I have the money... the house is just perfect.' Part of me wanted to stamp my feet in frustration and, at the risk of sounding like a spoilt child, I added, 'It really, really, is all I've ever wanted.'

I broke off as both Reardon-Jones and I turned to the man standing in the open door of the sitting room, arms folded, laughing in my direction.

'I think, Mr Estate Agent, she's trying to tell you she won't take no for an answer.' Tod laughed again and, regardless of the other man standing there, walked over, lifted my face to his and smiling down at me said, 'And neither will I. Welcome to the north, Jenny.'

Acknowledgements

My thanks must go to author Anna Stuart, aka the very lovely and clever Joanna Courtney, who, having been an undergraduate at Cambridge University herself, was able to advise me on, and guide me through, not only the many nuances of student life there, but particularly with regards the organisation of the much-revered FDC or Footlights Drama Club, run by the students themselves.

Thanks also to Dave Brewer, a Yorkshire friend of mine, who, as a Tic-tac bookmaker for many years at The Races, was a fount of knowledge on how top race horses are trained, including an explanation of "The Gallops", "Starting Stalls" and how bets are placed. I learned a lot!

Thanks, as always, to my lovely agent, Anne Williams at KHLA Literary Agency, for her unstinting help, advice and loyalty as well as to Thorne Ryan my editor at Aria, Head of Zeus who, with the rest of the team, have helped to make A Village Secret the best it can possibly be.

And finally, to all you wonderful readers who read my books and write such lovely things about them, a huge, heartfelt thank you.

About the Author

JULIE HOUSTON lives in Huddersfield, West Yorkshire where her novels are set, and her only claims to fame are that she teaches part-time at 'Bridget Jones' author Helen Fielding's old junior school and her neighbour is 'Chocolat' author, Joanne Harris. Julie is married, with two adult children and a ridiculous Cockerpoo called Lincoln. She runs and swims because she's been told it's good for her, but would really prefer a glass of wine, a sun lounger and a jolly good book – preferably with Dev Patel in attendance. You can contact Julie via the contact page, on Twitter or on Facebook. Twitter: @juliehouston2; facebook.com/ JulieHoustonauthor.